Dear Reader,

In so many of ~~my~~ ... ~~a~~nd heroine triumph ov~~er~~ ... ~~an~~d-expanding America. ... ~~we~~stern romances, hope you ... ~~an~~d still intend to write m~~ore~~ ...

Yet lately I've been longing t~~o te~~ll a story from a more recent time in our history, the period between World Wars I and II, years when young lovers faced a different kind of hardship: the Great Depression. Drama and romance flowered then as well. Gangsters, every bit as nefarious as Western outlaws, made violent headlines while young people danced to new jazz rhythms that shocked their elders. As always, strong family ties were the keys to survival.

With Hope is the first of at least three novels I'm writing set in the 1930s. It tells the story of a woman trying to keep her farm and misfit siblings together after her parents' deaths, and of the strong, kind-hearted man who helps her but can't offer her the one thing he wants to give her the most.

I hope you'll enjoy reading it.

With thanks to all my loyal readers,

Dorothy Garlock

Turn the page for more praise for Dorothy Garlock and her previous novel, *Sweetwater* . . .

ACCLAIM FOR DOROTHY GARLOCK AND HER MAJOR NATIONAL BESTSELLER, *Sweetwater*

"Garlock's narrative and dialogue lend rich visual, almost cinematic flavor . . . [and her] secondary story of a few brave souls attempting to restore justice is deftly handled."
—Publishers Weekly

"Dorothy Garlock has given us another adventurous romance, with her superb storytelling and a cast of characters so lifelike you hate to see the story end. For readers of romance, for historical fans, for anyone who enjoys a good read and a well-crafted plot, *Sweetwater* is a must-read and a keeper."
—CompuServe Romance Reviews

"*Sweetwater* is a slice of the Old West complete with the hardships and joys that settlers encoutered. Ms. Garlock is the diva of American Romance."
—Kathe Robin, *Romantic Times*

"Vintage Garlock. . . . Her characters are superb as they come alive in this multilayered tale."
—*Rendezvous*

"Fantastic! 5 bells!!! The Western frontier is brought to you in vivid colors and in wonderful detail by the renowned Ms. Garlock."
—*Bell, Book, and Candle*

"To read one of Dorothy Garlock's novels is to fall in love with the strong, heroic men and women she portrays, with the rugged Western Frontier she describes, and with her wonderful deeply held conviction that love can heal all wounds."
—*Dalton's Heart to Heart*

"Fans will definitely enjoy this entertaining work from one of the grand dames of romantic fiction."
—**Amazon.com**

"Captivating . . . a wonderful sense of time and place. . . . Rarely have I cared more about fictional characters than I did about Trell and Jenny. . . . The reader won't want this book to end."
—*Calico Trails*

A Featured Alternate of Doubleday Book Club®

Books by Dorothy Garlock

Published by WARNER BOOKS

DOROTHY GARLOCK

With Hope

WARNER BOOKS

A Time Warner Company

WARNER BOOKS EDITION

Copyright © 1998 by Dorothy Garlock
All rights reserved.

Cover design and illustration by Anthony Greco

Warner Books, Inc.
1271 Avenue of the Americas
New York, NY 10020

Visit our Web site at
http://warnerbooks.com

A Time Warner Company

Printed in the United States of America

First Printing: September, 1998

10 9 8 7 6 5 4 3 2

To Dr. James Hendricks for sharing his medical expertise not only in this book, but in previous books.

To Mary Ann Hendricks, for her enthusiasm, pinpoint suggestions and patient listening.

To Marjorie Theiss, for her quick mind, her sharp pencil, and for being such a good friend.

To Pete Carroll of Ringling, Oklahoma, for telling me about cotton patches, post oak brush, bull nettles and hard times during the '30's.

To Claude Woods, curator of the Healdton Oil Museum, Healdton, Oklahoma, for telling me about how it was back then.

To family and friends, especially Mary Ben Cretenoid of Dallas, Texas, who shared bits and pieces of their memories of the Great Depression.

And to my grandchildren, Adam Mix, Loraine and Amos Mix, who have a hard time believing people "back in the olden days" could live and be happy without television sets, computers, microwaves and Burger King.

"All this drudgery will kill me if once in a while I cannot hope for something for somebody. If I cannot see a bird fly and wave my hand to it."

--Willa Cather,
THE SONG OF THE LARK, 1915

WITH HENRY ANN

You open your eyes at the sound of her voice,
See her sweet face at the dawn.
Greet the new morn and rejoice, yes, rejoice
For you are so lucky, my son.
You are so lucky, my little man,
Staying with Henry Ann.

You close your eyes at the day's end now
When she sings you a lullaby,
You feel her dear kiss upon your brow
As off to dreamland you fly.
You are so blessed, my little man
'Biding with Henry Ann.

I miss you, my lad, back at our farm.
Your mother grows stranger each day.
Henry, I know, will guard you from harm.
For your sake, I keep you away.
Yes, you are safer, my little man,
Living with Henry Ann.

I know it is wrong that I envy you
The joy and the comfort you've found.
I want to be happy and carefree too,
From my miserable marriage unbound.
I want to be with you, my little man,
Loving with Henry Ann.

—F.S.I.

Prologue

1919 — JEFFERSON COUNTY, OKLAHOMA

*"How'er ya gonna keep 'em down on the farm
after they've seen Pa-ree?
How'er ya gonna keep 'em—da-da-da-da-da--"*

Dorene gazed into the mirror as she sang, adjusted the neckline of the thin sleeveless dress she wore, then licked her fingers and flattened the spit curl on her forehead.

"Are you leaving . . . again?" The small barefoot girl stood in the doorway and watched her young, pretty mother preen in front of the dresser mirror.

"Uh-huh."

"Why'd you come?"

"To pay you a visit."

Dorene Henry twisted from one side to the other so that the long fringe on the bottom of her sleeveless dress would swirl around her legs.

"Daddy said you come 'cause you wanted money."

"Your daddy owes me. I'm still his wife, and the law says he has to support me. But I wanted to see you, too."

"You really come for the money. Will you be back?"

"Maybe. Do you care?"

"I guess so." The child shrugged indifferently. Then, "Will you?"

"I don't know. Maybe, maybe not." Dorene gave the girl a casual pat on the head and closed the packed suitcase that lay on the bed.

"Daddy'd get you a pony . . . if you stay."

"Good Lord!" Dorene rolled her eyes. "I want a lot of things, snookums, but a pony ain't one of 'em."

"Don't call me that. My name's Henry Ann."

Dorene rolled her eyes again. "How could I possibly forget? Where's your daddy now?"

"In the field. Are you goin' to tell him good-bye?"

"Why should I? He knows I'm going."

Dorene's deep felt hat fit her head like a cap. She eased it on, careful not to disturb the spit curls on her cheeks.

"You could thank him for the money."

"He had to give it to me. I'm his wife. Your daddy don't like me much or he'd not have made me live out here in the sticks where I was lucky if I saw a motorcar go by once a week. Work is all he thinks about. You . . . and work, I should add."

"He likes you too. He just didn't want you to cut off your hair like a . . . like a flapper, rouge your cheeks, and wear dresses that show your legs. Daddy says it makes you look trashy."

"He wouldn't know trashy if it jumped up and bit him," Dorene sneered. "He likes me so much he wants me to walk behind a plow, hoe cotton, slop hogs, and have a string of younguns. I'm not doin' it. If God had meant for me to be a slave, he'd of made me black and ugly. And that's that."

"I like it here. I'm never going to leave," Henry Ann said defiantly.

"You may think so now. Wait until you grow up."

"Are you goin' to the city in a motorcar?"

"We're goin' to Ardmore in a motorcar and take the train to Oklahoma City. I've . . . got things to do there." Dorene put her foot on the chair, adjusted the beribboned garter above her knee, then straightened the bow on the vamp of her shoe. The child watched, but her mind was elsewhere.

Yeah, I know. I heard you tell Daddy that you've got a little boy back in the city. You've got to go take care of HIM! I've got Daddy to take care of me.

Dorene picked up her suitcase and went through the house to the porch. A touring car was parked in the road in front of the house. A man with a handlebar mustache came to the porch to take her suitcase. He wore a black suit and a white shirt with a high-necked collar. His felt hat tilted jauntily on his head, and he smelled strongly of hair tonic. He looked from the barefoot child to Dorene.

"This your kid?"

" 'Fraid so, lover. She's only six. I had her when I was fifteen and had no idea how to keep from havin' youn-guns."

"Six?" Henry Ann said with indignation. "I'm nine almost ten. And you were sixteen when I was born. Daddy said so."

Dorene glared at the child as if she'd like to slap her; but when she turned to the man, she was all smiles.

"This smart-mouthed little brat is Henry Henry. Ain't that the most god-awful name you ever heard of for a girl?

I named her Henry after her daddy. It was his idea to have her and my idea to name her."

"No doubt," he muttered.

"I pulled one over on old Ed and got the name on the birth certificate before he knew what was what." Dorene giggled, and her eyes shone like glass beads. "He 'bout had a calf! Lordy mercy, it was funny! He tore outta that room like a turpentined cat! He run darn near to town to catch the doctor and got 'Ann' stuck in between the Henrys. Ain't that rich?"

The man frowned. "Yeah, rich."

He looking from the child to the mother, thinking there was a resemblance and hoping for the child's sake it was only skin-deep.

"I like my name. No one else has one like it."

The child spoke quietly and with such dignity that the man felt a spark of embarrassment. *Damn this baggage.* He'd dump her right now if it were not for the favors promised when they reached Ardmore.

"Let's get goin'," he growled impatiently.

"I'm ready, sugar." Dorene failed to notice the man grimace in reaction to the pet name and gave him a bright smile.

He looked at the child again, then looked quickly away, picked up the suitcase, and headed back to the car.

"Are you going to kiss me good-bye?" Dorene hesitated before stepping off the porch.

"Not this time."

"My God!" Her musical laugh rang out. "You're gettin' more like your daddy every day." She stooped and kissed the child's cheek, then hurried across the yard to the car, teetering on her high heels, the six-inch fringe on the bottom of her dress dancing around her legs.

Henry Ann stood on the porch and watched her mother step up onto the running board and into the car. *I'll not be like you! I'll never go off and leave my little girl no matter how much I hate her daddy. You won't be back this time . . . and you know what? I don't care!*

The man cranked the motor, detached the crank, threw it behind the seat, and slid under the wheel. Dorene waved gaily as the motorcar took off in a cloud of dust.

Chapter One

RED ROCK, OKLAHOMA — 1932

The bus was an hour late but it didn't matter to the man who leaned against the side of Millie's Diner. He wasn't meeting anyone. When the bus finally arrived, the passengers poured out and hurried into the café to sit on the stools along the bar for the thirty-minute supper break. Converted from an old Union Pacific railroad car that had been moved to Main Street ten years ago, the café, one of two in town, had only two things on the menu this time of day: chili and hamburgers.

A woman with a skinny teenage girl slouching along behind her was the last to leave the bus. The woman patted the top of a ridiculously small, flower-trimmed hat firmly down on her head and walked behind the bus to where the driver was unloading a straw suitcase and a box tied with a rope.

Cupping the bowl of his pipe in his hand, the man watched the mid-calf-length skirt swish around her shapely legs. He enjoyed seeing the grace of her slender body, the tilt of her head, her curly brown hair, and heavy dark brows. He noticed the brows because most women had taken to plucking them to a pencil-slim line that, to him, made them look bald-faced. He knew who she was—Ed Henry's daughter. He judged her to be three or four years younger than his own age of twenty-eight.

He waited until the walk in front of the diner cleared, then headed for the lot behind the grocery store where he'd parked his Ford roadster. He had put the car together himself back in '25 when it was shipped, and he'd kept it in tip-top shape. When it was washed and polished, it looked brand-new. He treasured it next to his three-year-old son.

Stopping, he knocked the ashes from his pipe on the sole of his boot and put the pipe in his pocket. Sooner or later he might have to sell the car. That would depend on whether or not he had a fairly good cotton crop and what price he could get for it. But for now he'd put off having to make the decision by offering to install a new motor in the grocer's truck and taking pay in trade.

Henry Ann Henry thanked the bus driver and picked up the straw suitcase.

"We can leave the box at the store and come back for it later."

The girl snatched the box from the driver.

"I'll carry it. How far do we go?"

"A mile after we leave town."

"That far? Well. I'm not leavin' my stuff for some shit-kicker to glom onto."

"Mr. Anderson wouldn't let that happen. But never mind. Let's go. I want to be home before dark."

The few people passing them along the street nodded a greeting to Henry Ann Henry and curiously eyed the girl with her. Henrys had lived in the Red Rock area since the town's beginning. Ed Henry, Henry Ann's father, was a hardworking dependable man who had made the mistake of marrying Dorene Perry. According to the opinion of most folk here, the Perrys were trash then and the Perrys were trash now.

" 'Lo, Miss Henry." A small girl playing hopscotch moved off the sidewalk to allow them to pass.

" 'Lo, Mary Evelyn. How's your mother?"

"Fine."

Those who saw Henry Ann walking down the street, even the young girl, wondered about the stray waif she was bringing home this time. More than likely another one of Dorene's bastards. The last time Henry Ann had left town she'd returned with a surly fourteen-year-old boy.

Only a few miles and the Red River separated Red Rock, Oklahoma, from Texas. The business district of Red Rock consisted of two blocks of store buildings—a fourth of them now unoccupied. The grocery store, the bank, the shoe-repair shop, and the Phillips 66 gas station were across the street from Millie's Diner, the barbershop and the Five and Dime where Henry Ann had worked on Saturdays back when the owners could afford to hire help. But money was tight now, and the owners were very close to losing the business.

Red Rock was a place of ruined dreams, of good people facing bad times, of farms and ranches gone bust or on the verge of it. It was a town on the plains of Oklahoma hit hard by four years of drought and failed cotton crops. Cotton was bringing in only five cents a pound and wheat twenty-five cents a bushel. Beef was selling for seven cents a pound.

Men were out of work here as they were across the nation. In the cities entire families were lining up at soup kitchens to keep from starving. Rioting had erupted among men who were desperate for work. Hard times had led some folk to pack up and head west, where they had heard that jobs could be found in the fertile fields of California. Lack of respect for the laws of a nation that seemed unable or unwilling to help its people caused others to turn to the crime of bootlegging and robbing banks.

The row of small neat houses Henry Ann and the girl passed ended at the railroad tracks as if an invisible fence had been erected. A block farther on down the road they came to the smaller, tighter, shabbier row of dwellings that housed Red Rock's Negro community.

" 'Lo, Missy. Figured you be gettin' off the bus." A heavyset woman beamed at them from a rocking chair on a porch bright with pots of blooming moss rose. A blue cloth was tied about her head.

"Hello, Aunt Dozie. How's your rheumatiz?"

"Fair to middlin'. How was thin's up dere in the city? Cold up dere?"

"About the same as here."

"I allowed as dat dey might have snow up dere."

"Not this time a year, Aunt Dozie. Sorry I can't stop and visit. I want to get on home before dark." Henry Ann had known Dozie Jones all her life. Dozie knew about Dorene and about Johnny. Responding to her curiosity about Isabel would take too much time right now.

"Ain't blamin' ya, child. Keep yore eyes peeled for dem tramps. Hear? Dey'd steal yore eyeballs if ya warn't lookin'. Dey is thicker'n fleas on a dog's back after de train come in."

"I hear, Aunt Dozie. 'Bye."

Two more houses after Aunt Dozie's the dusty road stretched ahead.

"Tired?"

"A little. Where'd that old woman think ya went? Don't she know where Oklahoma City is?"

"It sounds a long way off to her." Henry Ann stopped, lowered the suitcase to the ground, and flexed her stiff fingers.

"He ain't goin' to want me, is he? And I ain't wantin' to go where I ain't wanted," Isabel said abruptly. "Mama said he was a shithead." The girl's small features hardened with a look of defiance.

Henry Ann studied the girl's face. She had to remember that Isabel had never had a normal childhood. She'd been exposed to things that most young girls had never heard about.

"You shouldn't use that language even if Mama did. Wait and judge Daddy for yourself."

"Your daddy. Not mine. The woman from the court-house wanted to put me in a home where I'd help take care of orphan kids and work for my keep. If she'd've took me, I'd've run off."

"I came as soon as I got Mama's letter."

"Why didn't you take me when you took Johnny?"

"I couldn't take you without Mama's permission. I offered, but she wouldn't let you come with me."

"She should'a died then." Catching the murmured words, Henry Ann shuddered at the thought of what this girl had seen during her short life. She thanked God that she had been left with her daddy. Her mother's selfishness had turned out to be a blessing in disguise.

"You shouldn't say such things," Henry Ann felt compelled to reply.

"Why not? She just wanted me there to keep house and cook while she went to the honky-tonks and flipped up her skirts."

"You . . . never . . . did—?"

"Whore? No. She made me stay out when new men come." Isabel snickered. "Reckon she was afraid they'd want me and not her."

"She loved you . . . in her own way."

"He ain't goin' to like me usin' his name."

"Who? Daddy?"

"Mama said he'd have a shit fit if she sent him another one of her kids!"

"I don't want to hear what Mama said about Daddy. She left us and went off with a car salesman. I was just three years old. Daddy had to work and take care of me, too. She came back from time to time . . . when she needed money. As far as I know Daddy gave her what little he could when she asked."

"She said he was a . . . tight-ass."

"Isabel! No more of that. She was far from perfect herself."

"She was a whore."

"Lord have mercy!"

"Poot! What do ya call a woman who changes men about as often as she changes the sheets, and sleeps with others on the side?"

Henry Ann looked into the face of the youngster and grieved for the sordid life she'd had with their mother. She'd had only a glimpse of her half sister four years ago when she had gone to fetch Johnny. Dorene had written to say that she was sending him to the State Reform School. Henry Ann had begged her father to let her go and get him. At the time they were milking six cows and taking milk and cream to town. She suggested that perhaps he would be a help on the farm. The boy had been so surly and resentful that it had taken a year for him to halfway adjust to a regular routine of work.

"You've got to put that life behind you, Isabel. Things will be different here. You'll have me and Daddy and Johnny to look out for you and love you."

"Johnny won't."

"You don't know that. It's been four years since you've seen him."

"Mama said he was just like his daddy—a hard-drinkin', hard-peckered blanket-ass."

"Goodness! I realize that vulgar words have been a part of your vocabulary all your life, but in our home, yours now, they are not acceptable."

"Who says?"

"I do . . . and Daddy, too. We will not allow it. You must break the habit before you start to school if you want to make friends."

"They ain't goin' to like me, and I ain't sure I'm goin'." Isabel picked up the box and started down the road.

Henry Ann had not seen her mother for four years when the letter came that said she was dying. She had journeyed to the city and found that her once-beautiful mother had become a wasted woman who looked twice her thirty-nine years. Less than six hours after Henry Ann arrived the end had come.

Ed Henry had adored his fifteen-year-old bride but had never been able to make her happy. She so despised being a wife and mother that she had bitterly named their baby girl Henry Henry. After all, it was his child; she hadn't wanted her. Dorene had left him and their child a few years later. Ed had not filed for divorce, and it had not seemed important to Dorene to make the break official.

Henry Ann was used to her name and liked it even though she'd had to endure a lot of good-natured teasing. Of course, the kids at school had thought it odd. Her musings were interrupted by the sound of an automobile coming up behind them. She urged Isabel to the side of the road, and they kept walking. The car slowed, then inched up beside them. It was a Ford roadster with a box on the back. She had seen the car go by the house several times but had never met the neighbor who owned it.

"Do you want a ride?" The hatless man was big, dark, and held a pipe clenched between his teeth. His midnight black hair was thick and unruly, his eyes dark, and his expression dour. "You're Ed Henry's girl. I'm Thomas Dolan. I live just beyond your place."

"I remember when you moved in. I met your wife."

"You can ride if you want. If not, I'll be getting on."

"We'd appreciate it."

"Put your suitcase in the back and climb up here. Careful. I've got a glass lamp back there." *I'm hoping it'll last longer than the last one. Glass lamps aren't made to be bounced off the wall.*

Isabel waited for Henry Ann to get in first so she'd not be next to the man. He started the car moving as soon as they were settled in the seat. Henry Ann turned so that her shoulder was behind the man's, but her hip was pressed tightly to his. In order to keep from looking at him, she kept her eyes straight ahead.

"How is Mrs. Dolan?"

"All right."

"She's very pretty."

He grunted, but didn't reply. An uncomfortable silence followed.

"We have a quilting bee twice a month at the church. I'd be glad to take Mrs. Dolan if she would like to go."

"I doubt she'd go." After a long pause, he added, "She doesn't go to church."

"Oh . . . well—"

The awkward silence that followed was broken when he stopped in the road in front of the Henry house, and Isabel asked, "Is this it?"

"This is it. Thank you, Mr. Dolan. Tell your wife I'd be happy to have her pay us a visit."

"Why? You didn't get much of a welcome when you called on her."

"How do you know? As I recall, you weren't even there." She looked at him then. His dark eyes caught and held hers.

"I know my wife."

Black hair flopped down on Dolan's forehead and hung over his ears. The shadow of black whiskers on his face made him look somewhat sinister. His dark eyes soberly searched her face. If she could believe what she saw in his eyes it was loneliness . . . pain. Big hands with a sprinkling of dark hair on the back gripped the steering wheel as he waited for her to step down from the car.

He's brittle and prickly as a cocklebur, she thought, but said, "You're . . . welcome to come in."

"I'll be gettin' on."

"Well. Thank you for the ride." Henry Ann backed

away, and the car moved on down the road, leaving a trail of dust in its wake.

Home looked good. It always seemed to when she had been away, even for a brief time. She had lived all her life in this neat white frame house with its two rooms across the front, two across the back, and lean-to porch that served as a kitchen stoop. A steep stairway led to the loft where Johnny slept. The rail-enclosed porch wrapped two sides of the house and hemmed in the two front doors. A half dozen huge pecan trees shaded the yard.

To the side of the house were a medium-sized barn, a shed, and the cow lot. There was a tight corral for the stock and beyond the barn a pigpen. A well, stone-enclosed, with a cylinder bucket hanging from the crossbar, was located between the house and the buildings; and near it was the storm cellar, with its slanting plank door.

"Ohhh—" Isabel let out a shriek when a large long-haired dog bounded from the back of the house, wagging its tail in delight.

"It's Shep. She won't hurt you." Henry Ann leaned down to scratch the woolly head. "Miss me, Shep? This is Isabel. When you get acquainted, I bet you'll be friends."

"I don't like dogs! It'll . . . bite me."

"She'll bite only to protect herself—or me. But never mind. Come on in."

Isabel followed Henry Ann into the house, casting fearful glances back at the dog. The house was cool and quiet.

"Guess Daddy isn't here."

"I'm here."

The voice came from the small room off the parlor. Henry Ann went to the door to see her father, fully clothed, lying on the bed.

"Are you sick, Daddy?" she asked with a worried frown as she went into the room to stand beside the bed.

"Just got a pain in my belly. It'll go away." He raised himself up and rested his feet on the floor.

Ed Henry was not a big man. He was slim and hard work had made him wiry. Henry Ann, who had seldom seen him sick, noted with alarm that his face was flushed beneath his deep tan and that his hands were clenched into fists. His thin gray hair looked as if he'd been in a Texas windstorm.

"Maybe if you drank some soda water, you'd throw up and feel better."

"I done that. Go on now. Get your hat off. Did you bring the girl?"

"Yes. Come in here, Isabel."

The girl came into the room, still holding her box. She stood close to Henry Ann and looked at the man sitting on the bed as if expecting him to spring up and bite her.

"Hello, girl." Ed looked steadily at the girl. "You look a mite like your ma when I first saw her."

Isabel looked down at the floor.

"She's tired. We both are." Henry Ann took off her hat. "We had a layover in Ardmore and walked halfway from town before Mr. Dolan picked us up."

"Go get her settled. I'll get up in a minute."

"You stay right there. I'll bring you some supper."

"I don't want anything."

"Where's Johnny?"

"I've not seen him for a day or two."

"He didn't help you drag logs in from the lower woods?"

"He took off with Pete Perry."

"Gosh darn it!" Henry Ann exclaimed. "I told him that if he didn't stay away from the Perrys, he'd end up in jail."

"He's got a right to know his kin, babe."

"Told ya." Isabel was close behind Henry Ann when she left the room. "Mama said he warn't no good. Jist like his pa."

Henry Ann went to the room off the kitchen.

"This is my room. We'll share it. Put your things here in the wardrobe." She took off her traveling dress and hung it on a hanger. Sitting on the bed in her slip, she took off her shoes and stockings.

"Mama was pretty . . . once. Did he mean that I'm pretty?"

"Of course. But being pretty is not an asset if you don't have any horse sense to go with it. Look what happened to our mother."

"She was a floozy, but men were crazy about her."

"She was dumb, selfish, self-centered, and completely lacking in morals. Being pretty may have been her downfall. It attracted the wrong kind of men."

"Well! I never! You're talkin' about my mama and she's . . . dead! That's mean of you."

Henry Ann shook her head. A while ago Isabel was calling their mother a whore. Now she was defending her. Henry Ann slipped a work dress over her head, buttoned it up, and reached for her everyday shoes.

"I didn't mean to be unkind, but every word I said is true. You can follow in her footsteps and end up as she did, or you can make a decent life for yourself. All Daddy and I can do for you is offer you a home, as we did Johnny. It's up to you."

"Maybe I should'a gone to the county home."

"If you want to go, Daddy'll give you bus fare. You've just turned fifteen. Mama's age when she married Daddy. We'd like you to be a part of our family, finish school, and have a better life than Mama had. But, as I said, it's up to you."

"I came with you, didn't I? I could've got a job and stayed in the city."

"A job doing what? Jobs are as scarce as hen's teeth, in case you haven't noticed." Henry Ann turned her back so Isabel wouldn't see how hard she was trying to hold on to her patience.

"I could've worked in a five and dime . . . maybe," she retorted stubbornly.

"Change into one of your old dresses. We'll have to do chores before supper."

"What chores? I ain't goin' to be no hired hand."

"Did you think you were going to be a guest here? This is your home now. We share the work."

"I bet Johnny don't," she mumbled as she pulled her dress off over her head.

Henry Ann left her. She'd suffered Isabel's grumblings all the way from Oklahoma City, and she didn't know how much more she could take before she lost her temper. She paused in the doorway of her father's room. He had lain back down on the bed.

"What needs to be done, Daddy?"

"Pen up the chickens, babe, and fork some hay to the cows. I did a poor job of milkin', but what I got is on the porch. And . . . I didn't get around to separating the morning milk."

"That's all right. I'll do it in the morning. I'm worried

about you." Henry Ann went to the bed and placed her palm on his forehead. "You've got a fever."

"Just a little one. I'll be all right."

"I brought you a newspaper. President Hoover is threatening to send the troops in to clear out the veterans who marched on Washington demanding a bonus. They've been there a couple of months and have built a tent city. It would be disgraceful to turn armed soldiers on our veterans who saved us from the Kaiser."

"Yeah, it would. Have they caught the man who kidnapped the Lindbergh baby?"

"Not yet, but there are several articles in the paper about it. Would you like to read them now? I'll get the paper and turn on the light."

"I'll read it tomorrow." His voice sounded strange, and he was breathing hard.

"Did you get the tube for the radio?"

"No, babe. I plumb forgot about it. Get along now. It's almost dark."

Ed Henry had a lot on his mind. He lay on his bed looking up through the dark to the ceiling, remembering the day he had come to this place. In his mid-twenties, he had inherited it from a childless uncle who had died in a flash flood. Ed had visited his uncle often and had loved the farm the minute he saw it—one hundred acres of good cotton land, two hundred acres of grazing, and a fine, stout house. There was not a nickel's debt against it, and he vowed that he'd never mortgage his land. To this day he had been able to keep that vow.

He had dreamed of raising a large family here, buying more land, and helping his sons get a start. It wasn't to be.

The young girl he had chosen to be his life's mate had had beauty, but it was only skin-deep. Inside she was ugly clear to the bone, a fact he'd discovered soon after they married. She had given him Henry Ann, and that gift had kept him from hating her.

When Henry Ann had come of age, he had transfered the deed to the land to her, fearing that if something happened to him, Dorene, as his legal wife, would inherit. Now, thank God, there was no danger of her stirring up trouble— but her kids were legally his kids.

Dear God, why hadn't he divorced her.

A month ago Doctor Hendricks had told him that he had a cancer growing in his belly. Soon his precious Henry Ann would be left alone to deal with Dorene's two kids. He had been willing for her to bring Isabel here, thinking the girl might have some of Henry Ann's good qualities and would be a help to her. Johnny was another matter. Something was eating at the boy, and, if he didn't settle down, he would more than likely end up in the pen in McAlester.

Ed had hoped to live long enough to see Henry Ann settled with a good man and children of her own. Now he had to face the fact that it wasn't to be. She was strong, his Henry Ann; strong, levelheaded, and smart as a whip. He had wanted her to go on to college, but that would have meant mortgaging the land, and she would not hear of it. During the past few weeks he had taken steps to make things as easy for her as possible after he was gone.

Ed went over in his mind the list of single men he knew. Most of them had come courting from time to time, but none of them had caught Henry Ann's fancy. Soon there would be plenty who would try to marry her. Times were hard, and even if they did get that fool Hoover out of office, Ed wasn't sure if things would ever get any better. A woman with three hundred acres free and clear would be a prize some men would kill for.

He was leaving his daughter better off than most. He had been careful with his money, careful not to go into debt. She would have a good crop of cotton, if some fool didn't bring in a piddly gusher and spray oil all over it. At the last count there were sixty-three steers. And he'd squirreled away some hard cash. Ed's mind raced to cotton-picking time. The thought crossed his mind that he'd not be here to see it.

He had met his new neighbor a time or two. Thomas Dolan wasn't exactly friendly, but he seemed a decent enough fellow. He had bought Perdie's farm after the old man died. From the looks of things they were living a hand-to-mouth existence over there. It was said that his wife, who came from moneyed folks down in Texas, had fought the move to the farm tooth and nail. Ed knew how hard it was to farm and care for a child without a woman's help.

Aunt Dozie said she'd heard that Mrs. Dolan seldom left the house, and when she did, it was only to sit on the porch all dressed up as if she was going to church. Once in a while Dolan would give a girl a quarter to come out and clean; but, as badly as the girl wanted the money, she wouldn't go back because she was afraid of Mrs. Dolan. The girl said Mr. Dolan did everything, even the washing, and lately had started taking his young son to the field with him.

The situation reminded Ed of the few years he'd spent with Dorene. He and Henry Ann had been better off without her, but at the time he had not known how he was going to farm and care for a young child.

Tom Dolan might be willing to help with the field work in exchange for the use of their mules to work his own land. Dolan's team was as sorry a team as Ed had ever seen pulling a plow.

Johnny was capable enough and had seemed to settle in lately. Then he'd become acquainted with some of his mother's relations who were known bootleggers and rustlers. It seemed that they might have convinced him that there were faster and easier ways to make money than riding behind a team of mules. Henry Ann would not be able to depend on him.

The first thing in the morning, Ed decided, he would go to town if he could get his car started. He'd see Doctor Hendricks, find out how much time he had left, then go have a talk with the sheriff and ask him to keep an eye on his girl.

Chapter Two

When morning came, Ed was half out of his mind with pain. He felt as if demons with hot pitchforks were inside his belly. His muffled cries brought Henry Ann rushing to his room.

"Daddy! Daddy—"

"Babe. Get . . . that bottle . . . in the top drawer."

She fetched the bottle and looked at it with an expression of horror.

"It's laudanum, Daddy!"

"Yes, yes. Put some in water."

"How long have you been taking this?"

"Don't fuss. I need it."

Henry Ann hurried to the kitchen for water. She returned, tipped the bottle and allowed a few drops to drip into the glass.

"More."

e added a few more drops and held his head up so he
drink.

"How long have you been taking this? The bottle is almost empty."

"I've got to . . . see Doc Hendricks." He was breathing hard through his open mouth. "When this takes away the pain . . . I'll get up."

"Daddy, you were sick when I left to go up to the city! Why didn't you tell me?"

"Babe—" His eyes, clouded with pain, sought hers. "If somethin' happens—"

"Nothing's going to happen, Daddy," she said quickly. "I'm getting you to the doctor and taking you on down to the hos . . . pital in Wichita Fa . . . lls." Her voice broke. She was choked with dread.

"Babe, listen." He panted and rolled his head. "Let me rest a minute."

Henry Ann knelt beside the bed.

"What can I do, Daddy? Is it your stomach?"

"Nothin' you can do, babe. There's somethin' you need to know. I've got money hidden away. Good thing too. I'm thinkin' the dang bank's goin' busted." He grabbed her arm, pulled her closer and whispered. "In an old rusty milk can in the weeds by the cow lot. The can's got a spot of black paint on it. Don't let anybody see ya gettin' it. Not the girl . . . not Johnny."

"You're scaring me."

"Ya hear me, girl?"

"I hear you, Daddy."

"Babe, you've been my life—" His hand moved down her arm to her hand, and he fell back on the bed.

"I know. And you're the best daddy anyone ever had."

Tears flooded her eyes. Ed's lids drooped. She smoothed the hair back from his forehead. He had always been thin.

But heavens! Why hadn't she noticed his hollow cheeks, bony forehead, and sunken eyes?

"What's the matter with him?" Isabel had come silently into the room.

"He's awful sick." Henry Ann resented the intrusion. She wanted to be alone with her daddy.

"What was he whisperin' about?"

"Nothing important."

"He was whisperin' 'cause he didn't want me to hear it."

"Were you listening?"

"No . . ."

You're lying. I heard the bedsprings when you got up. I heard the floor creak when you left the room, and came to the door. How much did you hear?

"Get dressed. We've got to do the chores while he's resting. Then I'll write a note for you to take to the doctor."

"In town? How'll I get there?"

"You can walk! You've got two legs, haven't you?" Henry Ann's voice was impatient. She looked down at the man who had loved her and had made a home for her after her mother deserted them.

As soon as she was sure her father was sleeping, Henry Ann dressed, washed, and went out to milk. The night before she had shown Isabel how to feed the chickens and had left her to do it. She was leaving the cow lot and taking the pail of milk to the porch when she heard a motorcar. She dropped the pail in the yard and hurried out to the road as the car approached. She waved both arms, and the black coupe she'd ridden in the night before stopped. She hurried to the driver's side of the car.

"Mr. Dolan, my father is awfully sick. Will you stop by and tell Doctor Hendricks to come out right away?"

"I'll be glad to, ma'am—"

"We're not going through Red Rock." Mrs. Dolan leaned forward to speak. She was small, had light blond hair and large blue eyes. A little dark-eyed boy stood between the couple, leaning heavily on his father's shoulder. "We're going to Wichita Falls and on to Conroy. My mother is expecting us for dinner."

"Well, in that case—" Henry Ann's face flushed darkly.

"You'll have to find someone else to run your errands." Mrs. Dolan sat back and waved her hand for her husband to drive on.

"We'll fetch the doctor." Dolan ignored the protest from his wife. "Shall I tell him it's urgent?"

"Tell him Daddy's in terrible pain."

"Thomas, we haven't time to go to Red Rock. Mama wants us to be there by noon. And . . . Jay wants to see his granny. Don't you, Jay?" Her voice rose shrilly. Her hand grasped the boy's shoulder and shook him. "Say you do, Jay!"

The man showed no visible emotion at his wife's outburst. He moved the child to sit on his lap. The little boy's eyes brightened. He flashed a smile at Henry Ann as his tiny hands grasped the steering wheel and moved it from side to side as if he were driving.

"I'll get the message to the doctor." Mr. Dolan spoke calmly.

"Thank you." Henry Ann stepped back.

Mrs. Dolan turned on her husband the instant the car began to move. Her voice was loud, shrill, and angry.

"We are not going to Red Rock!"

"Calm down, Emmajean. It'll not take but a few minutes—"

"We're going straight to Mama's. You promised. But you never keep your promises. Do you? You'd rather please an ignorant farmer than me. Have you got an itch for that bang-tail?"

Henry Ann watched the car disappear in a cloud of dust. The woman was the most selfish person she'd ever met. Her second encounter with Mrs. Dolan had been no more pleasant then the first.

It was no wonder Mr. Dolan was sour as a dill pickle.

Henry Ann had walked across the field to call on the new neighbors a week or two after they moved in. It was a hot May day. She had not been invited into the house or offered a drink of water. Mrs. Dolan, dressed in a pretty pink-organdy dress with a white-satin ribbon around her waist and one in her hair, had come out onto the porch and informed her that she only received callers on Sunday afternoon. Henry Ann had taken her leave feeling puzzled and terribly embarrassed.

She stood, now, in the road and watched the car carrying the strange couple until it rounded the bend in the road.

Tom Dolan thought that he'd gotten over being embarrassed by anything his wife said or did. But seeing the stricken look on Miss Henry's face when Emmajean had so cruelly refused to fetch the doctor had not only embarrassed him, but had made him so angry that he wanted to strangle her.

Godamighty! Was he going to have to pay for the rest of his life for one foolish night when he'd had the urge for sex and white lightning had addled his brain? He had taken it when it was so blatantly offered, and one hour had changed his life forever. The only good thing to come out of that night was Jay. During the last few years he had come to believe that he could tolerate Emmajean and her family for the sake of his son, because leaving Emmajean meant leaving the child. His in-laws had made that perfectly clear.

Tom was one of six children raised on a farm outside Dunlap, Nebraska. They had been known as "those wild Dolans." Wild and sinful! "Drinking, playing cards, and dancing their way to hell" is how a crazy old Holy Roller preacher described them. Of course, the old preacher thought all Catholics were heathens and doomed to the fiery furnace.

Heathens they might have been, but the Dolans were a happy family. Mike, one of the older boys, had gone to war, lived through it, and returned to search for and find Letty Pringle, the daughter the old preacher had thrown out when he discovered she was pregnant with Mike's child. Duncan, older than Mike, had been killed in a train wreck in Montana. One of his sisters had died during the influenza outbreak when she was small. Another sister had married a railroad man and moved to Lincoln. Hod, a year younger than Tom, was a Federal agent working out of Kansas City the last Tom heard. Tom's mother and father were gone now, and their offspring had scattered.

Tom's skill with motors of any kind had brought him to the oil boomtown of Healdton, Oklahoma. He found work near Wirt, commonly known as Rag Town, a hastily constructed tent city created by the massive influx of oil-field workers. Rag Town was a haven for bootleggers, gamblers, and prostitutes, ever willing to separate the oil-field worker from his pay.

Tom's job had been to keep the motors running at the gas- and oil-well drilling sites. When the drilling activities slowed, he drifted south, where he worked on cars, raced his motorcycle, and salted away his winnings in hopes of someday having his own dealership. It was a streak of bad luck, he thought now, that had brought him to Wichita Falls, where he'd met Emmajean. She was from Conroy, a town named for her grandfather, Judge Jason P. Conroy.

"And that's not all. Daddy won't like it a'tall that I'm living in that shack without electric lights. You just wait until I tell him that the Henrys down the road have electricity. It's not fair—"

"Mr. Henry paid to have the poles set and the wires run. It took everything I could scrape up just to get the farm." After that comment, Tom let Emmajean rant on. He had learned to turn off the sound of her voice when there was no reasoning with her.

"Daddy said in his letter that Marty was home and was going to work with him. They're goin' to dig an oil well and make a lot of money. Marty went to a school that taught him all about minerals and things like that. You don't know anything about how to make money. All you know is about greasy old motors and . . . being a dirt farmer—"

Emmajean's words floated over Tom's head. His thoughts were on Miss Henry. Nice woman from what he'd heard. She had the most beautiful soft brown eyes he'd ever looked into. There was not a whit of pretension or guile in them. Her hair, the color of polished pecan shells, hung in waves to her shoulders, natural-looking, unlike the short bob and spit curls Emmajean wore.

He'd not been in town long when he'd heard the tale about Dorene Henry, a member of the notorious Perry clan. Henry Ann's trip to Oklahoma City had been to bury the woman and bring back another one of her offspring. The boy and the girl couldn't be blamed for their mother's sins. He guessed that was the way Miss Henry looked at it.

"—And . . . if you're in there more than five minutes, I'm going to start screamin' and honkin' the horn—"

Tom pulled to the side of the house where the doctor had his office. He reached down, disconnected the horn, got out of the car, and reached for his son. He sat the boy astride his hip and went up the walk to the door.

Doctor Hendricks was a man in his early fifties with light hair and a friendly smile. He came out of his examining room when Tom opened the door.

"Morning, Tom."

"Hi, Doc."

"Hello there, Jay. You still mad at me for giving you that vaccination?" Jay hid his face against his father's shoulder. "Don't blame you a bit. It hurt, didn't it? What's his problem, Tom."

"He's all right, Doc. Miss Henry stopped me as I passed. She wanted me to tell you to come right out. Mr. Henry's in terrible pain."

"Uh-oh. I was afraid of that. I'll get on out there and take some morphine."

Doctor Hendricks began taking things from a cabinet and putting them in a bag. Tom could see from his expression that Mr. Henry was seriously ill.

"I'm sorry to hear he's bad off. I met him only a few times, but he seemed a decent fellow."

"He was . . . is. Ed's the salt of the earth." Doctor Hendricks broke off and turned to grab his coat off a hook.

"If there's anything I can do, let me know."

"Thanks for bringing the message, Tom. I'd better be getting on out there."

Henry Ann had time to say no more than hello after the doctor arrived. He went into the bedroom and closed the door.

She waited now, sitting on a straight-backed chair in the parlor beside the library table staring blankly at the framed picture of herself on her first pony, with her daddy holding the reins. Her thoughts were not on the picture. They were focused on her father and what the doctor would tell her when he came from the room. Thank heaven, Mr. Dolan had gone straight to his office, despite the objections of his snippy wife.

Isabel was shelling peas on the back porch. Henry Ann wished that the girl weren't here—wished that she had never brought her and Johnny to their home. She wished that she and her daddy were alone, here in their house as they had been for all those years that she was growing up.

Her daddy was dying. She had read it on the doctor's face when he came in the door. Daddy had been sick, maybe for months, and hadn't told her, wanting to spare her the worry. He'd carried the burden by himself as he'd always done—taking care of her without complaining or even making a derogatory comment about the woman who had abandoned them.

Whatever would she do without him!

The door opened. Doctor Hendricks moved the flatiron that served as a doorstop to hold it back so the air could circulate.

"He's sleeping. Let's go out into the yard."

He opened the screen door and she passed through. With

a heart heavy with dread, she went down the porch steps and out to lean against the trunk of the huge old pecan tree, where a piece of rope, what remained of her childhood swing, still dangled.

"He's dying, isn't he?" The words came from stiff lips.

"Yes. It won't be long now."

"Can't you do . . . something?" There were tears in her voice, but she held her head up and looked him in the eye.

"All I can do is keep him from suffering. He has a cancer in his stomach. When he came to me two months ago, he told me he was spitting up blood. I thought it could be an ulcer. Later I came to realize he had a cancer. I gave him laudanum. It's addictive, but I knew that he had only a short time left. Now he must have something stronger. I gave him morphine."

Henry Ann turned away and allowed the tears to trickle down her cheeks.

"I wasted a whole week up there when I could have been here with him."

"He wanted you to go. He told me so. He said that you needed to do what you could for your mother—for your sake, not hers."

"He's like . . . that."

"Is there someone you want to come stay with you?"

"My . . . half sister is here."

"You have no other relatives here?"

"None that I want."

"There's something else I want to tell you. Last week Ed came to town. He drew some money from the bank. He had me figure what my fee would be right up to the last and he paid me. He also paid Elmer over at the funeral home.

He said he figured that the bank was due to go busted, and he wanted his bills paid before it went under."

Henry Ann choked back a sob. "He knew his time would be soon, didn't he?"

"Yes. He worried about you being left with Johnny and the girl, if you brought her back. I see that you did."

"I must tell him not to worry—"

"You need to see a lawyer, Henry Ann. Those two kids carry Ed's name even if he didn't father them. You may have to share the inheritance with them."

"Daddy already thought of that, Doctor. He put the land in my name long ago. What little he had in the bank was in his name. I doubt there's any of that left."

"He was making it as easy for you as he could. Your daddy was quite a man."

"I know—"

"I'm going to have to leave for a while—"

"Oh, but—"

"I'll be back in a couple of hours. He should sleep while I'm gone."

"Will I get to talk to him . . . again?"

"I don't know if you'd want to, Henry Ann. During the night, the cancer . . . Well I won't go into that. His condition has worsened considerably. If he goes off the morphine, he'll be screaming with pain. I can keep him under until the end if that's what you want."

"I . . . don't want him to suffer."

"I'll check in at the office, then I'll be back." The doctor placed his hand on her shoulder and gave it a squeeze.

Henry Ann sat down on the porch and watched him turn his car around in the middle of the road and head back for town. It was all so . . . unreal. She should be down in the garden forking up potatoes or picking beans. Instead she was sitting here, wringing her hands, waiting for her father to die. Nothing would ever be the same again. All her life she had had him to depend on. Soon she would be alone.

Childhood memories flooded her mind.

Swing me, Daddy. Swing me higher.

Hold on tight, babe.

Daddy, guess what? Miss Brown said I had a voice like a bird. She chose me to sing at the Christmas party.

I've been tellin' you that all along.

I'm sorry I put too much salt in the corn bread.

It's all right, honey. Feed it to the chickens. We won't have to salt the eggs when we cook 'em.

Ah . . . Daddy, you're funny.

Not as funny as you, freckle-face.

Thank you, Daddy, for the new shoes and the button hook. I'll be the only girl in school with red shoes.

The screen door slammed, jarring Henry Ann from her thoughts.

"Is this enough peas?" Isabel held out the pan.

"Don't slam the door!"

"How'd I know the old thing would slam? Is this enough peas?"

"I guess it . . . is." Henry Ann stood. The doctor's car pulled to a stop in front of the house and a large woman got out. A blue cloth was tied around her head and a dark gingham granny dress hung to her ankles.

"Thanky for the ride," Aunt Dozie called, and came through the gate as the doctor turned his car around in the middle of the road and again headed back to town.

Henry Ann went down the steps to meet her. Dozie dropped a bundle to the ground and opened her arms.

"I knowed it. I knowed it. I knowed it when I saw de doctor's car go by comin' dis way. I said, Dozie, it's time to gets yore body on down de road. I was comin', chile, when Doctor turn 'round 'n' brung me."

She folded Henry Ann to her ample breast and held her while, for the first time, Henry Ann gave way to tears and cried as if her heart would break. After a while she pulled away.

"How did you know, Aunt Dozie?"

"Honey, yo're daddy come tol' me a while back that ya'd be needin' me. He told me again last week after he been to de doctor. Lawsy, I hates it, chile. But it's God's will, and we gots to endure."

"He told you that he—?"

"He say to me, Dozie, ya took care of my babe when she was little bitty. She love ya. She gonna need ya when I'm gone. And here I is, chile, fer as long as ya want me."

"I want you, Aunt Dozie. You and Daddy are the dearest things in the world to me."

"We's goin' to get through dis, chile. With God's help, we gets through it."

With their arms around each other they walked up onto the porch. Isabel eyed the woman's round black face with suspicion.

"This is Dozie Jones, Isabel. I've known her all my life. She took care of me when I was little."

"Lucky you. I took care of myself."

"Hello, girl. What ya got dere? Hummm . . . fresh peas. Day be mighty good eatin' cooked with taters."

"Then cook 'em." Isabel shoved the pan into Dozie's hands.

"Come on in, Aunt Dozie." Henry Ann took the pan of

peas from the surprised woman. "Doctor Hendricks said Daddy would sleep for a couple hours." In the kitchen, she set the pan on the table, took Isabel's arm, and pushed her out onto the back stoop. When they were away from the door, she spun her around and faced her. "I'm going to say this one time. If you are rude or sassy to Aunt Dozie again, I'll put you on the bus and send you out of here so fast you'll think you're in a tornado. Understand?"

Isabel jerked her arm free. "She's colored, ain't she? Ya can cozy up to her, if ya want. I ain't lowerin' myself to cuddle up to . . . no colored trash."

"It's a matter of opinion what's trash and what isn't. She came as a friend. I'm warning you. One nasty word to her and out you go!"

"I ain't sure ya can do that." A cunning look came over the girl's face making it hard to believe she was only fifteen. "My name's Henry same as yores even if ya do got it twice. Mama said she named ya Henry to get back at the old man for puttin' ya in her belly. Who's to say the old man didn't make a visit to Mama now and then. They was still married, wasn't they?"

Henry Ann looked at her as if seeing her for the first time. She had a sly smile on her face and a crafty look in her eyes. It took all Henry Ann's willpower to keep from slapping her face. Henry Ann remembered the muttered words her mother's last lover had said on the day of the burial when Isabel had shown no sign of grief.

"The girl's trouble. She ain't got no conscience at all."

At the time Henry Ann hadn't thought much about the statement. Now she wished she'd had more conversation with the man.

"Yes, they were married, Isabel. Papa believed in keeping his marriage vows. Mama didn't. Get it through your head right now . . . you have no claim here."

"We'll see." Isabel tossed her head. "Me'n Johnny's got as much right here as you have." She stepped off the porch and walked out into the yard toward the outhouse.

Leaving Henry Ann free to sit beside her father's bed, Aunt Dozie quietly and efficiently took over the work. She cleaned the kitchen, started a batch of bread to rise, put potatoes on to boil with the peas, and ran the milk through the separator. She sang softly while she worked.

> *"Sw . . . ing low, sweet char . . . i . . . ot—*
> *Comin' for ta carry me ho . . . me.*

The sound was comforting to Henry Ann. When she was small, Aunt Dozie would sit in the old rocking chair, take her on her lap, and sing to her. She had been a young woman then, widowed before she could have children of her own. She had focused her motherly love on Henry Ann and that love was returned.

A few months before, when Dozie's mother died, Ed Henry had taken a smoked ham and a peck of potatoes to the house to feed the mourners. Henry Ann and her father were the only white people at the burial in the cemetery behind the small Free Baptist Church. She was not surprised that he would confide in Aunt Dozie.

She left his bedside and went to the kitchen, where her dear friend sat in a chair working the dasher up and down in the churn. She placed her hand on Dozie's shoulder.

"It's good to have you here, Aunt Dozie."

"Where else would I be when my babe need me?"

"What'll I do? I don't know if I can cope with Isabel and Johnny."

"Ya will. Ya'll knows whats to do when de time come."

"Isabel is sly and sneaky. Johnny is just irresponsible. I'm afraid of what'll happen if he gets thick with the Perrys. They're the biggest bootleggers in the county. I don't know why the sheriff doesn't do something about them."

"Ya ain't the boy's mama. He be a man now. Old enough to fight in a war if there was one. Ya jist do de best ya can, but don't take no sass off 'em. Dey get de upper hand and dey run ya to de ground. See'd it done many a time."

Henry Ann heard a horse nicker and went to the door. Johnny and Pete Perry were putting their horses in the fenced area attached to the cow lot. Ed had given Johnny the black-and-white pinto a few months after he arrived. The boy had taken to riding as if he were born to it. Henry Ann had come to believe that the horse was the only thing in the world that Johnny loved.

As Henry Ann watched, Isabel came around from the front of the house and went toward them. They leaned against the corral rails and eyed her. Under their gaze she began to swing her shoulders and skinny hips to match her steps. She lifted a hand to her hair and tucked one side behind her ear. It was obvious that she was enjoying the male attention. Her mother's lover's words came back to Henry Ann. *The girl is trouble.*

Henry Ann went back to look in on her father. He was lying so still that her breath caught with fear. Then she saw the slight rise and fall of his chest, and his hand twitched. She eased down into the chair beside the bed, and after a while she began to pray.

"Dear God, please make his passing peaceful. He's been

such a good man. He's worked hard. Never cheated anyone, nor broke the law. He was kind—"

Loud talk and boisterous laughter broke the silence.
Henry Ann jumped to her feet and hurried to the kitchen.
Johnny and Pete Perry were horsing around on the porch.
Isabel, her arm around a porch post, watched with a broad
smile.

"I'll have to learn ya how to Indian wrestle. You'd take
to it like a duck to water considerin' ya got that wild blood
in ya." Pete's loud voice reached into every corner of the
house.

"Ya couldn't learn me nothin', ya . . . bunghead!"

Johnny escaped into the kitchen, allowing the screen
door to slam behind him. He looked around the kitchen and
grinned at Henry Ann. He was a slim, handsome youth
with the straight black hair and inky black eyes that suggested that the unknown man who had fathered him might
have been an American Indian

"That Isabel sure grew up. Didn't know her till she told
me who she was."

"Keep your voice down. Daddy's sleeping."

"Isabel said old Ed was 'bout to kick the bucket. Is that
right? He's not been so full a piss and vinegar lately, but I
never thought—"

Henry Ann took two quick steps, drew back her arm,
and slapped him across the face. An almost uncontrollable
rage washed over her.

"Don't you dare be disrespectful of him!" she hissed,
low-voiced. "My daddy put a roof over your head, fed you,
gave you work so you'd have a little money, all because he
thought it the decent thing to do. He had no obligation to
take you in."

Johnny was stunned. He lifted his hand to his cheek and looked at her as if he'd never seen her before.

"You ungrateful cur! He was sick!" Henry Ann continued heatedly and almost choked on the words. "He was . . . sick and you went off and left him to do the chores all by himself. You told me you'd help him drag deadwood in from the lower woods. You're . . . you're a sorry excuse for a human being, and I'm ashamed . . . totally ashamed that some of the same blood that flows in your veins flows in mine."

Johnny stood as still as a stone.. He had grown lately and stood two or three inches taller than Henry Ann but she was too angry to notice.

"Where were you while he was lying there . . . sick?" Henry Ann demanded.

"At Perry's."

"Delivering bootleg whiskey?"

Ignoring her question, the boy asked quietly, "Do you want me to leave?"

"It's up to you. But if you stay, you'll do your share of the work and you'll stop hanging out with thieves and bootleggers like Pete Perry. I don't want him here."

"I guess you're wishin' you hadn't brought me here."

"Daddy and I wanted to give you a chance for a decent life. If you want to go back to the city, go. If you want to go to the Perrys, go. But don't come back."

Johnny walked quickly out the door, stepped off the porch, and headed for the corral. Pete, who had been standing at the door listening, followed.

"What did you say to him?" Isabel demanded as she came into the kitchen.

"That's between me and Johnny and no business of

yours." Henry Ann wanted to cry. It seemed to her that the sky had opened and spilled grief all over her.

"It is, too, my business. He's my brother."

"Don't give me any sass, Isabel," Henry Ann said sharply. "Or I'll slap your face, too."

"Well! Try it and you'll get slapped back." She placed her thumb on the end of her nose and wiggled her fingers in a defiant gesture, before she flounced out the door, slamming it behind her, and hurried across the yard to the corral.

Pete Perry was in his middle twenties: a tall, lanky man with straw-colored hair, springing thickly from the scalp and pushed back in deep waves. He had hazel eyes, strong white teeth, and a deep dimple in his chin. He considered himself quite attractive to the female population. Henry Ann didn't know if he'd ever had a steady job, but he seemed always to have money in his pocket.

"She tryin' to run ya off?" Pete asked when Johnny came from the house, climbed atop the rail fence, sat down, and hooked his heels on the lower rail.

Silence from the boy on the rail fence.

"What she needs is a hour or two on her back with a man between her legs. A real man with a long pole'd take the sass outta her." Pete enjoyed talking nasty about women.

Johnny's dark eyes moved to the man and then away. It was impossible to know what the boy was thinking when he wore his Indian face.

"Listen, kid. With old Ed gone you stand to get a piece a this place. Ain't no mortgage on it far as I know. Hell. It ain't fair for that tightass woman to get it all. You could go to Dallas or New York— maybe even to California."

Again Johnny's eyes flicked to Pete's face and away.

"Ya and the girl's got as much right here as that stuck-up Henry Ann. Old Ed was still married to your mama, you know. Betcha he didn't make out no will."

Johnny slid off the fence, slipped the bridle on his pony, and sprang on its back. Without a word to Pete, he nudged open the gate and rode off down the lane toward the woods.

"Johnny! Wait—" Isabel called. "Where's he goin'?" She came to stand beside Pete.

"Ridin'."

"Where? What'd he say about what she did?"

"Nothin'." Pete looked down at the girl and grinned. "Don't worry 'bout it. He gets that way sometimes. He'll come around when he thinks about it."

"Are you really my cousin?"

"Name's Perry. Your mama was a Perry."

"Are we close kin?"

"Me and Dorene had the same grandma somewheres down the line—so Pa says."

"Ah . . . shoot!"

"Now why'd you go and say a thin' like that?"

"I'd just as soon you wasn't . . . kin."

"You flirtin' with me, honey? How old are you? You look like you ain't been outta diapers long."

"Seventeen," she lied.

"Then I reckon you're old enough." He chucked her beneath the chin with his fist, then let it fall to sweep lingeringly across her small breast. He turned to get his horse. "Got to be gettin' on home. See ya . . . cutie."

"Ain't ya got a car?" Isabel called.

"Yeah, I got one."

"Then why'er ya ridin' a horse?"

"So I can get places I can't get to in a car, sweet thin'. And so pretty little girls will ask questions." He finished saddling his horse. "If I'd knowed I wasn't gettin' an invite to dinner, I'd not a unsaddled my horse."

Isabel glanced toward the house, then back to Pete, who was sitting atop his horse rolling a cigarette.

"I'm askin' ya . . . to dinner."

With his eyes on her face, he licked the edge of the cigarette paper to seal the tobacco in, twisted the end, and stuck it between his lips. He lit it before he spoke.

"You ain't got 'nuff say 'round here yet, cutie. Maybe later . . . huh?" He dropped his lid in a flirtatious wink and put his heels to his horse.

Isabel watched him until he disappeared into the wood. Then, with her heart beating with excitement, she ran back to the house.

Chapter Three

CONROY, TEXAS

Tom Dolan sat in one of the white wicker chairs on the long veranda and listened to his father-in-law and Marty try to outtalk each other. They had ignored Tom as if the conversation were beyond him. Young Conroy was trying to impress his father with his knowledge of the oil industry.

"We'd not have to lease a whole section, Daddy. Hell, set a well a hundred feet from the section line and drill down at an angle. They do it all the time."

"I'd think a fellow can get himself in a mess of trouble draining oil out from under another man's land."

Marty laughed. "You have to get caught first, Daddy. How do you think Tom Slick made all his money? By hook and by crook, that's how. He went out and leased a hundred thousand acres, raised two hundred thousand dollars, and sank a dozen wells. We can do it with a lot less money. We can pick up leases from these sod-busters for next to nothing."

"That remains to be seen," The elder Conroy smiled indulgently at his son, as if he were a schoolboy.

"We're opening an office across the river." Marty glanced quickly at Tom. "An old wildcatter named Rigger Haines is drilling up there. The old bastard's a millionaire twice over, but he just keeps on drilling. I saw a map of where he's drilled, and it's headed straight down from the Healdton field."

"I've heard of Rigger Haines."

"He brought in a gusher in the old played-out Marlow field and made a pile of money."

"They say he's tough as a boot."

"Not so tough that he don't need a little . . . ah . . . protection now and then, huh, Daddy?" Marty smirked and glanced at Tom.

After each of the half dozen times Tom had met Marty Conroy he had come away with the impression that all that was on the man's mind was big money and how to get it without working for it.

Marty began to talk about the Chicago gangster, Al Capone.

"He made a hundred million a year, Daddy. More money than Henry Ford. He was only twenty-six years old, a year older than I am, when he took over the bootlegging and gambling in Chicago. He had to be smart to outwit the Feds for so long. They couldn't get a thing on him."

"I wouldn't say he outwitted them," Tom said drily. "He's in jail for income-tax evasion."

"Ha! He'll be out by the end of the year. He's too smart—"

Tom's mind suddenly turned off their conversation when he heard Jay's cry, and Emmajean's shrill voice scolding him. He got up and went into the house, not bothering to excuse himself.

Emmajean was holding the child's shoulders and shaking him vigorously.

"I told you not to touch anything. Mother'll not let us come again. You're bad . . . bad—" The last words were accompanied with a sharp slap on the cheek.

Tom hurried forward and picked up his son. The sobbing child wrapped his arms around his father's neck and hid his face.

"I've told you not to hit him in the face!"

"See, Mother? See what I have to put up with?" She turned to the frowning woman standing by the settee holding a satin pillow and examining it for damage. "When I try to make him mind, Tom pets him. I just don't know what I'm going to do. He just makes me so . . . mad!" Emmajean's voice got louder and more shrill.

"Here, here. Stop yelling, Emmajean. The neighbors will hear you." Mr. Conroy had come in, followed by Marty.

"He just makes me so mad!" Emmajean said again. "Let me stay here, Daddy. I hate that old dirt farm. Let me come back home. He can have Jay. I don't care. Mother? Daddy? Pl . . . ease! I don't even have electric lights or a radio out there, and I have to get water out of a well. And he wants me to . . . cook and wash his dirty old clothes. Please . . . let me stay—"

"We've gone over that before," Mrs. Conroy said patiently. "Your place is with your husband and child."

"But . . . but . . . I hate him!" Emmajean's voice had reached an hysterical pitch. "Mama—" she said pleadingly to the slim, elegant woman still holding the pillow and inspecting it. "Don't make me go back . . . there."

"Mother," Mrs. Conroy corrected. "Mama, is so . . . common."

"Calm down." Mr. Conroy shook his head at Marty when his son gave a snort of disgust. "Calm down. You're a grown woman now, Emmajean. A grown, *married* woman."

"I knew this would happen if they came." Mrs. Conroy looked accusingly at her husband then back to her daughter. "Emmajean, straighten up and behave," she said firmly.

Tom carried his son out onto the porch. A scene similar to this one took place each time they came for a visit which, thank God, wasn't very often. He was embarrassed for Emmajean, not because she didn't want to go back to the home he had provided for her, but because she was begging, pleading to stay when it was so obvious that her parents didn't want her.

He had known the morning he had taken her home and she had blurted out the fact that she had spent the night with him that these people were like none he'd ever known. There had been no outrage. They had calmly set about planning a quick wedding. It was not until after he became aware of his bride's erratic behavior that he realized the Conroys had found a respectable way to rid themselves of an embarrassing daughter. What had been their problem was now his.

A half hour later, when they headed back to Red Rock, Emmajean was still crying. Jay lay asleep on the seat between them, his head on his father's leg.

Tom was silent. What a mess he'd made of his life!

* * *

Henry Ann sat beside her father's bed and fanned him with a cardboard fan that advertised White's Drug Store in Red Rock. The doctor had come back, given Ed another shot of morphine, and promised to return before dark. As the afternoon lengthened, the breeze that had earlier stirred the window curtains stilled. The air in the room was hot and oppressive.

"What's the matter with the radio?" Isabel asked from the doorway.

"It needs a new tube."

"Well, poot! I wanted to listen to it. There's nothin' else to do 'round here."

Henry Ann didn't bother to reply. Isabel stood for a moment pouting, then left the room singing the theme to a popular radio show.

"When the moon comes over the mountain—"

How was it possible the girl could be so uncaring? The pain in Henry Ann's heart made her feel as though a wide chasm lay between her and the rest of the world.

Old Shep slunk into the house and under her father's bed as if waiting for something vague and fearful to happen.

Minutes spun into hours. In the late afternoon a car stopped out front. Aunt Dozie came to the bedroom door.

"Chile, Mr. Dolan is here."

Henry Ann reluctantly left the room and went out onto the porch. The man stood there with his hat in his hand.

"Thank you for sending the doctor."

"Glad to be of help. Is there anything I can do?"

"No. But thank you for offering."

She was aware of the big, dark man towering over her. Their eyes met and held. She was afraid if she said another word, she would burst into tears. That must not happen. Pride kept her head up and her eyes dry.

"Doctor Hendricks told me about Mr. Henry. I'm sure sorry. If I can help in any way, send the boy to fetch me."

"Thank you."

He turned and stepped off the porch. *So much pride. So much dignity.* The image of the woman's lovely haunted face stayed in his mind as he strode quickly to the car. Emmajean was on the verge of one of her rampages. When she was like that he feared leaving Jay alone with her, and, also, he wanted to get away from the Henrys' before she started yelling at him.

The end came for Ed Henry at dusk. It was symbolic that his life ended at the golden time of day when the sun had set and the birds were settling into the trees for the night—the time of day that he liked to take his guitar to the front porch, play a few chords, and sing his favorite songs for his own enjoyment and for that of his daughter. He knew dozens of ballads: "Strawberry Roan," "The Prisoner's Song," "Bury Me Not on the Lone Prairie," and his favorite, "Red River Valley."

Since he had bought the radio he and Henry Ann seldom missed listening to the *Grand Ole Opry* on Saturday night. Ed was especially fond of Uncle Dave Macon, known as "the Dixie Dewdrop," and Roy Acuff. Personally, Henry Ann thought her daddy played and sang better than any of them.

Just before Ed breathed his last, Aunt Dozie had come in and closed the door, shutting out the curious Isabel so that Henry Ann could be alone with her daddy. When it was over, Aunt Dozie closed his mouth and folded his arms across his chest. Henry Ann placed her head on the pillow beside his and cried. This day, at dusk, it was Aunt Dozie who sang. She stood at the end of the bed with the Henry family Bible in her hands.

> "A - maz - ing grace, how sweet the sound,
> That saved a wretch like me!
> I - once was lost, but now am found,
> Was blind, but - now I see."

At daybreak Henry Ann went to the kitchen. Aunt Dozie was there starting a fire in the cookstove.

"That old dominecker rooster came clear up to the door dis mornin'," Aunt Dozie said shaking her head. "It was plumb queer the way he jist stood an' crowed fit to kill. 'Twas as if that old rooster was sayin' his good-bye to Mr. Ed."

"I heard him. It seems strange not to have Daddy here. He always got up before I did."

Henry Ann batted the tears from her swollen eyes and went to the porch. She stood there and scratched old Shep's ears for a while before she headed for the barn to do the chores. To her surprise they were done. Johnny was drawing water from the well and filling the stock tank. She hadn't heard him when he came home last night, but she'd noticed him in the kitchen when the undertaker arrived. Then he had come to the porch and had stood silently and expressionless as Ed Henry was taken from his home for the last time.

"Johnny, I need to go to town to . . . make arrangements." He averted his eyes when Henry Ann spoke to him. "I'd like for you to take me."

"Why? You can drive."

"I can't crank the car. Here are the keys to the shed." She handed him a ring of keys she took from her pocket.

"He didn't have to lock it up." The boy looked straight at her. "I wasn't goin' to steal it."

"He knew that, but he wasn't sure about Pete Perry."

"I found a butchered steer down in the lower woods."

"Butchered? You mean someone killed it for the meat?"

"Looks like it."

"Well, forevermore. Did they take it all?"

"Only the front and hind quarters. Dogs and wolves tore up the rest."

"That means they took it to sell and not to eat. Were there tracks?"

"Motorcar tracks."

"Do you know whose?"

"No."

Henry Ann looked into her half brother's face and knew he was telling the truth. He seemed different this morning; not so hostile. Could it be that he *really* had felt something for her father?

"We can tell the sheriff, but I doubt he'll do anything. I'll be ready to go in a few minutes."

Ed Henry had not particularly wanted a car; he bought it only to take Henry Ann to school on the days she couldn't walk. Johnny, however, had been delighted that a car was available when he first came to live with them. Ed had taught him how to drive and how to take care of the machine. The enthusiasm for the car faded as soon as Ed bought him the pony.

The motor of the topless Model T balked at first when Johnny attempted to start it. He instructed Henry Ann to pull out the choke. He had worked up a good sweat turning the crank by the time the engine sputtered, caught, then began a steady hum.

When they reached the funeral parlor, located behind the furniture store, Henry Ann asked Johnny if he wanted to come in. He shook his head, and she went in alone. The mortician confirmed what Doctor Hendricks had told her. Ed had made the arrangements for his burial and had paid for it. He had not been interested in the services that would precede the burial and had left that up to Henry Ann.

She visited next with the Reverend Wesson, the minister who would conduct the services. His daughter, Karen, was her best friend. He told her that Karen had left only minutes ago for the Henry farm.

After reporting the slaughter of the steer to the sheriff's deputy, Henry Ann and Johnny headed back home. Two wagons and two cars were parked in the yard. One of the cars belonged to their neighbor, Tom Dolan, the other to Karen Wesson.

"Are you coming to the service?" Henry Ann asked when Johnny stopped in front of the shed to let her out.

"Do you want me to?" He stared straight ahead.

"Only if you want to."

"I . . . don't have a decent shirt."

"I'll wash one of Daddy's."

"What'll I have to do? I've not been to . . . one—"

"You don't have to do anything."

"I'll come."

A girl ran out the back door to meet Henry Ann. Her hazel eyes were red with weeping.

"Oh, Henry, I didn't even know your daddy was sick." She wrapped her arms around Henry Ann.

"I didn't either until I got home day before yesterday. He hadn't told me, Karen. He let me go off to Oklahoma City without saying a word."

"I heard about it last night at choir practice. It was late, or I'd have come out then."

"I'm glad you're here now. I just saw your daddy. I told him that I wanted you to sing at the service."

"You know I will."

With their arms about each other, they went into the house. On the kitchen table was a variety of food already brought in by the neighbors. Aunt Dozie was bustling from table to stove, and, sitting quietly in Henry Ann's old high chair with a slice of bread and jam in his hand, was a small boy.

"Yo a'right, chile?" Aunt Dozie asked anxiously.

"I think so. Is this Mr. Dolan's little boy?"

"Ain't he 'bout the cutest little tyke ya ever did see?"

"He sure is. He was in the car yesterday when—"

"Dat Mr. Dolan come right after yo left. Brought a bag a coffee fer the fixin's. Said ya got a fence down and he'd fix it 'fore yore cows got out. Said it looked like someone'd drove a car in. Was goin' to take da little boy with 'im, but I said ta leave 'im. Little feller's good as gold, he is. Loves ta eat dat plum jam."

"Hello." Henry Ann squatted down beside the chair. The child turned his head to the side and refused to look at her. "What's your name?" He still refused to look at her. His mouth puckered as if he were ready to cry, and he looked fearfully up at Aunt Dozie. She hurried to him, picked him up, and cuddled him to her ample breast, uncaring that his little face was sticky with jam.

"Dere, dere, little sugar. Yo ain't got no reason ter be

scared. Dat lady like little boys," she crooned. Then to Henry Ann, "Took a while 'fore he'd let me hold him. He a daddy boy." She added in a whisper, "Yo better go on in de parlor. Dat gal's in dere talkin' her head off to Miz Austin."

"I'll stay and help Aunt Dozie," Karen said, and took Henry Ann's hat when she removed it. "Go on. That busybody is picking the girl's brain for everything she can get out of her."

"Dat ain't goin' ta be much!" Aunt Dozie snorted. "Dat girl ain't got much brains ta pick at."

Mrs. Austin embraced Henry Ann when she came into the room.

"You poor dear child. We just feel so bad about poor Mr. Henry. Chris-to-pher wanted to come over, but he hired two coloreds to help hoe cotton; and when you're paying five cents a hour you got to stand over them and see that they earn it." Mrs. Austin always drew her son's name out as if she were reciting a poem or singing a hymn.

"I know Mr. Austin is busy—"

"Not Percy, dear. Chris—to—pher."

"I would like for Mr. Austin to be a pallbearer—"

"Chris—to—pher would be glad to."

"Daddy has known *Mr. Austin* for a long time. If you think he'll be unable to do it, I'll understand and ask someone else."

"He'd be glad to, dear. Do you need Chris—to—pher, too?"

"No, but thank you."

Henry Ann untangled herself from Mrs. Austin's arms and went to speak to the other neighbor.

"I'm just as sorry as I can be, Henry Ann. Yore daddy was as good a man as I ever knowed."

"Thank you, Mrs. Whalen. And thank you for the beet pickles."

With her legs crossed and showing a goodly amount of flesh above the knee, Isabel sat in the chair beside the door, swinging her foot back and forth. She wore her best dress, rouge, and lipstick. She had slid a yellow ribbon under the back of her hair and tied it in a bow on top of her head. Henry Ann looked at her, then looked back again. Isabel had also plucked her eyebrows to a thin arched line and had marked them with a pencil.

She looked like she had come off South Reno Street in Oklahoma City, the street that was notorious for honkytonks and speakeasies.

Mrs. Austin prepared to leave as did Mrs. Whalen. Henry Ann walked with them to the porch.

"It's a shame is what it is that Isabel didn't get to know her daddy. Poor child's all tore up about it and cried when she told me how her mother kept her from him."

Henry Ann stared for a moment at Mrs. Austin, then looked back to where Isabel stood in the doorway. Their eyes met. The girl stared straight at her, then tilted her chin and curved her lips into a thin smile.

Henry Ann turned back when she heard Mrs. Austin telling her husband he was to be a pallbearer.

"I'm honored to be one of Ed's friends."

"The service will be at ten o'clock tomorrow morning at the church."

"We'll be there," Mrs. Austin said, then added for the benefit of Mrs. Whalen as they walked toward the wagon,

"We'd have brought the car, but Chris—to—pher needed it."

Mrs. Austin was fond of "putting on the dog," as Aunt Dozie described it. For the last several years she'd been trying to make a match between her son and Henry Ann, who liked Chris, but not well enough to consider him husband material. Everyone in the county, except Mrs. Austin, knew that he paid regular visits to Opal Hastings, a girl who lived down on the river bottom with her grandpa. Opal had a child and had never been married. Some said she was a whore, others said she had been raped. Henry Ann thought she was a pretty girl who had had a lot of trouble.

By noon, visitors had ceased to come with offerings and condolences, and Henry Ann was glad for the respite. Others would come when noontime was over. Aunt Dozie had washed a shirt for Ed to be buried in and one for Johnny to wear at the funeral. Henry Ann fetched them from the line and walked past the woodpile, where Tom Dolan had cut a supply of wood for the cookstove. He was stacking it as she approached. Their eyes caught and held. Hers, he thought, were like empty stars; the desolate look on her pretty face was a sad thing to see.

Henry Ann stopped a dozen feet from him, and a sudden paralysis kept her rooted to where she stood. Intensely aware of the big man with the curly black hair and broad shoulders, she finally spoke.

"Thank you for . . . fixing the fence and for splitting the wood."

"It's the least I can do for a neighbor."

"Dinner is ready. We'd be pleased to have you join us."

"You don't need to feed me, ma'am."

"I insist, and not because of the work you've done. I don't think Aunt Dozie would let you take Jay if you wanted to. She promised him a chicken leg."

"He took to her right away and . . . it's strange. He's not been around many colored folk."

"I'm not surprised. Aunt Dozie has a way with little ones. There's plenty of food, Mr. Dolan."

"If you're sure we'd not be a bother."

"No bother at all. You can wash up at the well. Have you seen Johnny?"

"He went out to drive your steers into that pasture behind the barn. He showed me the one that had been slaughtered. We took the hide. The boy's handy with a knife."

"That's the first steer we've lost . . . like that. The Whalens and the Cookmans have lost a couple."

"Whoever killed it drove a car in to pack it out. I'll keep a lookout for the kind of tires that made the tracks. Johnny said there was grass enough for the steers up close to the house for a day or two."

"We won't wait dinner for him. He can eat when he gets back."

Tom watched her walk back to the house, his eyes fastening on her straight back and swaying hips. She was all woman! His insides felt warm and melting. Christamighty! What was the matter with him? His heart was thumping, and goose bumps were climbing up his arms.

Tom's eyes found Jay as soon as he entered the kitchen. The boy was in a high chair pulled up to the table.

"Daddy, looky—" The grinning child squeezed the rubber ball in his hand, and the green rubber frog attached to the ball by a tube jumped and made a croaking sound.

"Well, whata ya know. That's some frog." Tom went to his son and placed his hand on his head. "Be careful with it."

"Aunty." Jay's eyes sought Aunt Dozie.

"He ain't goin' to hurt dat frog none. It been here since Henry Ann was little bitty, same as dat chair."

"Do you know Karen Wesson, Mr. Dolan?" Henry Ann said, when her friend came into the kitchen, followed by Isabel.

"We've not met. Pleased to meet you."

"Same here." Karen stepped forward and extended her hand.

Henry Ann wasn't in the mood to eat, but she made an attempt so that Aunt Dozie wouldn't fuss. In the past Aunt Dozie had sat at the table with her and her Daddy, but with Isabel, Karen, and the Dolans present, she made herself busy by setting up the ironing board and ironing the shirt Karen would take back to the parlor for Ed Henry to be buried in. Isabel ate in a surly silence, but Karen talked easily to Tom.

"We haven't seen you in church, Mr. Dolan. We have a Sunday school class for toddlers Jay's age . . . and I'm the teacher."

Tom placed the spoon in his son's hand to prevent the child from using his fingers to carry mashed potatoes to his mouth. His dark eyes went first to Henry Ann and then to Karen.

"I was born and raised a Catholic, Miss Wesson."

"Oh, I see. This is Baptist country. The nearest Catholic church is in Wichita Falls. Were you married there?"

"No, ma'am. We were married by the justice of the peace in Conroy."

Karen, fearing that she was getting into touchy territory, changed the subject.

"Someone told Daddy that you're an automobile mechanic."

"Among other things."

"But you'd rather farm, is that it?"

"No. It's a matter of making a living. There's not enough mechanic's work now to support a family. So I'm doing a little of both." His eyes briefly caught Henry Ann's, and she saw a muscle jump in his jaw.

"We have an old Whippet that hasn't run for several years." Karen continued on, blissfully unaware that Tom Dolan was reluctant to talk about himself. "Daddy's had several mechanics look at it, but there's so much wrong that they suggested he sell it for junk."

"He might get something out of the parts."

"I don't think Daddy can stand to see it torn apart. It's the same with an old buggy he has." Karen laughed.

Henry Ann was so used to her friend that sometimes she forgot how pretty she was. There was not a single blemish on Karen's face. Her hazel eyes shone between rows of thick lashes only a shade darker than the dark blond hair that she had pressed into a perfect finger wave. Her friend even had a special name. Most of Henry Ann's friends had names like Betty Jo, Flossy Mae, or Sadie Irene. Karen was a special name for a special girl.

Did Mr. Dolan think she was pretty?

Karen was interested in everything with a compelling eagerness. When listening to someone, she was intent, as if what was said was terribly important to her. She was friendly, gay, and happy, yet deep down inside she thought as much about serious things as Henry Ann did. It was one of the things that made them such good friends.

"Every tire on the thing is flat—rotten in fact."

"Whippet is a good car." Tom's eyes went from Karen to Henry Ann and found her looking at him.

I wonder if she knows how long it's been since I've sat in a friendly kitchen at a cloth-covered table and eaten a meal that I didn't prepare myself. My son has never had this experience before. He wasn't allowed to eat at his grandmother's table lest he spill something on the tablecloth.

Oh, Lord! I must hurry and get out of here, or I may never want to leave.

"I hate to eat and run, Miss Henry, but I've chores to do at home." Tom stood and looked down at his son. "Can you thank the ladies for dinner, tadpole?" He picked the child up and set him on his arm.

Jay hid his face against his father's shoulder.

"Thank you for fixing the fence—"

"It was nothing—"

"Dat baby ain't leavin' dis place less'n he got him a handful a cookies." Aunt Dozie put several large round cookies in Jay's hand. "Yo come back'n see Aunt Dozie, hear?"

"And the frog. I'm glad Teddy, that's what I called him, has someone to play with him." Henry Ann held out the green frog. One of Jay's hands was full of cookies, but he quickly reached for the toy with the other hand.

"Are you sure you want to part with it?" Tom asked, looking into her calm face. There was a slight smile of amusement on his.

"Quite sure."

*I was saving it for a child of my own. But it seems to give
your child so much pleasure—*

Henry Ann followed Tom through the house and stood
on the porch while he put his son in the car. He got in,
lifted his hand in a salute, and drove away. Back in the
kitchen, Henry Ann urged Aunt Dozie to the table to eat.

"Isabel and I will do the dishes before I go back to
town," Karen said.

"I got things to do. 'Sides, what's *she* here for?" Isabel
started for the back door.

"Isabel!" Henry Ann's voice stopped her. "Aunt Dozie
has worked all morning, and Karen needn't stay when you
and I can do the cleanup."

"Oh . . . all right. But that kid made a mess."

"He's just a little boy. I thought he did quite well."

"I've been around enough married men to know when
one ain't in no hurry to get back to his *wife*," Isabel said
nastily. "That'n would hop in bed with either one of ya at
the drop of a hat. He's woman-hungry, is what he is."

"For crying out loud!" Henry Ann stood with her hands
on her hips, her disbelieving eyes on the young girl's face.
"I don't understand you at all, Isabel. That man is a neighbor who came to do a neighborly deed. Beside that . . . he's
married."

"What's being a neighbor got to do with it? And so what
that he's married? That don't mean nothin'. He's a man
with a pecker, ain't he?"

Henry Ann felt the tingling sensation of embarrassment
as blood rushed to redden her face. Her eyes flashed to
Karen, who was carrying dishes to the the workbench, then
to the door as Johnny came in.

He stood just inside the door as if sensing the tension.

"Come on to the table, Johnny. We didn't wait for you, but Aunt Dozie held back some chicken. She's got hot bread."

"Sit yoreself down, boy. I'll be loadin' yo up a plate." Aunt Dozie took a clean dish from the shelf and went to the stove.

Johnny looked at Isabel's pouting face and noticed the paint and the pencil-slim brows.

"Jeez . . ." he whistled between his teeth. "What'er you all gussied up for? You look like you just came off Reno Street."

"And . . . you look like you just came off a . . . off a reservation!" Isabel flounced out and let the screen door slam behind her.

"Ain't nothin' bad 'bout a reservation far as I can see." Aunt Dozie set Johnny's food down on the table. "Dem Indian folks was here long 'fore dem white man come."

Emmajean was waiting on the front porch when Tom drove into the yard. She had on one of her good dresses and was wearing her floppy-brimmed hat. Knowing there was going to be an unpleasant scene, Tom left the sleeping child in the front seat of the car and went toward the house.

"Where in the hell have you been? I've been waiting hours."

"You know where I've been. Mr. Henry died last night. I went there to pay my respects."

"Four hours. It took four hours to say you were sorry the old man died?"

"I fixed a fence that was down. They invited me and Jay to dinner."

"Well, now, isn't that just dandy? You were eating dinner while I waited for you to remember you have a wife."

"Waiting for what? You were still in bed when I left." Tom was trying to hold on to his patience.

"To go to town!" she shouted. "I told you last night I was out of embroidery thread. Didn't I? Didn't I?"

"We'd use ten cents' worth of gas to drive to town just to buy a one-cent thread. You should have said you needed it yesterday when we were in town."

Tom walked into the house, and Emmajean followed. The bed was not made, clothes she had tossed out of drawers were scattered over the floor that hadn't been swept since he last swept it. The place was a mess. The glass lamp was lit, and a curling iron in the chimney was red hot. He blew out the lamp.

Dear God! She gets more irresponsible every day.

"Don't you walk away from me." Emmajean was working herself into a full-blown tantrum. "I said I wanted to go to town."

"I've got work to do, and so have you. Why in God's name don't you clean up this place? I'm not taking you to town again until you do." He raised his voice and glared down at her.

"You'll take me if I tell you to!" she screamed. "Who'er you but a dirty old sod-buster. And what's this, but a old . . . a old dirt farm? I'm a Conroy. The town of Conroy, Texas, was named for my grandpa. There wasn't a town named for *your* grandpa."

"Clean the house, Emmajean."

"You've been over there smelling around that slut! I knew what she was when she came pussyfootin' over here to *welcome* the new neighbors. It wasn't *me* she came to see. No-sir-ee. It was big Thomas Dolan who's hung like a stallion and is horny as a billy goat." Her face now was distorted with fury, her voice filled with hate. "You won't sleep with me! But you're screwing *her*, aren't you?"

"Hush that kind of talk, Emmajean!" Tom was glad he had left Jay sleeping in the car.

"Hush that kind of talk, Emmajean," she mimicked. "Hush that! Hush that! That's all I ever hear. From Mama. From Papa and from you. Someday you'll be sorry for treating me like this. I wish Mama would die. I hate her. I hate you. I hate that stinking brat you made me have!" Her voice rose to a screech.

"Calm down. You're getting all worked up, and you'll be sick."

The words had no more than left his mouth when a plate went flying past his head, hit the wall, and smashed into pieces. Knowing what would come next was a crying jag that would last for several hours, Tom left the house, went to the well and began filling the stock tank.

Could hell be any worse than this?

Chapter Four

It seemed to Henry Ann that half the town had turned out for her father's funeral. There was standing room only in the church, and a string of motorcars followed the black hearse that carried his body to its final resting place.

That is not my daddy being put in the ground. It is only the house he lived in while he was here. The thought helped Henry Ann to get through the day.

Johnny had stood beside her, silent and expressionless. It would surprise her to think later that his presence had been a comfort. Isabel, on the other hand, had sulked because Henry Ann suggested firmly that she wash the paint off her face and wear a freshly ironed gingham dress instead of the green satin that had been their mother's.

Dozie had insisted on staying at the farm even though Henry Ann had asked her to come to the burial.

"Mr. Henry done knows that I's grievin' his passin'. I stay right here and get de fixin's ready for when de company comes."

"I hope that old woman's got the lemonade ready," Isabel said, as they left the cemetery and headed down the road toward the farm. "I'm 'bout to burn up."

Henry Ann had sent Johnny to town early that morning to get a block of ice. He had put it in a washtub and covered it with a couple of old quilts. The stoneware cooler for the lemonade would be set at the end of the tables lined up on the porch to hold the food.

With a heavy pain burdening her heart and wishing the day to be over, Henry Ann had helped Aunt Dozie with the food, then stood on the porch and greeted her father's friends. She thanked those who brought covered dishes and invited all to take plates from the end of the table and to help themselves. Shoulders stiffly erect to hide the pain within her, she accepted their condolences.

The yard filled quickly with cars and wagons. Ed Henry was well-known and respected in the community. Later Henry Ann would compare the number of friends who came to her father's funeral to the fewer than ten people who had come to say farewell to her mother just a week before.

Johnny chipped ice and carried it in a dishpan to the cooler for Aunt Dozie. He seemed to share none of Isabel's dislike for her. In fact, he hung around in the kitchen making himself available to help. Isabel, however, disappeared as soon as Pete Perry rode into the yard and let his horse into the back corral. Many of the people had passed the tables and filled a plate when Isabel came out of the house with her arm tucked in Pete's. She led him to the tables heaped with food and handed him a plate.

Anger kept Henry Ann's tears at bay. Pete Perry had never been welcome in her father's house, and he wasn't welcome now. How dare that little twit bring him here as if he were a member of the family! He smirked when he saw her glaring at them, left his plate on the table, and came to her.

"I'm sorry about Uncle Ed, Cousin Henry Ann," he said loudly enough for those sitting on the edge of the porch to hear. He touched her arm in a gesture of sympathy. She jerked away from his hand as if it were hot.

"Eat and go," she said in a low voice. "You're not welcome here."

"I'll be glad to," he said loudly. "I'll be over tomorrow to lend you a hand." He walked away before his words soaked in and she could demand to know what he was talking about. She stood numbly while those sitting within hearing distance looked at her in puzzlement.

Henry Ann pressed her lips together and gritted her teeth. She would not make a scene in front of the neighbors, but she certainly intended to have it out with Isabel. She turned her gaze to the man standing at the edge of the porch holding his son. Her eyes were caught and held by dark intent ones that conveyed understanding. *He had overheard the conversation! What in the world was he thinking?*

"Let me have dat sweet babe, Mista Dolan." Aunt Dozie came across the porch and reached for Jay. "Come ta Aunt Dozie so yo papa can fill him a plate. Aunty fix dis babe somethin' mighty good." Jay went eagerly to Aunt Dozie, and they disappeared into the house.

"He's really taken to her," Tom observed, groping for something appropriate to say as he stepped up onto the porch.

"I've not known a child who didn't take to Aunt Dozie,"

Henry Ann murmured. "Help yourself to dinner, Mr. Dolan."

"It was a nice service. Mr. Henry had a lot of friends."

"Yes, he did."

Tom searched her face for a long moment before he spoke again, noting the dark circles that ringed her eyes and lines of fatigue that bracketed her mouth.

"I'd like to talk with you . . . sometime within the next few days."

"Talk to me? About what?" A puzzled line appeared between her brows,

"About trading work."

"Oh. Well. I've not had time to think about how I'll get the work done."

"Then you are going to stay here."

"Of course. This is my home."

"I heard talk that you might lease out to an oil company."

"You can put the rumors to rest. I intend to stay here and farm the land just like my . . . daddy." Her voice caught, and she turned away to speak to a neighbor who had just arrived. "Hello, Mrs. Bradshaw."

"My, my, my. I was just so sorry to hear about poor Mr. Henry. Whatever will ya do, child?" The woman's weathered, wrinkled face was creased with lines of concern. "Yo're alone now, ain't ya? It's too bad ya ain't got ya a good man to run the place—"

"I'll be fine." Henry Ann straightened her shoulders. "Johnny and I will manage just fine."

"I ain't thinkin' ya can depend on . . . *him.*"

"We'll do fine, Mrs. Bradshaw. Take a plate and help yourself." Henry Ann turned to see that Tom Dolan still stood beside her, the plate she had handed him still unfilled. She left the porch and walked out into the yard to greet Karen and her father.

Times were hard. A funeral gathering was not only a time for neighbors to get together and remember the deceased, but to catch up on the news and discuss the terrible state of the economy and what the politicans planned to do about it.

A goodly amount of time was spent discussing the upcoming presidental election. Franklin Roosevelt, former New York governor, was promising the American people a "new deal" if he was the candidate chosen to run against President Hoover. Most of the people didn't know what the term "new deal" meant, but the majority of those present declared their intention to vote for him if he won the nomination.

"I'm thinkin' he can't do no worse than what Hoover's done." The man who spoke had lived in a sod dugout for five years, eaten beans and corn pone while waiting for a cotton crop that would allow him to build a frame shelter for his family. "Anybody been to see you fellers about a oil lease?"

"One a them slick-talkers come nosin' round my place. Promisin' to make me rich. Bullfoot!" Mr. Whalen snorted. "Ain't been nothin' come in near me but a little old piddlin' well that pumps 'bout fifty barrels a day. Fifteen cents a barrel is all it's goin' for. I'd be lucky to get two bits a day. All them oil fellers do, to my way of thinkin', is mess up the land so it ain't no good ever again for plantin'."

"Ain't it so?" Mr. Austin's head bobbed up and down. "I see what they done up 'round Marlow. Place looks like a cyclone struck it. Ain't nothin' worse lookin' than a old played-out field. Them drillers come in, tear up, and move on.

"There's another of them outfits comin' to Red Rock. Got some kind of connection with that feller that put on the air show down in Wichita Falls. Harrumph! Why anybody'd be such a fool as to stand on top one of them airplanes is beyond me."

"It ain't beyond me. Ain't much a feller won't do nowadays to get that jinglin' stuff in his pockets. Hell! I'd join up with that dance marathon that's coming to town if I wasn't so damn old."

"Ya can't dance nohow, Wilbur. Heard Pete Perry's already signed up."

"Wal, there's just one good thin' about that. If he's dancin', he ain't bootleggin'."

"That dance marathon'll bring folks to town. It'll be somethin' to gawk at, that's sure."

Tom listened to the talk. As a newcomer he didn't have much to add to the conversation. He had heard talk in town about Pete Perry. He reckoned the man was about as sorry a sort as they come. What game was he playing with Miss Henry? She was going to be in trouble up to her neck if she didn't put a rein on the little baggage she brought back from the city. That one had the makings of a *tramp* if he ever saw one.

A few of the women had asked him about his wife. He'd brought out the lame old excuse that she didn't feel well. Maybe she didn't. She'd still been in bed when he dressed himself and Jay and left the house. He would have found an excuse not to bring her even if she had wanted to come.

It seemed to Tom that Emmajean became more and more unstable as time went by. Last night she'd thrown a dipper of water in Jay's face, then later when she tried to hold him on her lap, he had screamed. It had infuriated her. She held on to him tightly, and Tom'd had to pry her arms loose from the terrified child.

In the saner light of day, Tom usually felt as if he could cope with the problems life had dealt him. It was at night, lying on the cot in the kitchen, that he was acutely aware that not only was his son deprived of a mother, he himself was deprived of a wife.

Henry Ann thought the afternoon would never end. She had been shooed out of the kitchen by Aunt Dozie and a couple of neighbor women who were washing the empty bowls and platters and arranging them on the table so the owners could pick them up as they were leaving. When Aunt Dozie whispered that the little boy should use the chamber pot, Henry Ann lifted him from the high chair. He went with her willingly.

She took him to her room and closed the door. The minute she brought out the pot the child looked up at her and said, "Pee, pee."

Henry Ann unbuttoned his overalls. "Can you do it by yourself?"

"I big boy."

"Of course, you are." She positioned him over the pot and was surprised at how well he handled himself. When he finished, he looked up at her with a pleased smile, clearly expecting praise. "You *are* a big boy."

"I Daddy's big boy."

"I can see that." She buttoned his clothes. "Shall we go outside for a while?"

The child looked at her with large dark eyes so like his

father's. The parallel between her life and that of this child suddenly came into focus. Her daddy had been both parents to her when her mother left. Mr. Dolan was trying to be both parents to his son. What in the world was the matter with the mother of this child?

If this little boy was mine, I wouldn't let him out of my sight.

A yearning for a husband and children of her own came over her. She was twenty-four years old. Considered an old maid by some. Karen was the only girl she knew anywhere near her age who hadn't married and had a child or two. Well, she'd never tie herself to any man unless she was absolutely sure that he was everything that she believed him to be.

"Mr. Dolan?"

Tom was jarred into awareness by the minister who had conducted the funeral services. He stood and held out his hand to the short, gray-haired man.

"Tom Dolan."

"Reverend Wesson." The man's hand was soft, but his grip firm. "We haven't met, but my daughter told me about meeting you . . . and your young son."

"I heard her sing this morning. She has a beautiful voice." The men sat back down on the bench.

"Yes, she does." There was pride in the minister's voice. "She says you're a mechanic."

"Among other things."

"I've got an old Whippet—"

"Whippet Six was a good car. They were among the first to have a seven-bearing crankshaft, full force-feed lubrication, and four-wheel brakes. I'm not sure they're making them anymore."

"I see you know your cars. This one is a 1916 model."

"I've not seen that model in years. It would be hard to find parts."

"I'd sure like to put the old girl back in running order."

"Why? It'll probably cost you more than you'll ever get out of it."

"Sentimental, I guess. She served me well. I hate to see her going to the junk pile." His blue eyes twinkled. "Will you take a look at her and tell me what she needs?"

"I'll be glad to take a look. It's impossible for me, at the present time, to be away from home for any length of time—"

"I understand. If you take on the job, we could tow her out to your place."

"All right. I'll take a look the next time I'm in town."

"I'd be obliged."

The sound of happy, childish laughter reached Tom and made him turn and look back over his shoulder. His son was hugging the neck of an old shaggy dog. Miss Henry was kneeling beside him and the dog. The dog shook his head and licked Jay's face. His son laughed and patted the dog's face with his small hands.

Tom couldn't tear his eyes from the woman, the child, and the dog. He was awed by the power of the feeling that washed over him. He had never before heard such spontaneous laughter from his son.

As he watched, Miss Henry stood and took Jay's hand. The pair walked toward the chicken pen, the dog following along behind. Inside the pen a big speckled rooster, unhappy about being penned for the day, was strutting around with ruffled feathers. Suddenly, squawking and flapping his wings, he ran at a lazy hen. Jay's childish laughter rang out. He clapped his hands.

There was a shining pain in Tom's eyes as he watched Miss Henry and his boy. *With a mother like Emmajean, the child was missing so much.*

"Henry Ann has a way with children." Reverend Wesson followed Tom's gaze to the pair beside the fence. "She should have been a teacher."

"Why isn't she?" Tom turned to look at him.

"I'm not sure. Ed would have sent her to college if she'd wanted to go. She's going to have it rough for a while. Every single man in the county will be after her thinking to get his hands on this farm."

"She . . . doesn't have a regular . . . fellow?"

"No one special."

"That's strange. She's a good-looking woman."

"But an independent one. She'll not take a man unless she loves him with all her heart." The minister stood. "I'd better collect Karen and head back to town. There's choir practice again tonight. Come by anytime, Mr. Dolan."

"Thank you, I will. I need to get home, too. I'll say good-bye to Miss Henry."

Henry Ann watched Jay run to his father, be snatched up and tossed in the air. The child giggled happily and wrapped his arms around his father's neck. The loving look on the man's face as he hugged his son disturbed Henry Ann so profoundly that she felt a tingling travel down her back.

"We've got to get along home, son. Can you tell Miss Henry good-bye?"

"Goo-bye."

"Good-bye, Jay. Come see us again."

"I'd like to talk about trading work, but I'll not bother you now—"

"I'm not sure there's anything I could do for you."

"If Johnny would give me a hand, I'll pay back—"

"Johnny?"

"An able hand as far as I can see."

"I'm not sure that he'd be willing."

"I'll be by one day soon, and we can ask him." He pressed his son's head to his shoulder. "This fellow's had quite a day. He'll be asleep before I get him home. If there's anything I can do, let me know."

His eyes locked with hers, and she knew that he was thinking of Pete Perry.

"Thank you, but I'll be able to handle it."

"The offer is there if you need it. I know quite a bit about car tires, and I'm still looking for the car that drove into your field and carried out the steer meat."

"I reported it to Sheriff Watson, but I'm not expecting much help from him. He has the whole county to patrol."

Henry Ann watched as Tom placed his son on the seat, backed his car out of the yard, and drove slowly away.

The Austins and the Newmans were the last to leave. When Christopher returned for the Austins, Henry Ann had to endure the gushing of Mrs. Austin, and had to ward off the offers to have Christopher come over to give her a hand. Christopher stood, hat in hand, while his mother did the talking. Henry Ann looked at him with pity. *Didn't he have enough gumption to speak for himself?*

"But, dear, your field is gettin' weedy. Christopher will bring over a couple of hands and take care of it before the weeds crowd out your plants."

"No, thank you. Johnny, Isabel, and I will make quick work of it."

"If you're sure, dear."

Henry Ann breathed a sigh of relief when they left. Johnny came to take the tables off the porch.

"You've been such a help today, Johnny. Everything went just as Daddy would have wanted. I don't know if I could have done it without you."

"You'd a got by."

"Where's Isabel?"

"Don't know." He shrugged his shoulders.

"Pete Perry still here?"

"His horse is."

"Well, if that doesn't beat all!"

Henry Ann stepped off the porch and marched around the house and toward the barn. The doors were closed. She flung them open. Isabel was not there, nor was she in the shed where they kept the car. Pete Perry was a good ten years older then Isabel. She had no business going off alone with him. Henry Ann scanned the edge of the woods that lined the creek, then turned back toward the house.

The slanting wooden door of the cellar began to open as she approached. Pete stepped out and reached down to pull a giggling Isabel out behind him. She blinked when she came into the bright sunlight. Neither of them noticed Henry Ann until she spoke. Her voice was loud and angry.

"Isabel! Have you lost your mind?"

Pete turned and grinned. "Hi, Cousin Henry Ann. We were countin' the fruit jars."

"I bet you were, you . . . you lowlife polecat. You stay away from her. Hear me. She's only fifteen years old."

"I am not!" Isabel yelled.

"My mama had me when she was fourteen, Cousin Henry Ann. Your mama wasn't hardly more'n that when she had you. 'Sides . . . all we done was a little kissin'. You jealous?" He continued to grin cockily.

"I'd sooner kiss the back end of a mule." She turned on Isabel. "I'm warning you. Stay away from this scoundrel or out you go. Out! You'll go back to Oklahoma City to the orphans' home."

"I ain't goin' to no orphans' home. I got a brother and a sister and I got part a this farm. Ain't that right, Pete?"

Pete lifted his shoulders in a noncommittal gesture.

"You've got no claim to this farm. Get that through your head right now. If you want to straighten up and act decent, you can stay here. If not . . . get out."

"Now ain't ya bein' hard on the girl, Cousin? She didn't do nothin' but help me count fruit jars."

Henry Ann was so angry she could hardly breathe. She took a couple of deep breaths before she spoke.

"Get your horse and get off my land. If you come back, I'll go to the sheriff and have you arrested."

"For what? Comin' to help my . . . cousin?"

"I don't want your help."

"He can come here anytime he wants to." Isabel snuggled up close to Pete and rubbed her cheek against his arm. "Me and Pete's goin' to enter the dance marathon. We'll win the prize, too."

"What dance marathon?"

"The one that's comin' to Red Rock." Pete rubbed his knuckles on Isabel's cheek. "They're goin' to build a platform on Main Street across from the Five and Dime. It'll bring folks to town. Already got ten couples signed up. I'd'a asked you, Cousin Henry Ann; but Isabel here is no bigger than a minute, and I figure I'll have to hold her up while she sleeps."

"Find someone else. She's not doing anything as idiotic as that. Go to the house, Isabel."

"I will not. You're not my boss."

"Ya better go, sugar. We got to keep old Henry Ann pacified . . . for a while."

"Will you be back?"

"He will not be back," Henry Ann interjected before Pete could speak.

"Oh . . . you make me so mad." Isabel stamped her foot. "You're just a prissy old maid."

"Old maid or not, I know what's decent and what isn't. You're too young to be messing around with the likes of Pete Perry."

"We'll see." A cunning look came over the girl's face. "I've got rights here, same as you."

Johnny came across the yard toward them.

"Howdy, boy," Pete called. "You been busy as a bee . . . helpin' the ladies with the fixin's. Me'n Isabel had to go to the cellar, 'cause there was so many folks around we couldn't find a place to do any kissin'." His bright blue eyes glittered when they flashed at Henry Ann.

Johnny walked past Pete without saying a word. He went to the corral and Pete followed.

"You goin', Pete?" Isabel's voice was anxious.

"Yeah, I'm goin'. See ya around, sugar."

" 'Bye, Pete." Isabel turned on Henry Ann like a spitting cat. "I hope you're satisfied. You've run him off. He said you'd be jealous if he paid more attention to me than to you. You're just like *her*. She didn't want me 'round when she was doin' *it* with a new man. I hate you. I hate you more'n I hated her." Isabel ran to the house, leaving Henry Ann shocked to the core of her being.

Tom had stayed at the Henrys' until it was time to do chores. The Austins and the Newmans seemed to be in no hurry to leave either. Pete Perry's horse was still in the corral, but there was no sign of him or the flitty young girl Miss Henry had brought back from Oklahoma City.

Jay had missed his afternoon nap and was asleep by the time he stopped the car in front of the shed. He decided to leave him there until he found out what kind of mood Emmajean was in. As he approached the house, she came out onto the porch.

"Where's Jay?" she called.

"Asleep in the car. I'll leave him there while I do chores."

"I've got a surprise for you." Emmajean was smiling.

Oh, Lord! What now?

She held the screen door open for him and followed him into the house. He could scarcely believe his eyes. There were no clothes scattered about, the bed was made, and the floor freshly swept. His face registered his surprise.

"That's not all," Emmajean trilled. "Come to the kitchen." She grabbed his hand and tugged.

The work counter had been cleaned off, the table was covered with a cloth, and a vase of flowers set in the middle of it. Something was cooking in a pot on the stove. His eyes scanned the room. *His cot was missing, but the crib he'd built for Jay was still there.*

"Well?" Emmajean waited like a child expecting praise.

"It's certainly an improvement."

"I worked all day." She went to him, wrapped her arms

about his waist, and snuggled her face into the curve of his neck. "I've not been a very good wife," she whispered sorrowfully, then added brightly, "but that's all changed now. You'll see. I'm going to keep house and cook and . . . be the best wife a man ever had."

"That's what you say now, but it seems that I've heard this many, many times before." He took her arms and peeled them from around him. "How about your son, Emmajean? How about Jay? You said nothing about taking care of him."

"I will! Oh, I will. I've missed him today. I've just been so lonely and so anxious to see my baby." Large blue eyes looked pleadingly into his.

Tom wished that he could believe her, but he couldn't. He studied her face. She had washed her hair and painted her face, thinking that it was what made her pretty. She was pretty. He had to admit that. She was pretty until she opened her mouth.

"I've got beans cooking. We'll have a nice supper, then sit on the porch."

"I've got to do chores."

"Yes, yes. Go do them. I'll have supper ready."

Tom left the house and headed for the barn. Leaning against the side of the house was his cot; the mattress and bedclothes in the dirt. He knew what Emmajean was up to. She was trying to force him into her bed. No matter how lonely he got, or how much he ached, it would never happen. He would never, never, take the chance that his seed would take root in her body; she would never have another child of his.

Chapter Five

During the following week Henry Ann not only had to cope with the grief of losing her father but had to adjust to all the responsibility of the farm and living with Isabel. Aunt Dozie stayed for three days after the burial. If not for Isabel, she would have stayed longer. Henry Ann spoke to her old friend about it.

"Aunt Dozie, you're going because of Isabel, aren't you?"

"I be like a sore toe in a tight shoe to the gal. It make thin's better if I go for a while."

"I'm so sorry. I worry about you. What are you doing for money?"

"I gettin' by. I does a little a this, little a that. I got chickens, I got a garden, I got a roof over my head. It more than some folks got."

"I'll always have room here for you. I hope you know that."

"I knows it, chile."

"Johnny will take you home when you're ready to go."

Many times Henry Ann wished that she'd never gone to Oklahoma City. She'd missed out on being with her daddy during his last days, and she had brought home a peck of trouble.

At daybreak several mornings after Aunt Dozie went home, Henry Ann awakened Isabel and insisted that she put on an old hat and come to the cotton field with her and Johnny. The girl had whined that it wasn't fair for her to do "nigger" work. She sulked through breakfast and all the way to the field.

Henry Ann was patient with her and showed her how to hoe the weeds from around the cotton plants. After watching her for a few minutes, Henry Ann started weeding down her own row. After a short while she looked back to see that Isabel had chopped out everything in the row; weeds, cotton plants and all. Twenty feet of cotton plants had been deliberately wiped out.

"Isabel! Stop!"

"There just ain't no pleasin' you, is there?" She leaned on the hoe handle and glared at Henry Ann.

"Don't you know a weed from a cotton plant?"

"No. I don't know a weed from a cotton plant," she echoed.

"Then you can learn."

"I ain't no field hand."

"Isabel, I'm getting sick and tired of your attitude. Why do you insist on being so unpleasant?"

"I hate this place. I understand why Mama left it."

"You haven't even tried to like it."

"And I ain't going to either. I'm goin' to the house."

"No, you're not. Sit down there in the shade where I can keep an eye on you. Johnny's finished a half row already."

"He knows 'bout diggin' in the dirt. He's a breed, ain't he?"

"What do you mean by that?"

"His daddy was a dirty old Indian. Mama said so."

"I don't want to hear you say that again. You've got a mouth on you like the Perrys. And I'm beginning to believe that you're just as rotten as they are."

"I take that as a compliment. Pete's goin' to take me to see them. He said they'd just love me 'cause I look like my mama."

"You're not going anywhere with Pete Perry. And that's that."

Isabel sank down on the grass with a smirk on her face.

"I'm thinkin' that pretty soon you ain't goin' to be so smart and know-it-all."

Henry Ann started down the row, her hoe expertly cutting the weeds from around the foot-high cotton plants. She had never met anyone like her half sister, and she didn't know how to handle her. She pondered about asking Johnny for help. Even though he had taken over the outdoor work, he was still uncommunicative, and most of the time limited his answers to yes and no.

Ahead Johnny had finished his row and was headed back toward her on the next one. When he got even with her, Henry Ann, on a sudden impulse, stopped him.

"Johnny, wait a minute."

Johnny wiped his wet forehead with the tail of his shirt. Then he took off his old felt hat, slapped it against his thigh, and slammed it back down on his head before he turned his expressionless face and dark eyes to her.

"What am I to do about Isabel?" Henry Ann wiped the sweat from her own face with a handkerchief she took from her dress pocket. "She refuses to help out, and she's so mouthy that I'm afraid that one day I'm going to lose my patience and slap her."

Johnny's dark eyes came alive, and the corners of his mouth lifted in a grin that lasted for only the space of a heartbeat.

"It worked with me."

"Oh, Johnny. I felt so bad about that. I've never struck another person in my life."

"I had it comin'."

"Please help me with Isabel. She's going to really be in trouble if she hangs around with Pete Perry."

"She slipped out and met him last night."

"Oh, no! Oh, Lord! I was so tired I slept like a rock. I'll talk to the sheriff and tell him that Isabel is underage."

"Won't do no good. She's like *her.* Let her go."

Henry Ann was shocked into silence for several minutes while she leaned on the hoe handle. In the four years Johnny had been with them he had never mentioned his mother, not even one time.

"Isabel keeps hinting that something is going to happen. Just now she said that soon I'd not be so know-it-all. I want you to know, Johnny, that when I came of age, Daddy deeded the farm to me. I think you can guess why he did it. He was afraid that if something happened to him, Mama would come and take it."

"She would've."

"Help me with the farm, Johnny. Even if it is in my name, I'll share it with you."

"I ain't no kin of Ed's. I've known that since I was knee-high. *She* told me lots of times that my pa was a blanket-ass."

"I don't like that word. It's obvious that my daddy wasn't yours, but you should be proud of your heritage. Never be ashamed of it."

He looked off toward the lower woods and didn't answer.

"You're my brother, Johnny. Whether we like it or not, she was our mother. And Isabel's. I'd like to help Isabel, but I don't think she'll let me."

"Let her go," he said again. "She won't do nothin' but drag you down." He began hoeing again and never looked back.

During the following week, Isabel grumbled continually about having to go to the field. She usually took a blanket and slept in the shade. Henry Ann offered her a book to read. She refused. One morning Johnny handed her a hoe and told her to have the weeds at the end of four rows chopped out by the time he returned or he would slap her silly. The threat worked.

Johnny worked from dawn to dusk, taking time out only to do the chores and to move the cattle to the lower pasture. Henry Ann wished that he had behaved this way when her daddy was alive. He had always wanted a son.

Rain was needed badly. The ground was as hard as a rock in some places and powdery dry in others. If rain didn't come soon, the cotton plants would be stunted, if they lived at all.

One evening, bone-weary after ten hours in the field, they walked back to the house to find a man standing beside the well drinking out of a tin cup.

"Who's that?" Isabel had pulled up the hem of her skirt to pull out the cockleburs that had stuck to it.

"I don't know, but put your dress down."

"Ma'am, I hope you don't mind that I helped myself to a drink of water."

"Of course we don't mind."

One glance told Henry Ann that the man was a transient, a hobo. He had a week's growth of light-colored whiskers on his sunken cheeks, and the pack that lay on the ground beside his feet probably held the sum of his belongings. He had removed a checkered cap when he spoke to her. Fair hair was plastered to his head with sweat.

Johnny drew a cylinder of water from the well and dumped it into the water bucket on the bench and into the washpan sitting beside it. Henry Ann removed her wide-brimmed straw hat, pushed up the sleeves of her father's old shirt that she wore over her sleeveless dress, and splashed water on her face with cupped hands. With her face dripping, she slicked her hair back with her wet palms. The skin on her face and neck had turned golden from the sun.

"I'd like to speak to your husband, ma'am, about doing a few days' work for some grub."

"She ain't got a husband," Isabel said with a snort. "And as prissy as she is, she'll probably never get one."

"Shut up!" Johnny hissed, and jerked her arm.

Henry Ann ignored her. "We've made it a rule not to hire from the road. I'll give you a meal and you can be on your way."

"I'd appreciate the meal, but I'll work for it."

"Johnny?" Henry Ann left the decision to her brother.

"He can fill the tanks while I mix the slop for the hogs."

"All right. I'll milk, then make supper. Feed the chickens, Isabel."

"Ma'am, I'm a right good hand at milkin'—"

Henry Ann looked into serious blue eyes. He was somewhere around thirty, she imagined. He spoke like an educated man. What bad luck, she wondered, had brought him to this stage in his life.

"Very well. But be sure to wash. I'll set the milk pail on the porch."

Henry Ann moved the soap dish over near the washpan, motioned to Johnny, and headed for the house. When they were a short distance away, she whispered, "Keep an eye on him."

"What'er ya whisperin' for?" Isabel asked loudly.

"Weren't you told to do chicken chores?" Johnny turned on his heel and left them.

Isabel stuck out her tongue. "Feed the chickens, water the chickens, gather the eggs," she chanted. "What's got into him? He acts as if he owns the place . . . already."

Henry Ann hung her shirt and hat on the peg beside the door and lit the two-burner kerosene cookstove they used during hot weather. She peeled potatoes and sliced them into a heavy iron skillet. After adding lard and a chopped onion, she placed the pan over the flame. She set the table for three, then added a fourth plate.

No need for the man to eat his plate of food on the porch as long as Johnny was here.

"That damned old hen pecked me again." Isabel came in and plunked down the egg basket. "Someday I'm goin' to wring her neck."

Henry Ann took the basket from the countertop where she was working at the cabinet and set it on the floor.

"I showed you how to get the eggs without disturbing the hen."

"Are you goin' to let that bum eat with us?" Isabel eyed the four plates on the table.

"Do you have any objections?" Henry Ann unscrewed the zinc lid from the fruit jar and forked spiced peaches into a bowl.

"I'll swear! You ain't got no pride a'tall. First you let that old nigger woman eat with us and now a bum."

"You can take your plate to the porch if you like."

"Thanks. Thanks a lot." Isabel peered into the mirror above the washstand. "Look at my face," she wailed. "I'm gettin' all freckled."

Henry Ann went out onto the porch to meet Johnny and the *bum* when they came from the barn with the milk.

"Set it here on the porch." She covered the full bucket of milk with a clean cloth. "After supper I'll run it with the morning milk through the separator."

"I'll be glad to do that for you, Miss—" The man snatched off his cap.

"Henry. You know how to run the separator?"

"Yes, ma'am. Necessity has turned me into a jack-of-all-trades. I've packed ten years of education into two." He smiled, showing exceptionally even white teeth. For all his ragged appearance, he oozed confidence. "Name is Grant Gifford, ma'am."

"Come in—both of you. Supper is ready."

Johnny stepped up on the porch. The man hesitated.

"I appreciate being asked in, Miss Henry. It's been a while since I put my feet under a table."

Henry Ann was almost too tired to eat. Isabel picked at her food, complaining that she didn't like raw-fried potatoes and why couldn't they have tomatoes and spaghetti. Johnny ate hungrily, as did Mr. Gifford.

"How come you're a bum?" Isabel asked with her eyes riveted on the stranger. "You'll not amount to anythin' roamin' around beggin' off folks."

"Isabel! Don't ask rude questions." Because she was tired, Henry Ann spoke more sharply than usual.

"I suppose you think you'll amount to somethin'," Johnny mumbled, his eyes on his plate.

Isabel heard. "More'n you, clodhopper!"

"Please," Henry Ann said tiredly.

"It's all right, Miss Henry. I'll answer the young lady. I'm a bum because I want to be. I have no one to look out for but myself. I'm satisfying my wanderlust. I've been from coast to coast and from border to border. I've learned things and seen things that I never would have experienced if I'd stayed in one place. And . . . I've never asked for a handout without offering to work for it first."

"You don't talk like a bum."

"How's a bum supposed to talk?"

"I don't know, but not like you do."

"Where are you going from here, Mr. Gifford?" Henry Ann asked.

"I was hoping to stay around Red Rock for a while."

"Good. He can help hoe weeds outta that cotton patch." Isabel spoke as if the decision were hers.

Grant's eyes met Henry Ann's. "I can do that, ma'am. For meals and a place to sleep."

"We've got a week's work left in that field."

"Not if three of you work."

"Shut up, Isabel." Johnny's patience had finally

snapped. "We'd be through by now if you'd done your share."

"You'll have to sleep in the barn or the shed." Henry Ann ignored both her brother and her sister.

"There's snakes out there," Isabel said.

"I'll throw my bedroll in the wagon bed."

The man had the bluest eyes Henry Ann had ever seen and the saddest. She also realized that her daddy would not allow anyone off the road to stay any longer than to work off a meal or two. There was something different about this man. His clothes were ragged, but reasonably clean and of good quality. She could not fault his manners, and he appeared to be a good worker.

Was he a criminal? Was he hiding from the law?

Henry Ann looked at Johnny, hoping to gauge his reaction. He was looking steadily back at her—waiting.

"Well, for goodness sake!" Isabel broke the silence. "There ain't nothin' to ponder about." She turned her eyes on Grant. "You're hired. I own a third a this place and—"

"Shut up!"

Henry Ann jumped. It was the first time she'd heard Johnny yell. He was on his feet, grabbed Isabel's arm, and yanked her out of the seat. Before she could gather her wits to protest, he had propelled her out the door and onto the back porch. She began to screech.

"Stop it! You . . . stupid . . . blanket-ass! Ain't ya goin' to stick up for what's ours? Ya goin' to just bow and scrape and lick her boots till—" The rest of her words were muffled when Johnny put his hand over her mouth.

Embarrassment caused the blood to rush to Henry Ann's face.

"My . . . half sister's a handful," she said lamely.

"I can see that. The boy's got a good head. I can see that, too." That shadow of sadness was back in his eyes.

"I'm the sole owner here."

"The boy told me that—in the barn, when I asked about staying on a while. He said your father died recently."

"Yes," she said quietly. Then, "I can afford to pay you a small wage."

"I'll work for meals. I've not stayed in any one place more than a week. You may wake up one morning and find me gone."

"A man who works deserves wages," she said. "I'll pay by the week."

Pale yellowish clouds were building in the west as Henry Ann watched Johnny and Grant, hoes on their shoulders, each with a jar of well water wrapped in a wet burlap bag tucked under his arm, walk away from the farm buildings. A weird half-light shadowed the farm yard. A dust storm was brewing somewhere along the dry, sandy riverbeds.

At the crack of dawn she had fired up the cookstove and made biscuits and pan gravy. The chores were done and the morning milk on the porch when Johnny and the new hired hand came to breakfast.

"I'll stay here at the house this morning, Johnny, and work in the garden. I've got green beans to pick and new potatoes to dig," she'd said.

Now, with the water in the copper boiler to sterilize the canning jars heating on the stove, she knocked on the door of her old room to wake Isabel.

"Isabel, get up. Hot biscuits are in the warming oven. I'm going to the garden. Eat and come on out."

Silence. Isabel usually grumbled and flopped over in bed when she was awakened.

"Isabel." Henry Ann listened, but didn't hear the squeaking of the bedsprings. She lifted her hand to rap again, then dropped it to the doorknob as a sudden premonition caused her to open the door.

The room was empty.

Henry Ann crossed the threshold to open the double doors of the wardrobe. She knew it would be bare, and it was. She looked beneath the bed where Isabel had put her suitcase. It wasn't there. She stood in the silent room where she'd slept all her life until the past week when she had moved her things into the room that had been her father's. Her eyes took in every detail. Isabel had taken everything she had brought with her and a couple of things she had not. The ivory-backed hand mirror Henry Ann had left was gone, as was a strand of long glass beads she'd left hanging on the post beside the beveled-glass dresser mirror.

Henry Ann went back into the kitchen. She didn't know whether to be glad or sad that Isabel was gone. She had longed for the peace she'd had before her half sister came to stay, but it troubled her that the young girl had probably gone to the Perrys.

After putting another stick of firewood in the stove and checking the firebox to be sure it was safe to leave the house, Henry Ann put on her old straw hat and went to the garden.

Carrying her suitcase, Isabel walked down the dusty road. She had tiptoed out of the house early while she was reasonably sure Henry Ann was still sleeping. *Johnny can hear a chicken fart and has eyes like a hawk*, she thought with a giggle. But if he heard her leave, he'd not care. He'd told her so last night—told her she was no-good, just like her mama.

The poor dumb-cluck red-ass! He'd fallen right into step with Miss Prissy-ass and wouldn't go see a lawyer. Their name was Henry too, wasn't it? Well! He could go sit on a hot skillet as far as she cared. Pete said he'd help her, said the Perrys would be glad to take her in until she could get what was lawfully hers, even if she wasn't old Ed's kid.

She'd had all she cared to take from Miss Prissy-ass Henry and Turn-tail Johnny. She set the suitcase down and sat on it to rest. She was too pretty to ruin her looks working in a cotton patch. Pete had said so. She'd let him feel between her legs the night she slipped out to meet him. He'd stopped when she told him to, but he'd not wanted to and was mad as a hornet. She giggled. It felt really good to have something a good-looking man like Pete wanted. Now she understood a little bit of how important her mama must have felt when a man was panting for her.

An hour after she left the farm, and after stopping several times to rest, Isabel came to the crossroads that Pete had told her about. One was a wagon trail, the other a road. No one lived at the end of the wagon trail, he'd said, but Perrys. There were so many Perrys living there that they could have a town of their own called Perrytown.

Walking down the wagon track, she visualized how it would be when she and Pete were married. They'd win the dance marathon and go to the city to live. Pete was too smart and too good-looking to spend the rest of his life living down on Mud Creek. In her prime, her mama would have latched on to him in a hurry, even if he was kin.

Maybe he was too close a kin for her mama, but not for her.
Second and third cousins wasn't too close. Pete had said
so.

Brush and blackjack oak grew close alongside the
wagon track. As she hurried along she stepped over horse
droppings from time to time. A long green snake slithered
into the track ahead. She barely repressed a scream. She
froze until it crossed and disappeared into the brush on the
other side. She waited to see if it would reappear. When it
didn't, she ran a good hundred feet, then stopped to catch
her breath.

Finally, she came to a clearing and saw a house ahead.
Smoke was coming from the chimney. The unpainted
house was set high off the ground on blocks. Beneath the
slanting roof that covered the front porch were two doors,
both of which were open. A sloppy woodpile was in the
front of the house and a tilting outhouse at the side. A flock
of red chickens, with a few white ones mixed in, roamed
the dirt yard, scratching, looking for a meal.

Suddenly a big black dog shot out from under the house,
barked furiously, and raced toward her. Isabel screeched
and hugged her suitcase to her for protection. She continued to screech as the dog bounded toward her. Suddenly a
shrill whistle from the house caused the dog to skid to a
stop.

"Hush up that caterwaulin'!" The harsh voice came
from behind her. "Yo're runnin' off the game."

She whirled around to see a grossly fat man with a thick
black beard come out of the woods. His overalls were fastened over only one shoulder, and his shirt, evidently the
top of his underwear, was dirty and sweat-stained. He cra-

dled a rifle in his arms. The dog, wagging his tail, went to the man who stooped and scratched its head.

"What'er ya doin' here?" His voice was mean. He was as scary as the shaggy dog. Isabel's knees began to shake.

"I . . . I . . . came to see Pete."

"Pete? Law! His women is gettin' younger all the time. Betch ya ain't stopped shittin' yellow yet. Pete got ya knocked up?"

"No! I'm . . . Isabel Henry. Ah . . . Dorene's girl."

"Bet it ain't 'cause he ain't tried. Hee, hee, hee!" When he laughed his stomach bounced up and down. "Yo're 'bout as juicy as a overripe peach."

Isabel took that to mean he thought her pretty. She preened and let the suitcase slide down her thighs to rest on the ground at her feet. With one hand she flipped her hair behind her ears. She wished she'd had time to use the curling iron. The man's eyes, made small by his fat face, were roaming hotly over her, making her leery of him.

"This is where he lives, ain't it?"

"Pete? Hell, no. He lives down yonder on the river bottom with his daddy and Jude. 'Course, way that boy roams ain't no tellin' where he's at. Ya say yo're Dorene's gal?"

"Yes. Mama's dead."

"That Dorene was one hot little twat. Time she got her bleedin', she had ever man on Mud Creek pantin' fer her—kin and all. Then she up and wed up with Ed Henry. Ever'body knew she'd not stay with him. Just wanted them pretty dresses he bought her. Last I heard she was in the city livin' high on the hog."

Isabel opened her mouth to ask if he thought going from man to man, living in rooms at a run-down flea-bitten rooming house was living "high on the hog," but thought better of it. Let them think her mama was something special. And she was. She'd shaken off the stink of Mud Creek and the dirt farm.

"Well, come on to the house. Ma's standin' there on the porch a wonderin' 'bout ya. Ain't no use me tryin' to get a mess a squirrels now. Yore screechin' plumb scared the hell outta 'em, and they're long gone."

The fat man led the way to the house, where a woman stood in the doorway. Her thin gray hair was fastened in a tight knot atop her head, and the wrinkled skin on her face was like dried leather. She wore a shapeless cotton dress and had a snuff stick in the corner of her mouth.

"Who ya got there, Fat?"

"Ma, this here's Dorene's kid."

"What's she here fer?"

"She ain't comin' here. She's goin' to Hardy's."

"What fer?"

"See Pete, I reckon."

"Harrumph! What's he been up to now? If he causes a ruckus and the law comes in, Hardy'll whop his 'hind."

"This one's kin, Ma."

"Kin, or not, wouldn't make no never mind to Pete."

So far the woman hadn't even looked at Isabel; now she did. Her eyes were an amazingly bright blue in her brown wrinkled face.

"Hello," Isabel said hesitantly.

"Ya watch yoreself down at Hardy's, or you'll find yoreself with a woods colt, if ya ain't a'ready. Yore mama'd lay down and spread her legs at the drop of a hat. It's in yore blood."

"Ah . . . who's Hardy?"

"Hardy Perry is Pete's pa." The man called Fat answered. "Hardy's 'bout the meanest son of a bitch on Mud Creek if ya cross him. But I reckon if Pete told ya to come, ya'll be welcome. Hardy thinks the sun rises and sets in that boy."

"Harrumph! That ain't all that 'rises and sets' in that boy. He's as horny as a two-peckered billy goat."

"Smart though, Pete is."

"Pete brung Dorene's boy here." The old lady spit snuff juice out into the yard, then wiped her toothless mouth on the end of her apron. "Didn't cotton to him much. Ain't got no use fer Indians. It's what he was. Plain as the nose on yer face. Screwin' a Indian brung Dorene down a peg or two to my way a thinkin'."

"My daddy wasn't no Indian," Isabel retorted hastily.

"I can tell that. I ain't blind."

"Come on in." Fat grabbed a post and pulled himself up onto the porch. "What'd ya say yore name was?"

"Isabel. What's yours?" *Surely he had a name other than . . . Fat.*

"Fat's what I is. Fat's what I'm called," he said belligerently.

"Ain't no call to get yore tail in a crack, Fat," his mother scolded.

"I ain't got my tail in no crack," he retorted. "Come on in, Issy. We'll eat a bait, and I'll take ya on down to Hardy's." He leaned his gun against the side of the house and put both hands through the sides of his overalls to scratch his belly. "I can't wait to see his face when he sees ya. Why, he's goin' to be plumb tickled havin' a young, tender piece like ya are a-switchin' her tail 'round his place."

"Ya stay outta Hardy's bed. Hear? Ain't nothin' causes

trouble faster'n two studs after the same bitch. When them two gets to fightin' they's like two ruttin' bulls with no quit a'tall."

"Could cause a killin'." Fat was now scratching his privates. "Seen it happen a time or two. Recollect, Ma, when the Powell Perrys got to feudin' over Minnie Mae's girl?"

"I recollect. They never did figure out who got to her first. Reckon ever' Perry on Mud Creek's got to her by now."

Fat was scratching now with both hands. Isabel kept her eyes on her feet.

"Ya got cooties down there, son? Might be ya ort to bathe yoreself with that lye soap or douse with coal oil."

"Yes, ma'am. I'll . . . go do it."

Chapter Six

When Henry Ann told Johnny that Isabel had taken her belongings and left, he merely shrugged.

"I'm worried about what will happen to her at the Perrys."

"She'll either get a belly full of 'em and come back or fit right in and stay."

"Aside from Pete, I haven't seen any of them in years."

"He's a cut above the rest."

"Lordy! I didn't think he could be a cut above anyone."

After the noon meal Johnny and Grant refilled their water jugs and prepared to go back to the field.

"Betcha a nickel I can beat you two rows out of three." Grant was sharpening his hoe on the grinder.

"If I'm goin' to bet, it'll be for something more than a nickel."

"Then name it."

Grant grinned, and his blue eyes flashed toward Henry Ann where she stood on the porch. The thought came to her that he was really a very nice man and not at all bad-looking.

"If you lose, you'll lance the boil under old Stanley's tail. We'll not be able to hitch him up till it's healed."

"Phew! I've got no fondness for boils . . . or mules, especially one as ornery as that one. He tried to bite me this morning. But I'll go along with it. It'll be one bet I'll not lose." Grant playfully slapped Johnny on the shoulder as if they had known each other for years

Henry Ann watched the two of them leave the yard. It was good that Johnny had someone like Grant to talk to. She could see a world of change in him. He seemed to have matured all of a sudden.

In the afternoon, while she was sitting on the front porch snapping green beans, Christopher Austin stopped by.

"Have a seat, Chris. I'll get you a cool drink."

"Don't bother. I'll just walk out to the well. I was passing by and thought maybe you didn't know that there's going to be an air show in town a week from Saturday. A couple of oil men are opening an office in town, and it's their way of giving the folks a treat."

"Just what Red Rock needs is another oil man."

Henry Ann walked beside him to the well. Christopher's pale hair was sun-streaked, his eyes a vivid green, and his skin deeply tanned. He had a stocky build, carrying most of his weight in his shoulders and chest.

"Yeah, that's what I think, too. But this pair is bringing in the air show to open their office with a bang. Folks in town are pretty excited about it."

"Daddy and I went to one in Ardmore a couple of summers ago."

"The notice says that there'll be two daredevil stunt pilots, a wing-walker, and parachute jumpers. They'll give plane rides, too."

"Not me. I can't see myself in an airplane riding on air."

"I'd like to try it," he said wistfully.

"It'll bring folks to town. That's sure."

"That and the dance marathon. I suppose you'll enter," Christopher teased.

"Oh, sure. You want to be my partner?" Henry Ann had known Christopher all her life and really liked him. He was a year or two older than she was. She just couldn't understand why a man his age would let his mother run his life.

"Now wouldn't you be surprised if I took you up on that?" He smiled one of his rare smiles and let the bucket down in the well. "Saw Karen in town. She said that if I stopped by to tell you she'd be out soon," he said while waiting for the bucket to fill.

"Christopher! Did you go to town just to see Karen?"

"No. I saw her at the store."

She knew better than that and didn't know why she said it. He had such a frown on his face that she was sorry she had teased him. She thought briefly about asking him about Opal Hastings, but thought better of it. He had a hard enough time dealing with his mother without having to fend off her questions. But, seeing the stress on his face, she placed her hand on his arm.

"We've been friends for a long time, Chris. If ever you want to talk to anyone, I'm here."

He looked at her a long while before he spoke. "I appreciate that, Henry Ann."

"Are you . . . ah . . . interested in someone, Chris?"

"You might say that."

"It'll work out."

"There's not much hope of that." There was a world of longing in his voice. He changed the subject quickly. "Oh, yes. We had another steer killed last night. I told the sheriff's deputy. He's usually in Red Rock."

"Do you have any idea who is doing it? You've lost two. We lost one and the Whalens have lost one that we know of."

"It isn't a big operation. Someone's killing for the meat. The talk is that it's the folks down on Mud Creek, but there's no proof yet."

"Mr. Dolan saw tire tracks in our field. He's watching for the tires that made them."

"A tire track is a tire track as far as I know."

"Most folks *know* the Perrys are bootlegging. I don't understand why the sheriff doesn't do something about it."

"I'm just glad I'm not the sheriff. He's got folks on his neck all the time to do something about something. How's Johnny doing?"

"Fine. We hired a man to help him clean the cotton field. We need a good rain soon, or we'll not make a decent crop."

"I was afraid that you'd bitten off more than you could chew when you brought him back from the city."

"He was a confused boy. He took Daddy's death harder than I imagined he would. He's really been a help to me these last few weeks."

"If there's anything I can do, you let me know. Hear?"

"I hear. And, Chris, the same goes for me."

He knew that she was referring to Opal. It was comforting to know that someone he admired and respected was not horrified at the thought of his being in love with a girl with Opal's background. Folks didn't really know her. His mother would never accept her. She'd not even give her a chance.

"I appreciate that. I really do." He put his arm across her shoulders and gave her a brotherly hug. "I'd better get crackin', Henry Henry," he teased to break the tension and headed for his car.

" 'Bye, Chris. Stop by again."

Emmajean had been exceptionally good—better than she'd been since she and Tom were married. For five days she had cooked and cleaned, cuddled and played with Jay, and even sung as she worked. She took Tom's refusal to come to her bed without a fuss. She flirted with him and at times even made him laugh. Jay became comfortable with her, and, for the past two days, Tom had left him in his mother's care for several hours at a time.

This morning when Tom left the house at sunrise, Jay was still sleeping in his crib. He loaded fence posts and wire in the wagon and headed for the back of the property to replace a downed fence so that he could turn his stock onto ungrazed grassland.

Before he realized it the sun was directly overhead, and he still had three more posts to set. He figured another hour or two would finish the job, so he continued to work. Finally he finished, threw his tools in the wagon bed, took up the reins, and headed back to the house. On the way, he began to feel uneasy. A sudden urgency caused him to cluck and snap the reins sharply on the mules' backs, and the wagon jolted recklessly along the rutted path.

Tom drove into the lot behind the barn, unhitched the mule, and checked the water tank before he headed through the barn toward the house. As soon as he stepped out into the bright sunlight, he heard Emmajean's shrill voice.

"Stop bawling, you ugly little beast!"

The sound of Jay sobbing reached him, and he began to run. He sprang up onto the porch and into the kitchen just as Emmajean's palm connected with the child's face so hard that his head hit the back of the chair.

"Stop that!" he shouted. "Are you crazy? He's only a baby, for God's sake."

Jay, still wearing his nightgown, was tied to a chair with a dish towel. Tom untied the sobbing child and lifted him in his arms. The child screamed when he tried to hug him close.

"My God! What have you done to him?" Tom put his arm under the little legs and cradled his son. The little boy continued to scream in pain.

"What did you do to him?" Tom demanded again, as frightened as he'd ever been in his life.

"He wet the bed and—"

"And what? If you've injured him, I swear I'll beat the living daylights out of you." Jay straightened his little legs as if he were going into convulsions. His cries were cries of intense pain. Tom placed him on the bed and knelt beside him. The child turned on his side, his hand fastened in Tom's shirt, his pleading eyes on his father's face.

"What's the matter, son? Where do you hurt?"

Tom pulled Jay's gown up to his waist to expose his little bottom. Raised red welts crisscrossed his buttocks.

"You dammed bitch! You've whipped him with the razor strop."

"He peed the bed! I told him what I'd do if he peed again. And I did it," she said proudly. Still in her nightclothes, she stood hands on her hips, a look of pure hatred on her face.

"She'll not whip you again, son. I'll see to that."

"I will if he needs it."

"Get the hell out of here!" Tom shouted, then in a strangled voice, "Oh my God!"

Jay's small hand had fluttered down toward his penis. Tom noticed for the first time that the little organ was swollen twice its normal size. The skin had turned a dark blue.

"Oh, my God!" It seemed to be all he could say. All he could see was the end of a string that had been tied tightly around the little penis. "You bitch! You bitch!" he shouted over the screams of his son. The string around the child's male member was concealed by the swelling. There was no way of getting it off the thrashing child without cutting him, and he couldn't depend on Emmajean to hold him.

"He peed. He peed, he peed," Emmajean kept repeating.

Indescribable panic assailed him. He picked up his son. Emmajean stood in the doorway when he reached it.

"Where are you going?"

"Get out of my way!"

"No! You're not taking him to *her*! He told me she'd given him the frog. I threw it in the stove—"

"Get out of my way," he shouted again, and before he could stop himself, he struck her with his open hand.

Tom didn't even wait for her to hit the floor. He ran out the door and to his car. He gently placed his son on the seat, started the car, and sped out of the yard. It seemed hours, but it could only have been minutes before he turned into the yard at the Henrys. *Thank God, Miss Henry was on the porch!*

"Please help me," he shouted as he got out and ran around to the other side to lift his screaming child into his arms.

Alarmed by the urgency of his shout, Henry Ann rushed out into the yard to meet him.

"Bring him in. What happened?" She turned to run ahead of him to hold open the door.

"The bitch tied a string around his little pecker. I can't get it off."

"In here." Henry Ann led the way to the kitchen and hurriedly moved the caster set from the middle of the table. "What can I do?"

"Hold him as still as you can. I've got to cut the string . . . if I can find it."

"Ah . . . baby . . ." she exclaimed when Tom pulled up the gown, and she could see the child's grossly swollen male organ.

"I'll get Daddy's razor. It's sharper," she said as Tom took a jackknife from his pocket.

"Hurry. I don't know how long it's been on there."

Seconds later, Henry Ann had one arm across the child's legs, the other holding his upper body. She murmured softly to Jay and kept her eyes averted from what Tom was doing. It seemed an eternity before he spoke.

"It's off. I nicked him," Tom groaned as blood dripped onto the table. The child continued to scream. "It'll hurt bad as the blood goes back in. Dear God, I don't know what to do."

"Get him to the doctor."

"Go with me. Hold him."

"Of course. Let's go."

Henry Ann didn't even take the time to take off her

apron. She hurried to the car and climbed in. Tom placed the child in her arms. Jay didn't want to leave his daddy and clung to Tom's shirt.

"I've got to drive, son. Henry Ann will hold you."

"Let me hold you, baby." Henry Ann cuddled the child in her lap. "It'll stop hurting soon," she promised, and smoothed the dark, wet curls from the child's face. "Ah . . . poor baby. Sweet baby." His head was wet with sweat, the print of a hand visible on his cheek.

"The crazy bitch whipped him with a strop too," Tom gritted as the car sped down the road. "It's my fault for leaving him with her. But . . . she seemed . . . better—"

"Don't cry, honey," Henry Ann crooned to the little boy, only half listening to Tom's angry words. "Your daddy's hurrying as fast as he can. Doctor Hendricks will make it better. Don't cry—"

"Damn her to hell! Damn all the blasted Conroys to hell!"

"It won't be long." Henry Ann rocked the child in her arms and kissed his forehead. "We're almost there. Soon the hurt will be gone and you can go to sleep. How could she do this?" she demanded of Tom, and turned to look at his angry face. "How could a mother hurt her own baby?"

"She's insane." He looked at her briefly. "I knew that something was wrong the day I married her, but there was nothing I could do." He drove recklessly into town and turned down the street to the doctor's house. "Thank God, Doc's car is here."

Henry Ann led the way up the walk and held the door open for Tom. He yelled for the doctor as soon as he stepped into the room. Doctor Hendricks came through a side door at the sound of the commotion.

"What's the matter, Tom?"

"He's hurting bad, Doc—"

"In here."

When the door closed behind them, Henry Ann turned to look at the two women in the waiting room. Both had their mouths open, their inquiring eyes on her.

"What in the world, Henry Ann? What happened? Did the child break an arm or a leg?" The woman who spoke was wearing a sunbonnet. Henry Ann had never seen her without her head covered. Karen had told her that the woman's hair was so thin that you could see every bump on her head and that she chose to always keep it covered.

Does she sleep in that bonnet?

"I'm . . . not sure if something is broken. How have you been, Mrs. Miller?"

"Fair to middlin'. How come you're with Mr. Dolan?"

"He needed someone to hold the baby so he could drive. I haven't seen you for a while, Mrs. Overton." Henry Ann spoke to the other woman, who was fanning herself with the brim of her hat.

"I was at your daddy's funeral, but with the crowd and all, you couldn't know everyone there. Are you makin' out all right, Henry Ann?"

"I think so. I've been awfully busy."

"It's good you got your brother and sister with you," Mrs. Miller said. "The Lord works in wondrous ways. When he took Dorene, he sent Isabel so you'd not be left here alone." She looked slyly at Henry Ann from beneath the stiff brim of her bonnet, waiting anxiously for a reply she could relay to her friends in the sewing circle.

Henry Ann kept her thoughts to herself. *God didn't send*

Isabel to me so that I'd not be alone. If anything, he sent her to punish me for caring so little about my mother.

"I understand that there's going to be an air show on Saturday." She addressed her remark to Mrs. Overton.

The woman clicked her tongue. "A bunch of foolishness. It's said them planes burn up ten dollars' worth of gasoline ever' time they take to the air. That oil man ought to take that money and feed the poor to my notion."

"He can spend his money anyway he wants to, Myrtle. If he wants to spend it givin' the folks in Red Rock a good time, it ain't none of our business."

"He ain't doin' it for nothin'. You can bet your buttons on that. He's hoping to get on the good side of folks so he can lease their land for next to nothin', go in there and tear it up so it ain't fit for farmin' or grazin'. They been drillin' dry holes 'round here for years."

"We're not too far from Healdton. That town is boomin'."

"Harrumph! A rag town, is what it is. Every wildcatter in the country flocked there. What'll they have once the field plays out?"

In the quiet that followed Henry Ann became aware that little Jay was no longer crying. She heard only the low murmur of male voices coming from the room. Her stiff shoulders sagged with relief.

"Is Mrs. Dolan ill? Is that why she's not here?" Mrs. Miller's inquiring voice dropped into the silence.

Henry Ann was saved from having to give an answer. The doctor opened the door for Tom, cradling his son in his arms, to pass through.

"I think he'll be all right, Tom, but bring him back in a

day or two. Hello, Henry Ann. It was a good thing you were nearby to help Tom."

Henry Ann knew that Doctor Hendricks was talking for the benefit of Mrs. Miller, who was the undisputable queen of gossip in Red Rock. He was making a plausible excuse for her being with Tom Dolan.

"I was glad I could help."

"What's wrong with him, Doctor?" Mrs. Miller stood and peered at the sleeping child. "There's several cases of diphtheria in town. I don't want to take the germs home."

"No danger of that. He hurt his little tally-whacker and balls. Little boys have to be careful with that little treasure." Doctor Hendricks spoke matter-of-factly to the suddenly red-faced woman. "It's the source of our future generations."

"Thanks, Doc. Put the charges on my tab, and I'll be in to pay." Tom crossed the room to the door, and Henry Ann went to open it.

"We won't worry about it. If any of the things I told you to watch for happen, bring him in at once."

After Tom passed through the door, Henry Ann turned and said good-bye to Mrs. Overton and Mrs. Miller, then followed him to the car. He settled Jay in her lap, then went around and got behind the wheel.

"We'd better get out of town. There'll be talk as it is." He turned the car around in the middle of the street and headed back toward the farm.

"The doctor set Mrs. Miller down. The old gossip! What did he say to look for?" Henry Ann liked the feel of the small boy in her arms.

"Fever, stomach pain, blood in his urine. He gave him

something to make him sleep. He'll be hurting for a while. Damn, damn her!"

"She slapped him, didn't she?" She brushed the hair back from the bruise on the child's cheek.

"And beat his little butt with a strop. Doc said if the string had been on there much longer not only would his little dinger have been ruined, but being unable to get rid of the urine in his bladder he could've died. As it is, he could still get a bladder infection. I was stupid to leave him with her. When I saw what she'd done, I wanted to kill her."

On the outer edge of town he stopped the car under a large pecan tree that grew close to the road.

"Do you mind if we stop here a minute?" Dark, hurt-filled eyes settled on Henry Ann's calm face. "I've got to think." She shook her head. He rested his forehead on the arms he had folded over the steering wheel.

The minutes slipped away. It was quiet and hot. Henry Ann's dress stuck to her damp back and moisture ran in a rivulet between her breasts. While she waited, she fanned Jay's face with a newspaper she found on the seat and wondered at the extent of the torment roiling inside of the man beside her. She wished for words to comfort him. He loved his child—there was no doubt of that. Did he love the boy's mother, too? Was that why he stayed with her?

Finally Tom lifted his head, turned sideways in the seat, and looked at his son sleeping in Henry Ann's lap. Tired dark eyes met hers. His cheeks were covered with a thin stubble of black whiskers, giving him a sinister look.

"I can't take him back," he whispered desperately. "He'll be terrified of her."

"What will she do if you don't?"

"She can do anything she wants to as long as she doesn't touch that boy. She could have killed him."

"It's hard to think of a mother doing such a thing to her child. Is she . . . is she really—?"

"Say it. I've thought it a million times. She's insane, or bordering on it," he said tiredly. "I can't help her. I've tried. I've got to think of what's best for Jay."

"Aunt Dozie will take care of him."

"Jay liked her. Is she staying with you?"

"She went home. Isabel was downright mean to her when I wasn't around. But now she's gone—" She halted, thinking she was telling too much.

"The girl left?"

"She went to the Perrys."

"What do you think about that?"

"I think that it's a sorry place for a young girl, but there's not much I can do about it. They're her kinfolk."

"I'm sorry she's causing you grief," Tom said softly.

"My troubles are nothing compared to yours. I have only myself to look after."

"Yes. Poor little fellow." He smoothed the child's hair with clumsy tenderness. "He's never had a real mother. She hates him."

"No! How could she?"

"Like I said, she's strange. I met her at a carnival in Wichita Falls. I was lonely and had been drinking. She was loving and willing. I took her home the next morning, and she blurted out that she had spent the night with me. We were married that afternoon." He didn't know why he was telling her this. He hadn't talked this freely with anyone for years. "Her folks had found a good excuse to get rid of her."

"Maybe she's to be pitied."

"I felt sorry for her . . . at first. After a week, I knew that I'd let myself in for a hell of a life. I only . . . slept with her twice," he murmured. Suddenly it was important to him to let Henry Ann know that his was not a *real* marriage. "I don't think she knew she was pregnant until she started showing. She went into a rage. I thought she was going berserk. I'd been trying to think of a way to get her folks to take her back. They said that if I left her, they'd take my child. They've got the money and influence to do it. I couldn't let that happen. Since then, I've been trying to make the best of it. But she's getting worse. More irrational. Now, I'm afraid for Jay."

Henry Ann was quiet for a moment, absorbing what he'd told her.

"Talk to Aunt Dozie."

"I can't pay her cash money right now."

"I don't think you'd have to."

He dropped his eyes before her unwavering glance, and was terribly moved to see her holding, cuddling his child as if he were her own. She intrigued him like no woman he had ever known. Since the day he had given her a ride home, he had thought about her. At night the image of her clean, fresh face had appeared time and again behind his closed lids.

A big touring car went by, stirring up a cloud of dust. Tom was so engrossed with his problems that he was only vaguely aware the car had slowed down as it came alongside his.

"Shall we ask Aunt Dozie?" he asked.

She nodded. Neither Tom nor Henry Ann had noticed that he'd included her in the decision. It was all part of this incredible afternoon that they would remember for the rest of their lives.

Tom stopped the car in front of Dozie's small unpainted frame house. The porch was crowded with people and a number of children chased each other in the yard. Dozie came out of her chair and down the dirt path to the car.

"Lawsy, chile, what ya doin' ridin' 'round in Mr. Dolan's automobile?"

"Hello, Aunt Dozie."

"Dis babe sick?" She reached in through the open window and laid the back of her hand on Jay's forehead.

"He was . . . hurt. We just came from the doctor."

"Lawd have mercy. Hurt bad?"

"We think he'll be all right," Tom answered. "I was wondering if I could leave him with you for a few days."

Aunt Dozie's eyes traveled back and forth from Henry Ann's face to Tom's. It jerked Tom's mind back to the fact that he had drawn Henry Ann into his problem with his wife and that by doing so he was damaging her reputation.

Henry Ann glanced at Tom's grim face, then said softly, "Jay's mama hurt him." Then to Tom, "Aunt Dozie won't tell."

"His mama? Lawsy! Lawsy! Dat's a pure-dee shame."

"He can't take him home right now," Henry Ann explained.

"Dis here ain't no place for a hurt chile, honey. I let my sister's boy move in. He ain't got no place for his woman and kids 'cause his house burnt plumb to de ground."

"They're going to live here?"

"Ain't no place else for 'em to go. I can't turn dem younguns out in de cold."

"Come live with me, Aunt Dozie," Henry Ann said

quickly. "You're very dear to me. Remember when you nursed me through the measles, the whooping cough, the chicken pox? You've been like a mother to me. Come live in my room. I'm in Daddy's. Isabel sneaked out in the middle of the night and went to the Perrys."

"If'n I leave my house, chile, I lose it." A deep look of concern came over Dozie's usually cheerful features.

"Then lose it. A good strong wind could blow it down anytime. You'll lose your mind living in two rooms with all those children. You're not going to be able to work forever. When you can't get around, I'll take care of you like you took care of me when I was little. I want to, Aunty, and Daddy would want me to."

Dozie's eyes slowly filled with tears.

"Land a livin'." She grabbed hold of Henry Ann's hand. "Ya be takin' on dis ole woman as fambly?"

"Now what's so surprising about that, Dozie Jones? You've always been family to me."

"Ya'll be gettin' wed someday—"

"Your biscuits may be the only thing that'll get a husband for me," she teased.

Tom was barely able to comprehend what he was hearing. This slim, sweet woman was everything he had imagined his life's mate would be. But fate had played a cruel joke, and he had to play the cards he was dealt.

"Dere be thin's I not want to leave here—"

"Of course. Bring whatever you want. I know you'll want to bring your rocking chair."

"My mama rock me in dat chair."

"And you rocked me. When can you be ready?" Henry Ann had a happy smile on her face. "I've got to get you out of there before you change your mind."

"I ain't a changin' it, honey. I be ready in not much more'n da switch of a dog's tail." Dozie's face was creased with smiles. "Truth is, all dem younguns goin' in and out and slammin' de door was 'bout to frazzle my mind."

Henry Ann turned to Tom. "We'll take care of Jay at my house until you can take him home."

"What will folks say? I don't want to cause you any trouble."

"We can say your wife is sick . . . if anyone asks."

"She is . . . in a way."

"Will it upset her if you don't bring him home?"

"Only that she wouldn't want him to be with you."

"Why me?"

Because you're young and pretty and . . . she knows she can't hold a candle to you.

"Well, probably because . . . you're handy," he said finally because she was waiting for an answer. *Heaven help me! If I'm not careful, I'll fall in love with you.*

They smiled into each other's eyes. *He really is a very nice man in spite of that frown and that wild hair.*

"I'll take Henry Ann home, Aunt Dozie, and be back for you."

"I be ready, Mistah Tom."

Chapter Seven

Emmajean lay on the floor where she had fallen when Tom struck her. At first she had been consumed with self-pity, cried, and pounded her forehead on the floor. Then a feeling of elation swept over her. The thrill that knifed through her settled in her genital area. Her hand went there, and she lay on the floor caressing herself as she did sometimes when she was in bed wishing her husband would come to her and do the things he had done the night they met. Until then she had only imagined what wonderful things went on between a man and a woman.

She had liked the pain when he took her virginity. She had liked it when, far too drunk to realize it, he had been rough with her. She had liked it so much that she was determined to have Tom for a husband, and knew that if she told her parents, they'd make him marry her.

She told.

And they did.

But only on their wedding night had he done that wonderful thing to her. And he had been so gentle that it had infuriated her. The next day he had looked at her as if she were a stray cat! She was sure that she could have persuaded him to stay in her bed if not for the damn kid that started growing in her body.

Almost immediately after they were married she was sick, then her stomach began to stick out, and her feet and legs became so swollen she couldn't even wear her high-heeled shoes. She became mean and irritable and had crying fits that lasted for hours.

After she delivered, she wanted nothing to do with the *ugly, wrinkled, bawling thing*. The idea of its sucking on her breasts was so repulsive to her that she had screamed when the midwife had tried to put the brat to her breasts. She hated it then, but hated it more when Tom turned all his attention to it. When she refused to take care of it, he took it to a woman to care for during the day, and at night he spent every possible minute with it.

Emmajean was lying on the kitchen floor thinking these thoughts and caressing herself when a car drove into the yard. It wasn't Tom's car, she could tell that by the sound of the motor. She got up off the floor and went to the front window when she heard a door slam.

A man stood beside a shiny black touring car, hands on his hips, surveying the homestead. Her brother, Marty. She ran to the door and out onto the porch.

"Marty! Marty! I'm so glad you've come—" She began to cry and wring her hands. "Look what he did to me! He beat me—" Her eyes were swollen, her cheek was red from Tom's blow and scratched from lying on the rough floor. She lifted her hair to show the bumps and cuts on her forehead.

Marty came up onto the porch. He knew his sister and had no doubt that if her husband had beaten her, she had deserved it. But it wouldn't do to tell her that. This just might be something he could make work to his advantage.

"Why did he hit you, Emmy?"

"He was going to leave, and I didn't want him to go. I was in his way and he . . . and he . . . knocked me to the floor."

"Where was he going?"

"I . . . don't know."

"I saw him sitting alongside the road just now. Someone was with him."

"It was *her*!" Emmajean's crying stopped as suddenly as if the tears had been turned off by a faucet. A look of extreme fury came over her face. "He goes there all the time. He fixes her fence, fetches the doctor, takes her . . . things—"

"Who?"

Marty had never liked his irrational sister. She had been strange all her life and was an embarrassment to the family. When they'd had an excuse to marry her off and get rid of her, they had taken it, thinking the man would take her and go back to Nebraska. But he had not been as docile as the family had expected him to be.

"That Henry slut. She lives on the next place. We hadn't been here a week until she came sashaying over here to see him. He takes Jay over there. She gives him toys—"

"Why aren't you dressed? It's the middle of the day." Marty knew that his sister often lied. He was fond of saying that she wouldn't know the truth if it jumped up and bit her.

"He . . . won't let me. He wants me in my gown all day

so that . . . so that when he comes in, I'm ready to do . . . it."

"It?"

"You know . . . in bed. He wants it three or four times a day."

"Three or four times a . . . day? Good Lord! He must be quite the stud."

"He . . . he wears me out." Emmajean allowed her voice to quiver.

"What do you do with the kid?"

"Oh, he don't care if he watches."

"Good Lord," Marty said again.

"Come in." Emmajean grabbed her brother's hand. "He won't want me to do it while you're here."

"Go get dressed. I'll wait on the porch."

"You won't go?"

"No. I'll be here."

Jay was asleep in Henry Ann's bed—the bed she had been born in, and the one where her daddy had died. She had brought out an oilcloth and put it under the sheet to protect the mattress should the little boy wet.

"He's been real good about . . . that," Tom said. "I take him out every night and then again in the morning."

"He may not have control for a while." Henry Ann covered the child with a sheet. "Don't worry about it."

"I don't know how to thank you." They looked at each other across the sleeping child.

"Thanks are not necessary. Neighbors should help neighbors."

"We never did get around to talking about exchanging help. I'm willing to help Johnny—teach him what I know."

"What can we do to help you?"

"I'll never get my crop out by myself. I've been taking Jay to the field with me. I wish to God I'd taken him this morning."

"We'll work something out. The man we hired doesn't seem to want much more than food and lodging."

"I can't offer him even that. A working man needs to put his feet under a table and have three squares a day."

"Supper's ready. Can ya stay, Mistah Tom?" Dozie came to the bedroom door. "Johnny and that other'n come and went to milk. They do chores later, they say."

"I'd like nothing more, but I've got chores of my own to do."

"Don't worry about Jay. We'll take care of him." Henry Ann left the room and Tom followed. "If we need to go back to the doctor, I'll send Johnny to get you."

"I'll be back tomorrow." He didn't want to leave but knew he had to. "I need to put water in my radiator before I go."

Henry Ann walked out onto the porch, picked up a bucket, and walked with Tom to the well. She heard a whoop coming from the barn and then laughter—Johnny's. Grant, carrying the milk bucket, came out of the barn first. *Lordy! She'd forgotten about milking.*

"Who won the bet, Grant?" Henry Ann called.

"You had doubts, Miss Henry? I gave him a chance at two more rows and still beat him four out of five."

"He took the easiest rows," Johnny yelled from inside the barn.

"Don't believe him. He's mad 'cause I won't help him with that mule."

Tom stood holding the bucket of water. The new hired

man didn't act like a stranger. Had Henry Ann known him for a long time? An unfamiliar feeling came over Tom. He felt sudden dislike for this friendly man who talked so easily to Henry Ann. My God! *He was jealous!*

"I'll put the milk on the porch, Miss Henry."

"Grant, this is our neighbor, Tom Dolan. Tom, Grant Gifford will be helping us for a while."

The two men shook hands while Henry Ann explained that Tom's land joined theirs on the south.

"You from around here, Gifford?" Tom asked.

"You could say that. I'm admiring the automobile. Is it yours?"

"Yes."

"You don't see many of that model anymore."

"I try to keep it up to snuff. I've got to be going, Henry Ann. I'll be over in the morning."

Henry Ann walked with Tom to the car and watched him remove the radiator cap and pour the water.

"Have you known Gifford long?" he asked.

"A week. Maybe a little longer. He stopped by for a drink of water and asked for work."

"He's from the road? A bum?" Tom turned to look at her with a frown drawing his dark brows together.

"I suppose so. He and Johnny hit it off—"

"You don't know anything about him. He could be a convict."

"I doubt that."

"Is he staying in the house?"

"In the barn."

"Do you lock the doors at night?"

Henry Ann laughed. "We don't have keys for the locks.

I suppose Daddy had them at one time. I can't remember the last time we felt a need to lock the doors."

"Things are different now. A third of the population is out of work. Not only are men roaming up and down the roads looking for a handout, outlaws are on the prowl looking for easy pickings. There's a bank robbery about every day. Some of these men are desperate. You're a woman alone."

"I'm not alone. I have Johnny."

"He's just a kid."

"Johnny is more of a man than you think he is. He can handle things," she said, with a note of irritation in her voice.

"How do you know? He came from the city, didn't he?"

"Are you worried about leaving Jay here?"

"No. I just . . . well, that fellow, Gifford—"

"He wouldn't have a chance between me, Johnny, and Aunt Dozie." Her face relaxed, and a smile tilted her lips. "Would you like to go up against Aunt Dozie with a skillet in her hand? I was taught how to take care of myself. I got to be even a better shot than Daddy."

Tom grinned in spite of himself.

She looped a strand of hair behind her ear and reached for the empty bucket. He was intensely aware that he had only to lift his hand to touch her. She was pretty and natural as a woman was meant to be. He wanted to keep on looking at her but feared that he would embarrass her—and himself. Instead he opened the car door.

"I'm sorry if I overstepped—"

"You didn't. We'll keep an eye on him."

"Thanks for keeping Jay."

"You've said that ten times."

He grinned. It was easy to do when he was with her.

"I guess I have."

She stood in the yard while he backed the car out and turned down the road. She didn't wave, just stood there until he rounded the curve and could no longer see her when he looked back.

He wanted something, wanted it badly.

For a while now he'd felt a deep hunger for the soft warmth and tenderness, the sweetness of a woman. He wanted a decent life, a family like his brother Mike had in Nebraska. And now the most amazing of all—*he wanted it with Henry Ann Henry.*

When his farm came in sight, Tom braced himself to do battle with Emmajean. He slowed when he saw the black touring car with the Texas license plate in the yard. He drove slowly around it and stopped in front of the shed. He debated about going directly to the barn and starting the chores, but dammit, this was *his* house and he had a right to know who was in it.

"So you finally came home." The words came from Emmajean the second he stepped into the room. "Marty has been here a long time."

Tom's glance took in his wife and her brother sitting at the kitchen table.

"I've got chores to do."

"Chores!" Emmajean said disgustedly. "He's always got *chores.*"

"How'er you doin', Tom?"

"How do you think I'm doing?" Tom looked squarely at his brother-in-law for the first time.

"I told Marty what you did to me," Emmajean said spitefully. "I showed him where you hit me."

"Did you tell him why?"

" 'Cause you were going to leave and wouldn't take me with you."

"Good Lord!" He muttered the words in disbelief and reached under a workbench for the milk bucket. At the door he stopped and looked back at his wife and her brother. Then, without another word, he left the house.

Emmajean had not even asked about their son.

Tom finished milking and returned to the house with a half a bucket of milk. The cow was going dry. She needed fresh green grass to produce. He'd not had time to stake her out, nor had he the money to buy feed. Emmajean and Marty were still sitting at the table when he entered the kitchen. She had made no effort to start supper. Tom placed the milk on the counter, covered the pail with a cloth to keep out the flies, and went back out to gather the eggs.

Marty was waiting for him when he came out of the chicken house. Pin-striped shirt, bow tie, and felt hat tilted at an angle; a Jelly-Bean, Tom thought with disgust.

"Where's the kid?"

"With friends."

"Emmajean said you beat her."

"I knocked her out of the way so I could get out the door, not that it's any business of yours."

Marty shrugged. "She's my sister."

"You're damn lucky she isn't your wife." Tom set the egg basket down and picked up a pitchfork.

"I realize she's kind of strange—"

"Strange?" Tom looked him in the eye. "She's crazy as a bedbug, and you know it. Your folks know it, too. They found a sucker to take her off their hands."

"Now listen here. Just because she's strange is no reason to beat her up."

"Did she tell you why I was in such a hurry to get out the door?"

"You were anxious to get over to the Henrys'."

"Oh, for God's sake!"

"She also told me that you made her stay in her nightgown all day so that she'd be ready anytime you wanted to screw her." Marty laughed. "That's not such a bad idea. A man could get used to that."

Tom glowered at him for so long that Marty became uneasy and shifted from one foot to the other. Finally he spoke.

"My . . . ah . . . partner and I have opened an office in Red Rock. To start it off we're bringing in an air show on Saturday."

"Bully for you." Tom began to pitch dried grass to the mules.

"We'll be offering oil leases. There's an underground river of oil running through here."

"Who says?"

"Geologist."

"Harrumph!"

"Dammit, don't you want to make a lot of money?"

Tom stopped and looked at him. "Who for? I haven't seen many farmers getting rich off oil around here. What are you offering, twenty-five cents an acre?"

"We're prepared to offer fifty cents an acre."

"Oil is going for fifteen cents a barrel—if you find any, and you'll be paying one-sixteenth of that to the landowner. Right?"

"Wrong. We'll pay one-eighth."

"But if you drill a dry hole and tear up the land, you'll put it back?" Tom asked sarcastically.

A look of practiced disgust covered Marty's face. "There isn't an oil company in the world that'll agree to that."

"So that poor sucker who leases his hundred acres to you for fifty bucks, with the promise of an eighth of fifteen cents per barrel of oil, is going to get rich. I'll take my chance on a cotton crop."

Marty was astounded that Tom knew so much about the oil business.

"Hell, man, you'll be lucky to make twenty bucks off that cotton patch. What's it selling for now? Five cents a pound? By the time you get it to the gin it'll probably go for three cents."

"Well, don't you worry your head about it."

"Goddammit, Tom. I'm trying to help—"

"Can it! You're trying to help yourself. You want to get your foot in so you can tell the others that a well on my land will drain the oil out from under theirs. You'll get them to sign up for a little or nothing and have control over their land."

"That's business, and if you're too dumb to know it—"

"I'm not so dumb that I'd sign my land away—if I was going to sign, without seeing a geologist's report. There's no reason to think that because there's oil south of here and north of here that it'll be here."

"Think what you like. If you're so damn smart, why are you a dirt farmer?"

"If *you* had the brains of a flea, you'd have found out who *owns* the mineral rights to this land before you came around making your pitch."

"Jesus Christ! Don't *you* own them?"

"No."

"Shit! Why didn't you say so in the first place?"

"Why should I tell you anything?"

"Did you sell off the rights?"

"They were kept by the heirs when I bought the place, and the heirs are now somewhere in China."

"What are they doing in China?"

"Making Christians out of the heathens, I reckon."

"How can I find them?"

"How the hell should I know?" Tom walked into the barn, picked up a long stick, opened a gate, and drove his cattle through to take them to the fresh grass along the creek.

Marty, wiping the sweat from his face with a snowy white handkerchief, got in his car and left without even saying good-bye to his sister. He hated to go back to town and tell Walter he'd not been able to swing the deal with his brother-in-law.

Johnny seemed to be genuinely glad Aunt Dozie had come back. When she went to the washbench, handed him a towel, and told him curtly not to drip water on the floor, he flashed her one of his rare smiles.

"Yes, ma'am," he said, and then said to Grant, "She gets cranky when things ain't goin' her way."

"I shore as shootin' does." Dozie shot back, her dark face creased with smiles even as she spoke gruffly, making it clear that she had a fondness for the coppery-skinned boy. "I ain't havin' no water sloshed on de floor, I ain't havin' no cow stuff tromped in de house, and I ain't havin' no sass outta a youngun like you is, Johnny Henry."

"Told ya," Johnny said to Grant. "No cow stuff tromped in the house," he repeated, and lifted up first one boot and then the other to make sure they were clean.

"Sit yoreselves down. You been foolin' 'round for so long dat dis corn bread is gettin' cold."

"Jay is still sleeping." Henry Ann came in and went to the cupboard for a jar of tomato preserves. "Last of last year's preserves, Aunt Dozie."

"I's hopin' dat babe sleep all night long."

"Sit down and say the blessing," Henry Ann said. "Johnny is about to gnaw on the table leg."

Dozie hesitated, glancing at Grant, who stood politely behind his chair waiting for Henry Ann to be seated.

"Sit," Henry Ann said again, then with a knowing look at Grant conveyed a silent message. *If you act in the least like you're offended to eat at the table with a colored woman, you can hit the road.*

He met her look squarely without the slightest change of expression.

After the blessing was said and the dishes of food were passed, Henry Ann asked how long it was going to take to weed the field.

"Shouldn't take more than a few more days if I could get this kid here to work," Grant said, teasing. "But I don't want to finish it too soon, I'll be out of a job. Ma'am," he said to Dozie, "I've eaten corn bread all over this country, and this is the best I've had in a donkey's age."

"Mr. Henry, he love my corn bread too. He say, Dozie, use as many eggs as yo want. He like it with milk gravy. Never could fatten up dat man. He work too hard to get him any fat on."

"I've got a dishpan of green beans ready to can." Henry

Ann helped herself to butter and passed the crock on down the table.

"I see dat. There's a mess of okra to pick and taters to dig. Lawsy, dat garden doin' mighty fine without rain."

"I watered while you were gone to the city." Johnny glanced at Henry Ann. "I did it again the night Ed passed on."

"You never told me that!"

He shrugged, his eyes on his plate.

"I saw where a trench had been dug down between the rows. I though maybe Daddy—"

"—He showed me how to irrigate. I did it at night."

"Why?"

"So the ground would stay wet longer."

"Johnny. You surprise me."

"Kid might know gardens, but he doesn't know beans about chopping cotton." Grant's eyes caught Henry Ann's, and he winked.

"You're not going to let that go, are you?" Johnny asked.

"Not on your life. I'm going to stand by and watch you pay your debt."

"Do you have to refer to that bet while we're eating?" Henry Ann put her fork back down on her plate.

"Sorry, ma'am. Guess I wasn't thinking."

Dozie had been quiet. The white man had called her ma'am, too. She didn't know what to think of that. Johnny liked him. Henry Ann seemed to like him, too. Dozie hoped that he stayed for a good while. That Mister Dolan could mean trouble for her girl. He was a married man, but he looked at Henry Ann like a man hungry for something he couldn't have.

* * *

"Wal, here ya are, purty little bird. This here's Hardy Perry's place."

Pudgy fingers suddenly gripped Isabel's elbow and squeezed. She jerked her arm free from the fat man's grasp, set the suitcase down, and moved to the other side of it.

"This is where Pete lives?"

"Yup. Ain't much to look at on the outside, but they got one of them iceboxes in there and a wind-up Victrola. Got a feller named Rudy Vallee singin' on it. Hardy's got a likin' for music. Sometimes he makes Jude dance with him 'nd Jude's dang near big as his paw. Hee, hee, hee." The fat man's beady eyes shone like glass as he eyed Isabel. "Hardy'll take a likin' for you, too, purty little bird."

"Who's Jude?"

"His kid. Only one he claims 'side of Pete. Hee, hee, hee. He ain't foolin' nobody. There's Perrys strung all up and down Mud Creek, and he's got kids by most of 'em."

"Relatives?"

"Hell. Cousins and aunts ain't close kinfolk. That Hardy is the limit. He's hornier than a bull moose," he said. " 'Course, I ain't no mouse myself," he added proudly.

The small unpainted house had appeared suddenly when they rounded a bend in the road. It squatted on blocks amid the weeds and scrub growing out of the sandy soil. Behind it was a lopsided outhouse and a shed with a new tin roof. To the side was the slanting door of a root cellar and the well. Chickens picked and scratched among the debris that littered the area around the house. It was worse than Fat's place. Isabel's heart sank. *This couldn't be where Pete lived!*

All was quiet except for the buzz of a dozen june bugs

and the call of a whippoorwill. From a distance a cowbell sounded gently, mellow and muted. Then from the house came music.

"Hardy's home. Ain't nobody touchin' that Victrola but Hardy. Listen. Ain't that pretty?"

> *"I'll see you in my dreams,*
> *hold you in my dreams—"*

"That's that Vallee feller singin'. He sure sings pretty. I'm goin' to have me a record player someday."

"Why don't you buy one," Isabel said absently.

" 'Cause I ain't . . . ready yet, that's why," he answered crossly. "There ain't no call for ya to get sassy. I brung ya over here when I could've been fishin' or huntin' squirrels."

"Let's go. I want to see Pete."

" 'Let's go. I wanna see Pete,' " he mocked, and walked away, leaving her to struggle in the deep sand with the suitcase.

A chorus of frenzied barking from dogs penned behind the house announced their arrival. The music stopped, and a man came out onto the porch. He was big, with a head of thick gray hair and hands like scoop shovels. Although he wasn't overly fat, he had a big belly that hung over the belt that held up his britches. His open shirt showed a mass of gray chest hair, and the stubble on his face said it had been some time since he'd shaved.

"Shut up!" he yelled at the dogs, and they stopped barking as suddenly as if their throats had been cut.

"Howdy, Hardy. I brung ya a visitor."

"Howdy, Fat. How's yore maw?"

"Fair to middlin'. How'er yore folks?"

"I ain't heard no complaint." Hardy's eyes had not left Isabel. "Who's the split?"

"Dorene Perry's girl from the city. Come to see Pete."

"Well, ain't that just dandy? That Pete. He draws women like flies to a syrup bucket. What's yore name, girl?"

"Isabel. Is Pete here?"

"He'll be along. Come on in. Have a drink from the well, Fat, before ya start back."

If the fat man was offended by being dismissed so abruptly, he didn't show it. He shuffled off toward the well. Isabel set her suitcase on the porch before she went up the steps and followed Hardy Perry into the house.

Isabel heard the clump of heavy steps going across a wooden floor. Then a screen door slammed. She stood just inside the door and sucked in a breath as she looked around at the clutter. A cot was piled high with clothes and bedding and in the middle of it all, a pair of muddy boots. The cot and a chair were the only furniture in the room beside the highly polished Victrola. The top lid was open, showing the picture of the small white dog with its ear tilted in a listening position. The doors below were open. All the record slots were full.

"Come in. Come in." Hardy Perry's big body seemed to fill the room.

"When will Pete be back?"

"He'll be along. Are ya hungry? There's a hunk a meat on the stove."

"I ate at Mrs. Perry's."

"You been sleepin' with Pete?"

"No!" The abrupt question took her breath away.

"If ya ain't lyin', Pete must be slowin' down some. Ain't

never knowed him to pass up a piece a ass if it was handy."
He laughed, showing stained teeth and a gaping hole in
front where one had been.

"Will he be gone long?"

Hardy ignored the question. He carefully turned the
crank that wound the Victrola and set a needle on the spin-
ning disc. Music filled the room.

> *"Girl of my dreams, I love you.*
> *Honest, I do. You are so sweet—"*

"Ya know how to dance, don't ya?" Hardy asked, then
before she could answer, " 'Course ya do. Dorene'd see to
it. Come on, gal. Come on, now." He grabbed her hand,
pulled her up against him, and began to sway with the
music.

Hardy held her so tightly against him that the buttons on
his shirt hurt her breasts. His chin on the top of her head
held her face pressed against his chest hair as he swayed
back and forth to the slow music.

Isabel's heart pounded so hard that she could hardly
breathe. When she finally gathered her wits, she wondered
why she couldn't feel her feet on the floor. Then, with sudden shock, she realized—*This hairy brute of a man was
holding her inches off the floor!*

Chapter Eight

Isabel could have wept with relief when, after she had danced an hour with Hardy, a car drove into the yard. Over the frenzied barking of the dogs, someone yelled his name.

"Shitfire! I plumb forgot 'bout Sandy comin'. I gotta be goin', gal." Hardy carefully lifted the needle from the record and closed the lid on the Victrola. He went to the door. "Hold yore horses," he yelled at the sound of a blast on the horn. Then to Isabel, "We'll do some more dancin' tonight. 'Bye, sugar."

Isabel stood in the middle of the room until she could no longer hear the sound of the car. Then she sat down on the edge of the cot, took off her shoes, and wiped the sand from the bottoms of her feet.

The room was as dirty and as cluttered as the ones she had grown up in. Dorene had never been concerned about keeping the apartment tidy. As long as there was a place to sit and a bed to lie on, it didn't matter if the place was strewn with clothes or the table was piled high with dirty dishes. Isabel paid no mind to the clutter but was disappointed that Pete lived in this run-down place with bare floors.

Pete's daddy wasn't exactly what she had expected either. After hearing Fat and his mother talk about him, she had feared that he would throw her on the cot and rape her. He had danced with her and that was all. After he changed the first record, he had loosened his grip on her, and she had been allowed to stand on her feet. Isabel had learned to dance at an early age. Dorene had loved to dance but scorned square dancing as countrified. She had taught her daughter to waltz, even how to do the Charleston.

Isabel heard the squeak of the screen door. Without bothering with her shoes, she hurried to the door leading to the back room.

"Pete?"

"I ain't Pete."

A boy about Johnny's age came into the kitchen. He was a younger, thinner version of Pete. His blond hair was long, and he had a scowl on his face.

"You look like him."

"I can't help that." He lifted a cloth from a pan on the table, cut off a hunk of meat, and began to eat.

"You're Jude?"

"That's my name."

"You're a lot younger than Pete."

"Smarter too."

"But not as good-looking. Pete's handsome."

"Your opinion."

"Fat told me your daddy makes you dance with him." She giggled.

"He's got you now. He likes 'em young and with bumps on their chests . . . even little bumps."

"You're nasty. I don't like you a bit."

"You're breaking my heart."

"Do you know when Pete'll be back?"

"When the notion strikes him. Sometimes he's gone for two, three days."

"Where does he go?"

"Ask him. Ain't you too young to be one a his women?"

"I'm seventeen," she lied.

"You look about fourteen."

"I can't help that either," she snapped. "Me and Pete are going to win the dance marathon."

"I heard him tellin' Pa. Pete'll do anythin' to keep from workin'. You stayin' here?"

"Pete said I'd be welcome. I'm a Perry."

"Lucky you."

"Why do you say that?"

"Ain't your name Henry?"

"Dorene Perry was my mother."

"Who was your pa? Bet you don't even know. If Dorene was like the rest of the Perry women, she was a slut."

"Who'er you to talk about my mother like that? At least I know who my mother was," she sneered.

"So do I."

"Then where is she?"

"In the graveyard. Why'd you leave the Henrys'?"

"Because that prissy-ass woman won't admit that part of that farm belongs to me. Pete's going to help me get my part of it. I'll sell it, and we'll go to California."

"Bullfoot! Ed Henry wasn't your pa. Ever'body knows that."

"Him and Dorene was married. I'm legally a Henry."

"Who says?"

"Pete says."

Jude snorted with disgust. "Pete'll say anythin' to get his hands on a dollar or get in a woman's drawers."

"Why don't you like him?"

" 'Cause he's a shit, that's why. He's got the balls of a brass monkey." He stalked to the door and went out. Isabel followed.

"What do you mean by that? Where'er you goin'? I don't like to be here by myself."

"Then go back to Fat. He'd be tickled pink to get Pete and Pa's leavin's."

"You're hateful and mean and . . . I hate you!"

"Clean up the place, *Issy*. The old man'll want to dance with you when he gets back." There was no mistaking the scorn in his voice.

"Maybe he'll want to dance with you, *Miss* Jude Perry."

He laughed. "With you here, that's 'bout as likely as me bitin' a dog."

"You're jealous!" she yelled as he disappeared around the end of the shed.

The afternoon wore on. Thinking to make a good impression on Pete when he came home and to work off her anger at his young brother, Isabel washed the dishes and swept the floor in the front room and the kitchen. The other two rooms, where the men slept, were cluttered with everything from saddles to animal hides to shiny new boots. There was only a path to the bed. The bedclothes consisted of a blanket thrown over a soiled mattress.

The rooms stank of dirty feet.

Isabel washed in the washpan, changed her dress, and

used the curling iron she had taken from Henry Ann's house after heating it in the chimney of a kerosene lamp. She checked the results with Henry Ann's ivory-backed mirror, then rouged her cheeks and applied lipstick. Slipping a ribbon under her freshly curled hair, she tied it in a bow on top of her head. With a drop of Blue Waltz perfume behind each ear, she went out onto the porch to wait for Pete.

He didn't come. Not that night. Hardy and Jude seemed to think nothing of it. After supper, Hardy wound up the Victrola and pulled Isabel out of the chair to dance with him. Jude disappeared.

They waltzed to the crooning music of Rudy Vallee. Hardy smelled of sweat and woodsmoke. Isabel tried to hold herself as far away from him as she could. He seemed to be in a dreamworld.

Later, Isabel lay on the cot fully clothed and listened fearfully for sounds coming from the other room. Hardy had looked at her with interest during supper, and when they danced, he had bent his head time and again for a whiff of the fragrance she had dabbed behind her ears. Fat Perry had said that he was the meanest man on Mud Creek and that he took whatever he wanted.

He hadn't tried to talk to her as they danced, not even to ask her what type of dancing she liked, or how long she had known Pete. He just danced, then turned off the Victrola, and went outside. She had heard him relieving himself at the end of the porch. When he came back in he blew out the lamp and went to the other room, leaving her in the darkness.

Was she safe from him because he thought she was Pete's girl?

Isabel was just beginning to relax when she heard a screen door squeaking. Someone had come into the kitchen. She jumped up.

"Pete?" she asked in a loud whisper.

"It ain't Pete." The voice that came out of the darkness was Jude's. "I need a blanket. You got my bed. I'll sleep on the porch unless you want to."

"I don't want to," she said irritably, when he came out of the back room.

"Get enough dancin'?" he whispered nastily, as he passed her on his way to the porch.

She followed him out the door. The moon, shining through a thin cloud, gave a sickly light. She saw the shape of him throwing the blanket down on the plank floor.

"Why don't you like me?" she whispered.

" 'Cause there ain't nothin' 'bout you to like."

"What's wrong with me—to your way a thinkin'?"

"You ain't nothin' but a snot-nosed, know-it-all kid chasing after a man twice your age. You'll get knocked up in a year and spend the rest of your life on Mud Creek havin' younguns that'll grow up living on Mud Creek having younguns."

"What'a you know about anything? You've never been anywhere or done anything."

"Think what you want."

"What've I done to you?"

"Nothin', and you ain't goin' to. Go to bed."

"What's that howling?"

"A coyote. Go to bed."

"I'm going to tell Pete how . . . how nasty you've been."

"Tell him."

"He'll beat you up."

"Go to bed."

She went back into the house and felt her way across the floor to the cot. *Damn him!* Who did he think he was to turn up his nose at her? When she got her money from the farm, she'd show him. He'd change his tune about her.

Jay recovered quickly and appeared to be perfectly at home at the Henrys'. Aunt Dozie doted on him. She was supremely happy to have a *youngun* to care for again. The child responded to the attention with smiles and childish chatter. To the surprise of both Dozie and Henry Ann, Johnny took a delight in playing with Jay and every day carried him on his shoulder out to the corral to see his pony.

The little boy never once mentioned his mother or going home. But when his daddy came, he was wildly happy to see him. He would run to meet him and be swept up in his arms and plant wet kisses on his cheek. It was a joy to see. Tom was not at all shy about kissing and cuddling his son, and telling him how much he missed him.

The first few nights Jay had slept fitfully in Henry Ann's bed and had awakened several times a night. Henry Ann had held him to her and crooned to him until he went back to sleep. She had become so attached to the little boy that she began to dread the day that Tom would take him home.

Johnny and Grant finished weeding the cotton field, set a row of fence posts, and strung a couple rows of barbed wire to keep the stock from wandering across the creek. Grant took over the garden and the milking chores. He was clean, cheerful, and good company; but at times Henry Ann had seen a sadness in his eyes and wondered what would cause a man, obviously rational and well educated, to take to the road.

Tom Dolan was still suspicious of him and scarcely gave him the time of day when he was around. Henry Ann wondered why. Grant's help was well worth the small wage she paid him, and she had enough money to continue it. The day after Isabel had left to go to the Perrys, she had gone to the rusty old milk can with the dab of paint on it and found the money her father had told her about. She had been dumbfounded to discover almost three hundred dollars—a fortune—and had put it in a fruit jar and buried it in the soft sand of the cellar floor.

One evening after supper as they sat on the porch, Jay asleep in Aunt Dozie's lap, Johnny asked Henry Ann if he could use her daddy's guitar.

"Grant says he can play it and will teach me to play chords."

"Goodness! Don't tell me you can play the guitar, too?" Henry Ann asked. "We'll have to add that to fixing the radio and the electric wires and lancing boils."

"Well . . . I was forced to lance the boil. Even if I did win the bet, the kid here was about to cut old Stanley's tail off—we couldn't have that."

He likes Johnny! And Johnny likes him.

Henry Ann watched the horseplay between the two and was glad Johnny was no longer under the influence of Pete Perry. It was strange how things happened. She never would have thought her young half brother's attitude toward her and the farm could have changed so quickly. He had more confidence, spoke out more often, and seemed to enjoy Grant's friendship.

"About all I can do on the guitar is make the dogs howl."

Grant strummed a couple of times, adjusted the tension on two strings, then strummed again. He picked at the strings making soft, quiet music. At first he hummed, then began to sing as night settled down around them.

"On a day like today, I pass the time away,
writing love letters in the sand—"

"Grant, that was beautiful," Henry Ann said, when he finished. She was near tears remembering the many warm summer evenings she and her daddy had sat on the porch and he had played that same guitar and sung songs like "Red River Valley" and "Yellow Rose of Texas."

"All I can say is that I'm glad I'm not trying to make a living singing. I'd starve to death." Grant's reply was followed by a small chuckle. He handed the guitar to Johnny. "All right, cowboy, let's get you started. Who knows, you might be the next Gene Autry, and we'll be listening to you on the radio." He placed Johnny's fingers on the strings and put the pick in his other hand.

Emmajean had almost stopped talking to Tom. She had asked, one time, where *the brat* was. Tom told her he was being taken care of, and she hadn't asked again. She had taken to walking along the creek bank and into the Henrys' woods. Several times Tom had seen her beneath a big pecan tree by the creek bank and on a sack swing that hung from one of its branches. The past few days he had found her wandering the yard in her nightdress, her hair a tangled mess, her bare feet dirty.

This evening, tired from working all day in the field, and anxious to go to the Henrys' to see Jay, Tom fried raw potatoes and opened a can of peaches. When it was on the table he went to call Emmajean. She was lying on the unmade bed.

"Supper's ready, Emmajean."

She didn't answer. Her eyes were on the ceiling, her hands folded behind her head.

"Come and eat or you'll be sick."

She appeared to be unmovable. Unreachable. It was the same as last night. Tom went back to the kitchen and ate, leaving a portion on a plate for her, then washed up the dishes. He looked in on her again just before he left the house. Her eyes were closed, but he wasn't sure if she was sleeping.

He was puzzled about what to do about her. She was his son's mother, his wife. It was his responsibility to keep her safe but, dear God, how could he make a living, see to his son, and keep a constant eye on this unstable woman?

He worried constantly that her parents would become aware that she was slipping into insanity and commit her to an institution. In that case they'd try to take the boy away from him. *That would not happen. He would take Jay and flee the country.*

It was clear that he'd never be able to bring his son home as long as Emmajean was there. Tonight Tom planned to speak to Henry Ann and make arrangements to pay for Jay's keep if she would allow him to stay there for a while longer.

Henry Ann. At times he could hardly think of anything else for the thoughts of her that crowded his mind. He struggled to think of something else, he really tried, but when evening came, he found himself hurrying, not only to see his son, but to see *her.* It was wrong, he knew. And God forbid that she ever know about his dreams of someday holding her . . . loving her. He ridiculed himself for the thoughts, then rationalized that he was allowed to daydream as long as he kept those dreams to himself.

Grant Gifford was a nagging threat in the back of Tom's mind. He had already admitted to himself that he was jealous of the man's being there day after day. Hell! He had no right to feel anything for Miss Henry but gratitude.

Grant had wandered off the road and made himself at home at the Henrys'. Tom had nothing against him personally. He worked hard. He'd been good for Johnny. It was just that he was there, a man who more than likely had snakes of his own to kill or he wouldn't have taken to the road, but also a man who could very well wriggle his way into Henry Ann's heart. The thought did not sit well with Tom, and he cursed himself for being a fool. It was insane even to think about her. *He was tied to Emmajean—for life.*

When he reached the Henry farm, Tom stopped beside the shed to watch what was going on in the yard. Gifford was tossing a ball to Jay. The shaggy old dog lay nearby, his head resting on his paws. His son's childish laughter and the man's low tones of encourgement mingled with the sounds of birds settling in the trees for the night and the squeak of the pulley as Johnny drew a bucket of water up out of the well.

The scene was peaceful, homelike. Tom was plagued by the ache of awful emptiness in his heart. He stood there in utter misery until his son looked up and spotted him.

"Daddy! Daddy!" The game was forgotten. Jay ran to him. He scooped his son up in his arms, loving the feel of the small arms that wrapped about his neck.

"How are you, son? I've missed you."

Jay's hair had been cut, and he was wearing new coveralls with a drop-down seat.

"Looky, Daddy." Jay pulled on the front of his coveralls. "Aunty make."

"Hey, now. That's great." He stood his son on his feet and took his hand. "Did you thank Aunty?"

"Uh-huh." Jay pulled on his hand. "Aunty make pie."

"Supper ready." Dozie came out onto the back porch. "Come on in, Mistah Tom. We's late eatin'. Henry Ann been to town."

"I'll wait out here on the porch—"

"Why yo do dat? Come on in dis house. Dar's plenty."

"Thanks, but I've had supper."

"Den have some more. Did yo have green tomato pie? Did yo have turnip greens and corn bread?"

"No use arguin', Tom." Johnny passed him with a bucket of water. "You'll not win an argument with her."

"An' yo ain't goin' to either, ya rascal. And don' ya slush no water on dat clean lin-ole-um floor. I 'bout scrubbed dem flowers off'n it a cleanin' up after yo muddy feet."

When Tom went into the kitchen, Henry Ann was setting another place on the oilcloth-covered table.

"Hello, Tom. I set a place for you there by Jay."

"Evening. I . . . didn't come to get a meal."

"We know that. You got to wash your hands, puddin'," she said to Jay. "Then you can sit by your daddy."

During the meal Henry Ann listened to the banter between Grant and Johnny, and the teasing of Jay. The child giggled, his dark eyes going often to the big, shaggy-haired man beside him. She marveled at the gentle way Tom's big hands cut up the food on Jay's plate and how the dark eyes beneath the thick brows rested lovingly on his son's face.

"Our peaches are about ready to pick." Henry Ann filled in the void in the conversation because she thought she should say something. "In another week or two we'll be busy canning."

"There's two good peach trees on my place, but someone slipped in and picked them. I doubt there's a half bushel left."

"I remember Daddy saying that someone always stripped those trees." In the silence that followed, Henry Ann said, "I was in town today. Everyone is excited about the air show. We plan to go. Do you mind if we take Jay?"

"No. I'd appreciate it. I thought I'd take Emmajean. She needs to get away from the house once in a while."

"Would you rather Jay go with you?"

"If . . ." Tom paused. His eyes circled the table quickly. "I think he'd have a better time with you. His mother isn't . . . up to taking care of him."

"We'd love to have him. Aunt Dozie is going to make a picnic. You and your wife are welcome to eat with us. My friend, Karen, will be there."

Henry Ann watched Tom fill his plate for the second time after urging from Aunt Dozie. He was hungry! Didn't his wife cook for him? The question hung in her mind during the meal and afterward as they sat on the porch. Jay was in his lap.

Shep came up to him and nuzzled at Jay's foot.

"Hello, Shep." The child reached down and patted the dog's shaggy head. Shep whined softly, his eyes peering upward, then lay down on the floor beside the chair. It was quiet and peaceful sitting in the dark with her family around her. The only sound was the squeak of the porch swing as Henry Ann rocked it gently with the toe of her foot.

"This fellow's all tuckered out," Tom said later, and got to his feet, holding his son.

"No, I ain't." Jay roused and put his arms around his daddy's neck.

"I think you are, son."

"I think he is, too." Henry Ann reached for the child.

"I'll take him to his bed."

Tom followed Henry Ann into the house. She switched the overhead light on in her room, and he saw the neatly made bed before she took off the cover and folded it as his mother used to do. The room with its pictures on the wall and a crocheted scarf on the dresser reminded him of how bleak his own home was.

He placed Jay on the bed and removed his shoes. Henry Ann took a nightshirt from beneath the pillow and held it out to Tom.

"I . . . ah . . . usually have him . . . go in the chamber under the bed. If you want to take care of that, I'll get a warm cloth to wash his face and hands." She was out the door before he could see the flush of embarrassment that covered her cheeks.

Tom was slipping the nightshirt over Jay's head when Henry Ann returned. She gently wiped the child's face, then his hands, and pulled the sheet up to cover him.

"It's warm tonight. Are you sure you want the cover?"

"Uh-huh."

"No matter how hot it is, he wants the cover. It must make him feel safe. Good night, puddin'. If you want me, call out. Aunt Dozie and I are never far away." She kissed him on the forehead and walked away to give Tom a few minutes alone with his son.

After Tom switched out the light in the bedroom, he went to the kitchen where Henry Ann was drinking from the dipper that hung over the water bucket. She lifted her gaze to his. Did she imagine a flicker of longing on his face?

"I don't know how to thank you. He's never been so . . . happy." His voice was a husky whisper.

"Are we going through *that* again?" she said in a teasing tone. Her palms grew damp and a wild desire rose in her to put her hands on his worried face, smooth the tired lines away, and comfort him.

"I guess not. I've got to get back, but first I'd like to talk with you. Will you walk with me? Just to the edge of the yard?"

He waited expectantly until she nodded. Then he opened the screened door, and she preceded him out onto the back porch and down the steps to the yard.

Chapter Nine

Henry Ann was unaware of the cloudless sky, the bright stars, and the quarter moon beginning its nightly journey across the sky. She knew only that she was alone in the dark with this big, wild-haired man who could break her in two with his two hands, yet was so gentle with his son.

She walked beside Tom to the place where the house yard ended and the cotton patch began. They stopped beneath a giant oak, the oldest tree on the farm.

"My daddy said this tree was here when the men fought at the Alamo and for Texas's independence at San Jacinto." Henry Ann placed her hand on the rough bark and traced her name, which had been cut into the trunk when she was a child. "Indians once camped where the house sits. We've found flint arrowheads and stone hatchets. The town of Red Rock got its name when a cowboy died here, and they marked his grave with a big red rock."

"Was he killed by the Indians?"

"No. He was bitten by a rattlesnake."

Henry Ann fell silent, realizing that she had been babbling on about something that was probably of little interest to him. She gripped her two hands together in front of her and stared silently out over the neat rows of cotton plants.

She didn't know that he was looking at her face and wishing with all his heart that he were free to reach out to her and tell her what being alone with her meant to him. She heard a coyote baying to the moon and an answering cry dying away in the still night. Looking up at the man beside her, Henry Ann thought she had never seen anyone who looked so sad, so lonely.

"How much longer"—Tom's voice came out hoarsely. He cleared his throat and continued—"will Gifford be here?"

"I'm not sure. Why?"

"I was going to ask for the use of your mules for a few days, but with two men here, you don't need my help in return."

"You don't have to pay back—"

"I can't take and not pay back. I owe you enough as—"

"I . . . understand you don't wish to be obligated."

"It isn't that. I've already imposed, and I've got to ask for more. Will it be all right if Jay stays a while longer?"

"Of course, he can. I'm begining to dread the day you take him home," she said with a soft laugh.

"Oh, God . . . oh God—" He leaned his forehead against the rough bark of the tree.

The moan that came from him startled her. "What's . . . what's wrong?"

"I'm just so glad he's got a safe place. I'm so glad you want him—like him."

"He's a sweet little boy. I don't see how anyone could not love him—want him." As soon as she said the words she wished that she could take them back. Tom had said Jay's mother didn't want him. "I'm sorry. I forgot for a moment that Mrs. Dolan is ill."

"Henry Ann—May I call you that, please?"

"Of course."

"You can't know what it means to me to know that Jay is taken care of. That he's with folks who . . . are fond of him. You're . . . you're . . . I . . . If ever I can do anything to repay—" Before he realized what he had done he had placed his hand on her arm.

She covered his hand with hers. It was a spontaneous gesture.

"Don't speak of payment."

"She threw the frog you gave him in the stove," he said softly, sorrowfully.

"He told me his frog had gone to heaven." Henry Ann stood rooted to the spot. She couldn't have moved away from him if her life had depended on it. "Aunt Dozie made him a bean bag, and he's been playing with a clown made out of stocking."

"Was it yours? When you were little?"

"No. I bought it at a church bazaar when I was about sixteen." She laughed a little and let her hand drop to her side. "I was a little too old for dolls, but I had my first pay from the Five and Dime, and it was burning a hole in my pocket."

The hand on her arm was warm and rough, and prickles of some undefinable something skidded up her spine. Her gaze slid over his face. She saw the hollows beneath his cheekbones, the dark circles that ringed his eyes. She longed to wrap her arms around him, comfort him, tell him that she would do everything she could to help him protect his son.

Grant's voice calling "Good night" blasted through her reverie and made her aware of her surroundings. She stepped back, and Tom's hand fell from her arm.

"Would you like Johnny to help you for a few days?"

"I'm thinking about giving up on the cotton crop. In another week it'll be too high to cultivate with a team; and if it's to be saved, it'll have to be hoed."

"Let us help you."

"I couldn't ask that. I—"

"—I've no way of paying back," she finished for him. "The time is coming when our car will need some work and—" She left the sentence unfinished.

"—Just let me know."

"I'll speak to Johnny about coming over on Monday. He's takin' a likin' to that team." She tried to speak lightly. "They're almost as stubborn as he is. I don't know about Grant."

"I can't offer them a meal."

"Aunt Dozie will pack a lunch. Now, about the air show. We'll park the car near the field north of town. We'd be happy if you and Mrs. Dolan—"

"No," he said quickly, "But thank you. I don't know if she will even go. She's been acting strange. Stranger," he corrected. "I want to get her to Doctor Hendricks."

"Well, if you change your mind . . ." His hand was on her elbow steering her back toward the house, and her thoughts became confused.

"I'd better be getting on back." Tom had seen movement along the brush that edged the field—the blur of something white. He stopped at the back steps, anxious suddenly to be gone. "Does Johnny sleep in the house?"

"Of course. Why?"

"Peaches being stolen and cattle slaughter tells me we have some night thieves." His hand dropped from her arm. "Good night, Henry Ann. Thank you for the supper."

"You're welcome, Tom. Good night."

Keeping alert, Tom hurried along the edge of the field. He saw nothing of the white blur that he had glimpsed before. When he reached his house, he lighted the kitchen lamp and opened the door to Emmajean's room.

She lay in bed, the covers pulled up to her chin.

Fully clothed, Tom stretched out on his cot, his hands beneath his head, his ears straining for sounds from the other room. He heard the floor squeak. What was she doing? He eased up and looked out the door to see if a light was coming from her window. It was dark. She hadn't lit the lamp. Although she had been in bed when he came home from the Henrys', he was almost sure she wasn't sleeping.

He played over in his mind every minute he'd spent with Henry Ann. *Lord! He had no business thinking about her.* He had no business thinking about anything but how he was going to live out his life with a woman who was mad or close to it and how he was going to make a living while raising his son.

When he had seen the white blur moving along the edge of the field, he had thought sure that it was Emmajean and that she had followed him to the Henrys'. After she had come so close to killing Jay, Tom was not sure of what other cruelties she was capable. Sometimes in the moments just before he fell asleep, he envisioned the long lonely years ahead and wondered if he had the strength to endure them.

He slept, but restlessly.

Morning came. Tom started a fire in the cookstove and put on the coffee, then went out to do the chores. When he returned, Emmajean was sitting at the table drinking coffee. She was smiling. Her hair was combed and she was wearing one of her frilly robes.

"Would you like to go see the air show?" Tom asked, after he had washed.

"Oh, yes. And I can see Marty."

"We'll go about noon. I've got to fix a hole in the bottom of the water tank first."

"I can hardly wait. I need to look my best so Marty will be proud of me. I'll wear my white dress with the puffed sleeves and the hat with the big floppy brim. I wonder how it would look with a pink-satin rose pinned on it. And—I'll wear my high-heeled shoes. Oh, dear. Do I have time to wash my hair?"

"I would think so."

Tom watched her hand flutter up to her face and down to the neck of her robe. Then with her eyes on his face she pulled on it until the tops of her breasts showed. Suddenly, she was on her feet and around the table to lean on his back and with her arms around him. He could feel her breath on the side of his face.

"It's just like it used to be, isn't it, sweet man? Just you and me. You'll be proud of me. When we walk down the street, people will say—'Look at Mrs. Dolan—isn't she pretty? Tom Dolan is a lucky man.' We'll go to the restaurant and—"

"We'd better eat a bite here before we go. The restaurants will be crowded."

He was suffocating. He wanted to tear her arms from around him. She nuzzled the side of his face with her lips, and it took all his willpower to keep from shoving her away. He sat as still as a stone. Suddenly her sharp teeth sank into his earlobe and she bit him, viciously. He yelped and jumped to his feet. She backed away laughing.

"I've always wanted to do that."

A steady drip of blood fell on his shirt. At the washbench he wet a towel and held it to his ear.

"I hope it leaves a scar." She giggled happily. "Little old me put a scar on big Tom Dolan." She went to him. "Let me see."

Tom turned on his heel and went out the door.

Red Rock was teeming with several times its normal population when Johnny, with Grant beside him, and Henry Ann, Aunt Dozie, and Jay in the back, left town and parked the car along the edge of the flat pasture which served as an airfield. People had come from miles around, and wagons far outnumbered cars. Teams were staked out, quilts spread on the grass, children ran and played. People streamed from town carrying blankets to sit on and umbrellas to protect them from the hot Oklahoma sun.

Grant lifted Jay from the car while Johnny, wearing a clean white shirt and a wide-brimmed hat, offered a hand to Henry Ann. His black eyes sparkled with excitement. In just a few short weeks she had become terribly fond of him.

"I ain't a movin' from dis here seat," Aunt Dozie announced when Johnny reached for her hand. She unfurled a big black umbrella and held it over her head. " 'Sides, I ain't wantin' to get eat up by no chiggers. Watch dat baby. I tie his britches down to keep dem chiggers off his legs."

They had stopped at the ice dock in town and bought ten pounds of ice for the water cooler. Grant lifted the cooler from the car and covered it with the two old comforters Henry Ann had brought along to insulate it from the hot sun. While she was spreading a quilt on the ground for Jay to sit on, the Austins pulled up and parked beside them. Christopher was driving, Mrs. Austin beside him and Mr. Austin in the backseat.

"Yoo—hoo, Henry Ann," Mrs. Austin called.

Henry Ann groaned. Of all the people she knew, why did it have to be the Austins who parked next to them? She lifted her hand and waved, then smiled at Christopher.

"Are you going to ride in the airplane?"

"I'm not sure yet."

"Not me. I can't climb up on a chair without feeling dizzy," she said with a laugh. *Thank goodness*, she thought, when someone pulled in on the other side of the Austins and drew Mrs. Austin's attention.

Johnny and Grant went out to where a group of men were gathered around one of the planes. Henry Ann returned Jay to the car seat so that he could sit behind the wheel and pretend he was driving the car.

"Dat ole hen a-lookin' at dat child." Aunt Dozie leaned over and spoke in a low voice. "What yo goin' to tell her?"

"The truth. I'll not tell her anything if I don't have to. If I do, I'll say that Mrs. Dolan is ill and we're helping a neighbor."

"Yo best get yo mouth set. Dat Miz Austin, she comin' dis way."

"How are you, Henry Ann?" Mrs. Austin ignored Dozie. "Are you holdin' up?" She clicked her tongue and shook her head sadly. "My, my, I still can't believe Ed is gone."

"I'm doing fine. Have you been to an air show before?"

"No. I was not for coming, but young folk want to see the sights. What could I do?"

You could have stayed at home.

"Now what do we have here?" Mrs. Austin patted Jay's head. "It's the little Dolan boy, isn't it?"

"Yes, *he's* the little Dolan boy. His name is Jay."

"Well, well. Are the Dolans going to picnic with you?"

"I'm not sure. Oh, hello, Karen. I was wondering if you would find us."

Karen, wearing a large-brimmed straw hat, her full skirt swirling around her legs, came quickly toward them.

"Hello, Mrs. Austin. Hi there, Aunt Dozie. Hello, sugarfoot." She kissed Jay on the cheek. "Are you driving this car?"

"Daddy let me." Jay continued to turn the wheel. "Ooo . . . gaa, ooo . . . gaa," he shouted in imitation of a car horn.

Karen's laugh rang out. She was the sunniest person! In all the years Henry Ann had known her, she had seldom seen her without a smile on her face. Karen turned now to Aunt Dozie and squeezed her arm.

"I've been looking forward to your picnic, Aunt Dozie. Did you bring enough for me?"

"I did dat, chile. I shore 'nuff did. I made dem devilish eggs yo like and dat tater salad. Where's yo daddy at?"

"He was invited to eat with the Andersons. I saw you driving in. Where's Johnny?"

"He and Grant went out to look at the plane."

"We heard you had a hired hand." Mrs. Austin jumped

into the conversation quickly. "How's he workin' out? My, but most are a lazy bunch of good-for-nothings. They'll eat you out of house and home. Did he come recommended?"

Henry Ann ignored the question. "Grant's more like a friend than a hired hand." She turned and lifted Jay out of the car. "We'll walk out to the plane, Aunt Dozie. See you later, Mrs. Austin."

With Jay walking between them, each holding a hand, Karen and Henry Ann crossed the field and approached the plane that had been brought out for the crowd to inspect. Another plane sat at the end of the field with a crew of men working on it.

"That woman gets my hackles up," Henry Ann admitted.

"I could tell." Karen's tinkling laugh rang out.

"Was it that obvious?"

"Only to me and Aunty. You'd have to hit Mrs. Austin on the head with a hammer to get through to her."

"Johnny, Johnny," Jay yelled, when he spied Johnny and Grant. He would have run to them, but Henry Ann held tightly to his hand.

Johnny turned when he heard his name. He tipped his hat to Karen, then with a broad smile picked Jay up and set him on his shoulder.

"Howdy, cowboy."

"Howdy, cowboy," Jay echoed and giggled.

Johnny carried Jay up to where he could touch the tail of the plane.

"Well, isn't that thoughtful?" Karen turned her smiling eyes on Henry Ann. "He's changed."

"Yes, he has. I'm proud of him." She glanced at Grant and saw his eyes on Karen . "You don't know Grant. Grant Gifford, Karen Wesson."

"Hello." Karen offered her hand. "Have we met before? Your face seems familiar."

Grant laughed and took her hand. "That's supposed to be my line. And no, I don't think so. I would have remembered meeting *you*, you can be sure of that."

"What time does the show start?" Henry Ann asked.

"In about an hour. Afterward they'll give rides."

"Are you going up?" Karen asked.

"No, but Johnny is."

"Johnny?" Henry Ann said with alarm. "Oh, I don't know—"

"All right, Mother Hen," Grant teased. "Give the boy a little rope."

"Have you been up in a plane?" Karen lifted her face to look at him.

"A few times. I lost a bet to Johnny, so I'm paying off with a ride."

"What was the bet about this time?" Henry Ann watched Johnny coming back with Jay perched on his shoulder.

"I don't think you want to know." Grant's eyes flicked to Henry Ann and then back to Karen.

"I'll ask Johnny."

"You do that." Grant laughed, causing Karen to say, "Maybe you'd better not, Henry Ann. I think it has something to do with *man talk*." Karen smiled up at Grant. "You seem to be the authority here on airplanes, maybe you can tell me if this is the kind of plane Amelia Earhart flew across the ocean."

"It might be. She crossed solo just last week."

"I heard about it on the radio."

"I don't know what kind of plane she flew."

"Well, glory! Here's a man who doesn't know everything."

They walked back across the field past a tent with an American flag flying from the center pole. Inside a man standing in front of a large map was speaking to a group of men who gathered around. Beside him a young man indicated specific places on the plat map with a pointer stick.

"It's a certainty the oil boom is coming this way. Oil runs in rivers beneath the ground just as water runs in rivers on top of it. It only makes sense that from Healdton south to Wichita Falls the river of oil should run right here or very near it. Now you can get in on the ground floor, or you can let someone else drain the oil from beneath your land."

"That's a line of bull if I ever heard one," Grant said, as they moved on toward the car. "I hope folks will get a lawyer to look over any contract before they sign."

"Are you an oil man, Mr. Gifford?" Karen asked.

"No. I'm a bum."

Karen laughed, as if he had made a joke. "The oil man is willing to pay them on the chance oil is under their land."

"Yeah, fifty cents an acre."

"Fifty dollars for a hundred acres is a lot of money nowadays." Then to an older man in ragged overalls using a cane, Karen called out, "Hello, Mr. Jacobs. My, you're getting along great! You'll be dancing a jig next. It's good to see you out."

"Howdy, Miss Wesson. I be doin' tolerable."

"Glad to hear it." They walked on, and Karen said, "Sorry to interrupt. He's been awfully sick."

"I was just going to say that these birds will not lease a

hundred acres. They'd probably only lease ten acres from a landowner for five bucks. And they'll make sure that the ten acres lie on the property line on the corner next to a couple of properties they didn't lease. They'll resell the leases for a big profit if a big outfit comes in. If not, they'll drill on a couple of them if they can raise the money. If they get a piddling amount of oil, it isn't worth it to have the land torn up."

"You think they're crooks?"

"Legal crooks."

"Where did you learn so much about the oil business?"

"Newspaper." He grinned down at her.

She removed her hat and ran her fingers through blond wavy hair—cut short—practical, hair for a woman with no time or desire to fuss. She wore almost no makeup except for a little color on her lips. She had an inquisitive mind, was pretty, and sparkled like a new penny. *A wholesome small-town girl.* How could he be sure? Women as a rule were like chameleons.

"Have you seen Mr. Dolan?" Henry Ann asked, when they reached the car and Johnny set Jay on his feet.

"Nope. Have you, Grant?"

"I've not seen him."

"I invited him and Mrs. Dolan to eat with us. He wasn't sure they were coming today."

Aunt Dozie climbed out of the car, and Johnny carried the food basket to the quilts spread in front of the car. After the food was laid out, Dozie went back to the car.

"What are you doing here?" Henry Ann followed her to ask.

"I ain't a gettin' on de ground to eat," she replied, and

lifted the umbrella to make a shade. "It'd take all a yo to get me up. I sittin' right here, and dat's dat!"

"I'll bring your plate." Henry Ann reached in and kissed her dear friend on the cheek. "You're part of my family, Aunt Dozie."

"Dat Miz Austin ain't carin' 'bout dat, honey. Her mouth be goin' like one a them whirly-winds if she see me sittin' an' eatin' with white folks."

Henry Ann took Dozie a plate filled with fried chicken, potato salad, and pickled beets. Grant filled a glass with lemonade, added a piece of chipped ice, and placed it on the car floor within Dozie's reach.

Along the edge of the field picnic lunches were laid out, excited children ran and played, and neighbors were caught up on the latest gossip.

"Yoo-hoo, Henry Ann. Have you seen Chris-to-pher? Mr. Austin is wanting to eat," Mrs. Austin called.

"I haven't seen him," Henry Ann replied and tied a cloth around Jay's neck to keep his new coveralls clean.

"I saw him," Karen murmured. "He was heading for the other end of the field where Opal Hastings and her grandpa were sitting beside their wagon."

"Chris is in love with her." Henry Ann glanced over her shoulder to be sure Mrs. Austin hadn't approached.

"Then why doesn't he stand up to his mother and say so?" Karen whispered. Her snapping blue eyes darted a glance at the Austins, then back to Grant, who had fastened an umbrella to the front of the car to provide shade for the ladies and Jay. "Well, you're just about as handy as a pocket on a shirt."

"I try to be."

Grant was mystified by this totally unaffected girl. There

was nothing flirtatious about her. It had been less than an hour since they met, yet she acted as if she had known him for years. He didn't flatter himself that it was personal. She had been just as open and friendly in the way she had greeted people as they walked from the plane.

Henry Ann was wiping jam from Jay's face when she saw Pete Perry with Isabel clinging to his arm coming toward them. She glanced at Johnny. He was pulling his hat brim farther down on his forehead.

"Hello, Cousin Henry Ann. Sorry we're late." Pete squatted down on the ground and helped himself to a piece of chicken. "Dolan and that little hot pepper of his asked us to stay with them, but I knew you'd want me to eat with you."

"You are not invited to eat," Henry Ann said crossly.

" 'Course, we are. Here, sugar." He speared a deviled egg with a fork and held it up to Isabel. "We're kin, honey. You going to refuse to feed yore little sis?"

"Yes. She left my house. She's your responsibility now."

"And a sweet and juicy responsibility she is." Pete lifted his bushy brows several times in a racy gesture.

Isabel giggled.

Johnny made a snorting noise.

Pete turned and hit Johnny on the back so hard that the lemonade in the glass he was holding sloshed over onto his shirt.

"Ain't seen ya since the hogs ate my little brother, chief. Ya still on the warpath?" He laughed with his mouth full of food. "Didn't take long for ya to knuckle under once the old wolf was gone and his cub got her claws in ya."

Johnny bristled. "Keep your hands to yourself."

"Ooh, ooh. I'm scared!" Pete stood and looked down at

Jay. "Ain't that Dolan's kid? You 'n' Dolan got somethin' goin', Cousin?"

"Watch your mouth." Grant got slowly to his feet.

"Well, now. Who'er you?" Then to Isabel, "Is this the bum ya told me 'bout, honey?" Without waiting for an answer he spoke to Henry Ann. "Cousin, yo're more of a woman than I thought ya was if ya can service this road bum and Dolan—"

In a lightning move, Grant hit him a solid blow on the mouth.

Pete backtracked, then regained his balance. To the surprise of all, he laughed.

"Not bad for a roady. Ya must a been feedin' him good, Cousin." He shook off Isabel's hand and dabbed the cut on his lip with the back of his hand. "Anytime ya want to meet me behind the barn, road bum, I'll give ya a chance at me."

"Why behind the barn, big mouth? Are you afraid your reputation as a bully will suffer if folks see you eat dirt?"

"Stop this." Henry Ann stood. "People are looking."

"Let 'em." Isabel, her face painted and her hair frizzed with a curling iron, clung to Pete's arm. "Tell 'em, Pete. Tell 'em we got us a lawyer who'll make her give me and Johnny what's ours."

"Count me out of any a that," Johnny said. He was on his feet, his arms folded across his chest. "I want no part of it."

"You think you'll get more if you side with her? I ain't met a Indian yet that had any backbone," Isabel taunted.

"Ed wasn't my daddy and he wasn't yours. You know that."

"Anybody with half a eye could see he wasn't yours.

Your daddy was a blanket-ass. Mama said he was big, dumb, and lazy—"

"And yours was a sot with jake leg from drinkin' rotgut whiskey."

"He had money. All yours had was a big pecker."

"It was what *she* wanted. You're just like *her*."

"So's she." She glared at Henry Ann. "Mama admitted she liked *it*. *She's* keepin' Dolan's kid, and if he ain't already got in her pants, he will. Mama always said nasty nice *ladies* were like bitches in heat once a man got 'em—"

"—Hush your filthy mouth," Johnny said.

"Leave." Henry Ann's heart beat rapidly, her ears rang, and her voice came out louder than she wanted. "And take her with you."

"The lawyer will serve papers on you." Isabel looked so smug Henry Ann wanted to slap her, but she addressed her reply to Pete.

"What will you pay a lawyer with—bootleg whiskey?"

"It's good as gold. Come on, sugar," he said with his arm across Isabel's shoulder. "Let's find us a place in the shade to watch the show. One more thing, *Cousin*, when yo're out behind the house with Dolan, stay in the shadows. Ain't no tellin' who'll be out there watchin'. Might even be Miz Dolan. Jealous wives can be . . . mighty dangerous."

As they walked away, Isabel looked over her shoulder and stuck out her tongue. The gesture was childish. Henry Ann could have felt sorry for her if she had not made that vicious remark about her and Tom Dolan. She could feel the fire in her cheeks, and in order to cover her humiliation, she looked down at little Jay who had crawled into Karen's lap. Her arms were wrapped around him. His face was hidden against her shoulder.

"Oh, my goodness!"

"He sensed the tension even before . . . what could loosely be considered a fight." Karen glared at Grant. "While you were at it, why didn't you knock his teeth out instead of giving him a little peck on the chin?"

"I promise to do better next time." Grant grinned down at her, his eyes alight with amusement.

"Let's not let this unpleasantness spoil the day." Henry Ann's voice was not quite steady. "Aunt Dozie, do you want anything else? If not, we can put away the food."

"I had plenty. Jist let me get down from dis car an' I pack it up."

"Sit still. Karen and I can do it."

One of the planes was preparing to take off by the time the picnic basket was stowed in the car. Henry Ann whispered to Jay, then took him behind the car and held up a blanket while the child relieved himself. Grant and Johnny walked away; Henry Ann and Karen settled down on the quilt with Jay to watch the show.

The plane took off, circled the field emitting red smoke, then climbed and began a rolling and looping routine. As the crowd watched, the plane swooped low over the field and then shot almost straight up. After another loop the loop, the plane straightened out and a man jumped. The crowd held its collective breath until the chute opened, then cheered his safe descent. The parachute, red with white stripes, floated the man gently to the ground.

While waiting for the other plane to take off, someone spoke on a loudspeaker, but it was difficult to understand what he was saying. Henry Ann determinedly tried to keep her mind on the show, but she found herself recalling Pete's and Isabel's hateful words.

"Don't worry about it." Karen's words reached into her mind as if she knew what was there.

"I can't help it."

"Have you seen a lawyer?"

"O.B. Phillips. He didn't think I'd have a problem."

"Mr. Phillips is sixty if he's a day, Henry Ann."

"Daddy trusted him. He's the one who told him to put the farm in my name. What makes me mad is the other things they said."

"About Mr. Dolan?"

"He's a terribly nice man, Karen, and he's got a peck of trouble with that wife of his."

"Trouble or not, she's still his wife." Karen reached over and squeezed Henry Ann's hand.

"I know."

"Isabel wanted to say something to get your goat. Forget about it."

The second plane took off, and they turned their attention to it. Jay lay with his head in Henry Ann's lap. She cooled him with a cardboard fan. The wing-walker put on a show that left the crowd gasping. Then it was time for the rides. Johnny and Grant were among the men lined up at the ticket stand.

Later, Henry Ann was grateful that she hadn't known whether or not Johnny was in a plane when it took off. The rides lasted about ten minutes. First one plane went up and then the other.

Cars were leaving the field, and teams were being hitched to the wagons by the time Grant and Johnny came back to where Henry Ann and Karen waited. Johnny was excited.

"Did you ride? Oh, I don't need to ask," Henry Ann said.

"It was great, sis. Just great."

He had never called her sis, had seldom even called her by name. Henry Ann felt a tide of affection for the slim boy and wished that her daddy could know how he had stood by her today.

"Were you afraid when you looked down?"

"Not a bit. Someday I'm going to fly one of those."

"Took to it like a duck to water," Grant said.

"I'd never have done it . . . if not for the bet," Johnny admitted, unable to keep the grin off his face. "I wanted you to have to put out that two dollars."

"Two dollars? Is that what it costs? Grant? You shouldn't have—"

"Sure he should." Karen fanned her face with the brim of her hat. "A gentleman never weasels on a debt."

"Well, now, who ever heard of a bum's being a gentleman." Grant's eyes teased her.

"Or a gentleman's being a bum," she countered.

"We'd better be going," Henry Ann said. "Aunt Dozie is hot. We'll drop Karen off on the way."

Johnny picked up the sleeping child and placed him in Aunt Dozie's lap. Henry Ann shook out the quilt, folded it, and got in the backseat leaving Karen to sit in the front seat between Johnny and Grant.

"I haven't sat this close to a good-looking man in a long time." Karen grinned at Johnny.

"Thanky, ma'am."

"She was talking about me, Johnny boy," Grant told him.

Karen's gay laughter rang out.

Chapter Ten

All the way to town Tom regretted his decision to take Emmajean to the air show. She was too exuberant, too keyed up. She hadn't even glanced at the Henry place when they passed it and had not been still for an instant since she got into the car. Her hands moved constantly in a fluttering motion, her feet beat a tattoo on the floor—and she hadn't stopped talking.

"Did I tell you about Bob Crain? He had a terrible crush on me while we were in school. It was more than a crush—let me tell you. He was wild about me. He'd follow me around . . . like a stray puppy. It was so annoying! One night I let him take me to a dance at the Twilight—that's a fancy ballroom in Wichita Falls—and afterward, 'cause he'd been so nice, I let him feel under my dress. Was I surprised! He knew just how to do *it* and he did *it* real good. When I found out he was so . . . ah experienced and all, I let him do anything he wanted to me. Oh my, it was the best I'd ever had, and I didn't get home until dawn. Daddy was waiting on the porch madder than a hornet, and Mama was in a snit!" Emmajean giggled.

Lies, lies. Tom felt a surge of pity for the woman beside him. She had dressed in ribbons and lace as if she were going to a party and had doused herself with toilet water. Her face was painted, her eyelashes coated with mascara, and her brows marked with a dark pencil. He had to keep reminding himself that she was his wife, the mother of his son.

Emmajean talked nonstop all the way to town, telling him that while she was still in school, she had gone on a church picnic and had slipped away with one of the deacons and the choir director. The three of them had made love all afternoon, and they had told her that they had never met a girl who could make them as horny as she could. She leaned close to Tom and looked him in the face to see his reaction to her words.

"I made you horny, too, didn't I, big man?"

He glanced at her and away. *More lies.* He was alarmed that she was talking so freely about sex—telling him her sexual fantasies. She had never been with a man until the night she was with him. Her being a virgin had added to his guilt. Had she been a loose woman, he would never have felt obliged to marry her.

The town was crowded with cars and wagons. Men on horseback mingled among them. Tom drove by the doctor's office. His car was gone, and the sign was in the window that said the office was closed. When they reached the field, cars were lined up along one side. Tom spotted the Henry car almost immediately. It was one of a few without tops. Aunt Dozie sat in the back with a big black umbrella over her head. He turned in the opposite direction and stopped at the far end of the field, making sure the tent where Marty Conroy would be was nearby so that Emmajean would have no reason to go near the Henrys.

He glanced at Emmajean to see if she had spotted Henry Ann and Johnny with Jay sitting astride Johnny's neck, crossing the field toward their car. His heart lurched when he saw his son. He should be the one showing him the airplane for the first time. The group would pass the tent, so he placed his hand on Emmajean's arm to hold her attention so that she wouldn't look that way until after they had gone by.

"Look. I think that's the man who will jump from the plane. He's putting on his parachute."

"Wouldn't it be funny if it didn't open?" She held up the floppy brim of her hat so that she could see.

"I don't think it would be funny at all. The man would be killed."

"Why do you care? You don't know him . . . or do you?"

"No, I don't know him."

"Well—I guess it would spoil the day—for some. I think it would be exciting."

Oh, Lord. What's going to keep ME from going as crazy as she is?

When Henry Ann's group had passed the tent, Tom let go Emmajean's arm. She opened the door and bounced out.

"Ohhh . . . Damn!" She stooped and pulled the spike heel of one of her shoes out of a pile of cow manure. Tears flooded her eyes, and she began to cry. "What'll I do?"

"Stand there by the car. I'll wipe it off."

Tom rummaged in the box that replaced the rumble seat

of his Ford roadster and found a rag. He carefully wiped the heel and gave the shoe back to Emmajean.

"Be careful where you step; the ground is soft in places."

"You're sweet today." Her tears had miraculously disappeared, leaving behind dark smears of mascara. She clung to his arm with both hands. "Why can't you be this sweet all the time?" She laughed shrilly. "You don't have to tell me. It's because we're alone, like it was before we got that unwelcome addition."

"We're not alone." Tom wanted to ask her how she could talk that way about her child. Instead he said, "There must be several hundred people here."

"You know what I mean." She giggled happily and hooked her fingers in the fly of his trousers.

"Stop it!" He removed her hand.

"You're an old fuddy-duddy. Nobody can see. You're not any fun at all. Let's go find Marty."

"He's busy now. Let's look at the airplane first."

Tom shook free of her clinging hands and gripped her elbow firmly to steer her out toward the plane. The crowd had thinned out, and he hoped not to see anyone to whom he would have to stop and speak. The first person they met was Christopher Austin. His gaze slid over Emmajean, and he nodded to Tom while his eyes searched the area.

"Hello, Dolan. Come to town to see the sights?"

"This should be worth seeing."

"Yeah. If you're looking for—"

"We're going out to the plane. See you later."

"We'll see you later," Emmajean echoed. "And what's your name?"

Christopher paused and turned. "Christopher Austin."

"My name's Emmajean . . . Christopher."

Christopher tipped his hat. "How do you do, ma'am?"

"Why don't you ever come over to our house?"

He glanced at Tom, then said, "Well, ah . . . maybe I will sometime."

"Come on, Emmajean." Tom tried to move her, but she had dug in her heels.

"You're awfully cute . . . for a sod-buster."

Tom read the look of puzzlement on Christopher's face before he turned and walked away.

"Where does he live?"

"I'm not sure."

"Where did you meet him? Will he ever come to our house?"

"I don't remember where I met him, and, no, he'll not come to our house."

"I wish he would. He's so . . . cute."

She clung to his arm as they went slowly toward the plane. Walking on the prairie sod was difficult in the spike-heeled shoes. Tom was becoming increasingly alarmed by her bizarre behavior. For almost a week she had said hardly anything to him, and now it was as if a dam had broken and she chattered continually. His hope was to get through the day and get her back home without a scene.

They reached the plane as the last of the sightseers were leaving and came face-to-face with Pete Perry and Isabel.

"Well, now, looky who's here. The great man and his lady." Pete's admiring gaze moved over Emmajean. "Hello, pretty lady."

"Hel . . . lo," Emmajean said breathlessly, her eyes devouring Pete's face. "I've seen you before."

"Naw, ya couldn't have—"

"Oh, yes, I have," she said coyly. "And I know where. But . . . I won't tell."

"Come on, Emmajean." Tom tugged on her arm to pull her along.

"Hold on, Dolan," Pete said, stepping in front of them. "Come on back with us to Henry Ann's picnic. You're goin' to eat with your kid, ain't ya? There'll be fried chicken and tater salad. She sent me a special invite to come eat. Don't want to disappoint her, or I'd watch the show with this here pretty lady." He chucked Emmajean beneath the chin.

"Get your hands off her and get the hell out of the way," Tom gritted angrily.

"Pete." Isabel jerked on his arm. "Come on."

"Just a minute, honey. No need to get yore ass in a crack, Dolan. Ya got the prettiest woman in the county. Ain't that enough? But . . . reckon one woman ain't enough for a horny Irish sod-buster. Huh?" Pete stepped aside and tipped his hat to Emmajean. "See ya later, sugar."

"I think you're cute," Emmajean called over her shoulder as Tom pulled her away before he gave way to the urge to plant his fist in Pete's mouth and cause a scene that would be gossiped about for months.

"Perry is not a man you should flirt with."

"Why not? I saw him one day when I was out walking. He was riding his horse."

"Did he see you?"

"I hid." She began to whine. "Why can't we stay with him? You're jealous 'cause he thought I was pretty. Next time I see him, I won't hide, and I'll talk to him all I want to. Stop pushing me! I like him. He liked me, too. I could tell. He'd not say, 'Stop, Emmajean. Don't touch me there,

Emmajean.' Oh, you make me so mad," she fumed, her voice getting louder and louder. "I don't want to see an old airplane. I want to go see Marty. Why can't I go see Marty?"

"We'll go see Marty." Tom swore under his breath.

It had been a *big* mistake to bring her to town, he thought now as he turned her around and headed for the red-and-white-striped tent. The crowd had thinned out, and only a few men stood out in front, one of them Marty.

"Mar . . . ty!" Emmajean squealed when she saw her brother, and tried to break away from the grip Tom had on her elbow.

Marty came quickly toward them, obviously to head them off.

"Hello, Emmajean, Dolan."

Emmajean grabbed his arm and tried to kiss him. The brim of her hat hit his cheek and fell to the ground. Marty retrieved it and held it between them.

"Come to see the show?"

A stupid question, Tom thought. Why else would they be here?

"I wanted to see you, Marty." Emmajean clung tightly to his arm.

"Show's about to start. Better get her back in the car outta the sun, Tom."

"I'm not going back to that old car. I'm staying with you."

"You can't. I've got work to do."

"I'll help—"

"Who do we have here, Marty? Introduce me to your friends." A handsomely dressed man in a pin-striped suit came up beside them. He had a large nose, a rugged face, and dark red hair. His bright eyes fastened on Emmajean.

"Hel . . . lo. I'm Emmajean." She smiled up at him.

"Hello. I'm Walter Harrison."

"I'll call you Walt. You can call me Emma." She transferred her hands from Marty's arm to his. "I'm Marty's sister."

"You don't say. You never told me you had such a pretty little sister, Marty." The cigarette between his lips lobbed out smoke; his hard eyes crawled over Emmajean like beetles.

"This is her husband—Tom Dolan," Marty said quickly.

Harrison glanced at Tom. "Howdy."

Tom said nothing. He was watching Emmajean with growing concern. Marty was watching, too; he tried to capture Walt's attention.

"Walt, I told Mr. Callahan we'd be over to—"

"—You don't have to go, do you, Walt?" Emmajean was flirting outrageously with the man, sliding her hand back and forth over his and leaning heavily on his arm. When she leaned her head against his shoulder, Marty looked at Tom with alarm.

"We'd best get back to the car, Emmajean. The show is about to start." Tom reached to take her arm.

She batted his hand away. "I'm staying here."

"We've got work to do, Emmajean," Marty said, and tried to give her back the hat he was still holding. "You'd better go with Tom." She knocked it out of his hand, and it fell to the ground.

"Go, Tom. I'm staying here. Say you want me to stay, Walt. Pl . . . ee . . . ase, please, pretty please with sugar on it. You like me, don't you? We can go in the tent. No one can see us in there and—" She let her words trail suggestively and trailed her fingers over his chest.

Harrison raised one eyebrow at Marty in an expression that asked: *What's going on?*

"It's hot out here in the sun." Marty tried to loosen his sister's hands from Walt's arm.

"I don't care."

Marty turned to Tom and lowered his voice until it was barely more than a whisper. "Get her . . . away from here."

Tom reached for her arm and pulled her forcibly away from Harrison. "Let's go, Emmajean."

"No . . . ooooo! Damn you!" She exploded in fury. As she struck out at Tom, her sharp heels sank in the dirt, and she almost fell. "I want to stay here. You never let me do anything. I hate you!" she yelled shrilly. Her coy expression had changed in an instant to one of hysterical outrage.

Tom knew that there would be no reasoning with her, when she struck out with her fist and hit him in the face. He swung her up in his arms to carry her back to the car, leaving Marty to explain to Harrison.

"Shithead! Horsecock! Bastard! Sonofabitch!" Every foul word she had ever heard exploded from her mouth as Tom carried her kicking and screaming toward the car. "Put me down!" She tried to bite him and scratch his face.

People stared.

Tom prayed that Henry Ann was not witnessing his humiliation.

Marty, head down, carrying his sister's hat, hurried to catch up with Tom. He reached the car ahead of them and opened the door. Tom sat Emmajean on the seat, gripped her shoulders, and shook her.

"Emmajean! Calm down! You're making a show of yourself."

"Ugly, stupid old . . . turd! Stinkin' . . . shit—" She tried to hit his crotch with her fist and when he countered the blow, she spit. It landed on his cheek. "I'm a Conroy. Mama said Conroys were special, not trash like you. I'll tell my daddy on you." Dark smudges surrounded her tear-wet eyes. "Marty!" She looked over Tom's shoulder. "Let me stay with you," she pleaded. "I'll be good. He'll hurt me. He'll tie me up and . . . rape me!"

The pity Tom had felt for her was washed away by anger at the situation he found himself in. He wanted to shake her until her teeth fell out. Instead he held her on the seat gently, but firmly, and said to Marty, "I can't drive and hold her."

Marty looked at his sister with revulsion, then back to Tom. He tossed her hat into the car and backed away.

"She's your wife. You married her quick enough, thinking you'd feather your nest with Daddy's money. Just get her out of here and keep her away from me."

Emmajean broke down in a storm of weeping. She threw herself down on the seat and Tom closed the door.

"She's getting worse every day. You'd better tell your folks that I may not be able to take care of her much longer."

"I'm sure they'll say it's your problem, not theirs." Marty turned and walked away.

Tom stood beside the car for a moment to be sure Emmajean was going to stay in the seat. His eyes swept the crowd of people who were watching and had heard Marty's words.

To hell with them. Let them think what they please!

He went around the car and got under the wheel. In his haste to get the car started, he almost flooded it. Finally, the motor caught. He backed up and drove out of the field, circled the town, and headed back to the farm, feeling the weight of the world resting on his shoulders.

Emmajean stopped sobbing about halfway home. She sat up, folded her arms across her chest, and stared straight ahead. When they reached the farm she made no move to get out. Tom went around and opened the door.

"Come on. Go in and wash your face. I'll fix us something to eat."

When she got out of the car, her big, floppy-brimmed hat fell on the ground. She stomped on it viciously, the heels of her shoes making holes and catching in the straw crown. She would have fallen if Tom had not grabbed her arm. She jerked free of him, looked at him as if she would like to kill him, slipped out of the shoes, and went to the house in her stocking feet. He watched her, then followed. She stamped into the bedroom and slammed the door.

As they left the field and all through town, Henry Ann looked for a Ford roadster with a box on the back. Relief was mixed with disappointment when she didn't see it. Her mind drifted back to the night before when she had stood under the oak tree with *him*. She shook her head to rid her mind of the memories that had played over and over in her mind: memories of his hand on her arm, the careful way he had ushered her back to the house, the concerned look in his eyes when he cautioned her to be careful.

He's married, he's married, he's married. You have no right to think about him.

The car stopped in front of the parsonage. Grant got out and extended his hand to Karen .

"See you tomorrow, Henry Ann. Bring Jay to Sunday school," Karen said, when she stood on the sidewalk.

"I'd have to ask his . . . daddy about taking him to a Baptist church. He's Catholic. I'll stay home tomorrow so Aunt Dozie can go to her church."

"Jay can stay with me and Grant while both of you go," Johnny said.

"That problem is solved." Karen looked up at Grant. "Are you not a churchgoing man, Mr. Gifford?"

"Who's Mr. Gifford?" Grant looked up and down the street. "Yes, I go once in a while, Karen."

"If you're planning on beating up that bully, you'll need the Lord on your side. You'd better go to church more than once in a while."

"If I'd known you had so little confidence in me, I'd have put more muscle behind the punch I gave Big Mouth. I was afraid I'd hurt him and he'd bleed all over the picnic."

Karen rolled her eyes toward the heavens. "Henry Ann, I want to be invited for Round Two. I'll bring the first-aid kit."

"I'll see that you get a front-row seat."

"Mercy me. What yo younguns talkin' 'bout?"

"The next big heavyweight fight, Aunt Dozie." Karen's cheery laughter rang out. "Pete Perry'll not forget that punch. Watch your back, Mr. Jack Dempsey Gifford. 'Bye. Thanks for the lunch, Aunt Dozie. See you tomorrow."

Grant watched as she ran up the steps to the porch, then waited as she turned and waved before he got back in the car.

On the way back to the farm Henry Ann felt a sudden

tinge of alarm. Karen was attracted to Grant and he to her. Lordy. She knew nothing at all about him. Tom could be right about his being a jailbird and that it was risky taking in a man off the road. Grant was pleasant company, but people said that about Al Capone and Clyde Barrow. She'd heard that Baby Face Nelson was as nice a fellow as you'd meet, but he was a bank robber and kidnapper.

One thing was sure: Grant Gifford was no *ordinary* bum.

Chapter Eleven

"Why didn't ya hit him back?"

Isabel was worried. Pete hadn't been acting as she had expected he would when she left Henry Ann's to go to the Perrys', at Mud Creek. He hadn't come home for three days and when he had, he hadn't seemed particularly glad to see her.

"What you doin' here, sugar? I told ya to hang in there so we'd know what was goin' on at the Henrys'. Ya gotta get Johnny to go along with us."

"He ain't goin' to. He called me a slut. I just couldn't stay there, Pete, and I come here to my own folks."

"It's all right, honey. Ya can stay here . . . or over at Fat's."

Later she had heard him arguing with Hardy.

"Son, I ain't understandin' why ya ain't takin' yore pleasure with 'er. Hell! She's old enough and got all the bumps in the right places. I could've had her on her back in two shakes of a dog's tail if I'd a half tried. Got Dorene's blood in her, ain't she?"

"Stay outta her, Hardy. I ain't takin' no chance of her gettin' knocked up. I'm goin' ta wait until I find out if she's got a real claim on that farm; if she does, I'll marry her. Meanwhile I want to partner her in the dance marathon. I could use that five hundred bucks."

"Hell, it'll take ya two months' a dancin' to get it. We could get that much in one or two jobs."

Isabel paid attention only to Pete's promise to marry her and his expressed desire to dance with her in the marathon. She worried some that he was gone a lot, and she never could find out where he went. He and Hardy went off together and were gone for a day at a time—sometimes overnight. That damn Jude was always making remarks about how stupid she was to think that Pete would marry her. Lately, when Pete was so cross and not even interested in kissing her, she had begun to believe Jude was right.

"I said, why didn't you hit him back." She trotted to keep up with Pete's long legs as they went toward where Jude sat in an old Model T truck. Isabel had ridden to town with Jude. Pete had ridden ahead on his horse, a palamino with a flowing white mane and tail. The animal was Pete's pride and joy. When he had an audience, he liked to show off his riding skills by causing the horse to rear up on its hind legs.

"Because I didn't want to. Now shut up!"

"Were you afraid you couldn't whip him?"

"I could've cut his gizzard out before he laid a hand on me." Pete drew a switchblade knife from his pocket and shook it in her face. "I've got more important thin's to do than beatin' up on a road bum and gettin' the sheriff down on me."

"Because of the bootleggin'?"

Pete turned on her. "You keep your mouth shut 'bout that. Hear?"

"Henry Ann said it."

"You ain't Henry Ann. Don't forget it."

"You're sweet on *her*!"

"Ah . . . for God's sake! This is what I get for gettin' mixed up with a harebrained kid."

"Where'd you see that Mrs. Dolan? She was painted up like a slut. Reminded me of Dorene and how she flirted. At the last she put on more and more paint, tryin' to hide how old and sick she was."

Pete didn't answer, and Isabel, never knowing when to keep her mouth shut, continued on.

"I'm thinkin' that Dolan won't put up with you screwin' his wife, even if she is crazy as a loon. Are you screwin' her? Are you? If you are, I'll tell Henry Ann—"

They had reached the car where Jude waited. Pete grabbed Isabel's arm and jerked her behind it.

"Yo're a whinin' brat. And I'm gettin' sick a ya. Ya say a word to Henry Ann about anythin' I do, and I'll shake the stuffin's out of ya. Hear me? I'm gettin' tired of yore naggin'. Straighten up or I'll send ya over to Fat's. He'd think he'd died and gone to heaven. I bet that he ain't had no pussy since old Rosie was sent to the nuthouse. Now get in there with Jude and drive him crazy for a while."

Holding her arm in a tight grip, he jerked her around and flung open the car door.

"Take her home," he snarled.

"I come to see the show and I'm seein' it. If you want her outta here, take her yourself." Jude was never cowed, not by Pete nor by Hardy. They usually left him alone.

"Then keep her here in the car."

Isabel began to cry. "Pete . . . why'er ya so mad?"

"Ah . . . hell—" He stomped off to where he had tied his horse, mounted, and rode back toward town.

Isabel sniffed. Pete would change his mind when she got her part of the Henry farm. The lawyer said that if Ed Henry didn't have a will, she was in good shape to collect something. Of course, the farm would have to be sold before she could get the money; and, as he explained, there were not many folks who had money to buy a farm, and the banks were going broke every day. Nevertheless, he would look into the matter.

Pete asked about money Ed had in the bank and if Isabel had the right to take her part of the cattle and sell them. The lawyer mulled that over and said he would look into it. After Isabel signed some papers they had left the office.

"Told you." Jude's voice broke into her thoughts.

"Hush up your fat mouth!"

"He's not goin' to marry a little pissant like you. He's always had his sights set on Henry Ann Henry."

" 'Cause of the farm?"

"I'm not so sure. But if you get a third, he might marry up with you so Henry Ann'd have to deal with him. It's Henry Ann he wants."

"I don't believe it! What's that snooty bitch got? She thinks her shit don't stink."

"She's got respect. It rankles Pete to be called Mud Creek trash."

"It don't seem to bother you none."

"How do you know? You don't know anything about me . . . or Pete, or Hardy. You're just a snot-nosed kid who thinks she's grown-up. If you had any sense, you'd of stayed where ya was well off."

"And where was that? Oklahoma City?"

"And become a whore like your ma? No, stupid. The Henrys'. She'd a sent you to a school where you could've made somethin' of yourself."

"I wasn't stayin' there to be bossed by *her*!"

"You're dumber than a stump. You'd fit in just fine over with Fat. He's so dumb he don't know his ass from a hole in the ground."

"If you're so damn smart, why'er you still on Mud Creek?"

"I'm a bidin' my time, smarty. I got one more year at school. Then I'm outta there. I . . . I might get me a scholarship at a university."

"What's that?"

"Don't you know anything? A scholarship is money give to someone smart enough to go to college."

"You're not *that* smart."

"Not to your way of thinking. My teacher thinks I am. I'm going to study and be a doctor someday."

"Ha, ha, ha. You've got about as much chance a being a doctor as I've got flyin' to the moon."

"Then you better start sprouting wings, smart-ass."

"I want to go."

"Go. I'm staying. I already seen one sideshow. I'm staying to see the air show."

"What ya mean, sideshow?"

"Saw Dolan carryin' a woman to the car. I reckon it was his wife. The talk is she's queer-acting. She was kickin' and screamin' and carryin' on. The little dude from the tent was trottin' along with him, carryin' her hat."

"Where are they now?"

"He calmed her down and drove off. Folks got a good sideshow."

"Henry Ann's takin' care of his kid."

"Good of her. Man's got his hands full with that woman."

"He's wantin' to get his hands in Henry Ann's pants."

"How do you know that?"

"All men want it."

"All men want to get in Henry Ann's pants?"

"No, stupid. Dolan."

"And Pete."

"And you, if you got the chance."

"That's where you're wrong," he said softly. "I respect *her.*"

"What's that mean?"

"If you're too dumb to know, I'm not telling you."

"Bullshit, Jude! Bullshit!"

An airplane took off. Jude got out of the car and went to sit on the front fender. Isabel sat in the car glaring at his back and feeling that she didn't amount to any more than a dirt clod. Jude always made her feel like that. It rankled her that he respected Henry Ann and not her. He hadn't liked her from the start, considered her trash, and had told her so almost every day she had been on Mud Creek.

Why should she care? She didn't like him, either.

Jay was so tired from the exciting day in town that he was ready for bed shortly after Henry Ann and Aunt Dozie cleaned up the supper dishes. She washed him, put on his nightshirt, and tucked him in bed.

" 'Night, sweetheart." She kissed him on the forehead. He put his arms around her neck.

"Night, Mama."

Henry Ann was so shocked that breath left her.

"Oh, honey. You shouldn't call me that. You've got a mama. She's very sick."

"Her hurt me."

"She didn't know what she was doing. She won't do it again."

"Her will. Don't like me."

"I'm sure she does. Your daddy loves you, too."

"Love my daddy. Don't like her."

For a long moment Henry Ann didn't know what to say. She just stroked his hair, her mind searching for the right words.

"Your daddy will come tomorrow to see you."

"He take me back?"

"I don't know about that."

"Want to stay with you . . . and Aunty . . . and Johnny."

"We love having you. But we'll have to wait and see what your daddy says."

"Daddy stay here, too."

The pleading expression on Jay's face was so like the one on Tom's last night that Henry Ann felt a sudden quivering in the region of her heart. She smoothed the dark hair back from the child's face and cupped his cheek with her palm. *Oh, sweetheart, I wish with all my heart that your daddy could come stay and that you were my little boy.* She leaned down and kissed his forehead again, shocked and confused by her thoughts.

"You'd better get to sleep. Tomorrow afternoon we're going to make a freezer of ice cream. Aunt Dozie says we have enough cream."

"She let me churn," Jay said sleepily.

"She calls you her good little helper."

At the door, Henry Ann looked back at the small boy in her bed. A feeling of loneliness washed over her. All her life she had dreamed of being a part of a family where there was a mother and a daddy and brothers and sisters like many of her school friends had. That dream was what had driven her to plead with her daddy to let her go to Oklahoma City to get Johnny. She wished her daddy had lived to know how Johnny was shaping up and taking on responsibility.

On the front porch, Grant was strumming the guitar and singing in his soft husky voice.

"From this valley they say you are going.
We will miss your bright eyes and sweet smile."

Henry Ann went through the house to the back porch and stood looking toward the Dolan farm. Somehow she had known that Tom wouldn't come over tonight. What was he doing? Thinking? She knew that it eased his mind that his son was here with her.

"Come sit by my side if you love me—"

It was a fact of life that some women were not cut out to be mothers. Hers, for instance. Dorene hadn't wanted her just as Mrs. Dolan didn't want Jay—and she hadn't had the excuse that she was crazy. Her mother had been a selfish, self-centered woman. And Isabel was just like her.

"But remember the Red River Valley—"

Little Jay needed a mother's love. It had been a long time ago, but Henry Ann remembered how, when she was small, she had looked on with envy when one of her little friends would sit on her mother's lap and be cuddled and loved. She'd had her daddy, but daddies were not mothers—

The screen door opened behind Henry Ann. Grant came out. She had been so deep in her thoughts that she hadn't realized when he had stopped singing and the light had come on in Aunt Dozie's room.

"Warm night. We could get a storm out of those clouds." He stepped off the porch.

"We need the rain."

"Miss Henry . . . do you mind if I butt into your business?"

"I don't know if I mind or not until I know what business you're planning on butting into."

"This business about your sister's trying to lay claim to your farm."

"She has no claim here. The farm has been in my name for almost five years. I pay the taxes. My name is in the plat book."

"She would have no claim to the land and the buildings, but there is the machinery, the livestock, the household furniture, and even the crop that she could say belonged to Mr. Henry. Go see a good lawyer, Miss Henry."

"You mean . . . you mean she can lay claim to the cattle? The car? My . . . bedroom set?"

"She can file suit to get a third of everything that belonged to Mr. Henry when he died."

"She's only fifteen. She isn't even of age. How could she?"

"Does she have a court-appointed guardian?"

"Not that I know of. Johnny and I are her only relatives except for Dorene's folks. The Perrys all live down on Mud Creek. Dorene, her . . . our mother's affairs didn't last long. I doubt if Isabel even knows who her father is."

"As far as the law is concerned, Miss Henry, she's your father's daughter. Johnny tells me that his mother and your father were never divorced. If that's the case, he was legally married to her mother when Isabel was born."

"That's right. Daddy never got a divorce."

"One of the Perrys could get himself appointed guardian and file suit on her behalf."

"Now wouldn't that be just dandy!"

"I just wanted you to be aware of what could happen."

"How do you know all this?"

"Well—" His laugh was soft as the warm summer night. "I've been floating around for a while and picked up bits of this and that along the way."

"Do you plan to stay on here for a while?"

"I haven't decided. I like it here—in this area. I've got to land sometime—somewhere."

"You've taught Johnny a lot. He . . . needs a steadying influence, and I think you've provided that."

"I'm glad you think so. He's a good kid. Guess he's really not a kid, but compared to me he is."

"You can move into the attic room with Johnny, if you like."

"Thanks. I am getting tired of sleeping on a bedroll in that wagon." He stooped to scratch the head of the shaggy dog. "Are you wondering why I don't go to bed, Shep?" Then to Henry Ann, "He's been sleeping with me."

"Fine watchdog you are, Shep, sleeping on the job."

"Not much goes on that he doesn't know about. He's been up several times a night lately. I thought someone was prowling around, but I've not seen anyone."

"It's probably Pete Perry. He knew—"

"Yes. I caught that. He was here spying and saw you walk to the edge of the yard with Dolan."

"Mr. Dolan is—a friend," she felt compelled to say. "He was just telling me—that he wants to trade work. I said that he could use the mules and that Johnny would help him for a few days. He'll work on the car . . . if it needs it," she finished lamely.

"Do you want me to go along and help, too? He hasn't weeded his cotton patch. He'll not get much of a crop if it isn't weeded soon."

"Do you plan to stick around through cotton picking?"

"I guess I am." He said nothing for a minute. Henry Ann would have been surprised to know that his mind had switched to a blond-haired girl with dancing blue eyes and a merry laugh.

After Grant left, Henry Ann stood for a while longer on the porch. The moon had come up over the treetops and in the distance a coyote bayed. She waited for the answering call. When it came, it was closer.

Was it the same coyote who bayed the other night when she was standing under the tree with Tom, his hand warm on her arm, the darkness wrapped around them?

As Henry Ann stood looking up at the sky, she began to realize that her heart had been captured, roped, and tied by a wild-haired man with dark, sad eyes. It was a secret that she would never, could never, share with anyone.

Tom stood behind the house and looked toward the

Henry farm. He heard a coyote calling for his mate, and a feeling of loneliness washed over him. He longed to set his feet in motion and go to where he would be greeted with a welcoming smile, but he was afraid to leave Emmajean alone lest she get it into her head to set fire to the place. She was still lying on the bed where she had thrown herself when they came home from the air show. She had refused to come out when he called her to supper.

Tom began sifting through his thoughts. He would remember last evening, alone with Henry Ann in the moonlight, as one of the most special times in his life. He remembered every word that each of them said, then remembered every move, every gesture.

Henry Ann, is it possible that you dream the same dreams that I dream? Do you dream of my holding you, kissing you, in soft moonlight? Can you imagine our naked bodies pressed closely together? Would you hate seeing your belly grow big with my child? Dear, sweet woman, you would be so beautiful—

Tom looked up at the dark sky and thought of the empty nights he had spent since he'd met her. It was impossible to press down the feelings that surfaced when he thought of her. He had tried to deny the stirrings that sifted and swirled within him, but now he realized that he didn't want them to stop. They were too new and too wonderful. He wanted to make love to her and to have her love him in return.

But, he thought bitterly, it would never be. He was married to Emmajean until death parted them. And he would never dishonor Henry Ann by declaring a love that could not be fulfilled.

*   *   *

Five miles south, near the Red River, Christopher Austin was walking beside a slender, dark-haired girl. Holding tightly to her hand, he heard the lonely call of a coyote. Months ago he would not even have heard the mournful sound. It wouldn't have penetrated into his consciousness. Now he was more sensitive to sounds of loneliness, love, and laughter. His life had been changed forever. Love did that to a man.

"I hate to go, but I must."

"I know."

Christopher turned, put his arms around Opal, and held her close. He could smell her, soft like a warm spring rain. She was sweet, loving, and giving. He loved her so much that he ached. How he longed to make a home with her and little Rosemary. Opal's grandpa was getting up in years, and soon she would be alone.

There were times when Christopher was certain that he hated his mother with a hatred that almost made him sick. She was a narrow-minded, selfish woman and would never accept Opal should he bring her home. He was not sure about his daddy. If he married Opal, he would be forced to leave the farm that he had toiled on and helped to make into one of the most prosperous in southern Oklahoma.

If he gave up his heritage and left home, how could he make a living for Opal and her child? If he could get a job that paid enough, regardless of what it was, he'd work his fingers to the bone for them. But there were no jobs. He had no way to support a wife without the help of his folks.

"I love you," he whispered desperately. "I hate it that we can't be together."

"I know."

"It's unfair that you're blamed—"

"Shhh . . ." She put her fingers over his lips. "I've told you that in spite of the *way* I got Rosemary, I've no regrets. Next to you, she's the most wonderful thing that ever happened to me."

"You still won't tell me . . . who?"

"I don't know, Christopher. I've told you that."

"The miserable bastard. I'd kill him!"

"I know. Then I'd lose you forever." Her voice was beginning to crack. He could feel her trembling warmth.

"You'll never lose me," he said with feeling. "It has to be like this for a while. We don't have a choice. We're meant to be together. I know that as sure as I'm standing with two feet on the ground." He lifted her chin and kissed her gently. "I've told you, sweetheart, that Rosemary will have a daddy. She'll be my little girl, and I'll love her as much as I'll love the children we have together."

"You're so good. You deserve someone special."

"I have someone special." He cupped her cheek with his palm and felt her tears. "Kiss me, sweetheart. It's got to be enough for a while."

Wrapped in each other's arms, lips pressed tightly together, they were lost in a world of their own. Until—

"Well, well. Look who sneaked here to see my girl." Pete Perry came out of the shadows and stopped several yards from them. His arms were folded across his chest.

Chris whirled around, his arm sweeping Opal behind him.

"What the hell are you doing here?"

"What'a ya think I'm doin' here? I came to see my girl."

"Your girl? Stay away from Opal."

"Ya got a claim?"

"Yes, I've got a claim."

"Well, now . . . I may have somethin' to say about that."

"You've nothing to say about anything that concerns Opal."

"Maybe it's the other girl I come to see. *My* little . . . kinfolk."

A low growl came from Chris's throat, and he took a step forward. Opal dragged on his arm.

"No, Chris! He's not worth it. He's drunk and lookin' for an excuse to fight."

"You son of a bitch!"

"Yeah, I'm probably just that." Pete laughed. "Don't bother me a damned bit."

"I've told you before that I don't want you around here," Opal said firmly. "Now go."

"Go and leave ya to smooch with mama's boy? Not on yore life, sugar-puss. I'm stayin'. I brought yore grandpa a fruit jar full of good bootleg whiskey."

"He don't need that rotgut."

"I ain't sayin' he *needs* it, but he wants it. Ask him."

"I'll do no such thing. Take it and go."

"You heard her, Perry," Chris said.

"Stay outta this, mama's boy—"

Chris lunged. A hard fist landed square on Pete's chin. He backtracked several steps before he sat down hard on the ground.

"Don't ever call me that again," Chris snarled, ready to strike out again as soon as Pete got to his feet.

Pete took his time standing. He rubbed his chin, then

suddenly there was a knife in his hand. He crouched, ready to spring.

"Yo're close to bein' gutted, *mama's boy!*"

"No!" Opal cried.

"Back off, Pete." Grandpa Hastings, shotgun in hand, appeared out of the darkness. "Back off, or I'll blow ya in half."

Pete turned. "Ya got shells in that thin', grandpa?"

"Ya betcha."

"I ain't believin' ya."

"Wal . . . there be a way to find out. I'm gettin' plenty fed up, by grab, on the likes of ya comin' round here pesterin' Opal."

"Ya shoot me and the whole shebang down on Mud Creek'll kick up a stink and be all over ya like a swarm a hornets."

"Not if they don't find ya, they won't. Got me a dry well out back that needs fillin'."

Pete laughed. "Is this any way to treat a suitor comin' to call on yore granddaughter? Brung ya a jar of white lightnin', too."

"It's Opal's call who comes courtin', not mine. Now get. Don't come back till ya can act decent."

"Maybe I wanted to see my little sis . . . or cousin."

The old man lifted the shotgun.

"No!" Opal shouted, and rushed toward her grandpa. "He's just rattlin', talkin' big."

"Was it him, girl? Or his . . . pa?"

Drunk as he was, Pete realized that he was close to dying.

"I told you it was dark, and I couldn't tell who it was."

"I was just a pullin' yore leg, Mr. Hastings," Pete said, trying to put a note of laughter in his voice.

"It ain't nothin' to joke 'bout, boy. Now, if ya ain't wantin' to see yore guts nailed to that tree behind ya, ya better get."

Pete looked at Chris. "Ya ain't always goin' to have a old man with a shotgun backin' ya."

Grandpa Hastings followed Pete down the lane to where he had left his horse.

"I allus liked ya, Pete. Thought ya a cut above the rest down on Mud Creek. Now I ain't so sure. Don't pull this stunt again."

"I ain't likin' that mama's boy hangin' around."

"As I said, it ain't yore call. Opal ain't wantin' ya for her man, and that's that."

"I ain't courtin' her. I got bigger fish to fry than a—" Pete caught himself.

"Than a what?"

"Than a gal young as Opal."

"I'm hopin' that's what ya meant to say."

Pete swung up in the saddle. Anger was like a burning fire in his belly. He couldn't leave without doing something to soothe his injured pride. He took a glass jar from his saddlebag and, with all his strength, threw it against a tree trunk. The sound of breaking glass and the smell of moonshine whiskey reached them.

"There's yore white lightnin', old man."

"Thanky."

Grandpa Hastings watched Pete spin his horse around and ride off in the night. He waited until he was sure Pete had left before he turned and went back to where Opal and Chris waited.

Opal went to him immediately. "Grandpa, I swear! You scared me to death. You don't have any shells in that gun."

"Maybe I saved one back."

"And maybe you didn't. You haven't had shells for a week or more."

"Good Lord!" Chris exclaimed. "That was some bluff you were running. Pete Perry can be mean."

" 'Twarn't nothin' to it. Kinda fun. Ya better watch yore back. Pete's turned ugly lately even when he ain't drunk."

"Why didn't you tell me your grandpa was out of shells?" Chris asked. "There's tramps and bootleggers roaming up and down the roads. They say that somewhere in southern Oklahoma there's a bank robbed every day."

"Nobody'd come here lookin' for money," Grandpa Hastings said.

"I'll bring a box of shells tomorrow . . . or the next day."

"You don't need to, Chris." Opal clasped his arm with both hands. "You've already brought us flour and sugar and coffee—"

"I'll see to it that you have shells, Mr. Hastings. I don't want you folks out here without protection."

"As long as I'm livin', they'll have it." The old man walked back to the house.

"Grandpa's got pride. It almost kills him for folks to think we're trash. If he could, he'd take me and Rosemary away from here."

"Oh, Lord, no!" Chris groaned. "I'm glad he can't. Hold on a little longer, sweetheart. Something's bound to happen to make things better."

"Be careful. Watch out for Pete. I've never seen him so mean."

"Does he come here often?"

"Not often. He comes once in a while and visits with Grandpa. Usually I take Rosemary and go to the garden."

"I'll try to be back tomorrow or the next day. Kiss me, sweetheart. I love you so much."

"I love you, too. Be careful."

Chapter Twelve

Early on Monday morning, Johnny and Grant hitched the mules to the wagon and left for the Dolan farm. Aunt Dozie had packed lunch in a bucket for the two of them and Henry Ann carried it to the wagon. She stood in the yard as they prepared to leave and waved as they headed down the road. After a trip to the privy, she went into the house to see if Jay had awakened. He was in the kitchen with Aunt Dozie.

"Morning, sleepyhead."

"I gotta go out."

"You can use the chamber."

"Gotta go doo-doo."

"In that case, come here. I'll carry you. There are cockleburrs on the path to the privy."

"Yo break yo back carryin' that youngun. I get his shoes." Aunt Dozie hurried to the bedroom while Henry Ann lifted the child and set him on the end of the wash-bench.

After Henry Ann put on one shoe and Aunt Dozie the other, Henry Ann set the child on his feet and took his hand.

"Hold up your nightshirt, honey," she said, as they went out the door.

Dozie turned a pan of bread dough out onto a floured board and began to knead it with her strong hands. Her brow was furrowed. Henry Ann had been unusually quiet lately. She had announced at breakfast this morning that while it was cool she would walk to town. She had looked at Grant, and he had nodded his head in approval. Dozie wondered what that was all about. One thing was sure: Henry Ann was becoming too fond of another woman's youngun, and Dozie suspected that she was liking the woman's man too much, too. Dozie could see nothing but heartbreak ahead for her girl.

"Yo ort to a let Johnny drive ya. It'll be hot'ern a oven come noon," Dozie said later, as Henry Ann tied a ribbon around her hair to keep it back from her face.

"There's a breeze, and I'll take the parasol."

"Can I go?"

"If you go, sugarfoot, who'll help Aunt Dozie churn?" Henry Ann stooped and placed a kiss on Jay's cheek. "I'll be back before you have time to miss me. And I'll bring you a candy stick."

"Can . . . can ya . . . can ya bring me a frog that jumps?"

"I don't know, honey. I may not find one like the one you had, but I'll try."

Henry Ann smiled and waved gaily at Jay and Aunt Dozie. As she started down the dusty road, it was a relief to let her face relax. She'd not felt much like smiling lately. Since Grant had told her that Isabel could lay claim to a third of everything but the land and buildings, she'd not had much else on her mind. She was anxious to talk to Mr. Phillips, her daddy's old friend who had drawn up the papers when the farm was put in her name.

How can things go so wrong in such a short time, she wondered, and tilted the parasol so the breeze could hit her face. Her daddy was gone, Isabel had been a disappointment and . . . she had lost her heart to a married man. Oh, he was grateful to her for taking care of his child during a trying time with his wife and for neighborly help with his field, but other than that he'd not really seen her as a woman with dreams of a man who would love her, give her children, and grow old with her. Anyway, if he were free, he'd probably be more interested in a friendly, sparkly girl like Karen rather than an old maid like her. Yet the night she and Tom had put Jay to bed together, his dark eyes had held a definite look of yearning in them. Of course, that could have been because he was nervous about asking her for the loan of the mules.

Henry Ann was so deep in her thoughts that a car pulled up beside her before she heard the sound of the motor.

"Hello, my pretty. Jump into my jalopy, and I'll give you a ride." Christopher Austin leered at her and twisted the ends of an imaginary mustache imitating a movie villain.

"My daddy told me not to ride with strangers," Henry Ann replied in a little-girl voice.

"Never fear, my pretty little lady, I promise to be a perfect gentleman."

"Well, in that case, I'll accept the ride." Henry Ann folded her parasol and got into the car. "How come you're going to town? Are you caught up with your work?"

"You're never caught up on a farm, H.A. You know that. I decided to run in and pick up a few things."

"How are your folks?"

"They're fine. I saw Johnny and your team in Dolan's field when I passed."

"We're trading work."

"I saw Dolan and his wife at the air show. That man's got a peck of trouble riding on his shoulders. Is his little boy still with you?"

"Yes. His . . . wife is not well."

"She's ah . . . strange. I heard that she put on quite a show on Saturday. Tom carried her kicking and yelling to the car, then took off before the show even started."

"Really?"

"Mrs. Miller told Mama about it. They were parked nearby."

"If Mrs. Miller saw it, it'll be all over town."

"She said that Mrs. Dolan could swear like a well-digger."

"She exaggerates."

"Her sympathy was with Mrs. Dolan. Made Dolan out as a man who was mean to his wife. Wouldn't even let her stay and see the show."

Henry Ann turned her head sharply. "Mean to her? That's the most ridiculous thing I ever heard. She's the one who's mean! Why do you think Jay is staying at my house?"

"Don't get excited, H.A.," Chris said quickly. "I'm just telling you what Mrs. Miller told Mama."

"She's an old busybody. I hope your mother didn't believe her."

"Don't count on it. Mama soaked in every word as gospel," Chris said dryly.

"Mrs. Miller was in the office the day Tom took Jay to see Doctor Hendricks. She . . . Oh, never mind."

"She told Mama about that, too. And that you were with him."

"Oh, good Lord! Maybe if my reputation is tarnished enough, it'll knock me out of the running for your hand."

"Don't count on that either."

They didn't speak again until they neared town.

"Will you be here long?" Chris asked. "I'm going to pick up some shotgun shells. I'll wait—"

"I don't know how long I'll be. You'd better not wait."

"I thought maybe . . . maybe you'd have time to ride with me out to Opal's," he said quietly, and turned his head so she couldn't see the anxious look on his face.

"Out to Opal's? I'd love to go if it wouldn't take more than an hour. I need to pick peaches later this afternoon."

"We'll not stay long. I thought it would be a good time for you and Opal to visit. She doesn't see many women her age."

"Thanks for the compliment." Henry Ann laughed dryly. "I'm at least five years older than Opal. Maybe more."

"She needs a friend, Henry Ann."

The sad look on Chris's face touched her heart. *You don't know it, Chris, but we both have troubles of the heart. Though yours aren't as hopeless as mine.*

"Of course, I'll go. But first I want to see Mr. Phillips, then go to the store. I won't be long." She smiled, and when she did, Chris thought his childhood friend was not only pretty, but terribly nice. "When we come into town together and then leave together, Mrs. Miller is sure to make something of it."

"Let her. I don't care if you don't."

"I'm willing to do my part to keep Mrs. Miller supplied with gossip to spread. Let me out at the corner, Chris. I'll see Mr. Phillips first."

"I'll park over by the store."

Mr. Phillips's law practice didn't take up much of his time. The only reason he had an office uptown was because he owned the property. The sandstone building was one of the oldest in town and had an iron stairway to the second story attached to the side. Two dirty glass windows with a door in between faced the street. On one of the windows was a chipped and faded sign in gold paint: O.B. PHILLIPS, ATTORNEY AT LAW.

Henry Ann opened the screened door and stood for a minute beneath the slow-whirling blades of the fan that extended down from the ceiling on a long pipe. Mr. Phillips sat in his swivel chair, his booted feet on his desk. His shaggy gray head was tilted to the side, his mouth beneath the bushy, drooping mustache hung open.

Henry Ann rapped on the door that was folded back to the wall. The old man came awake with a snort. His feet slid off the desk and hit the floor with a thump.

"Morning, Mr. Phillips. Sorry to wake you."

"That's all right, Henry Ann." He removed his glasses and pinched the bridge of his nose. "Just catchin' up on my sleep. Had to go over to the county seat last night. Sheriff Watson jailed one of my clients. Damned fool got in a fight and hit a deputy."

"I'll try not to take up much of your time."

"Sit. Sit, Henry Ann. What's on your mind?"

Henry Ann told him as briefly as possible about Isabel going to the Perrys and about her getting a lawyer.

"She can't get any part of the farm."

"How about the cattle, the crops, the household things?" Henry Ann's nose twitched when the old man held a match to a foul-smelling cigar and blew smoke across the desk. His appearance and his manner seemed unfit for a lawyer, but some folks swore by him. Henry Ann continued, "She'll say that they belonged to Daddy and that she is entitled to a third of them."

"Hummm—" He puffed for a minute. "Good thinking on your part."

"I didn't think of it. A man working for us did."

"Good thinking," he said again, swinging his chair around to spit in the spittoon behind him. "Who's her lawyer?"

"She didn't say. She was with Pete Perry."

"Don't think it was Mendosa, or he'd be crowin' about it. They might have called on that shyster over at Ringling."

"Can she force me to sell everything and give her a third?"

"How about the boy?"

"He hasn't sided with her. He hasn't mentioned wanting anything. He knows, and so does Isabel, that my daddy wasn't theirs."

"No tellin' how many more of Dorene's kids will show up. She was loose as a goose," he said with a snort of disgust, and Henry Ann cringed. "What's important as far as the law is concerned is that Ed was married to her when the kids were born. Ed knew that."

"I've not heard of any more kids. What can I do?"

"Hummm—" He puffed on the cigar. The smoke made her nostrils sting. "I'll have to think on it. I told Ed he ought to make out a will, but he thought putting the farm in your name was enough. I did, too, at the time."

Henry Ann stood. "He had twelve dollars left in the bank after he paid Doctor Hendricks and for his burial."

"Harrumph! If I know old Arnston, he'll not turn it loose without a court order, so you might as well forget it. Rumor has it the bank'll be going bust soon anyway."

"I don't want to give up what Daddy and I worked for. I offered Isabel a home and a chance to go to school, but she turned it down and went to the Perrys. I don't feel that I should have to sell my cattle and livestock at today's prices so she can have a third."

"I'll think on it."

Henry Ann went to the door. "Don't think too long, Mr. Phillips. I may be hearing from her lawyer."

"Run on home, Henry Ann. Leave it to me."

As she crossed the street to the store, his words played over in her mind. *Leave it to me.* Bullfoot! She'd wanted him to tell her that Isabel had no claim, but he hadn't. Thank goodness for the money her daddy had put in the milk can. It was safely buried in the cellar. The Perrys would never get their hands on that.

The store was typical of many small-town stores, although it was stocked better than most with groceries, feed, and some dry goods. Mr. Anderson was a good businessman, and he had a heart. He traded with his customers when possible, carried on credit the ones he was sure would pay when they could, and kept his prices low.

Henry Ann came face-to-face with Karen when she stepped into the store.

"Well, hello. I didn't see your car. Did you walk in?"

"I rode in with Christopher Austin."

"Oh, my!" Karen's blue eyes danced. "His mama will dance a jig over that."

"I hope she won't find out about it. I need to get a few things, then I'll ride back with Christopher. Hello, Mr. Anderson," she said to the white-aproned man who came from behind the counter.

"Howdy, Miss Henry."

"I want three peppermint sticks, a tin of Copenhagen, and a box of allspice. We're putting up pickled peaches," she explained to Karen. "I've got to pick peaches when I get home."

"You dipping snuff now?" Karen asked with a grin.

"It's for Aunt Dozie and you know it, smarty."

"The peach ice cream we had Sunday was good." Karen waited while Mr. Anderson put the spice, the tin of snuff, and the candy in a small sack.

Henry Ann dug into her purse and placed a fifty-cent piece on the counter. She accepted the change, waved good-bye to the grocer, and followed Karen out of the store.

"I wasn't sure you knew what you were eating on Sunday," Henry Ann said with a teasing grin as they stood on the store porch. "You and Grant were so busy flirting with each other."

"Flirting?" Karen's mouth dropped, and her cheeks fired up.

"Yes, flirting. Be careful, Karen. He's admitted that he's a bum with roaming feet and has been for several years. He's a good worker and a good influence on Johnny. Other than that, we know nothing about him. We never know when we get up in the morning if he'll still be there."

"Well, for crying out loud! I was . . . was just having a . . .

good time. If you don't want me to come out anymore, I won't." Karen's lips trembled. She turned quickly and rushed to the end of the porch.

Henry Ann hurried after her and grabbed her arm. "I didn't mean that, and you know it. Grant is good-looking enough to turn any woman's head—"

"—But not yours?"

"No, not mine. He's got personality and is smart," Henry Ann continued. "But he could be a crook and running from the law—"

"—He is not! If you think that, why are you letting him stay there?"

"I didn't say that I thought that. I said he could be. I don't want you to fall in love with Grant and be hurt when he suddenly pulls foot and takes to the road again."

"Henry Ann Henry! Who said anything about falling in love with the man? My goodness! He's fun to be with. He's not stuffy and serious like most of the men around here. If you think our teasing each other is more than just having a good time, your brain's on vacation."

Karen, my dear, sweet friend. You're protesting too much. You're already in love with him or close to it!

"All right. Let's forget about it for now. Come out anytime, Karen. I couldn't bear it if I lost you for a friend."

"You'll not lose me, hon. We've had differences of opinion before, and our friendship survived." Karen put her arm around Henry Ann and hugged her. "Is the candy for little Jay?"

"He asked for a frog like the one I gave him. I'm going over to the Five and Dime and see if they have one."

"What happened to the one you gave him?"

"His mother put it in the stove."

"Ah . . . no! Poor little boy. I don't think they have one at the Five and Dime. The tables are almost bare. The store will be closing any time now."

"Really? I hate to see it go."

"Mr. Anderson has bought out some of their stock. Daddy and I are going to Ardmore tomorrow. Do you want me to look for a frog there?"

"Would you?" Henry Ann opened her purse. "I'll give you some money."

"Not now." Karen covered Henry Ann's hand. "I may not find one."

"If you do, I'll pay you."

"I'm hoping to go to the picture show. I'd have to sneak in and sneak out. Some of Daddy's *flock* think you'll go to hell if you go to picture shows. I don't want to cause him any trouble. Did you hear what happened at the air show?"

"About Tom and Mrs. Dolan?" Henry Ann raised her brows. "Oh, yes. Mrs. Miller and her sewing circle are making sure that everyone in town knows about it, and they're making it look like Tom is mean to his wife."

"You got it right. I don't know why we need a weekly newspaper. That old busybody is making out that Mr. Dolan is a black-hearted, jealous Irishman who wants to keep his pretty wife all to himself."

"Is that what she's saying?"

"That, and more. She says he has an eye for other women."

"That's untrue and unfair!" Now it was time for Henry Ann's cheeks to flame.

"Mrs. Miller doesn't care if it's fair or not as long as she has center stage at the sewing circle."

"That woman is a gossip of the worst kind! I've got to go, Karen. Chris is waiting. Come out when you can."

"Daddy and I would like some peaches to eat and for a pie or two, if you have some to spare. I don't want too many, or I might have to can them."

"You're lazy and . . . the church ladies have spoiled you."

"Only the widows have spoiled me. They butter me up so I'll put in a good word for them with Daddy. If they want to make jelly and can beans for us, I'm all for it."

"Karen, you're the limit." Henry Ann squeezed her friend's arm and headed for Chris's car parked beside the curb.

"Yoo . . . hoo, Henry Ann."

Henry Ann turned to see Mrs. Miller, her sunbonnet tied snugly under her double chin, coming toward her on the other side of the street. She pretended not to have heard the woman calling her and quickly got into the car and glanced at Chris.

"Let's go. She's heading this way," Henry Ann urged.

The motor sprang to life and moved swiftly away from the curb. Henry Ann didn't breathe easily until they were a block away.

"Whee . . ." She puffed her cheeks and blew. "That was close."

"She got an eyeful. It'll be all over town that we were together."

"That isn't all bad, Chris. If they think we're a couple, they'll not connect you with Opal until you're ready."

"I don't know when that'll be. If I had a job that would pay enough for me to support Opal and Rosemary, I'd be ready right this minute." Chris swung around the block and turned the car into the Phillips 66 station just as a car was pulling out. "I'm 'bout out of gas. This won't take long."

A short thin man in a pair of greasy overalls stood looking after the touring car. He held several bills in his hand. He screwed his battered felt hat down on his head and came toward the car. He had a huge smile on his sun-baked wrinkled face and a chin dusty with three days' beard.

"Golly-bum, Chris. You just missed seeing Frank Hamer."

"Who's Frank Hamer?" Chris asked as he got out of the car.

"Don't ya read the newspaper? Frank Hamer's the famous Texas Ranger. He's a Federal man now. Gol . . . ly! I never thought I'd see Frank Hamer here in Red Rock."

"Give me five gallons, Vern."

"Frank Hamer come right in here and bought gas. He said, 'Fill'er up, friend.' He said that." Vern unscrewed the cap and stuck the nozzle in the gas tank. "Yessiree—I never thought I'd see Frank Hamer. Recognized him right off. Then I asked him, just bold as ya please. 'Ain't ya Frank Hamer?' I said. 'Was the last time I saw myself in a lookin' glass,' he said."

"Careful, Vern. I just want five gallon."

"Wonder what they're gonna do out at Dolan's." Vern cut off the flow of gas and replaced the cap on the gas tank. "Ya reckon he's run afoul a the law? Heard he beat the tar outta his wife at the air show, but Frank Hamer's got more to do than hunt up a wife beater."

"Tom Dolan does not beat his wife regardless of what you've heard." Henry Ann got out of the car and glared at Vern over the top of it.

"Just sayin' what I heard, Miss Henry."

"You heard the lies of a malicious gossiper."

"I was just—"

"He . . . does . . . not . . . beat . . . his . . . wife!" Henry Ann spaced the words to give them more emphasis.

"Ya got no call to get mad. I was just—"

"I know. You were just repeating the gossip that you heard, not stopping to think if it was true or not."

" 'Twas the man with Frank Hamer that wanted to know where to find Tom Dolan. Ain't ever'day a man like Frank Hamer comes to Red Rock."

"You've got a right to be excited, Vern. What did the man have to say about Dolan?" Chris asked, aware that Henry Ann wanted to know, but would not ask.

"Nothin'. Just how to get to Dolan's place."

"You told them?"

"Sure. Why not?"

"No reason."

"Reckon Dolan's tied in with the bootleggers? The bank at Duncan was robbed the other night—" He left his words hanging.

"Not a chance, Vern. I see him in the fields every day." Chris spoke matter-of-factly. "If he was getting easy money from bootleg whiskey or from a bank robbery, he'd not be breaking his back day in and day out in a cotton patch."

"Yeah . . . still, ya know, Frank Hamer ain't got time to chase petty crooks. He's got bigger fish to fry."

"He'll not fry them at the Dolan farm," Henry Ann said testily, got into the car, and slammed the door.

"What's eatin' her?" Vern asked. "I ain't never seen Miss Henry riled."

"She hates gossip—"

"—And people who spread it!" Henry Ann scooted across the seat and leaned out the window on the driver's side to add. "You're jabbering about something you heard from the town gossip. Shame on you, Mr. Neal."

Chris got into the car. "See you, Vern."

"Yeah. Thanks, Chris. 'Bye, Miss Henry."

Henry Ann looked straight ahead and didn't answer.

"You gave old Vern an earful, H.A. He's harmless."

"Harmless? I don't call repeating untrue things and ruining a man's reputation . . . harmless."

"Maybe I should've said dumb."

"He's ignorant and stupid just like most of the people in Red Rock."

"Gosh, Henry Ann, you sound like a sore-backed heifer with a mouthful of larkspur."

"I get tired of narrow-minded people and . . . Red Rock is full of them."

"These are hard times. If anything brings out the meanness in people, it's hard times."

Retreating into their thoughts, they didn't speak again until almost fifteen minutes later. Chris had turned down a road which was not much more than a lane and came to a halt in front of a small unpainted frame house.

"It's pretty back in here, isn't it?" Chris said, as he parked the car beside a dented old washtub filled to overflowing with colorful moss rose.

The house, not more than two rooms, sat off the ground on blocks. A narrow porch stretched across the front of it. On a clothesline in the back of the house, squares of white cloth fluttered in the gentle breeze. A thin girl wearing a faded gingham dress belted at the waist came out of the house and stood waiting on the edge of the porch. She had dark red hair and was carrying a small child on her hip.

"Get out, Henry Ann. Opal's shy as a doe, and she's scared." Chris had eyes only for the girl and the child.

"Because of me?"

"She's not sure if you'll be friendly." He went quickly to the porch. "Hello, honey. How's my girl?" He spoke first to Opal and then to the child. He bent and kissed the girl square on the mouth. She tried to back away, her eyes on Henry Ann, but Chris held her firmly to his side with his arm about her waist. "You know Henry Ann, honey."

"Hello, Opal. I've not seen you for a long time."

"I remember."

"This is Rosemary," Chris said proudly, the little girl's hand wrapped tight around his finger.

"My, how pretty she is." Henry Ann reached out and touched the dark red curls that hugged the child's neck. The little girl cowered away from her and hid her face against her mother's shoulder.

"Come here to me, little pretty." Chris reached for the toddler, who went to him willingly and rested her head on his shoulder. "Soon you'll be too big for your mama to carry." The child stuck her thumb in her mouth and turned large brown eyes on Henry Ann.

"Won't you . . . sit down?" Opal asked hesitantly, indicating the straight-backed chair with the rush-covered seat.

"For a few minutes." Henry Ann's mind searched for a way to put the girl at ease. "Chris gave me a ride to town—"

"I asked Henry Ann to come with me, honey. She knows about us."

"I . . . I—" Opal's eyes seemed to have a hard time leaving Chris. Finally, she turned to Henry Ann. "Can I get you a drink of water?"

"No, thank you. I'm fine. How old is Rosemary?"

"A year."

"She's a beautiful child. Would it be all right if I gave her a candy stick?"

"You don't have to do that . . . ma'am."

"Call me Henry Ann, Opal. I hope we can be friends."

"Oh, yes, ma'am."

Henry Ann went to the car and got a stick of candy from her grocery bag. When she returned to the porch, Opal sat in one of the chairs with Rosemary on her lap. Chris passed her on his way to the car and gave her a grateful smile.

Rosemary hid her face against her mother when Henry Ann tried to give her the candy.

"She's bashful," Opal explained. "She don't see many folks."

"She can have it for later." Henry Ann pressed the stick into Opal's hand and sat back down.

Chris was going around to the back of the house with a package under his arm. Opal's gaze followed him.

"Chris and I went to school together." When Henry Ann spoke, Opal's eyes went quickly to her and then away. "We've been friends for a long time and have . . . confided in each other. I know he loves you and wants to marry you."

"Folks'd look down on him." Tears shimmered in Opal's eyes. "I can't let him—"

"He doesn't care what folks think. It's you he cares for. You're a lucky girl. Chris is one of the finest men I know."

"I know it. He's too good for a girl like me." Opal's shoulders suddenly squared, and she tilted her head to give

Henry Ann a defiant stare. "I ain't ashamed of Rosemary. It ain't her fault . . . what happened."

"It isn't yours either, Opal," Henry Ann said gently.

"Folks think I'm . . . loose."

"Chris doesn't think so, and that's all that matters."

"I couldn't help . . . what was done to me. But I got Rosemary out of it and . . . I'm not sorry."

"God wanted to make up for what you had to endure."

"I never thought a that—"

Chris returned and stood at the end of the porch.

"I'm glad I got to see you again, Opal." Henry Ann rose and stepped off the porch. "Chris, I'll make ice cream next Sunday afternoon. Why don't you come and bring Opal and Rosemary?"

"Oh, no, ma'am. I couldn't."

"You'd like Johnny, my brother, and Karen Wesson, my friend, would come out. Aunt Dozie would spoil Rosemary. Do come, Opal."

Henry Ann went to the car to give Chris and Opal a minute or two alone. The car seat was hot against her legs. As she waited for Chris, she thought about how lonely it must be for a young girl to live out here with just her grandpa. And how unfair it was that Chris had to sneak around to see the girl he loved.

Chris was quiet on the way back. When he spoke it was with passion.

"If I knew who raped Opal, I'd kill him."

"That wouldn't solve anything. You'd spend the rest of your life in the pen, if they didn't hang you, and Opal would be alone."

"I wish I could take her and Rosemary and go to California."

"Why can't you?"

"Because someday the farm will be mine," he said with his face set in grim lines. "Since I was old enough to walk behind a plow, I've worked my butt off on that farm. Daddy knows that, but Mama—"

"Would your daddy stand with you against your mother?"

"I don't know. She rules the roost."

"Then fight for your right to marry Opal. Start by bringing her to my house on Sunday."

"I don't know. It would cause a hell of a squabble at home. I might even have to leave."

"I don't think it would come to that, Chris. You're needed there. Your daddy couldn't handle that big herd of cattle by himself. Has it ever occurred to you that your mother might back down if you and Mr. Austin stuck together?"

"I can't imagine Daddy bucking her."

"Talk to him. Tell him that you love Opal and ask him to go with you to visit her and her grandpa. He's a good man. You're his only son. He won't want to lose you."

"I'll think about it. You're a good friend, Henry Ann. I wish that I'd fallen in love with you."

"I don't know why your mother is so set on me."

"You're nice and pretty and have land that could be added to ours. She also thinks that in time she could manage you like she does me and Daddy."

"She must think that I'm pretty weak to knuckle under and let her boss me around. That doesn't say much for me."

"That's just what she'd do to Opal, and Opal would be too scared to stand up to her."

"Then it would be up to you to show some backbone and see to it that your mother didn't boss her. Folks will lose respect for you, Chris, if you continue to follow in your daddy's footsteps and let her dominate you."

Chris was silent during the ride to the Henry farm. Henry Ann did not care if he was offended by what she had said. It was time for him to take control of his life.

Chapter Thirteen

When the hot Oklahoma sun was directly overhead, Johnny stopped the team at the end of Dolan's field. Tom dropped his hoe and hurried to help unhitch them. He led the team to the creek to drink. Grant and Johnny followed to splash water on their sweaty faces. They sank down in the shade with the bucket of lunch prepared by Aunt Dozie between them.

"Come eat, Tom," Johnny called, after Tom had allowed the team to drink, then staked them out to eat the grass growing along the creek bank. "Aunt Dozie packed plenty."

"Thanks, but I'd better go up to the house and see about a few things."

Johnny and Grant watched Tom as he cut across the field and disappeared among the trees that grew along the edge of it.

"His wife is loony," Johnny said, after taking a long gulp of buttermilk from the fruit jar.

Grant nodded in agreement. "That man's got a bear riding on his back. He hasn't time to eat. He has to go see what she's up to."

"I've seen her a time or two in the woods. One time she saw me and waved for me to come to her, but I acted like I hadn't seen her and rode on."

"A woman who acts like she does is mentally disturbed."

"There's got to be something wrong or she wouldn't've tied a string about little Jay's pecker to keep him from wetting."

"I think that there's more here than meets the eye. Dolan's no fool. He must know that he can put her in an institution."

"He don't appear to have that kind of money." Johnny bit into a biscuit filled with butter and jam.

"Her folks are the Conroys down in Texas. They're loaded."

"How do you know that?"

"You'd be surprised, Johnny-boy, what you can learn by keeping your eyes and ears open and your mouth shut."

Tom never knew what he would find after being away from the house for a few hours. After the time he found the lamp turned over and kerosene spilled on the floor, he had hidden it in the barn. He feared that she would burn down the house with her in it or set herself on fire. He thanked God every day that he didn't have to worry about Jay's safety.

Emmajean's moods had become darker. She seldom talked to him in a normal tone of voice. She yelled, screeched, or hissed. He was in a quandary about what to do about her. He doubted that her folks would stand for his putting her in an asylum; and even if they did, they would try to take Jay away from him.

The house was quiet when he reached it. He entered the kitchen to find it exactly as he had left it The dishes were still in the dishpan where he had put them to soak. He had not expected them to be washed. Tom opened a can of pork and beans, went out to sit on the back step and eat out of the can.

He heard the door to her room open and knew that she had come into the kitchen. Then the screen door opened behind him. He turned to look at her. She was in her night-dress, her gaunt face streaked with eyelash blackener, and she had painted her lips bright red.

"Where's the lamp? I want to curl my hair."

"We're out of lamp oil."

"You're lying. You don't want me to curl my hair and be pretty."

"Your hair would be pretty if you just combed it."

"Men came here this morning, but you got them away before they could see me."

"They came to help me in the field. Have you eaten anything today?"

"I'm going to town to eat. Daddy's coming to get me."

Tom had no answer to that. She flounced back in the house, and Tom finished the beans and went to the well for a drink of water. Just as he was raising the dipper to his mouth, a black sedan pulled into the yard. He squinted his eyes to see who it was, and recognition brought a happy smile to his lips. He hung the dipper on the nail and hurried to the car as one of the men got out. He was tall but not as heavily built as Tom. He had the same inky black shaggy hair.

"Hod! My God! Is that you?"

"It sure as hell is. How'er you, Tom?"

The two men shook hands then pounded each other on the shoulders.

"You're looking great, Hod. Hell, you're looking more and more like our big brother."

"Better not tell Mike that." Hod turned to the other man who had gotten out of the car and stood smiling while the two brothers met. "Frank, this is my brother, Tom. Tom, shake hands with Frank Hamer."

"Howdy, Mr. Hamer." Tom shook his hand. "You've got to be a patient man to put up with Hod Dolan. He was the orneriest little critter you ever did see when we were growing up. Ma was sure he'd be the death of her."

"We," Hod corrected. "You were just a year older than me. You did your part to make her life miserable."

"Come on over, and I'll draw up a bucket of fresh water. This is the best water in the county."

Hod looked around while Tom lowered the bucket into the well.

"I never suspected you'd turn out to be a farmer. I thought you'd be designing engines for race cars."

"Sometimes life takes an unexpected turn. I'm still interested in engines, but I don't dislike farm work. I sold a couple of cars and paid for this place. It's not much now, but it could be. What are you doing in this part of the country?"

"Heading up north to do a little investigating. Frank was willing to go a little out of the way so I could see you. How long's it been? Five years?"

"Near that, I reckon. How did you find me?"

"I hear from Sis. She told me you were married, lived here near Red Rock, and that you had a son."

"Yeah, well, that's right. How about you?"

"I stay in one place only long enough to get my washing done."

Tom turned to look at the man who was a legend in Texas, a former Ranger who was relentless in hunting down outlaws. He looked to be in his late forties, had thick iron gray hair and deep lines around his eyes and mouth. Tom was embarrassed that he couldn't invite his brother and Hamer in for a meal.

"How old is your boy, Tom?"

"He's three. He's staying with a neighbor ... ah ... my wife has been sick."

"Sorry to hear it."

Hod was looking past Tom. Tom turned and almost groaned aloud. Emmajean had come out of the house and was walking toward them. She had hurriedly changed into the dress she had worn to the air show. Her cheeks were two red splotches, her mouth shaped into a cupid's bow with bright red lipstick, her hair was a mass of tangles. She had stuck a silk flower from one of her hats behind her ear. She stumbled toward them in high-heeled shoes.

Tom didn't look at his brother or Mr. Hamer. He didn't want to see the expressions on their faces. As Tom approached her, he could see that she didn't have a stitch of clothing on under the thin dress. Her nipples and dark pubic hair were clearly visible. When he reached her, he took her arm and spoke calmly.

"Go back in the house, Emmajean. Your lipstick is

smeared and you forgot to put your underwear on under your dress."

"I don't care." She jerked her arm from his grasp, lurched toward Hod, and grabbed his arm. "I'm Emmajean. Who're you?"

"I'm Hod Dolan."

"Are you going to town? Can I go with you?"

Hod glanced at Tom and saw the misery in his brother's eyes before he answered.

"I'm not going to town, Emmajean."

"Where are you going?"

"I'm not sure yet."

"When will you know?"

Hod ignored the question. "That's a pretty flower you have in your hair."

"I put it there for you." Emmajean beamed. "I don't like him." She stuck her tongue out at Tom. "He's mean and ugly and . . . I hate him."

"Let's walk up to the porch and talk about it." Hod spoke as if he were talking to a child.

"All right." She clung to his arm. "I like you. You're cute."

"Thank you. I like you, too."

"You do? Will you let me go with you?"

Hod walked Emmajean to the porch and very courteously assisted her into a chair before he sat down.

"She isn't drunk, is she?" Hamer asked.

"No. I wish to God that was all that was wrong with her."

"Hod's good in a situation like this. Once I saw him calm down a crazy who had killed two people. I was sure we'd have to kill him to get his gun."

"He caught on right away that . . . she wasn't right."

"He senses things. That's why he's so good at his job."

"She's getting worse. I had to leave my son with a neighbor. She hurt him. I was afraid that she might kill him."

"Has she tried to harm you, or herself?"

"Not yet. She roams in the woods. So far she's come home." Tom's eyes were on his brother.

Lord, but it was good to see Hod.

Hod got out of his chair and reached for Emmajean's hand. She stood, but he gently pressed her back down in the chair. He squatted before her and spoke to her for a while, then left the porch and came to where Tom and Frank stood beside the well. Emmajean waved to him and he waved back.

"We're going to have to go, Tom."

"I'd just as soon you didn't let the folks back home know about . . . her."

"I'll keep it to myself. How long has she been like this?"

"She was strange from the start and she's getting worse, much worse, and fast. I suppose you wonder why I married her. Rotgut whiskey and a powerful urge to get my ashes hauled. She was pretty and willing, and I was too drunk to realize that she was . . . like she is. It was a shotgun wedding, pure and simple. Her folks are well off. You might know of them, the Conroys of Conroy, Texas."

"Martin Conroy," Frank said, and it wasn't a question.

"You know him."

"Tried to be a big-time politician but couldn't cut the mustard. He's got more pride than brains."

"Fits him to a tee. Emmajean was an embarrassment to

them. They thought that I'd take her back to Nebraska, and they'd be rid of her."

"Too bad. I'm sorry, Tom. I told her that I'd be back. Will she remember?"

"I'm not sure. I'd like for you to see my boy, Hod. He's a pistol." Tom's pride in his son wiped the worry from his face. "If you have time, stop at the next farm on your way back to town. He's there with Miss Henry and a colored woman named Dozie Jones. They're fine folk. They'll make you welcome."

Hod and Tom shook hands and Tom got into the car. Hamer got behind the wheel.

"Good luck, brother. If you ever need me, send me a wire in care of Federal Law Enforcement Headquarters in Kansas City, Missouri. I work out of that office. They'll know where to find me. Keep your eye on that woman. I've heard of people like her dropping off the deep edge in the middle of the night and killing someone."

"I'm glad you stopped by, Hod. It was a pleasure to meet you, Mr. Hamer."

"Same here. Good luck to you." Hamer started the car.

"We'll stop and see your boy, Tom. Take care."

"You, too, Hod."

Tom had a sick feeling in the pit of his stomach as he turned back toward the house. Seeing Hod brought back the memories of home and family, of boyhood dreams. Hod had always wanted to be a policeman. He had fulfilled his dream. Tom, however, had been certain that he would build motors, race cars, and be another Barney Oldfield, his childhood hero. But who could hope to fulfill his dreams when his life had become a nightmare?

*   *   *

It was noon when Chris let Henry Ann out of the car in front of her house.

"Come in and eat, Chris."

"Thanks, but I'll get on home."

"You'll come over Sunday?"

"I'm not sure."

"Well, thanks for the ride."

As Henry Ann approached the house, Jay threw wide the screen door and came out onto the porch.

"Hen-Ann!" he shouted.

"Hi, punkin, come give me a lovin'." She held her arms wide and he ran to her. She picked him up and gave him a kiss before setting him on his feet. "I didn't find a frog, but I brought you a candy. You can't eat it until after dinner." Holding his hand, she led him into the house, where the aroma of freshly baked bread filled the air.

"Bread smells good, Aunt Dozie," she called from her room, where she had slipped off her shoes and stockings.

She was in the middle of taking off her dress and putting on an everyday one when Jay called that someone was coming. Henry Ann let the dress settle back down over her hips and went barefoot to the door. A black car had stopped in the yard and a man was coming to the house. As Henry Ann stepped out onto the porch, she recognized the black touring car as the one they had seen at the gas station in town.

What were they doing here? Had they found Tom? Please, God, don't let more trouble pile on him.

The man stopped several yards back from the porch and removed his hat. He was wearing dark trousers, a white shirt, and a tie. His sleeves were rolled to his elbows and his shirt had wet circles under his arms. His resemblance to Tom Dolan sent shock waves through Henry Ann.

"Miss Henry?"

"Yes."

"My name is Hod Dolan. I'm a brother to Tom—"

"Yes, I can see that." Her shoulders relaxed with relief.

"He told me that his little boy was here and that you'd not mind if I stopped by to see him."

"Of course I don't mind. Come in. Ask your friend to come in. I know that it's hot in that car. I just came from town myself."

"I sees clear as day dat dis is family of Mister Tom." Aunt Dozie's large frame blocked the doorway. "We got us company for dinner, honey. I's just putting de eats on de table and'll put out more dishes."

"Thank you, but we wouldn't want to put you out—"

"Ain't no put out to it, boy. We gots plenty. Can't yo smell that fresh light bread? Jist get yoreself on in here."

Henry Ann laughed. "We've all learned around here not to argue with Aunt Dozie. You may as well give up and come in."

Hod waved to Frank Hamer, and he came to the house. "We've been invited to dinner, Frank. Ma'am, this is Frank Hamer."

"How do you do." Henry Ann extended her hand. "Please excuse my bare feet. I just came from town, and it felt mighty good to get out of my shoes and stockings."

This is the man Vern was raving about. He looks like an ordinary man to me.

"Think nothing of it. I'm tempted to do the same."

"Sit here on the porch while Aunt Dozie sets the table. Would you like a cool drink?"

"Thank you, but we had one at Tom's."

"Is that fresh bread I smell?" Frank asked.

"Right out of the oven."

"I've not smelled bread like that since I was home on the farm in Nebraska." Hod sat down in one of the homemade, straight-backed chairs that had been at the farm since Ed Henry was a little boy.

"There'll be plenty of it. I'll get Jay. He may be hiding. He's shy of strangers."

Henry Ann went into the house and returned a minute or two later with Jay's hand clasped in hers. She had taken time to brush his hair and see to it that his face and hands were clean.

"Jay, this is your uncle." Henry Ann stopped in front of Hod Dolan and bent down to speak to Jay. "Remember when I told you that Johnny was my brother? This man is your daddy's brother."

"Hello, Jay." Hod held out his hand, but Jay lowered his chin to his chest and moved closer to Henry Ann.

"Your daddy would shake hands," Henry Ann whispered in the boy's ear.

Shyly, Jay put his hand in Hod's.

"You look a lot like your daddy did when he was a boy."

Jay looked up. "I love my daddy."

"I'm glad to hear that. I like him a lot, too. One time when we were about your age, I fell in the horse tank. Your daddy grabbed the back of my overalls and kept my head above the water. He yelled for help and our big brother, Mike, came and pulled me out."

"I Daddy's big boy."

"You sure are."

Jay had edged closer until he was leaning against Hod's

knees. Henry Ann backed away, smiled at Mr. Hamer, and went into the house.

When called to dinner, the two men seemed to be right at home sitting at the table with Aunt Dozie, although Henry Ann suspected it was a novel experience for them. Henry Ann had warned Dozie that if she didn't sit at the table, she wouldn't sit there either.

Jay appeared to be enamored of his uncle. Every time he spoke, the child's eyes fastened on his face. Hod's resemblance to Tom was uncanny, even to the tone of his voice.

As soon as Hod and Frank Hamer entered the kitchen, they had noticed that it was spotlessly clean and devoid of pesky houseflies. The table was covered with clean white oilcloth and loaves of fresh bread were cooling on the counter. They ate the strips of fried bacon, gravy, new potatoes, and peas. The thick slabs of fresh bread they covered with butter brought up from the cellar. When the meal was over they accepted second cups of coffee.

"It's been a while since I put my feet under a kitchen table and ate such a fine meal."

"I'm glad you enjoyed it, Mr. Hamer."

"The government gives us an allowance for meals. We'll pay—"

"—You'll do nothing of the kind. Mr. Dolan is our neighbor and . . . friend. My brother and our hired man are over there today. We're helping him with his field work, and he's going to fix our car."

"It's a relief to know that my brother has good friends close by, ma'am. He needs them." Hod Dolan's dark eyes caught and held Henry Ann's.

"Hen Ann gave me a frog." Jay's childish voice broke the silence that followed Hod's words.

"A frog? What'a ya know about that. Your daddy and I used to catch frogs."

"Mama burned it in the stove."

Hod tried to think of an answer to that. His dark eyes flicked again to Henry Ann. She plucked a sack from on top of the sewing machine behind her and pulled out a candy stick.

"Now's a good time for you to have this."

"Dat youngun goin' be one sticky mess." Aunt Dozie adjusted the cloth she had tied around Jay's neck when she sat him in the high chair.

Henry Ann laughed at the expression of delight on the child's face.

"He'll wash up, Aunt Dozie."

The men got to their feet. "Thank you for the meal, ladies," Hod said. "I don't know when I've had a better one."

"You're welcome."

"Yo 'bout as good a eater as Mistah Tom. Dat man pack away grub like he gonna get hanged. He come here, and Lordy, I do think his legs is holler."

"All of us Dolans are big eaters." Hod grinned, as if remembering. "Good-bye, Jay. I'll be back to see you one of these days."

" 'Bye." The child took the candy out of his mouth long enough to speak.

Henry Ann walked with the men to the porch.

"I'd like to ask you"—she hesitated—"if in your work you've run across the name Grant Gifford. My hired man came off the road. I know that I took a chance hiring a man that I knew nothing about and just wondered—"

Hod looked at Frank Hamer and waited for him to speak.

"Can you describe him?"

"He's around thirty, thin, this much taller than I am"—she held her hands about six inches apart—"blond hair, very well educated. He plays the guitar and sings. He knows a lot about a lot of things. He said that he learned them while bumming around for the past two years. I don't know whether to believe him or not. He's terribly nice and a good worker, but I worry about having him here when I know nothing of his background."

I worry because my friend Karen is falling in love with him.

"I've not heard of a man by that name wanted by the law. But I'll make some inquiries, and if anything turns up, I'll let you know."

"I'd appreciate that. Grant's been a big help to us, and my brother likes him a lot. He's thinking of settling down around here."

"It's a good idea to find out about a man's past before you get romantically involved with him."

"Oh, that isn't it at all. I'm not in the least interested in him . . . that way, nor is he interested in me. I guess I'm overcautious."

"It pays to be cautious nowadays."

"Well, thanks for the advice."

"I appreciate the help you're giving Tom," Hod said. "If I wasn't tied up right now, I would stay on. Things will have to change over there . . . and soon."

"Yes, I know what you mean. Good-bye, Mr. Dolan, and good-bye to you, Mr. Hamer. Good luck with your . . . ah . . . catching outlaws."

The car pulled away from the farm with its neat shady yard, hollyhocks growing along the fence and around the mailbox, and beds of flowering petunias.

"That's one nice place," Frank said.

"And one nice woman," Hod added.

"Strange how things happen. I'd almost forgotten about Grant Gifford. Who'd have thought he'd turn up working in a cotton patch?"

"It may not be the Gifford we know about. There must be more than one Grant Gifford."

"Hardly one that fits that description and was raised in this part of the country."

"It's been several years. Reckon he's been wandering around all this time?"

"He took what happened pretty hard."

"Yeah. But he was damn good. He did his damnedest, and he was convinced he was right." Hod took off his hat and placed it on the seat between them.

"Sometimes being right isn't enough."

"Too bad to lose a man like him. Too bad, too, that Tom couldn't have married a woman like Miss Henry."

"Sometimes a pretty woman causes a man to think with his pecker instead of his brain."

"What do you know about Martin Conroy? I've never heard of him."

"Not many folks outside of Texas have. He's one of those dudes who thinks they're better'n everybody else 'cause they've got money."

"Rich, rich, or kinda rich?"

"He's not a Rockefeller or an Astor, but he has money. He tried to run for governor while I was a Ranger. He's one of these fellers who thought he'd go right to the top ridin' on his granddaddy's coattails. He went over to Mineral Wells thinking he'd get the backing of the boys who own the Crazy Crystal Hotel. They laughed at him. I heard that they told him they'd rather back a horned toad. He got smart and made threats. It was the wrong thing to do. Out on a dark street a night or two later he met up with a couple of birds and came away looking like he'd tangled with a freight train. His campaign never got off the ground."

"Money talks though."

"I think old Granddaddy Conroy knew what his son and grandson were like. I heard that he put everything in a trust, and Martin gets only so much a year. Yet, it must be quite a hunk."

"Goddamn! I hate to leave Tom in this mess. He sure doesn't deserve a lifetime of hell with that woman."

"Sometimes fate kicks a man in the teeth, and there's not a damn thing he can do about it but get new teeth and ride out the storm." Frank pressed his foot down on the gas pedal and the big car picked up speed. "Look at the map, Hod, and see how far it is up to Lawton."

Chapter Fourteen

CONROY, TEXAS

Marty Conroy stopped his car in front of the Victorian-style house that had been his home all his life. He slammed the door of the car when he left it and ran up the steps to the porch. His heart was beating like a hammer in his chest. Teeny, the colored housemaid, opened one of the twin beveled-glass doors and Marty entered the foyer.

"How is he?" Marty roughly slapped his hat into her hand.

"He upstairs."

"I didn't say *where*, dammit. I said *how*," he snapped.

Without waiting for the maid to answer, Marty hurried across the polished wood floor, his clicking bootheels echoing through the quiet house. He looked up as he reached the stairs to see his mother coming down.

"Do you have to be so noisy? You sound like a herd of cows."

"How is he?"

"Not good, I'm afraid."

"What happened? He was all right when I left here a couple of weeks ago."

"His heart is failing. He'll go anytime now."

"Why isn't he in the hospital?"

"Are you questioning my judgment?"

"You know I'm not, Mama."

"If you can't call me Mother, don't call me anything."

"I'm sorry. I'm upset. I wish you'd wired me sooner."

"I didn't know sooner. I didn't know until he keeled over night before last. The doctor said he'd told Martin a year ago that his heart was weak. He also said that he could either die here in the bed where his father and grandfather died or in the hospital. It would make not one whit of difference in how long he lived. When it was time to go, he'd go."

"Can I see him?"

"The nurse is with him now. When she comes out, you can go in." Alice Conroy, her head held high, her face calm and emotionless, moved on down the stairs. "Take off those boots. I've told you repeatedly not to wear them in the house." She went past her son and into the dining room. "I'm ready for my lunch now, Teeny."

Marty climbed to the top of the stairs, sat down, took off his boots, and waited for the nurse to come out of his father's room. In all his life, he'd never seen Alice Conroy's calm reserve shaken except when it concerned his sister, Emmajean. His mother had doted on her when she was a child, dressed her like a doll, showed her off. All that changed when Emmajean was about twelve years old and began to act rebellious and have temper fits.

At that time Alice Conroy's attitude toward her daughter completely changed. She cut off all emotional ties to her child. Her main concern, then, was to get her out of their lives and as far away as possible with the least possible fuss. Marty had heard arguments between his parents as they tried to find the best way to accomplish this without causing damage to the Conroys' standing in the community. They had thought the problem solved when Tom Dolan married Emmajean. He had not taken her back to Nebraska as the Conroys had expected, however, but had stayed in the area.

The nurse, in a starched white uniform, came out of his father's room, interrupting his thoughts. Marty got quickly to his feet to face her.

"How is he?"

"Who are you?"

"His son, dammit. How is he?"

"I was told to report only to Mrs. Conroy, but—he's awake."

Marty brushed past her. He stood in the doorway of a room he'd entered only a few times in his life. It had been off-limits to him and to Emmajean for as long as he could remember. He saw nothing of the heavy walnut furnishings, only the figure of the man lying in the snow-white bed with the carved headboard that reached almost to the ceiling.

"Daddy?"

Martin Conroy lifted a hand only inches from the bed and beckoned his son to him. Marty hurried to the bedside. His father was gasping for every breath. Marty dropped to his knees beside the bed.

"Why didn't you tell me you were sick?"

"You're . . . the last . . . Conroy. Name and trust fund . . . goes to you. I want you to take . . . care of Emmajean. It's

not her . . . fault . . . she's like she is. Try to get her—"
Martin paused to catch his breath before speaking again.

"Daddy! Isn't there something we can do?" Marty held
his father's hand.

"Nothing. For . . . one time . . . in your life . . . listen—"

"I will. What do you want me to do?"

"Try to get her . . . into a home . . . where they'll be . . .
kind to her. I was . . . working . . . on it." He stopped, and
minutes passed. Marty wasn't sure his father could speak
again. His mouth hung open.

"But Mama won't like it, Daddy—"

"She's . . . a . . . cold bitch—" he gasped. "I shouldn't
have let her . . . treat . . . Emmajean that . . . way." His
eyes closed, then opened quickly.

"Rest a minute, Daddy—"

"No time. A . . . place in Dallas. Asylum. No one . . .
would know. Keep shame from . . . Conroy name."

"I'll take care of things . . . don't worry—"

"Alice . . . won't—" The words came out on a breath
and were so weak that Marty wasn't sure what he said.

"What, Daddy?"

"Alice . . . won't—" The eyes remained on Marty's
face. The hand in Marty's seemed to spasm.

"Daddy! Daddy!"

A minute passed, then another. The only sound in the
room was the rasping as Martin Conroy struggled to
breathe. Marty was not sure how long he had knelt there
holding his father's hand when he became aware that the
sound had ceased. There was only deathly silence in the
room. His father's mouth sagged on one side, his eyes remained open and unblinking.

The battle for breath was over.

"Nurse!"

Marty ran from the room, down the stairs, and out onto the porch. In the few short hours since he'd received the telegram, his life had changed drastically. His daddy was gone.

He felt a stir of excitement. *He* was The Conroy.

At dusk Johnny and Grant returned from the Dolan farm. They had stayed late to finish cultivating the field and had come back through the pasture, stopping to enjoy a dip in one of the deep holes in the creek that was mostly dry.

"Dolan said to tell you that he'd try and get over tonight to see Jay," Johnny said as soon as he came in the door. "Guess what? Tom's brother and Frank Hamer, the famous Texas Ranger, were at Tom's today."

"They were here to see Jay and ate dinner with us. You can sure tell that Hod Dolan is Tom's brother."

"Oh, shoot! Grant, we missed eatin' with Frank Hamer."

"He eats like any other man," Henry Ann said with a laugh. "My goodness, you'd think he was President Hoover the way you carry on."

"That old Hoover won't be president much longer. Grant thinks Roosevelt will be elected. I wish I was old enough to vote."

"Don't wish your life away."

"I'll wash and go milk." Grant ladled water into the washpan.

"I thought you might be late, Grant. I went ahead and milked."

"I'd sure like to a seen Mr. Hamer," Johnny said later, while placing a slab of corn bread on his plate and spooning pinto beans cooked with tomatoes and hot peppers over it. It was his second helping.

"Land o' Goshen! What'a yo do with dat bucket a grub I fix for noonin'?"

"Ate it." Johnny grinned. There was real affection between him and Aunt Dozie. "This is better'n good, Aunt Dozie. I ain't marryin' till I find a woman who cooks as good as you."

"Den yo goin' be without one till yo're old and toothless and can't eat nothin' but mush! Hee, hee, hee! Yo wantin' me to make ya a sweet-tater pie, is what yo is wantin' wid all dat sweet talk."

"Well, now that you mention it, I reckon I've not had a sweet-tater pie in a month of Sundays."

Henry Ann watched Johnny's eyes flash as he teased Aunt Dozie. He had changed so much from the silent, sullen boy who had come here four years before. He was so different from Isabel. He seemed to be happy, and she had to credit some of it to Grant. Grant, on the other hand, appeared to be genuinely fond of her brother. She hoped that Frank Hamer and Hod Dolan didn't find out anything bad about Grant.

"Bet Tom's not eatin' corn bread and pinto beans," Johnny remarked.

"He be eatin' 'em when he get here, lessin' yo eat 'em up."

"That woman a his is—" Johnny glanced at Jay and let his words trail off.

Henry Ann noticed that Grant had been quiet during the meal and assumed that he was just tired from a hard day's work.

"I wish you and Johnny had been here to meet Hod and

Mr. Hamer. Vern Neal, at the gas station, said Mr. Hamer's picture is in the paper sometimes."

"Yes, it is. I've seen it there," he said. "Johnny and I think we'd better take a water wagon out to the steers. The creek will be stone-dry in a week if we don't get a rain."

"To the north the sky is dark with dust clouds."

"The ground is so hard now, if we get a gully washer, it'll wash out the plants before the water can soak in."

"Let's hope for a nice gentle rain." Henry Ann carried the dishes from the table to the counter.

"And as long as we're at it, let's hope the country can get turned around so that there's jobs for people."

"How can that possibly happen?" *It wasn't logical that that was what worried Grant.*

"If we elect Franklin Roosevelt. I think that he'd be good for the country."

Later, Jay went to the porch with Grant and Johnny, while Henry Ann and Aunt Dozie tidied the kitchen.

"I'd not had to make no corn bread if'n dem fellers hadn't a gone down so hard on dat light bread. Hee, hee, hee. Dey sure 'nuff did fill demselves up. I's puttin' what's left of dis corn bread in de warmin' oven. Mistah Tom might be hungry."

"I wonder if Tom's . . . if Mrs. Dolan cooks at all." Henry Ann couldn't bring herself to say *wife.*

"I ain't knowing dat, honey. A woman sittin' 'round, doin' nothin' ain't needin' to be eatin' much as a workin' man."

When Henry Ann went to the porch, she found Jay asleep in Johnny's lap. He carried him to bed. Henry Ann glanced at the clock ticking on her bureau after tucking Jay in. Nine o'clock. It had been dark for almost an hour. Tom would have been here by now if he was coming, she thought. Henry Ann leaned across the bed and kissed his son on the forehead, turned out the light, and went through the darkened house to stand at the back door.

Aunt Dozie was on the porch with Johnny and Grant and was no doubt waiting for her to join them. All her life she and her daddy had spent evenings on the porch when the weather permited. He had told her stories about the olden days: about the Alamo and when the large herds of cattle were driven up the Chisholm Trail, a few miles west of their farm, to the railroads in Kansas.

He told her about the oil boom at Healdton in 1913. Looking for his father, he had visited the tent city set up to house oil-field workers. It was called Rag Town and was a haven for bootleggers, gamblers, and prostitutes. By that time she had known what a prostitute was and was reasonably sure that her mother was one, although her father never even hinted that it was true.

Later Ed Henry had learned that his father had been killed when a wooden derrick collapsed. The only relative he had left was the uncle who left him the farm.

Henry Ann's thoughts were interrupted when she heard Aunt Dozie coming in from the porch to go to bed. She slipped out onto the back porch and stood with her arm around the porch post. It was a dark night. Only a few stars twinkled through the clouds that hovered with the promise of rain.

He was only a few feet away when his voice came out of the darkness.

"Henry Ann? It's me, Tom."

"Oh, goodness! You . . . scared me."

"I was afraid I might."

"It's awfully dark . . . tonight." Suddenly she was breathless and her stupid heart was thumping like a tom-tom. She could see his outline. He was hatless, his shirt a light color and open at the neck.

"When the clouds came up, I thought we might get rain. But they're thinning out now."

"Jay's asleep."

"I figured he would be. Can I just look at him? I've missed the little rascal."

"Sure, come on in. I'll turn on the light."

Henry Ann fumbled around until she found the lightbulb hanging in the middle of the kitchen. The sudden light blinded her for a few seconds, then she looked at Tom. He was clean-shaven, and his hair was wet. He was big, strong, yet standing there beside the kitchen door, holding her eyes with his, he appeared to be as uncertain as she. Henry Ann's stomach pitched, and panic that somehow he was able to read her thoughts rose up to nearly suffocate her.

She went through the parlor to the bedroom, aware that he was following close behind her. The room was faintly lit by the bulb in the kitchen.

"No need to turn on the light. I can see him," Tom whispered. He stood beside the bed and looked down at his son. Jay was sleeping on his side, his palm under his cheek. Tom bent down and stroked his hair.

Henry Ann quietly left the room. Her feet felt as if they were embedded in cement blocks. She tried to shake off her nervousness. Heavens! She'd was acting like a frustrated old maid! She waited in the kitchen until he came silently to the doorway.

"Have you had supper?" she blurted as soon as she saw

him. "Aunt Dozie put back some pintos and corn bread when Johnny said you might be coming over."

"Thanks, but I've eaten."

"Are you sure you don't want something more?" She lifted the lid on the pot of beans and the aroma of onions and peppers and tomatoes wafted up.

"Smells good, but I shouldn't be eating off you . . . too. Besides, I'd better be getting back." They stared at each other for a second of suspended time.

"If Aunt Dozie were still up"—she drew in a shallow breath—"she'd not take no for an answer."

He smiled at that. "She wouldn't, would she?"

"She'll be disappointed," she coaxed.

"I'd hate to disappoint Aunt Dozie." He grinned, and to her amazement, a dimple popped into his cheek. *She'd not noticed it before.* She gazed at it for the space of a dozen heartbeats before she was able to pick up her train of thought.

"If you don't want to take the time to eat here, you can take it with you."

"I'll take time. My stomach would never forgive me if I didn't."

She busied herself dishing up the food, then sat across from him while he ate.

"Your brother came by to see Jay."

"I'm glad he got to see him." Pride in his son lightened his expression. "Did he take to Hod?"

"Oh, yes. Hod told him about the two of you when you were kids. Jay finally opened up and talked to him. He told him that he was his daddy's big boy."

"He said that?" A pleased smile tilted Tom's lips.

"Hod looks a lot like you—"

"Hod has a way of making people trust him."

"No more than you do," she said with spirit, then wished it hadn't sounded as if she were defending him. "How long has it been since you've seen him?" she added quickly.

"Five years. I saw him just before I left Nebraska to come down here."

"You look a lot alike—but I said that, didn't I?" She laughed nervously.

"Folks in Nebraska used to say you could tell a Dolan from a mile away. We all looked like our pa—black Irish Catholics, dancing their way to hell, is how an old preacher put it."

"If that's true, maybe you should consider entering the marathon," she teased, suddenly feeling light and young and happy.

"Will you be my partner?"

"I've not danced . . . much. Daddy and I went to a few country square dances. The neighbors would get together and hold them under a brush arbor when a fiddler was available. They'd have watermelon feeds sometimes and dinner on the ground."

She spoke in a distinctive Texas/Oklahoma drawl. Tom wished that she would keep talking, but she suddenly became quiet, thinking she was rambling on about things he had little interest in.

He finished eating, stood, and stacked the bowl and eating utensils on his plate and placed them on the work counter.

"Thank you for the meal," he said, looking down at her. His eyes that fastened to her calm, beautiful face held the familiar hint of sadness.

"You're welcome."

"I'm beginning to feel like a beggar."

"I don't know why. Neighbors around here always help neighbors." Feeling her face began to heat, Henry Ann rushed into speech. "Grant and Johnny are on the porch if you have time to sit a while and visit."

"No, I'd better get on back." He went to the kitchen door.

Henry Ann reached up, switched off the light, and followed him to the porch. She didn't want him to leave . . . yet. She pushed open the screen door and stepped out of the kitchen, her eyes searching the darkness, and walked into him. The jolt of bumping into his hard body sent her rocking back on her heels. He grabbed at her arm to steady her.

"I'm sorry," she gasped. "It's dark out here."

Feeling the warm skin of her arm under his hand, and with the sweet, clean scent of her filling his senses, Tom realized that he was trapped as securely as a fly on a sticky strip. He had to have a few more minutes with her. Throwing any niggling misgivings, together with caution, to the wind, his fingers tightened caressingly on her arm.

"Walk with me to the oak tree." His whisper was urgent.

"Someone could be watching," she murmured breathlessly.

"Who?"

"Pete Perry, your . . . Mrs. Dolan."

"I made sure she was asleep before I left. I'll beat hell out of Perry if I catch him out here spying on you."

Henry Ann stepped off the porch. Tom's hand had somehow slid under her arm and was holding it close to his side. The soft, scented darkness closed around them. They reached the tree at the edge of the farm yard. Henry Ann moved without thinking from the time they left the porch until he turned her to face him. Her awareness sprang to life now as her eyes fastened on the buttons of his shirt.

Oh, my goodness! What am I doing? This is wrong. He has a wife. He's married, he's married, he's married—

"There's so much . . . I'd like to tell you—"

She lifted her face to look into the dark eyes.

"About Jay?"

He sighed deeply. "Jay is part of it."

"I've told you not to worry about him. I love having him here. He's a dear little boy."

"Sweet, sweet woman—" The words came on a breath and so softly she wasn't sure she'd heard them.

Without realizing that he'd made the decision to do so, Tom slowly, almost haltingly, lowered his mouth to hers. It was a gentle, sweet, and lingering kiss. Her lips were moist and slightly parted in surprise. At the first gentle touch of his lips, the ground beneath her feet fell away. With his hands on her elbows, he gently drew her to him and almost groaned when her soft breasts first touched his chest and when he felt the heat of her hands through his shirt, as they slid around his waist. Their lips clung.

A moment became eternity.

When they drew apart, he gasped as if he were drowning. It was an effort that brought no relief to his pounding heart. *She had not been outraged. She had not pulled away.* He buried his face in her neck, kissing it and rubbing his cheek against it. He nuzzled her earlobe, her cheek, felt her breath quicken. Their mouths found each other again. The heat of this kiss was intense.

Reality was swept away in a blinding flash. He became lost in her beauty, her strength, her goodness. They clung desperately to each other, their lips inseparable. His hands moved up and down her back, hungry to feel every inch of her, to mold her to him.

He should stop! But he wouldn't, couldn't!

Something was happening to Tom's restraint. But he didn't care. He could feel himself slipping away. He was becoming one with the woman pressed tightly to him, joining more than bodies; merging minds . . . souls. She felt so . . . goddamn good! Her hands stroking and caressing his sides and back were driving him to the sweetest sort of insanity. He drank from her mouth like a starving man.

Time passed unnoticed.

The madness had to end. Tom lifted his head. Her face was still tilted to his; her eyes were closed. Panic welled inside him, and he fought against it. *Would his foolish action cause him to lose her?*

"I . . . can't say that I'm sorry," he gasped. "I wanted it . . . so much."

Loving the feel of his lean, muscular body pressed to hers, she wrapped her arms even more tightly around him.

"It's all right." She stood in his embrace, her head bowed. Their hearts beat together in one rhythm, protesting any move to separate.

Her sweetness and her vulnerability made him feel guilty, unworthy.

"I didn't plan to do that. But God help me! I can think of nothing but you."

"It's . . . wrong—" The spoken words forced her to face reality, and she pushed away from him. His arms fell from around her, but his hands slid down her arms to capture hers and grasp them tightly.

"I would have come here tonight if I'd had to walk

through a valley of rattlesnakes. I kept telling myself it was to see Jay, but it was to see you."

"It's wrong," she said again more forcefully, as if to convince herself.

"I know. I know. Emmajean is helpless and sick with a kind of sickness that's hard to deal with. She hurt Jay, and at times she tries my patience to the limit, but she's to be pitied. I'm all she has. Her folks don't want her. They would be pleased never to see her again."

"You don't have to . . . explain."

"I do!" he said desperately. "I told you how I came to marry her. I never loved her, not for one minute, but I've got to stay with her, take care of her. I can't help it if . . . I have feelings for you. I tried to hide how I felt about you because I knew nothing could come of it. But now you know, and it's even worse. Henry Ann, look at me. Please." He tilted her chin with a gentle finger and gazed into her eyes. "I took a vow and I must honor it. I owe her. She gave me my son."

The face close to hers was the same face she had dreamed about . . . only dearer now. *Please say you love me.* The unspoken wish jarred her, then filled her with fear and dismay. This was a destructive path they were on. She loved him and wanted him to love her. What was she thinking of now? Folks would believe that very flaw they condemned in her mother had been passed on to her.

"Does this change things?" His breath fanned her wet lips.

"What things?"

"Will you still keep Jay? Will you let me come over?"

"Why . . . why, of course, I'll keep Jay and . . . I want you to come over."

Henry Ann was still stunned by the enormity of what had happened between them. She had come to terms with the fact that she was in love, deeply and forever, with Tom Dolan, a married man. She loved his wild manliness, his complexity, his dedication to his child. She even loved his loyalty to the vows he had taken.

That he could have feelings for *her* was almost unbelievable. Then, it occurred to her that perhaps his feelings were mere . . . gratitude. She noted that he'd said he had *feelings* for her, not that he loved her. She swallowed the lump that rose in her throat.

"I'd better go in."

"I . . . can't let you go until . . . this thing is understood between us."

"Don't worry about it."

"Don't worry about it?" he echoed and his hands gripped her shoulders, his face so close she could see the intensity there. "How can I not worry about it? You're everything in the world to me—you and Jay. I've never been in love before. Never."

"You mean . . . you mean that you—" She couldn't bring herself to ask. It was too important to her.

"I mean that I'm in love with you, you sweet, wonderful woman. I'm crazy in love with you and will be until the day I die!"

"You can't be!"

"I love you. I can't keep my eyes off you. I don't go around kissing women I merely like. Oh, sweetheart, I don't know why it happened, but I've known for days now that I'd gladly give up an arm and a leg to be free to have you by my side for just a little while." He couldn't see the tears, but he knew that she was crying.

"Don't cry, my love. I'd not have told you if I had thought it would upset you. Doesn't it make you a little happier to know, even if . . ."

"I am glad that you love me. I'm happy tonight, but tomorrow I'll realize how hopeless it is and think myself a fool for daring to dream about you."

"Then you care for me? Tell me. You'd not let me kiss you or hold you if you didn't."

He wrapped her in his arms and held her. Her face fit in the curve of his neck. He closed his eyes and breathed in the essence of her. This was woman as she was meant to be: warm, caring, giving, wonderful and sweet. He had never questioned God's wisdom before, but how could He have let them find each other and yet keep the barrier of Emmajean between them?

"I've wanted to kiss you almost from the first time we met. You were wearing that crazy hat and trying so hard to be patient with Isabel. Then the morning after your daddy died, when I was at the woodpile and saw you coming across the yard toward me, I felt that somehow we were connected, and that fate had brought us together."

"I never imagined that love could be so complicated, or that when I met the man I loved, he'd already be married." Her breath was warm and moist against the skin of his neck. "We can't do this again."

He groaned deep in his throat. "I can't promise it won't happen again, my love."

Feelings she couldn't express choked her, numbing her brain. In his arms she was mindlessly savoring his strength, loving the feeling of being close to his warm, hard body. She had never felt so protected, so cherished.

This is all I'll ever have, and it will be over all too soon. But I'll have something to remember.

Tom leaned back and brushed her forehead with a feathery kiss. His hand moved up her back and under her hair at the nape of her neck.

"Go back to the house, sweetheart. I'll watch until you're inside."

"When will you be back?"

"You want me to come back?"

"I do . . . and I don't. Oh, I do!"

"I can't stay away!"

Henry Ann was aware of the tremor in his arms and the intensity in his voice. Impetuously she pressed her lips to his cheek. His face turned and his mouth was suddenly there, tasting hers with a hunger they both shared. Breath left her. They were in a world alone. She clung to him with eagerness, their lips blending with an impatient urgency and rode on golden waves of pleasure as the kiss went on and on. As his mouth caressed hers and his tongue branded her with its fiery touch, she trembled with the fervor that built within her. He raised his head and she looked up into dark smoldering eyes.

"I want to think of you as my wife, my partner, my lover. Please let me—" There was a ragged edge to his pleading voice, a roughness to his breathing.

"It's hopeless! It can . . . never be—" she whispered.

"It can! In our hearts."

Henry Ann closed her eyes, reveling in the enchantment of being in the circle of his arms. Never had she felt this magic, this closeness to another human being. When she turned her face, his lips were there and she welcomed them, savored the sweet ecstasy that his mouth created with its warm exploration of hers and returned the pressure, the nibbling, giving as much as she was receiving.

"I didn't mean to kiss you like that." When he looked at her, he saw the glimmer of tears.

"I'm glad you . . . did."

He dipped his head again. The brush of his lips was gentle and familiar now. The kiss was quick and terribly sweet. His arms dropped from around her, but he held her hand tightly in his as she moved back, her eyes still on his face. He dropped her hand. She turned and almost ran to the house. On the porch she looked back, but the darkness was too dense for her to see him. Yet she knew that he stood there . . . yearning for her, as she yearned for him.

Chapter Fifteen

Martin Conroy's death made the front page of the Conroy paper but, much to the annoyance of Alice Conroy, received only a small notice in the paper in Wichita Falls. She was determined that the services to be held two days later would be a funeral to be remembered and made the decision not to notify Emmajean until after her father was buried.

"She'd make a scene," she said to her son. "She'd bring that disgusting child and that dirt clod of a man with her. I will not have this occasion ruined by her irresponsible behavior. Imagine the talk!"

Marty, still in shock and unable to grasp the power of his new position in the family, allowed his mother to make the decisions. The service was held in a church overflowing with mourners and gawkers who, with nothing better to do, came to hear the flowery eulogies and the voices of the singers brought in from Wichita Falls.

Alice Conroy, dressed elegantly in black, a thin veil

covering her wide-brimmed hat and flowing down over her head and shoulders, acted the role of the grande dame. Regal and unapproachable, she was a picture of quiet dignity. With a dry-eyed Martin Jr. by her side, she led the procession out of the church and to the cemetery, where her husband was laid to rest in the Conroy mausoleum alongside his father and grandfather.

After the burial, county and state dignitaries and a few close friends were invited back to the Conroy family home for a private dinner honoring the deceased. Marty stood by his mother's side, greeted the guests, and then stood beside the door to bid them good-bye when they left. He was glad to see the last of them.

The family lawyer was waiting in the study to read his father's will.

Shellenberger and Shellenberger, the oldest law firm in northwest Texas, had set up the Conroy family trust back in the 1860s. Great-grandfather Conroy had been a close friend of Stuart Shellenberger, the founder. Now, Stuart's great-grandson, Luther Shellenberger, was head of the firm.

Luther, a small man with sharp features, took a sheaf of papers from his briefcase and placed it on the desk. Feeling the importance of the moment, he glanced first at Marty, sitting in a straight-backed chair, then at Mrs. Conroy, standing beside the window. He rubbed his hands together nervously.

"I didn't see Miss Emmajean at the service. Is she ill?"

"Yes." Alice Conroy uttered the word sharply while keeping her back to the room.

"I'm sorry to hear that. Well . . . let's get on with it. You know about the trust, so I need only tell you about the part that concerns you. A few months ago Martin came to the office and made some changes in his will." He paused as Mrs. Conroy came quickly to the center of the room and frowned at him.

"He did what?" she asked in her most superior tone.

"He came to the office—"

"You said that. The trust is still solvent?"

"Of course, it is. The bulk of the yearly trust will go to Marty as the only male heir, with the stipulation that he take care of you for the rest of your life."

"I expected that. It's one of the conditions in the trust. What about his personal estate? By all accounts it should be considerable."

"It is. The house is yours, Mrs. Conroy, for your lifetime. It then goes to Marty. One-third of the estate was bequeathed to you, his widow. The other two-thirds is to be divided between his two children, Martin, Jr. and Emmajean."

"Emmajean?" For a moment, and only a moment, Alice Conroy's face registered total loathing. Then the look was wiped from her face. She straightened her back, tilted her head, and looked down her nose at the man even though they were of equal height. "Was the new will drawn recently?"

"As I said, a few months ago."

"Well, out with it. What other fool thing did Martin do?"

Mr. Shellenberger glanced at Marty. Mrs. Conroy's attitude made him acutely uncomfortable.

"Mr. Conroy made a condition regarding the trust, which had to be approved by the trustees. I've made copies of the codicil and the will, so you may read them for yourself."

"What is the condition?" Mrs. Conroy refused to take the paper he held out to her.

"Out of the yearly ten-thousand-dollar trust, two thousand five hundred of it will go to take care of Emmajean in a private sanitarium should she have to be . . . ah . . . put there."

Mrs. Conroy gasped. Her face turned a fiery red. When finally she could speak, her voice was shrill.

"That is ridiculous! Uncalled for. It's an insult to the family."

"He explained to the trustees that his daughter was, at times—"

"—High-strung," Alice interjected. "She is merely high-strung, as some young women are. She is married, has a baby, and lives in Oklahoma."

"Daddy wanted to be sure that she would be taken care of, should something happen, Mother."

"What would you know about what Martin wanted?" Alice frowned at her son for daring to speak up. She faced the young lawyer. "He had no right to go behind my back and make these arrangements."

"He had the right, Mrs. Conroy," Luther said firmly. "The law and the trustees are on his side. I doubt you could reverse their decision even in the highest court."

"Who's in charge of Emmajean's windfall?"

"Mr. Conroy seemed to think that Marty would carry out his wishes," Luther said, glad that Mr. Conroy had warned them that his wife might be difficult.

"Marty? He can't even manage the allowance Martin gave him."

"I can do it, Mother," Marty said quickly. "If it should become necessary."

"Is there anything else, Mr. Shellenberger?" Alice asked frostily.

"No, ma'am. I'll leave the copies of the will here on the desk."

"Then excuse me. I have things to attend to."

As soon as Mrs. Conroy left the room, Mr. Shellenberger arranged two neat stacks of paper on the desk and closed his briefcase.

"I'm sorry she's upset, but Mr. Conroy talked over these conditions at length with the trustees, and they agreed. It wasn't my doing."

"Mother will be all right. Losing Daddy has been a shock to her."

"Well, I'll be going unless you have any questions."

"How will the money set aside for Emmajean be handled?"

"It will remain with the trustees until you find it necessary to draw on it. At that time you will come before the trusteess and make a formal request. It's all there in the will."

"If she should not require the use of it, what happens?"

"It will accumulate. At some future date should the trustees think she is capable of handling it, they will turn it over to her. But in case of her death, the conditions in the trust will be void; and you will receive the full yearly payment from the trust. Her inheritance, the one-third of Mr. Conroy's personal estate, will go in trust for her and will be used for her at your discretion. Again, should Emmajean die, the inheritance will remain in trust for her son with you as administrator. Mr. Conroy didn't want her husband to have control of the inheritance."

"Daddy was wise to do that." Marty extended his hand to the lawyer, then walked him down the hall to the door.

"Come see me. There'll be papers to sign before I can turn over the bulk of the estate." Mr. Shellenberger lifted his hat from the rack beside the hall tree and placed it carefully on his head. "Strange, isn't it, how my great-grandfather and yours got together way back then."

"Yes. Daddy told me. I'm glad they didn't kill each other over that barrel of whiskey."

"So am I."

Mr. Shellenberger got into his car and drove away. Marty stood on the porch and watched him leave. He wasn't as shocked as his mother that his daddy had left money to Emmajean. He had not told her what his father had said just before he died, knowing how angry she would be.

Marty dreaded going back into the house and facing his mother. She was furious at what his father had done, going behind her back to the trustees and exposing the shame that Emmajean wasn't *right*.

One thing was sure, Marty thought. His mother would do her best to see that Emmajean didn't get one cent of the money her daddy left her. The best thing for him to do, he decided now, was just to sit back and see where the chips fell. He wasn't happy about crazy Emmajean getting the money either, but there were things that could be done about it.

Whistling a tune under his breath, he went back to the study that was his now. All his.

Henry Ann's nerves were frazzled to the breaking point. It had been almost a week since Tom had been to the farm. Jay had become so much a part of the Henry family that now he seldom mentioned his daddy. Johnny and Grant told of seeing Mrs. Dolan walking along a fence line heading for the creek. Shortly after they had seen her with Tom; he was taking her back to the house.

Henry Ann sometimes wondered if Tom was sorry that he had kissed her, held her in his arms, and told her that he was crazy in love with her. She searched her memory time and again for every word he had uttered. She had only to close her eyes to feel his kiss on her lips. Thank heavens this was the canning season. Henry Ann welcomed the hard work. It helped to keep her thoughts at bay.

Jars of pickled peaches, chowchow, piccalilli and bread-and-butter pickles lined the shelves in the cellar. Green beans were packed in clean jars. Then six jars at a time were placed on a rack in the copper boiler and given a hot-water bath until sealed. The same process was used to can the tomatoes, okra, and corn that had been cut from the cob. The kitchen was like an oven most of the time, even though they used the kerosene stove on the porch.

On Friday morning Henry Ann picked the last of the beans. The vines had produced exceptionally well thanks to the irrigation system. As she was leaving the garden, Johnny came riding up on his horse. He and Grant were stringing a temporary fence to keep the steers out of a small patch of corn down by the creek. He got off the horse and went to the house. She could tell by the jerky way he walked that he was angry. She followed and met him coming out the door with the rifle.

"What's going on? What are you doing with the gun?"

"Two more of our steers were butchered. I'm on my way to Mud Creek."

"How do you know they did it?"

"I'm pretty damn sure it's Pete and that bunch he runs with. The tracks showed a shod horse was there as well as a car. They're not getting away with it."

"Where's Grant?"

"He's down there working on the fence."

"I don't want you going to Mud Creek, Johnny. Go to the sheriff."

"He'll not do anything."

"Does Grant know what you intend to do?"

"I didn't tell him."

"If you're determinded to go to Mud Creek, I'm going with you. Get out the car while I change my dress."

"Sis . . . I don't want you mixed up in this."

"The steers belong to both of us. Isabel, if she's still there, might claim that she was taking her third. I'm going."

"I'll put up my horse."

Fifteen minutes later Henry Ann, in a clean housedress, her hair tied back with a narrow ribbon, climbed into the car. She glanced at her brother's set face, hoping his temper would cool by the time they reached the Perrys'. When they passed the Dolan farm, Henry Ann searched for a glimpse of Tom, but he was nowhere in sight. The place looked almost deserted.

Johnny turned down a lane where grass was so high between the ruts that it slapped the underside of the car. Henry Ann had not been to Mud Creek since she was a small child and was shocked by the trash along the roadway and in the yard of the ramshackle, unpainted house they came to.

"Who lives here?"

"Fat Perry and his ma. He's mean and stupid."

Chickens scattered with angry squawks as Johnny stopped beside a porch with a sagging roof. He pressed on the horn repeatedly until a grossly fat man came out of the house. He paused on the porch, stuck his hands down the sides of his overalls, and scratched his stomach before he came down the steps to the car.

"Howdy, Johnny."

"I'm here to give you a warning, Fat. If I find out that you had anything to do with killing and butchering our steers or even eating the meat, you're going to wake up some night thinking you've died and gone to hell. After this shack burns down around you, there'll be nothing left of you but a big grease spot."

"Whoa, now. That's big talk for a redskin who ain't got no *braves* a backin' him up." Fat's little pig eyes strayed to Henry Ann's face while he spoke.

"I don't need backup to come around here some dark night and burn this place to the ground."

"Try it, sonny, and Perrys'd be all over ya like flies on a pile of fresh cow shit." Fat put his foot up on the running board, leaned closer, and looked down at Henry Ann's legs. "Ain't ya Ed Henry's filly outta Dorene?"

"That's a crude way of putting it," Henry Ann said coolly. "But yes, I'm Ed Henry's daughter, and I back my brother all the way."

"Brother, huh?"

"Yes, my brother. He's more of a man than you'll ever be."

"Hee, hee, hee! Feisty, ain't ya? Damn near feisty as Isabel. Pure Perry, that gal."

"What a pity."

"Mark my words, Fat. Stay away from Henry beef."

Johnny stepped on the gas. The car shot ahead, the fender brushing Fat and almost knocking him to the ground. The roar of the motor overrode the curses that followed them.

"What a disgusting man!"

"He's stupid. He'd not do anything on his own, but if Pete told him to poke his head in the fire, he'd do it. This next place is Hardy Perry's, where Pete lives."

Over the barking of penned dogs, Henry Ann heard the sound of music when they stopped in front of the house. Johnny honked the horn. The music stopped and a man with a head of thick gray hair came to the door.

"What'a ya want?"

"Where's Pete?"

"How the hell do I know? He let go a the teat a long time ago." The man came out onto the porch. Bright blue eyes honed in on Henry Ann. "What's Miss Rich-bitch Henry doin' callin' on us *poor* Perrys? Did ya come to dance, honey?"

"No." Henry Ann looked past him to where Isabel stood in the doorway. She had cut her hair. With her painted face and short dress, her resemblance to their mother was startling. Henry Ann felt a spark of pity for the foolish girl. "Hello, Isabel."

"You can just get on outta here. I ain't going back there till I come to get what's mine." She came out to stand beside Hardy. He put his arm around her and pulled her close to his side. She snuggled against him.

"Two more of our steers have been butchered, Hardy." Johnny ignored Isabel.

"What'er ya tellin' me for?"

"I'm tellin' ya because if I find a sign that you and Pete are in on the butchering that's been going on, I'll go to the rest of the folk that's been losing steers, and you'll find yourself facing a mob who won't wait for the sheriff."

"He ain't goin' to do nothin', Hardy," Isabel said. "He's just talkin' big in front of *her.*"

"Don't be worryin' yore pretty little head, sugar-teat. Go on in there and pick out a record for us to dance to."

Isabel snuggled closer to Hardy and looked smugly at Henry Ann from his embrace.

"You heard from my lawyer yet, Miss Rich-bitch Henry?"

"No. He probably tucked *his tail* and went on down the road after he heard from my lawyer." The pity Henry Ann felt for the foolhardy girl was fading.

"Tell Pete what I said." Johnny revved the motor.

"Sure ya don't want to come in for a while?" Hardy leered at Henry Ann.

"I was never more sure of anything in my life."

The car lurched ahead and turned around in the yard, stirring up a cloud of dust. Johnny gritted his teeth. If Henry Ann hadn't been with him, he would have looked around for evidence of fresh meat. He promised himself that he would come back some dark night and see what he could find.

They passed Jude coming out of the pasture with a snarling dog on a leash.

"Who is that?"

"Jude Perry. The only decent Perry on Mud Creek," Johnny gritted out angrily.

"Pete's brother?"

"Yeah. He'll not stay decent if he stays here."

"You like him?"

"He's not like the rest. He wants to make something of himself."

"You mean he doesn't look up to Pete and want to be like him?"

"He doesn't want to be like him, that's sure."

"Isabel has settled in with the Perrys."

"I told you she would. Her daddy was trash." Johnny said nothing more until they were almost home. "Ed told me that even if Mama was . . . well, the way she was, I had my daddy's blood, too. The Cherokees, he said, are proud people, and I had a choice which way I wanted to go."

"How did he know that your daddy was a Cherokee?"

"I was too dang bullheaded to ask him and too dumb to heed his advice."

"I wish he could know you as you are now. I was proud of you today, Johnny."

"Yeah. Well, I wish I could tell Ed how sorry I am that I didn't listen to him when I had a chance."

Jude waited for the car to pass, then went on toward the house and put the dog in the pen. The damn Victrola was playing a song he'd heard a hundred times.

"Falling in love again. Never wanted to—"

The old man was dancing with Isabel. Jude snorted with disgust. She was so stupid that she thought she'd have a chance with Pete if she cozied up to the old man. She was playing with fire. Pete would never tie himself to a woman like her. Jude suspected that his brother liked to flaunt the young girl before Hardy, knowing Hardy would want to get her in bed. He didn't know how much longer Hardy would hold out. It wasn't natural for him to be around a young gal and not get in her drawers.

Jude went around to the back of the house and let himself in the kitchen. Music filled the house. He went across to the door and glanced in. Isabel was dancing with Hardy; her cheek rested on his shoulder and his hand was on her buttock.

It won't be long, Jude mused. He went to the pan on the stove and cut himself a large slice of roasted beef and carried it to the back step and sat down. Pete and his cronies were getting bolder and bolder, killing other folks' beef and selling the meat to stores in Wichita Falls. The last two kills were no doubt from the Henry farm. That must have been why Johnny and Miss Henry were here.

Pete rode in and tied his horse where he could reach the water tank. He wasn't staying, or he'd have put his mount in the corral.

"I saw Henry Ann and Johnny go by. What was she doing here?" he demanded as he walked swiftly toward the house.

Jude chewed and swallowed before he answered. "Don't know. I wasn't here."

"Was she in the house?"

"Told you I wasn't here. You deaf or somethin'?"

Pete sprang up onto the porch. By the time the screen door slammed, he was passing through the kitchen and striding toward the other room. He went directly to the Victrola and lifted the needle from the record.

"What'd ya do that for?" Hardy snarled.

"You'll not listen long as that thin's goin'. What was Henry Ann doin' here? Was she in the house? Did she see that slab of meat on the stove?"

"She didn't get out of the car."

"What'd she come here for?"

"She come 'cause Johnny thinks yo're butcherin' their beef. They lost two last night." Hardy continued to dance even without music.

"Two? Shitfire! If that Sandy's cuttin' off on his own, I'll stomp his ass in the ground," Pete snarled. "What did Henry Ann say?"

"Well, now let me see. Do you remember what she said, honey?" Hardy stopped dancing, but kept his arms around Isabel.

"She said, 'Hello, Isabel.' " Isabel giggled.

"Don't get smart, wiggle-ass." Pete ran forked fingers through his thick blond hair in a gesture of nervous frustration. "What'd she say, Hardy?"

"Not much. Johnny did the talking. Said that he knows you and yore cronics is rustlin' beef, and he'll stir folks up against ya if it don't stop."

"Bullshit! He *knows* nothin'."

"Yore frettin' for Henry Ann Henry, ain't ya, boy? By granny! That nasty-nice filly's got yore pecker up." He slapped his thigh with his hand. "Now wouldn't that just frost yore balls?"

"Keep your mouth shut about her," Pete snarled.

"Boy, when a man's pecker gets hard, his brain gets soft. That gal can't see ya for dirt."

"Shut up! And stay outta Isabel's drawers. I ain't wantin' her knocked up and pukin' durin' the marathon. It starts in a few weeks. She's got to eat a bunch of that beef and get lots of sleep."

"Whose gonna make yore deliveries while yo're marathonin'? I can't make 'em all."

"Jude'll make 'em."

"I won't." Jude spoke from the doorway.

"Ya will if I tell ya to." Pete turned on his younger brother. "You'll take my place and work with Hardy while I'm gone."

"I'm not going to deliver your moonshine. I've told you that I want nothing to do with that."

"We'll see about *what yo're not goin' to do.* Yo're gettin' a little big for yore britches." Pete's voice was exceptionally quiet.

Suddenly, like a whiplash, his fist shot out. The blow knocked Jude to the floor. Blood spurted from his split lips. He lay there, shaking his head to clear it.

"Don't be tellin' me what you'll not do." Pete stood over him, ready to hit him again if he got up.

"Leave him be." Hardy's voice thundered.

Pete whirled, his fist drawn back. "Ya ready to take me on, old man?"

Hardy crouched. "If I hafta."

"Ya never let me back-talk. Look at 'em. Big, soft daddy's boy. He wouldn't fight to keep from eatin' shit."

"What the hell's buggin' you?" Hardy demanded. "Yo're like a sore-peckered bull."

"I'm gettin' sick a this place."

"You got no right to be mean to Jude," Isabel yelled.

"Shut up, whore!" Jude jumped to his feet. "I don't need any help from you." He headed for the door.

"Hold on, Jude." Hardy stepped in front of his son. "You've got no call to talk to Isabel that way. She's no whore."

"Not yet," Jude replied, stepping around his father and going out the door.

"Well, dog my cats." Pete had the old familiar smirk on his face. "You got the hots for my girl, *Daddy*?"

Isabel looked from one big man to the other. A thrill of excitement passed through her. *Both father and son wanted her!* Not even her mama'd had a father and son after her at the same time. She looked from one to the other. Hardy was mad. She gripped his arm with both hands and looked up into his face as if he were the most important thing in the world to her.

"I like to dance with you, Hardy," Isabel said in a pouty voice. "We have a good time together. What's wrong with that?"

"Not a thin', sweety."

"Not a thin', sweety," Pete mimicked, and chucked Isabel under the chin with his fist. "Go ahead and rub up against my daddy all ya want. Just don't let yore cherry get busted or I'll bust your butt with the razor strop and the old man's head with a two-by-four. Hear?"

Chapter Sixteen

Johnny and Grant had just finished the evening chores and reached the porch when the sky overhead opened up and released a deluge of rain. It came suddenly in wind-driven sheets out of the dark clouds that had hovered overhead since late afternoon. Old Shep whined and hugged Johnny's legs.

"Rain at last." Henry Ann stood on the porch and breathed in the rain-washed air.

"We sure need it. The pasture is about dried up." Johnny followed Henry Ann into the house. He let old Shep in, and the dog, fearing the storm, crept behind the cookstove.

"Dat lightnin' can come right down outta dat bulb," Aunt Dozie explained, as she turned off the electric light and lit the kerosene lamp.

"That's the way it is in southern Oklahoma." Grant hung the towel on the rod beside the washbench. "It doesn't rain for a month, then we have a gully washer."

"The ground is hard. I'm afraid it'll wash everything

away before the water can soak in." Henry Ann set a bowl of potatoes on the table.

"I don't think it'll hurt the cotton. The soil out there is pretty sandy. The pasture will hold the water. This is good grassland."

"Daddy talked about giving up trying to grow cotton and turning all the fields into pasture. He said the future of this part of the country could be in beef cattle."

"He may be right."

"There's a dark cloud bank in the southwest," Johnny said from the doorway. "Looks like there's hail in it."

"Just what—" A loud crack of thunder, followed by a flash of lightning, drowned out Henry Ann's words. She went to the door to look out. "Do you think we should go to the storm cellar?"

"Not yet. Let's wait and see how much wind is in those clouds."

"Den sit yoreselfs down and eat yore supper while I gather me up some quilts to make a bed for dis babe when we does go."

"Sit and eat, too, Aunty." Johnny came to the table. "We'll keep an eye on the clouds."

"Ain't nothin' scares me like when dat wind blows and dat lightnin' comes down. Well, guess dem whirly-winds does scare me more."

Jay went to Johnny and climbed in his lap. He was so quiet that Henry Ann had forgotten that the child might be frightened.

"Daddy." Jay looked up at Johnny, his mouth drawn down as if he were about to cry. Johnny looked helplessly at Henry Ann. She went to him and knelt. Jay immediately put his arms around her neck. She stood and then sat down with the child on her lap.

"Your daddy's all right. I bet he's looking out the door right now and thinking about his little boy. If it storms, he's got a cellar to go to just as we have here."

By the time supper was over, the wind and hail clouds had gone, but the rain clouds remained. Rain came down steadily. Johnny turned on the radio so that Aunt Dozie could hear her favorite show, *Amos and Andy*. The set crackled and popped, making listening impossible. Later they tried to listen to Ed Wynn, the Texaco Fire Chief, but had to give that up, too, because of the static.

"Too much electricity in the air. I guess we'll have to listen to Grant sing." Johnny flipped off the radio.

"You could plug up your ears," Grant retorted, picking up the guitar and strumming a few chords.

"Go ahead and sing, Grant. All Johnny can do is whistle and yodel," Henry Ann teased.

"Who says I can't sing?" Johnny stretched his long legs out in front of him and leaned his head back against the wall.

"Admit it. You can't carry a tune in a bucket." Grant winked at Henry Ann.

"I can too. I just don't want to get Gene Autry worried I'll knock him off the radio and outta a job."

"Give us a sample," Henry Ann urged.

> *"Arm in arm over meadow and farm,*
> *walkin' my baby back home,*
> *Cows go by and — da, da—"*

Grant snorted. "That's enough to make a dog sick. He doesn't even know the words. You'd better stick to 'Home on the Range,' cowboy."

A heavy knock on the back door caused a sudden quiet. Johnny glanced at Henry Ann and got up. Grant stood the guitar against the wall and followed him. Henry Ann carried the child sleeping on her lap to the bedroom, placed him on the bed, and hurried to the kitchen. Aunt Dozie hovered in the doorway. It was an unusual event to have a caller this time of night.

Johnny and Grant were on the back porch when Henry Ann reached the kitchen. She heard Tom's voice. It had a worried tone. Her heart jumped out of rhythm, then began to beat rapidly.

"I hate to ask you to come out in this weather, but I've looked all over for her. She's been gone since early afternoon. She usually comes home before dark—"

Tom held a lantern. Water dripped off an old felt hat on his head. He was wearing a slicker that came only to his hips. His pant legs and boots were covered with mud. Henry Ann stayed back away from the door, her eyes drinking in the sight of him.

"I'll get my boots and a slicker," Johnny said. He took the garment from the peg beside the door. "Here, Grant, take this slicker, and I'll get another."

"There's another lantern in the barn." Grant threw the slicker over his head and stepped out into the pelting rain.

With Tom standing alone on the porch, Henry Ann couldn't resist slipping out the door for a brief minute alone with him.

"This is a bad night to be out. Does she do this often?" Her voice had a nervous tremor.

Tom took a step nearer to her, then stopped. His eyes swept over her face like loving fingers.

"She runs off, but I can usually find her."

"Where does she go?"

"Into the woods. She's made a little place and takes things there. It's almost like a child's playhouse. She wasn't there—Are you all right?"

"Sure. I'm fine. Jay's fine, too.

"I saw you pass by today—with Johnny."

"Two more of our steers were butchered. I went with him to Mud Creek."

"You shouldn't've!"

"It went all right. Nothing to worry about."

"My whole herd could be rustled, and I'd not know it. I've been so busy keeping an eye on Emmajean."

"Jay asked about you tonight. He was worried you might be out in the storm."

"Ah . . . hell! I've missed him. And . . . you—"

Johnny came out of the house with the lantern usually kept in the kitchen.

"I'll saddle my horse, Tom." He took off on the run for the barn. Grant came to the porch. The lantern he carried emitted a faint light.

"Tell us where you've been and where you want us to go."

"I've been up and down the creek bank. Maybe you and I should spread out and go through the pasture. Johnny could search the lower woods. If you find her, whistle two long and one short."

"Would she have gone to town?"

"She's never gone that way. Good Lord. I never thought

about her doing that. If we don't find her soon, I'll take the car and go there."

"The road'll be muddy as hell by now. Johnny could make it on his horse."

"Let's try the woods first."

Henry Ann stood on the porch and watched as Tom and Grant disappeared. Their voices reached her when Johnny, on horseback, joined them. Then they were gone.

"Dat woman goin' to come to a bad end a roamin' 'round like she does."

"You'd think that she'd go home when it started to rain."

"Dat man got him a heap of trouble." Dozie's large, expressive eyes turned to Henry Ann. "Honey, yo be mindful to remember dat man got him a wife, crazy as she be, de law say she his wife."

"I've not forgotten."

"I got me a feelin' dat her'll end up bad."

"I think I'll sit on the porch for a while. Go on to bed, Aunt Dozie. I'll wait for Johnny and Grant."

"I be sayin' my prayers for dat po' woman."

"You should say a few for the man who's trying to look after her."

"I do dat, too, child."

Henry Ann took a chair from the kitchen to the back porch and sat down. The rain had let up and was now a steady drizzle. The darkness was tomblike, and only the drip, drip, of raindrops falling from the porch eave intruded upon the stillness. She tried to imagine how it would feel to be lost out in the rain. Perhaps Mrs. Dolan wasn't lost. Perhaps she was hiding somewhere and didn't want to be found. *What a cruel joke to play on Tom.*

Johnny pulled his battered old hat low on his forehead to protect his face from the water shaken from the trees as each gust of wind passed through them. It was dark here in the woods. Every once in a while he would stop, hold the lantern high, and call out.

"Em . . . ma. Em . . . ma . . . jean—"

The quiet was absolute. Not a coyote or an owl was on the prowl tonight.

As the horse picked its way among the trees and over deadfalls, Johnny's eyes tried to penetrate the darkness beyond the small circle of light provided by the lantern. The area was overgrown with post oak brush and bull nettles. A woman on foot would get tangled up pretty quickly. He searched his memory for a place where she could hide, if she was hiding, or a place where she might crawl in to wait out the storm.

The only place that came to mind was down where this wooded patch joined that of the Austins. Several months earlier he and Pete had ridden by an old three-sided shed that had been used to store water barrels. It had been abandoned when the well nearby went dry.

"I had me a red-hot time here four or five summers ago. I used to meet a gal here," Pete had bragged. "After I cleared out the rattlers, we'd have us a party that'd curl even yore hair, chief. That gal was hotter'n a fake fifty-dollar bill. She could turn me inside out. Wow!" He had laughed and slapped his thigh with his palm. "I used to wonder how long her old man'd last if he didn't have me to take the edge off'n her cravin' for poontang. She was something."

"Did he ever catch you?"

"Naw. They moved over to Ringling." Pete had laughed again. "She's got a couple kids now, and I heard she was 'bout to pop out another'n. She's still givin' it to somebody."

Pete liked to boast. Johnny believed only half his stories. He was glad he'd told him this one or he'd not have remembered the shed. It was quite a ways from the Dolan farm and unlikely the woman would have found it, but he decided to take a look anyway.

Johnny turned his horse around and slowly made his way out of the nettle patch and headed for a thick stand of cottonwood trees with a few pecan trees scattered among them. One thing was sure, Johnny thought as nettles grabbed at his pant legs, Mrs. Dolan wouldn't have made it out of that patch on foot in the dark.

The rain had turned into a fine mist by the time he reached the shed. He approached it from the side and called out while holding the lantern high.

"Em . . . ma. Emma . . . jean."

"I hate you!" The voice came from inside the shed.

Johnny moved his horse around to the front and held the lantern under the sagging roof so he could see inside. She was snuggled down in a corner, her knees drawn up under her chin, her arms wrapped around her legs.

"Mrs. Dolan?"

"You said you'd come back."

"Mrs. Dolan, I'm Johnny Henry. Your husband is looking for you."

"I waited and waited. I tried to go home . . . but— I don't like you anymore!" she yelled. Her wet dress was plastered to her body, her wet hair stuck to her cheeks. She had been in the nettles. Her arms had bloody scratches and there were tears in her dress.

Johnny got off his horse and set the lantern on the ground.

"I'll take you home."

"I want to stay here."

"You can't. You need to get home and out of those wet clothes."

"Stay here with me."

"Come on, get up—"

"I'll take off my dress."

"No, don't do that," Johnny said quickly. He didn't know what to do. She wasn't making sense.

"You said my titties were pretty." She looked at him as if she was about to cry. "I did what you told me. Why are you being mean?"

"Mrs. Dolan, I'm . . . not the one that was here. I'm Johnny Henry."

"I don't care." She pulled her bodice apart exposing her breasts.

"Don't do that. Come on, get up." He pulled on her hand. She stood; and before he knew it, her arms were wrapped around him. "Hey, now, stop that."

"Don't you want to do it some more?" She leaned back, looked into his face, and rubbed her groin against his. "I'll let you do it the other way, if you're nice."

"Lady, you've got me mixed up with someone else." Johnny shrugged out of his slicker and put it around her. "Put your arms in the sleeves," he ordered in a no-nonsense tone, and she obeyed. He realized that he couldn't handle her and the lantern, so he put out the flame and set it in the back of the shed to pick up later.

"Are we going to town?"

He lifted her up onto the saddle telling her to hold on to the pommel, then jumped up onto the rear of the horse. Not understanding the double weight, the horse danced nervously.

"Steady, steady—" Johnny talked soothingly to the animal until he settled down. Then he put his arms around Emmajean to hold her in the saddle, and they moved away from the shed.

Presently, Emmajean, sitting sideways on the saddle, wrapped her arms around Johnny and snuggled close. He tried to concentrate on where they were going and keeping both of them from sliding off the horse. She kept nibbling at his neck.

"You oughtn't to do that, Mrs. Dolan." He tried to move back from her but there was nowhere to go. "Who was with you in the shed?"

"A man."

"What man?"

"I like you better. You won't slap me, will you?"

"Did the man slap you?"

"Uh-huh. I pulled my dress up. He told me to take it off. I did, and he pinched my titties, slapped my butt, and put his thing in me. He slapped me when I wouldn't let him put it in the other place."

Johnny was so shocked, he stuttered when he asked:

"Wh . . . at was . . . his name?"

"I don't know."

Good Lord! Poor Tom. She's loony as a bedbug. What'll he ever do with her?

"Have you . . . ah . . . met this man before?"

"Down at . . . the place I go sometimes. He was nice then."

"Was his name Pete?"

"I don't know."

They reached the pasture behind the Henry farm. Johnny put two fingers to his lips and whistled. He waited a bit then whistled again. The answering call came, and Johnny trotted his horse toward the faint glow of light at the edge of the woods, anxious to turn this confused woman over to her husband.

The rain now was no more than a mist, but in the southwest the lightning continued to flash. The clock struck midnight. Shortly after, Shep, lying beside Henry Ann's chair, rose up with a low growl.

"Someone coming, Shep?" Henry Ann put her hand on the dog's head and peered into the dark night.

The growl changed into a whine of welcome when Grant emerged from the darkness, the unlighted lantern swinging from his hand.

"Grant. Did you find her?"

"Johnny did. She's all right." Grant came to the porch. "I'm one muddy mess. If you'll get my clean shirt and pants, I'll change in the barn."

"I'll get them, and then go inside. You can change here on the porch. Where did Johnny find her?"

"In an old shed at the far end of the woods."

"I know where that is. It's on Austin's land. How in the world did she get way down there?"

"Johnny will have to tell you that, if he knows. He went with Tom to take her home. He'll be back soon."

Henry Ann waited in the kitchen while Grant changed

out of his wet clothes. When he came in, he left his muddy boots on the porch.

"The electricity is out." She had lit the lamp on the table.

"There may have been a cyclone west of here."

"Go on to bed, Grant. I'll wait for Johnny."

"It was hard going through the mud. Tom is probably worn-out and still has to deal with that demented woman."

"Do you think she's . . . dangerous?"

"It's hard to say. Some perfectly sane people are dangerous. It could be that she's more of a danger to herself than to anyone else. The man's got his problems, that's sure."

"It's too bad," she said quietly, and turned so that he couldn't see her face. "We're making ice cream Sunday afternoon. Karen's coming out. I invited Chris Austin to come and bring his girlfriend." She turned to look at Grant. "Karen is my best friend."

Grant studied her for a moment with eyes that had taken on the deep sadness she had seen from time to time.

"What are you trying to tell me about Miss Wesson?"

"I don't want you to amuse yourself by flirting with her. She was hurt once. It took a while for her to get over it."

"What happened?"

"She fell for a man, then found out he had a wife and two children."

"He was still married?"

"Yes. He was a charming, handsome cad who took great pleasure in making young girls fall in love with him."

"A man who'd do that isn't worth the powder it would take to shoot him."

"My thoughts exactly."

"I'm not married. Never have been."

"As much as I like you, Grant, I . . . we know nothing about you. You'll be moving on, you said so yourself."

"Would it displease you if I decided to settle near here?"

"Not at all. But . . . don't play fast and loose with Karen's affections. She's really very innocent of what goes on in the world."

"More innocent than you?"

"Much more. My lessons on the sorry side of life began before I started to school."

"Johnny's told me some of it."

"He didn't have a very happy childhood with our mother."

"I'm not sure where they came from, but he has deep-seated principles now."

"It's hard to understand how Johnny and Isabel, both raised in sorry surroundings, could be so different."

"Human nature is funny. I've known of bank robbers and murderers whose parents were good, churchgoing people." Grant rubbed his eyes. "I'd better get to bed."

Too keyed up to sleep, Henry Ann went back out onto the porch to wait for Johnny. She left the lamp on even though it was an extravagant use of lamp oil. Her conversation with Grant played back in her mind. He had, once again, evaded telling her anything about himself except that he wasn't married. Somehow she believed him.

It amazed her how he had fitted into the life here on the farm. He smiled more than when he first arrived, but at times the sadness came back in his eyes. She wondered what had happened in his life to put it there.

Tom was bone-tired. His boots, covered with heavy red clay that stuck like glue, made his feet feel as if they weighed fifty pounds each. He trudged alongside the horse that carried Johnny and Emmajean.

When they reached the house, Johnny waited beside the back stoop while Tom went in and lit a lamp. He shed his slicker and boots before he came and lifted Emmajean, sleeping in Johnny's arms, to carry her into the house.

"Thanks, Johnny."

"Anything I can do?"

"You've already done plenty. I'll wash her up some and put her to bed. Sure appreciate your help."

Tom carried Emmajean through the kitchen to the bedroom and lowered her to the bed. Even in the dim light he could see that her arms and legs were scratched and blood oozed in a dozen or more places. Her bobbed hair was wet and muddy. There was a swelling and a bruise on the side of her face.

Days ago Tom had discovered the place in a hollowed-out clay bank by the creek she had made for her secret haven. He often found her there, sitting on the quilt she'd brought, looking into a small mirror, combing her hair, or singing to herself. If he awakened in the morning and found her gone, he'd check the clay bank. Her hideaway had seemed harmless until today when he had gone there and found several match sticks and butts of hand-rolled cigarettes, but no sign of Emmajean.

Tom went to the kitchen and returned with a pan of warm water and the lamp. Emmajean didn't awaken as he eased the wet dress off her shoulders. It was the only garment she wore. Embarrassed to look at her naked body, he covered the lower part of it with a sheet while he washed her face and arms. He had not realized how thin she was until now. Her arms were mere sticks. It was a distasteful task, but he washed her legs and thighs. There was blood and fluid on her thighs indicating that she'd had sex with a man and that she had been cruelly used.

Johnny had pulled no punches when telling him how she had behaved and what she had said when he found her. Tom drew in a quivering, angry breath. A man who would use a woman as disturbed as Emmajean was not much more than an animal. If he found out who had taken advantage of her, he'd beat him to within an inch of his life.

Names flitted through his mind. Pete Perry or some of his kin would be first on the list, then the flimflammer that Marty worked with. Tom had been disgusted by the man's response to Emmajean's deranged flirting. He actually seemed to be interested in her sexual advances and might have gone along with her had Tom not carried her away.

Then, there was Chris Austin, on whose land the shed was located. Emmajean had seen Chris at the air show. He seemed a nice enough fellow, but when a woman offered herself as Emmajean did, a man might lose his head.

She might have been wandering around and come onto the shed. A hobo could have been using it to sleep in. Or maybe someone had met her and taken her there.

Grant didn't seem to be the kind of man who would rape a woman, that is if it was rape. Nevertheless, he would like to know where Grant had been all afternoon. Johnny, he knew, had been with Henry Ann. Tom dropped the cloth in the washbasin, and closed his eyes.

Henry Ann. Oh, Henry Ann, my dear one—

Chapter Seventeen

The rain had not only given the crops and the grasses a good soaking, it had left the roads a quagmire of mud, but by Sunday the hot June sun had dried them out enough so that Grant could drive Aunt Dozie and Henry Ann to their respective churches. Johnny stayed at home with Jay. Henry Ann had no idea of how Grant spent his time during the service, but he was there when it ended. She waited beside the car for Karen, who was going home with them, and groaned when Mrs. Austin came out of the church and hurried down the walk toward her.

"Henry Ann." Mrs. Austin eyed Grant, who sat behind the wheel of the car, with a sour expression before she smiled sweetly at Henry Ann. "We'll pick you up any time you want to come to church, dear. It would save Johnny a trip, and gasoline, well, you know how expensive it is. Many of our friends had to give up their motorcars because of the price of gasoline."

"Thank you for the offer, but so far we're able to afford

the gas. And Johnny or Grant would have to make the trip anyway to take Aunt Dozie to her church. Oh, there's Karen." She waved to her friend. "She's going home with us. Nice seeing you, Mrs. Austin."

"Are you still taking care of the poor little Dolan boy?"

"Why do you ask?" Henry Ann's tone was frosty.

"Just wondered, dear. I thought I would call on Mrs. Dolan and see if there's anything I can do for her. She's ill, isn't she?"

"Why else would I be taking care of her child? Ready to go, Karen?"

Henry Ann got into the car to sit next to Grant. Karen crowded in, slammed the door, and the car pulled away, leaving Mrs. Austin standing beside the curb.

"I hate being rude, but that woman gets my back up."

"She hasn't given up on getting you for her daughter-in-law," Karen teased. "Where's Johnny?"

"At home with Jay. I decided just this minute that I'm bringing him to Sunday school next Sunday."

"Oh, my! Aren't we brave? You do want the tongues to wag, don't you?"

"Let them wag."

"Hello, Karen." Grant had pulled up to the ice dock. He bent forward to look past Henry Ann so that he could see her.

"Hello, Mr. Gifford."

"Have you forgotten my name already?" he said, then told the man on the dock, "Fifty pounds."

"I didn't forget, George." Karen's cheeks had reddened, and her eyes sparkled.

"George? I had a dog once named George."

"So did I. A big ugly dog."

The iceman came out of the icehouse, his tongs firmly embedded in a block of ice. "Where ya want it?"

"In the back. Behind me."

"I got it," Grant said, when Henry Ann began to dig in her purse for a coin.

"You didn't need to do that."

"It's done. I fully intend to eat my share of the ice cream."

Aunt Dozie, Bible in hand, was waiting in front of her church energetically waving her cherished church fan to cool herself.

"Lawd have mercy! Sun's 'bout cooked my brains. I got me a notion not to come to church no more till wintertime." She settled herself in the backseat of the car.

"What about your sins, Aunt Dozie?" Grant teased. "By winter you'll be guzzling moonshine by the quart."

"Hush yo mouth! I ain't goin' to be doin' nothin' like dat, and ya knows it!"

"Pay him no mind, Aunty," Henry Ann said laughingly. "He's getting more mouthy every day."

Homemade ice cream was one of Aunt Dozie's specialities. She was called upon at times to make it for church socials and wedding receptions. Before going to church, she had scalded the milk while Henry Ann beat together the eggs, sugar, and several spoonfuls of flour. Aunt Dozie poured the hot milk over this mixture and cooked it until it thickened, then set it aside to cool. Now she added the cream and the flavoring.

On the back porch Johnny and Grant chipped the ice and packed it around the galvanized cylinder in the wooden two-gallon freezer. They took turns turning the crank until it became difficult to turn, then the dasher was removed, the lid replaced on the can, and the freezer repacked with salt and ice. Several old quilts covered it to help keep the ice from melting before the cream hardened.

"Do you think Chris will come and bring Opal?" Karen and Henry Ann sat in the porch swing after the noon meal. They had come outside to enjoy the southern breeze.

"I invited them. Chris didn't say no."

"I wish he had more backbone." Karen's eyes were on Johnny and Grant heading for the well, Jay riding on Johnny's shoulders and sucking on a chip of ice. "That little boy seems right at home here. He won't want to go back."

"I think he will. He's very attached to his daddy," Henry Ann murmured.

"Tom's good-looking in a rough, masculine sort of way. I bet he had plenty of women after him when he was single." Karen watched Henry Ann as she spoke and noted the slight flush that came to her cheeks.

"Probably did."

"The talk in town is that his wife is crazy as a bedbug and roams around in the woods . . . sometimes at night."

"Who started that rumor?"

"Who else but the Perrys?"

"And Mrs. Miller is spreading it like butter on hot bread."

"Her main aim in life is to keep the citizens of Red Rock informed of all the rumors floating around . . . and to embroider them."

"She's a nosy old . . . hen."

Later, as they sat on the porch, Jay in Henry Ann's lap, she noticed that Karen and Grant appeared to be shyly aware of each other. Karen was not as spontaneous with her retorts to Grant's jibes as she had been before, and Henry Ann figured that she had taken to heart the cautionary advice she'd offered her the day they met in the store. When Jay whispered to Henry Ann that he needed to go potty, she left the porch and took him to the outhouse.

Johnny lingered, and a long silence ensued. He left the porch with the excuse he should check on the freezer.

"That was kind of Johnny." Grant moved to sit in a chair near Karen.

"What do you mean?"

"He gave me a chance to talk to you."

"You've been talking to me." She spoke without looking at him.

"Not alone."

"What do you want to talk about?" Karen drew in a shaky breath, aware that her heart was thumping beneath the bodice of the dress she had made especially to wear today. It had a round neck, puffed sleeves, and a circular skirt. The small blue-and-white-checked material was especially becoming, accenting her blond hair and blue eyes.

"Will you go with me to the picture show? I'm sure I can borrow the car."

"There isn't a picture show in Red Rock."

"There's one in Ringling."

"That's more than thirty miles."

"We could just go for a ride if you'd rather do that."

"When? Why?"

"Next Sunday afternoon. And because, well . . . I'd like to know you better. I think we could be . . . friends."

"Why go to all the trouble? You'll be moving on soon."

"Maybe not."

"I don't think I should——"

"Do you think I'm some sort of flimflammer who'll make promises, then run out on you?"

"It's possible." When no answer came, Karen pressed on stubbornly, refusing to be sidetracked. "Well. It is possible, isn't it?"

"Anything is possible." A bemused expression came over Grant's face as he regarded her. "But it isn't likely. I keep my word . . . if at all possible."

"This is a silly conversation. I don't expect you to *promise* me anything, so why are we discussing it?"

"I'm not the worthless bum you think I am." He looked away, then back to meet her blue eyes with his.

Karen turned away from the sadness in his eyes and pushed the swing with one foot. While she waited for him to say more, she listened to the squeak of the chain and watched a june bug hovering over the bed of moss rose. A definite, almost tangible silence hung between them.

"Then what are you?" Karen asked, unable to bear the suspense.

"A man trying to find himself."

"So you're lost."

"I was. Not now. About next Sunday——"

"I'll think about it."

"Fair enough," Grant said, and looked toward the road as a car came into the yard.

"Well, glory be!" Karen stopped the swing with her foot. "It's Christopher, and he's brought Opal. Good for him!"

When Chris came to the porch, carrying Rosemary, he urged Opal along with his hand in the middle of her back. Henry Ann came out of the house to greet them.

"Opal! I'm so glad you came."

"Howdy."

"Do you know Karen?"

"Of course she knows me. Daddy baptized Rosemary. Hello, Opal. Hello, pretty thing. Oh, she's still bashful," Karen said, when the child hid her face against Chris's shoulder.

Henry Ann introduced Grant and then Johnny when he came from the house. Opal murmured the polite responses, but said nothing more. She sat down in a bentwood rocker and reached for her little girl. Chris set Rosemary in her lap, then lowered himself to the step nearby. He seemed anxious that Opal be at ease. He knew that coming here and meeting his friends was difficult for her.

"We should have entertainment while we wait for the ice cream to harden." Henry Ann looked at Chris. "Do you remember when you used to come over and sing with Daddy? I wish I'd told you to bring your guitar. I'll get Daddy's if you'll play for us."

"I hear Grant does a fair job of playing and singing."

"Singing?" Johnny let out a sound of disgust. "I'd sooner listen to a hog rooting in a mud hole."

"I'll tell you what, Johnny. I'll play if you do the singing. Didn't he treat us to a song the night of the storm, Henry Ann?"

"I think it was wishful thinking and not even a song," Henry Ann said seriously. "It was something about walking his baby back home."

"They're all against me," Johnny complained to Karen.

"Get the guitar and I'll sing with you. I know 'Walking My Baby Back Home.'" Karen's cheerful laughter rang out.

Before Johnny could answer, a horse nickered, then a voice came from the end of the porch.

"We're just in time for the party, sugar." Pete Perry on his horse with Isabel perched behind came to a stop in the flower bed beside the front step. "Thanky for the invite, Cousin Henry Ann."

"You're not invited, and get that horse out of my yard." Pete gave her a cheeky grin but showed no sign of moving. She jumped to her feet. "Get that horse out of my flower bed," she ordered angrily.

"I know you're glad to see me, sweet thing, but you don't have to be so loud about it. You'll scare little Rosie." His eyes settled on Opal in the chair with Rosemary on her lap.

"Get the horse—"

Henry Ann cut off her words when Johnny snatched the hat from his head and whacked the horse sharply across the nose. The startled animal shied back and reared. Isabel screamed and clutched Pete around the waist. He cursed and worked to control the horse. Jay scooted behind Henry Ann and hid his face in her skirt.

"Get the goddamn horse out of her flowers," Johnny shouted.

"Don't get yore bowels in a uproar, boy," Pete answered coolly. He guided the horse to the side of the house and dismounted. After lifting Isabel to the ground, he took his time and led the animal to the corral fence and tied him there. He put his arm across Isabel's shoulders as they approached the house.

"That's ice cream on the back porch or I miss my guess." Pete grinned his cocky devil-may-care grin.

"You're not invited to stay."

" 'Course I am, sugar. Me'n' this here road bum got business to settle." He jerked his head toward Grant, then ignored him and went to stand in front of Opal. "Didn't know I'd get to see little Rosie." He reached out a hand to pat the child and Opal slapped it away.

"Get away!"

"She's a Perry. Betcha a dime against a doughnut she's a Perry."

"Leave her alone, Pete." Chris got to his feet, his face red with anger.

"I ain't forgettin' I owe ya one," Pete said to Chris without turning, his eyes still on Opal. Then to her, "Yore gettin' prettier ever'day, sugar teat."

"Come on, Pete, let's go." Isabel cast worried glances at Johnny, who remained standing, his arms folded over his chest, his narrowed eyes watching Pete.

"Not till I do what I come for, sugar," Pete said in a chiding tone, then suddenly he whirled and charged Grant who was standing a couple yards away.

Pete went low into a crouch, swinging both fists high. One of them struck Grant's left shoulder like a thrown brick. Taken by surprise Grant fell to the ground. He rolled over, but not before Pete slammed the toe of his boot into his ribs.

Johnny and Chris acted in unison. They jumped on Pete's back and bore him to the ground. Grant got to his feet.

"Let him up. If he wants a fight, we'll fight. But behind the house. Not here in front of the kids."

"Get yore hands off me," Pete snarled. Chris and Johnny backed off, and Pete stood up.

"Come on out back," Grant invited. "That is, if you've got the guts to meet me head-on in a fair fight."

"Don't worry 'bout that, *Roady*."

"Don't fight, Pete," Isabel pleaded. "They'll gang up on ya."

"Shut up and stay outta the way."

"It's all your fault!" Isabel turned on Henry Ann. "Ya wanted a man so bad ya took in that . . . tramp! Trash is what *you* are!"

"You've got a nerve calling me . . . trash!" Henry Ann retorted angrily.

Johnny grabbed Isabel's arm, propelled her to the side of the house, and shoved her down.

"Sit there and shut up! Say one more bad thing about Henry Ann, and I'll shut your mouth for you! You've not got a decent bone in your skinny body. You're nothing but a . . . whore!"

"I won't stay here!" Isabel tried to get to her feet. Johnny shoved her back down. She landed hard on her behind, her head bounced against the side of the house, and she burst into tears.

"Stay here, honey," Chris said to Opal.

"I hadn't ort to a come."

"This has nothing to do with you." Chris gave her a fleeting kiss and hurried toward the back of the house.

Aunt Dozie came out onto the porch and picked Jay up in her arms.

"Me'n Miss Opal'll stay wid dese younguns right here. Yawl go on and see dat Mr. Grant don' get hurt too bad. Dat Mud Creek trash is meaner dan a rattlesnake in a hot skillet."

"That's pretty mean, Aunty," Karen said.

"It be de God's truth."

When Henry Ann and Karen passed Isabel sitting with her back to the house, her head on her knees, Henry Ann paused.

"Bitch! Bitch! I'll have *all* the Perrys on you!" Isabel screeched, and kicked out at Henry Ann with her foot.

Henry Ann stepped out of the way, shook her head in disgust, and followed Karen past the cellar door to where Grant waited beneath the oak tree. He had removed his shirt and pulled on the leather gloves he used when he cut wood. Pete's shirt lay across the saddle on his horse; he had gone to duck his head in the watering tank.

"Grant?" Karen was clearly distressed.

"You wanted me to knock out a few of his teeth the day of the air show. I'll oblige you now." Grant's hard blue eyes swept past her to watch Pete.

"I didn't mean it. You don't have to do this."

"I do. It'll be all right. Trust me."

"It isn't that, but—" She was pulled away by Chris's hand on her arm.

"Come on, Karen—"

"I heard that Pete fights dirty, Chris. I want to warn Grant."

"Grant knows. If you and Henry Ann are going to watch, stay back by the house. Johnny and I will make sure the fight is fair."

"Be careful," Karen called, and feeling as if her heart would jump right out of her breast, backed away to stand beside Henry Ann.

Right away Grant could tell that, whatever else Pete was, he wasn't a coward. And that he'd learned from experience that the man who struck the first blow had an advantage. He had powerful arms and shoulders. He came barreling in close, slamming and butting beneath Grant's chin with his head. Grant managed to ram a fist into Pete's ribs before he threw him off, but he knew that wasn't how he could win the fight.

Pete charged in again, punching, driving, stomping on Grant's instep when he got close. At first, Grant didn't realize that Pete was basically a brawler or that anger was making him reckless. Grant took a few wicked punches, then retaliated by jabbing an elbow into the side of Pete's face with such force that it cut to the bone. When his blood began to flow, Pete went berserk. His fists worked like pistons.

Every punch hurt Grant, but he bided his time, and when the opportunity came, he caught Pete square on the mouth with a hard, gloved fist. It smashed his lips back into his teeth, shook him to his heels, and stopped his rush. Grant was able to land a left and then, as he crouched, he swung a right to the split cheekbone that ripped the cut wider. Pete grabbed his arm to throw him to the ground, but Grant took him down with him.

Pete landed hard with Grant on top. Grant ground the man's face in the loose dirt and had half smothered him before he suddenly jumped back and let him up. He wanted to whip him, not kill him.

Karen clutched Henry Ann's arm with both hands. Tears streamed down her cheeks. She wished over and over that she hadn't chided Grant for not whipping Pete the day of the air show. Somehow she felt that this was her fault, and if Grant were injured, or badly scarred, she would never forgive herself.

Henry Ann appeared calm, but anxiety was making her ill. She was so totally consumed with what was happening that she was unaware of Tom's presence until his hand touched her back. Her head jerked around, and she was looking into his face.

"What's this about?"

"Pete came picking a fight. How did you— Where is she?"

"In that place where she goes sometimes. She'll be all right for a while." His hand continued to stroke her back as if he had to touch her.

"I'm afraid—" Henry Ann leaned back against Tom's hand, seeking the comfort of his touch.

"Looks to me like Grant knows what he's doing."

When Pete came up off the ground, he staggered, wiped the dirt from his eyes, located Grant, and rushed. Grant put another fist to Pete's mouth that shoved him back, then took advantage of the opening to land a stunning blow as Pete tried to come in again. Pete went down hard in the dust. He got to his hands and knees, then threw himself at Grant's legs. A knee smashed him in the face, and he fell again, but rolled and slowly struggled to his feet.

"You're a good fighter, Pete, but don't you think this is enough? In the condition you're in now, I could hurt you bad. I don't want to do that." Grant's face was bruised and battered, although he had no cuts. His ribs hurt like hell where Pete had kicked him.

Pete tried to wipe the blood from his face with his sweat-slick arm. His cheek had been laid open, and his lips were bloody. One eye was almost closed, but he stood there, the hatred in his eyes as strong as ever.

"If you want to continue, I'm game." Grant waited to

see what his opponent would do. "We can stop now and try it again later on. Maybe you'll win next time."

"Next time," Pete snarled. "Next time it'll be different."

Pete had been stopped, but not beaten. He cherished his reputation of being tough. He gloried in the feeling of power, enjoyed going into town and having folks step out of the way. He wasn't giving all that up because he'd lost one fight to a road bum. What hit him hardest was being whipped in front of Henry Ann. He glanced in her direction and found Tom Dolan standing close beside her. He knew how to get back at him. They were all looking at *him* now as if he was a skunk that had been dead for a week. He'd get even with all of them.

"This isn't over," he said to Grant, his split lips hardly moving.

"It is as far as I'm concerned."

"And you," Pete's one good eye homed in on Chris. He felt the need to inflict as much hurt as he could. "I'm not finished with you. Stay away from Opal. She's not for a sissy mama's boy."

"Goddamn you!" Chris exploded. "If you weren't already whipped like a cur dog, I'd beat you to a pulp."

"You couldn't whip a sick whore with one arm tied behind her back." Pete spit a mouthful of blood on the ground. "As for you," he said to Johnny, "there's nothin' worse than kin turnin' against kin."

"I couldn't choose my kin, but if I could've, you'd not a been one of them. Stay away from here or a *wild Indian* might shoot a fire-arrow onto your roof some dark night."

Pete looked with surprise at the young boy before walking to the watering tank on legs spread wide to maintain his balance. He dunked his head before untying and mounting his horse.

When Isabel realized that he was leaving, she ran after him as he walked the horse down the fence line toward the creek.

"Pete! Pete! Wait, Pete."

Karen went to the house, returned with a towel, and took it to the well, where Johnny was pouring a bucket of water over Grant's head.

Henry Ann felt Tom's hand fall from her back and turned to look at him.

"It's been almost a week since I've seen you." His dark eyes mirrored his longing.

"Jay will be glad to see you."

"And you, Henry Ann?"

She flushed and lowered her gaze. For a little while she was wholly still, fighting down her desire to lean toward him, to rest in his arms. She gazed into his eyes, unable to keep the yearning from hers, and nodded.

"Henry Ann, I meant every word that I said the other night. You mean the world to me."

"We can't do anything . . . about it."

"I look over this way at night and wish that I was here."

"I . . . wish it, too."

"I'm afraid to leave her alone. She was with a man the night I couldn't find her. I've no idea who he was, but he hit her. She's pitiful, Henry Ann."

"I know."

"I can't watch her and work, too. I put off installing the motor in the grocer's truck, and he got someone else to do it. As soon as I can, I'm going down to Conroy and talk to her folks. They told me before that if I put her away, they'd go to court to get Jay. If that happens, I've no money to fight them. I'd have no choice but to take him and leave here."

"Nooo—" Henry Ann's hand went to her mouth.

Tom looked past her and saw the others coming toward them.

"Will you come outside tonight? Meet me out there by the tree?" he asked in a quick whisper. Then when she hesitated, "Please, sweetheart—"

She nodded, then turned to Grant. "You all right?"

"I couldn't be better. If I'd known I was going to get this much attention, I'd have fought him sooner." His grin was lopsided, his eyes on Karen.

"You sure like to talk," Karen retorted. Then to Tom, "You're just in time for the ice cream."

"It should be ready by now." Henry Ann had a nervous tremor in her voice which did not go unnoticed by Grant and Karen. "Jay's going to be surprised to see you."

Henry Ann and Karen went to the kitchen to get bowls and spoons. Tom and Johnny carried the freezer to the front porch.

"Grant whipped Pete Perry good," Karen said with a lilt to her voice.

"Maybe he was a prizefighter before he took to the road." Henry Ann set bowls on a wooden tray.

"He asked me to go to a picture show, but I'm not going. I did say I'd think about going for a ride next Sunday. He's going to ask to borrow the car, but I think I'll bring mine out and take *him* for a ride." She giggled happily.

"I hope you know what you're doing."

"I hope *you* do, too, Henry Ann." Karen spoke seriously.

"What do you mean?"

"You know. The man is still married even if his wife is . . . not right in the head. The town gossips will tear you apart."

"I know."

* * *

Jay was wildly happy to see his daddy. He insisted on sitting beside him on the step to eat his ice cream. Henry Ann's glance lingered on the two dark heads when Tom bent to say something to his son.

Opal became more at ease, even laughed a time or two. Chris had Rosemary on his lap and fed her ice cream out of his own bowl. The love he had for the pair and they for him was evident. Henry Ann had never seen him so happy as when he was with them.

"I'll take more." Johnny handed his bowl to Aunt Dozie, who was sitting on a chair beside the freezer refilling the bowls. "I got to get mine before Grant gets here," he said confidentially to Aunt Dozie. "I was hoping Pete'd knock his teeth out and he wouldn't be able to eat."

"Dat ain't nice ta be sayin' sich as dat. 'Sides, don' take no teeth ta eat dis ice cream."

Henry Ann was listening to the exchange and smiling fondly at her brother when a car slowed to a stop in front of the house, backed up, and pulled into the yard.

"Oh, no," she murmured, when Mrs. Miller got out and came toward the house. Henry Ann rose to meet her.

"Having a social, Henry Ann?"

"I suppose that you could call it that."

"We're on our way to the Austins'. I saw their car here and"—her small bright eyes honed in on Christopher with Rosemary on his lap—"I said to Wilbur . . . stop, stop. The Austins are here."

"As far as I know the folks are at home, Mrs. Miller."

Chris spoke up, then wiped Rosemary's mouth with the bib tied around her neck, making it clear to the woman that Opal and her child were here with him.

Henry Ann silently applauded.

"Well . . . Oh, hello, Karen. Your daddy preached a fine sermon this morning."

"I'll tell him you said so."

"Hello, Mr. Dolan."

"Ma'am."

"Is Mrs. Dolan here? I've not met her yet."

"No, ma'am."

"She's been ill, hasn't she? I've been meaning to stop by and visit with her. We need our young people on our committees. The time just slips by, ya know, what with all the quilting projects, the canning, and helping with the soup kitchen. So many *tramps* coming through these days."

"Yes, ma'am."

"You're lucky to have a neighbor like Henry Ann who'll take care of your little boy."

"I realize that."

"Before I forget, Henry Ann, there'll be a meeting of the committee planning the church budget next Wednesday."

"I'm not on the committee, Mrs. Miller."

"You're daddy was. We thought—"

"No. I'm not on the committee," she repeated.

Never before in her life had Henry Ann been rude to someone who had come to her home. She did not invite Mrs. Miller or her husband waiting in the car to come in. Nor did she offer them ice cream.

It seemed to her that the world and all around her stood still while the woman took in the scene: Rosemary on

Chris's lap, Karen sitting in the porch swing with a man with a bruised face and swollen eye and . . . of all things, Dozie Jones, a colored, sitting in a chair among them eating from a bowl of ice cream. It wasn't difficult to read the woman's thoughts.

Scandalous! What in the world is the matter with Henry Ann? Is she carrying on with Mr. Dolan? Ed Henry would turn over in his grave. Wait till I tell poor Pernie Austin that her Chris is here with that whore from down on the river. And oh, dear. Our Karen, our sweet and innocent Karen, is here in the midst of all this.

"Tell the folks that I'll be late getting home, Mrs. Miller, and that I arranged for the Whalen boy to come help with the chores." Chris seemed determined that the woman get the message that he and Opal were here as a couple.

"I'll tell them. 'Bye, Henry Ann. 'Bye, Karen." She ignored the others and headed for the car.

"Good-bye, Mrs. Miller."

All were quiet until after the dust from the car had drifted away.

"The fat's in the fire," Karen muttered. "It'll be all over town that Grant has been in a fight, that Chris was here with Opal, and that Mr. Dolan was here without his wife."

"This is a regular den of iniquity." Henry Ann laughed nervously.

Tom stood quickly and faced her. "I don't want you talked about because of me."

"She'll mostly talk about me and Opal," Chris said. "I don't care. Do you, sweetheart?"

Opal lifted her shoulders. "I'm used to it, but you—"

"I can get used to it, too."

Chapter Eighteen

There was only an hour of daylight left when Johnny came to the kitchen where Henry Ann was running milk through the separator and Aunt Dozie was washing dishes.

"If it's all right with you, Grant'll take Karen back to town."

"Is this Grant's idea?"

"No, it's mine."

"I don't know—"

"You don't trust him, do you?

"We don't really know anything about him."

"You didn't know anything about me when I came here."

"But you were my brother."

"It's up to you. They like each other, and I thought it would be a good time for them to be together without us around."

"Johnny! You're a regular matchmaker." Henry Ann

smiled fondly at her brother, seeing new depth to his character.

"Well? Shall I ride out and check the herd, or take Karen to town?"

"Check the herd." Henry Ann spoke as soon as Johnny left the room, "Aunt Dozie, am I doing the right thing?"

"Dey is kinda stuck on each other. Dat plain as day. I ain't seein' it hurt none. Miss Karen ain't no youngun no more. She old as you is."

Karen came to the kitchen, followed by Grant.

"I'm going, Henry Ann."

"Johnny's going out to the south pasture. Do you want to ride along with me to take Karen home?"

"I don't think so, Grant. You go ahead. I'll see you sometime this week, Karen."

Karen went to the bedroom to get her purse and hat. Grant lingered in the doorway.

"I understand your concerns. Thank you for trusting me."

When Aunt Dozie went to her room, Henry Ann went to sit in the porch swing and enjoy the quiet sounds of evening and the breeze coming from the south. She mulled over in her mind the happenings of the day.

No one could say that life on the Henry farm was dull.

Grant had handled himself well during the fight with Pete. The thought came to her that he wasn't a cruel man, or he would have really hurt Pete when he was no longer able to fight back. She searched her memory for a fault to find with Grant but could find only the fact that he didn't talk much about himself.

If he was a wanted criminal, Mr. Hamer and Tom's brother would have known about it—that is if Grant Gifford was his real name. Johnny said it was. He had found a letter addressed to Grant that had fallen from his pack. Karen was attracted to the blond-haired man. She sparkled even more than usual when she was around him. Henry Ann hoped that her friend wouldn't be disappointed again.

Trying not to dwell on the meeting she would have later with Tom, Henry Ann concentrated on Chris Austin and Opal. She had been proud of him today when he confronted Mrs. Miller, knowing that she would tell his mother that he had been here with Opal. This had been an exciting day for Mrs. Miller. She had stumbled onto a gold mine of things to gossip about. Could it be that Pete's taunting had embarrassed Chris and stiffened his backbone? He would never be able to take Opal and Rosemary home to live on the farm with his mother. Henry Ann was sure of that. Poor Chris. If he wanted Opal, he would have to leave the farm and all that was familiar to him.

When the lightning bugs began to flit about, Henry Ann went into the darkened house. A light was on in the upstairs room. Johnny had come home. As she ran a wet washcloth over her face and a comb through her hair, she wondered what Johnny would think about her sneaking out in the night to meet Tom. Would he lose respect for her and think that she was a loose woman like their mother? If she was lucky, Johnny would never know.

I love Tom! She fervently wished that she could shout the words.

With anticipation making her heart race, she slipped out the back door and almost stepped on Shep, who was lying on the porch. The dog stood and followed her out into the yard.

"Oh, Shep, I know that I shouldn't be doing this." The words came out on a breath.

As they neared the deep shadows of the tree at the far end of the house yard, Shep growled. Henry Ann stopped, put her hand on the dog's neck, and strained to see if someone was there. Shep continued to growl low in his throat.

"I'm here, Henry Ann." Tom's voice whispering from the darkness quickened her heartbeat.

"It is all right, Shep."

She patted the dog's head and moved on toward the man who appeared and held out his hand. Mindlessly, she put hers in it and allowed him to draw her deeper into the shadows. Shep followed. When they stopped and stood facing each other, the dog looked at his mistress and, deciding that she was where she wanted to be, lay down and dropped his head on his crossed paws.

"I was afraid you'd not come," Tom said anxiously.

"I shouldn't have. How were you able to leave the house?"

"Emmajean's been sick with a cold and sleeps a lot since the night Johnny found her in the shed." Tom held tightly to Henry Ann's hand when she would have pulled it from his. "I need to have a talk with Doctor Hendricks. I'll ask him to help me put her someplace where she won't be a danger to herself and to others. I don't know what else to do."

"Did you find out how she got down to the Austins' shed or who she was with?"

"No. She doesn't say much of anything that makes sense. She says that her daddy is coming to take her to a party."

"You can't let her roam around at will. Some scoundrel may take advantage of her again."

"I worry about that, but I can't watch her every minute."

"Jay never mentions her. It's sad—"

"She asked one time where he was. I told her he was with friends, and she hasn't asked again. She never wanted him—"

"He had a big day today. He was tired and went to . . . sleep—" Her words trailed off.

Tom was looking down at her. She felt a curious kind of panic as if her body, her mind, her soul were being merged with his. Long moments passed while her legs felt weak, her throat tight, and her eyes could focus on nothing but him. She was breathing fast, and so was he. She was unbearably aware of his towering strength.

"I've never loved a woman before. I think of you every minute of the day. I didn't know it would be like this— both wonderful and like a knife in my heart." The strangled voice sounded miles from her ears.

Abruptly he moved and gathered her into his arms. His mouth had found hers before she could turn her head. She felt his lips, his teeth, his tongue. She opened her mouth to his as the intimacy of the kiss increased and felt a strange helplessness in her limbs, as if he were absorbing her very being. A surge of sensual pleasure coursed through her. It was so strong, so unfamiliar . . . so wonderful that she feared her legs wouldn't hold her.

"Sweetheart, this feels so . . . right, so good. I couldn't wait to hold you—" He whispered the words, then feathered light kisses along her brow, her temples, and her chin.

Finally, when she thought that she could not bear the yearning an instant longer, she turned her mouth to meet his in a kiss that engaged her soul. His lips became demanding, and her own parted under them, admitting him, submitting. She touched the tip of her tongue delicately against his mouth and felt the tremor that shook him. Winding her arms tightly around his neck, she pressed the length of her body to his.

"I love you, my heart. I love you so very much." The muttered words were barely coherent, thickly groaned in her ear as he kissed the bare warm curve of her neck, following it to her ear and back to the hollow in her shoulder. He cupped a hand behind her head, thrust strong fingers into the disarray of her hair, and drew her flushed face into his shoulder.

"This is unfair of me. I've given you the burden of my love. I'm sorry, my sweet, sweet, wonderful woman." He stroked a strand of hair behind her ear.

"Don't be sorry, my dear . . . love. I'll treasure your love for the rest of my life. How can all this be so . . . wrong?" Her mouth moved against the skin of his neck and the words came from the center of her being.

"Am I? Am I really your . . . love?" His voice was a hoarse whisper.

"Yes. God forgive me. I love you, but you . . . belong to someone else." With a deep sobbing breath, she hid her face against his neck.

"I don't belong to her," he replied quickly. "I never did. But, sweetheart, I'm tied to her. Please, let me have some time with you once in a while. And don't stop caring for me. Right now you're all that's keeping me sane."

Headlights swept across the yard and Grant drove the car from the road into the shed. Henry Ann backed out of Tom's embrace.

"Grant's come back from taking Karen home. He'll be wondering where Shep is. He's always on the back porch."

"I thought that something was developing between them. I'm glad. I worried about Grant being here with you day after day. In my nightmares you fell in love with him."

They watched Grant come from the car shed, cross the yard, and step up onto the porch. He paused, looked around, then went into the house.

"Do you think he knows I'm out here . . . with you?" she whispered.

"I don't know, sweetheart." He cupped her cheek with his palm. "It kills me that we have to hide what we feel for each other."

"Johnny is just now getting to like and respect me. If he thought I was trying to take . . . another woman's . . . husband, he'd decide that I was like our mother after all."

"I'll talk to him, tell him I'm the one doing the pursuing. I'll make sure that he knows that you've done nothing wrong. It'll be all right. Johnny's a levelheaded boy."

"He saw a lot during his first fourteen years. I wasn't sure that he'd ever straighten out."

"He's got a good head on his shoulders, learns fast, and he isn't afraid to work. I'll be happy if Jay grows up to be as good. Don't worry about Johnny, sweetheart. If he finds out about us, I'll explain that we fell in love with each other, but that we know for now it's a hopeless situation."

"It is hopeless, isn't it?"

"I see only one way out. If I can get her into an institution, I may be able to get a divorce. But I know that her folks will fight me every step of the way." He groaned as he pulled her to him. "I should go, but God, I hate to leave you."

When he lowered his face, she raised hers. Their mouths met and were no longer gentle. They kissed deeply, hungrily. The kiss was slow and long, a joining of their hearts as well as their lips. She could feel the heavy beat of his heart and the pounding of her own.

"I want you to be mine," he said in anguish against her mouth, her ear, her nose.

"I am yours!" Her hands moved frantically over his back, up to the nape of his neck, and into his thick dark hair. "I'll be here for you . . . I'll wait forever if I have to."

His arms were wrapped around her, the palms of his hands on the sides of her breasts, his fingers stroking. She felt the breath expelled harshly from his lungs. She trembled beneath his touch, and her eyes filled with tears. She wanted to hold this big, dark, wild-haired man and comfort him.

"Can I come back?" The agonized plea was whispered against her cheek.

"Of course. As long as Jay is here—"

"To see you . . . and Jay. Sweetheart, I live for the times I'm alone with you."

"We'll find a way."

"I'll never give up the hope of spending the rest of my life with you."

Summoning up all her willpower, Henry Ann drew back until only their hands were touching.

"I must go."

"I'll see you to the porch."

"No. Shep will be with me."

She turned and stumbled away from him while she still had the strength to leave him. She crossed the yard in the moonlight, not caring if Johnny or Grant looked out the window and saw her.

Chris Austin parked the car in the open shed and sat for a moment, preparing himself for the battle ahead. A light in the kitchen told him that his mother, and possibly his father, was waiting for him. Mrs. Miller had, no doubt, done what he had known she would do when she saw him with Opal at Henry Ann's.

When Chris opened the screen door and stepped into the well-lighted kitchen, he blinked, then saw his parents sitting at the kitchen table.

"What are you two doing up this time of night?" he asked, well aware of why they were waiting for him.

"I think you know," Mrs. Austin retorted. "Have you no concern for your daddy? He works hard and needs his rest. The least you could do would be to leave . . . to get home at a decent hour."

"It's only ten o'clock." Chris spun a chair around and straddled it, resting his arms on the back. "Mrs. Miller, the town gossip, saw me at Henry Ann's with Opal Hastings and her little girl. I doubt that her dress-tail touched her behind before she told you. For once the old biddy didn't lie. That's the reason you two waited up for me. It's the reason why you're as mad as a couple of hornets. So get whatever you want to say, said. I'm going to bed."

"How . . . could you? You've shamed us as this family has never been shamed before."

Chris snorted.

Mrs. Austin's eyes filled with tears, and her lips trembled in a way that had always before been effective in getting her menfolk to do as she wanted.

"It'll be all over town, all over the county, that you've . . . you've been seen with that hussy and her bastard. We didn't raise you to chum up with . . . trash!"

"How do you know that she's trash?" Chris felt a burst of anger, but kept his voice calm. "You're taking the word of that old gossip, Mrs. Miller."

"Don't blame Mrs. Miller for seeing what's plain as the nose on your face. That girl had a little bastard, didn't she? She's not married, is she? How much plainer can it be?"

"Did you ever stop to think that maybe Opal had been raped?"

"Ha! Is that her story? Raped! I've never heard of a whore being raped. Don't you dare leave when I'm talking to you," she said angrily when Chris got to his feet. "I had such high hopes for you. There are plenty of *decent* girls you could have had."

Chris looked at his father. He was staring down at his half-empty coffee cup. *No help there.*

"Since I was in high school you've done everything you could to force me on Henry Ann. You could never understand that we were *friends* and nothing more."

"There is no such thing as *friends* between a healthy male and a young female."

"Godamighty!"

"Don't you swear in my house!"

"That's just it, Mama. It's always been *your* house, not *our* house." Chris threw up his hands. Tonight he was seeing his mother as he'd not seen her before. He had always known that she was overbearing and manipulative, but now he realized that she was also mean.

"I'll admit that I was wrong about Henry Ann. She's Dorene Perry's daughter after all. She would've never been allowed to carry on with a *married* man if Ed Henry had lived. Breaking up that poor woman's home with her sick in bed is a shame, is what it is."

"What in the world are you talking about?" Chris demanded, his hands going to the back of the chair. He leaned over the table to glare at his mother's angry face.

"You know perfectly well what I'm talking about. She's had Tom Dolan's boy living with her for over a month now. Everyone knows he slips over there at night and . . . makes himself at home."

"Tom Dolan goes to see his boy. Mrs. Dolan is too ill to take care of him. Instead of praising Henry Ann for doing a good neighborly deed, you accuse her of having an affair with a married man."

"That isn't all. Your daddy said someone's been in that old shed at the end of the woods. He found a pair of women's drawers there. It's a handy place for Henry Ann to meet her lover," Mrs. Austin said spitefully. "Wait until the church folks hear that Karen has been a party to what's going on over there."

"And what else is going on?" Chris asked calmly.

"That brother of Henry Ann's isn't worth shooting. I never saw a half-breed that was. Pete Perry hangs around over there, and everyone knows what he is. She took in a hobo off the road, didn't she? What for, pray tell? I offered to send you over to help her. And I declare. I never thought a Henry would sink so low as to take a colored in and treat her like a member of the family. How could you sit there on the porch and eat with a darkie?"

"It was easy, if you must know." Chris glanced at his father who sat with his head bowed, then back to his mother. "So *you* offered to send me over to help Henry Ann. That was generous of you, Mama. How do you feel about this, Daddy?"

"I've . . . not given it much thought, son." Mr. Austin looked pained.

"I'll never forgive Henry Ann for ruining your reputation by inviting you to her home with that woman there and not explaining to Mrs. Miller that . . . that it was an accidental meeting."

"Why should she do that? It wasn't an accidental meeting. She invited me to come for ice cream, and I took Opal with me. She wasn't obliged to tell that old busybody anything."

"You . . . took her in *our* car!" His mother gasped and looked as if she would swoon.

"Yes, Mama. It may shock you to know that I consider that car as much mine as yours and Daddy's. The money to buy it came from this farm. I've worked my butt off here since I was big enough to walk behind a plow."

"You were fed and clothed and—"

"It's a waste of time to argue with you. You've made up your mind about Henry Ann as well as about Opal, and there's nothing I can do to change it. I'm going to bed."

As Chris left the room, his mother broke into a storm of weeping.

On Mud Creek, Pete Perry sat at the kitchen table and sipped whiskey from a fruit jar. His eyes were swollen and ringed with dark bruises. The cut on his cheekbone had stopped bleeding. Hardy had pulled it together and held it there with a strip of sticky tape.

"Feller musta been some fighter," Hardy remarked.

"It wasn't fair. That old road bum wore leather gloves."

Isabel sat at the table restringing the glass beads she had taken from Henry Ann's room.

"Shut up harpin' 'bout it not bein' fair," Pete snapped. "It was fair. I got whopped, and I ain't denyin' it."

"But he wore . . . gloves."

"I could've wore gloves. Didn't have any." He flexed the fingers on his right hand. "I'm gonna get some."

"Will we still dance at the marathon?" Isabel asked timidly.

"Use your brains. Of course we'll dance at the marathon."

"Ain't no reason to snap at the girl," Hardy growled, and sprinkled loose tobacco into a cigarette paper. Then to Isabel, "Hand me that box of matches, honey."

Pete snorted with disgust. "Honey! You got the hots for her, Hardy? Ain't she a mite young even for you?"

"Yore ma was fourteen when she had you, and I wasn't the first to get to her. Issy, here, is a mite older'n that."

"Yeah? How old was Jude's ma?"

"Don't likely remember. Som'er's around there."

"You like that tender stuff, don't you, Hardy?" Pete asked nastily.

Hardy knew that his son was in a fighting mood. His pride was hurt when he was whipped in front of Henry Ann, yet he was man enough to admit that it had been a fair fight. Hardy knew when to hold on to his temper. He did that now.

"Issy says that Opal and her kid were at the Henrys' with Austin."

"Yeah? What about it?"

"Ain't he gettin' in yore henhouse, boy?"

"It botherin' you that Opal's got a feller?"

"I don't give a shit if she's got a hundred fellers!" Hardy's control snapped, and he shouted so loudly the dogs began to bark. "She ain't the only willin' woman on Mud Creek."

"She ain't willin'! Damn you to hell! I been tellin' ya that!" Pete shouted back then winced as it hurt his jaw to open his mouth so wide. "Stay away from her."

"What the hell's the matter with ya, boy? Ya ain't got a rope on ever' woman in the county jist cause most of them is willin' to spread for ya."

"I ain't got a rope on *ever'* woman, just a few. But them that's mine is mine, old man. You can have Issy after the marathon."

"Ain't I gonna have no say in that?" Isabel blurted. The men ignored her.

"Cousin Wally come on to a pretty woman along that creek that runs by the Henry place." Hardy spoke after a small silence. "She was sitting on a quilt a combin' her hair. He said she was right friendly."

"That'd be Tom Dolan's wife. She's pretty but somethin's screwed up in her head. She's got a loose spring. I ain't never seen a woman who wanted a man so bad 'cept maybe for a whore who needed to pay the rent."

"Cousin Wally wouldn't care if somethin' was wrong with her head as long as the other end was in working order."

The screen door opened, and Jude came in. For a moment he stood looking at them.

"Where've you been?" Hardy growled.

"Well, let's see. The governor invited me to a party. Didn't see you there, Brother. You must'a been busy somewhere else from the looks of your ugly mug. Did you finally meet up with somebody you couldn't bully?"

"What do you care?"

"I don't. Just wish I'd been there to see you get busted in the mouth."

"Yore smart mouth is goin' to get yore jaws slapped," Pete threatened.

"Yeah? Well, it's happened before." Jude picked up a knife and cut himself off a hunk of meat from the pan on the stove. "All we ever have anymore is beef. Why don't we have potatoes and bread and garden stuff?"

"Potatoes are in the cellar. Cook up a mess anytimes ya want." Hardy said.

"Why don't you make *Miss Issy Belle* cook?" Jude pointed the knife at Isabel as he chewed. She stuck her tongue out at him. "She ought to be good for something beside dancing and whoring."

"Watch your mouth, boy," Hardy snarled.

"And I'm getting tired sleeping on the porch. I want my bed back. Let her sleep with Pete. It's what she come here for," he said, ignoring his father's warning.

"You'll get yore bed back as soon as she and Pete go to the marathon."

"When's that going to be?"

"Another week, Mr. Smarty," Isabel said. "T'll be glad to see the last of you. You ain't nothin' but a wet-eared kid."

"So you're not coming back here? That's the best news I've heard since Hardy broke the spring on the Victrola. What'er you going to do? Set up your own house with a red light out front? You'll starve. Who'd want to hump your skinny bones?"

"Enough!" Hardy shouted so loud that Isabel winced. "You show a little respect. Hear?"

"Respect?" Jude stuck the knife back in the hunk of meat in the pan, put his hands on his hips and glared at the older man.

"Ya heard me!"

"Are you plannin' on makin' that little twister my new stepmama, Hardy? Huh? Huh?"

There was no answer, and Jude stomped out.

Chapter Nineteen

The rain had given new life to the pastures as well as the cotton patch, and the creek flowed with water as red as its clay banks.

Red Rock was preparing for the Fourth of July Celebration and the beginning of the dance marathon. Those with radios were listening for news and rejoicing that Franklin Roosevelt would be the man to run against Hoover. Although most Oklahomans didn't understand the "New Deal," they were looking to Roosevelt with hope.

Johnny had taken Henry Ann to town in the middle of the week. She had planned to see Mr. Phillips, the attorney, and find out if he had heard from Isabel's lawyer. A sign on his door stated that he would be out of town until after the Fourth of July. She had also intended to visit Karen, but she and her father had gone to Ardmore.

In the grocery store she had come face-to-face with Myrtle Overton who had given her only a grunt of a greeting before brushing past. Mr. Anderson welcomed her as usual, and she forgot the woman's snub until she and Johnny stopped at the ice dock and met Mr. and Mrs. Potter. The couple had for years owned the Five and Dime and employed Henry Ann on Saturdays during her high-school years. Mrs. Potter passed the car without as much as a nod when Henry Ann called out to her.

The rudeness hurt, and it told her that Mrs. Miller had been busy spreading her embellished tales about what she had witnessed last Sunday afternoon. On the way home Johnny surprised her by saying:

"Don't let the old hens bother you, Sis."

"Mrs. Miller has done a good job in a short time. Do they think that because I'm keeping Jay that—that Tom and I—"

"Yeah, but what do you care what they think?"

"I care, Johnny. I've known most of these people all my life."

It was haying time at the Henry farm. With only sixty acres to harvest it was no more than a two-man job. As Johnny cut, Grant raked, then both men forked the grass onto the wagon to be taken to the barn. Working in the sun had bleached Grant's blond hair and tanned his skin until he was almost as dark as Johnny. He had not said any more about settling down here and had not mentioned Karen's name since the night he took her home.

Henry Ann and Aunt Dozie made watermelon pickles and canned tomatoes and the last of the peaches. During this time several transients came by the house and asked for food. They were always fed out in the yard, and most of them offered to do some kind of work in return. Henry

Ann usually allowed them to draw water from the well and fill the stock tanks.

Henry Ann was pushing Jay in the swing that hung from the pecan tree one afternoon when a fancy, black, one-seater car passed by. It was covered with a thin coat of red dust and stirred up more dust as it raced down the road. Henry Ann had not seen a car in the area like that one and wondered if it was going to Tom's or to the Austins'.

At the moment the car passed the Henry farm, Tom was crossing the field with Emmajean's hand firmly in his. He had let her stay in her "playhouse," until he finished the outdoor chores and dug a row of potatoes. After boiling some of them and making a pan of corn bread, he went to bring her home and to coax her to eat. She was terribly thin. Her cheek- and jawbones were prominent, and her eyes appeared large and sunken. He planned to take her to town to see Doctor Hendricks if she was in a docile mood.

They were coming into the yard behind the house when the car turned in and stopped beside the well. Marty Conroy got out and waited for them to come to him. Instead, Tom headed for the porch and gently pushed Emmajean into a chair.

"Who is it?" she demanded shrilly. "Am I going in the car? What's his name?" She jumped up. "I'll put on my pink dress."

"Wait a minute." Tom took her arm and seated her again.

Marty came to the steps leading to the porch. He took off his hat and wiped his face with a white handkerchief.

"Hello, Emmajean, Tom. Christ, but it's hot up here."

"My name's Emmajean. What's yours?"

Startled, Marty frowned first at his sister and then at Tom.

"My name's Emmajean," she repeated. "What's yours? Want me to take off my dress?"

"No," Marty said quickly. Then under his breath, "What the hell—!"

"Are you going to take me in the car? I'll take off my dress." Emmajean reached out and tried to take Marty's hand, but he backed away.

"Emmajean, I'm Marty, your brother."

"That's nice." She jumped to her feet before Tom could press her down and reached for the hem of her dress. She had pulled it up to her thighs before he stopped her.

"Don't do it now," Tom said gently. "You can take it off later."

"When?"

"Later. After you eat."

"I don't wanna eat."

Before Tom could grab her, she jumped off the porch and went running toward the car. He ran after her and caught her hand as she was opening the car door.

"You can't go anywhere until you eat."

"Get away! Get away!" she shrieked, and tried to pull away from him. Failing that, she spit at him. As he pulled her along with him toward the porch, she continued to shriek, calling him every foul name she had ever heard. At the steps, he took hold of her shoulders and gently shook her.

"Emmajean. Emmajean." He kept repeating her name until she looked at him. "Go in the house and wash your face. Put on your pink dress and make yourself pretty. Tie a ribbon in your hair."

"Tie a ribbon?"

"Yes. Make yourself real pretty."

"All right." She smiled at him, then smiled at Marty when she stepped up onto the porch. "I'm going to a party."

"Good grief," Marty said, when his sister had gone into the house. "How long has she been like this?"

"This is the best day she's had in weeks," Tom said drily. "She's been getting steadily worse since the day at the air show."

"Does she ever make sense?"

"Not for the past week or two. I was hoping to take her in to see Doctor Hendricks today. I can't keep her here much longer. Tell Emmajean's daddy that he should come see her. I won't attempt to take her down to Conroy by myself. She might jump out of the car."

Marty's thoughts raced. *Was it possible that Tom hadn't heard that their daddy was dead?*

"You want . . . Daddy to come here?"

"As soon as possible."

"Why do you want him to see her?"

"For Christ's sake! Isn't it obvious?" Tom retorted heatedly. "She's got to be put someplace where she's not a danger to herself or to anyone else. I have to watch her constantly. The neighbors helped me with my crop, they're looking after my livestock and my son. I can't continue to impose on them while I watch over Emmajean. Her family should take some responsibility. They knew that she was unstable when they married her off to me."

"I'll . . . tell him." Marty looked away from him. "Where do you want to put her?"

"I'll talk to Doctor Hendricks. It'll have to be a state institution. I can't afford a private one. If he can't get her in some place soon, he may have some pills or something that will calm her down and make her eat. She's starving herself."

"Where's the boy?"

"With friends. Why?"

"Did she get worse after you took the boy away from her?"

"She almost killed him." Tom said irritably. "I had to get him away from her. She asked about him only one time. She has no motherly instincts. Never has had. She hates him."

"I'll talk to . . . Daddy. He and Mother talked about taking the boy—"

"Get that idea out of your head," Tom said quickly. "He's my son. He stays with me."

"I'll talk to . . . I'll see what I can do. Don't do anything until you hear from me."

"I'll wait a few days and that's all."

"I see your problem, Tom. You'll be hearing from me."

Marty could hardly wait to leave so that he could think. He backed up the car and took off down the road in a cloud of dust.

"Goddamn!" he cursed, and pounded the steering wheel with his fist.

He'd not stand by and see two thousand five hundred dollars a year being wasted on that lunatic. She'd never had enough brains to pound sand down a rathole, and now she was plain *crazy!*

Godamighty!

Suddenly he began to laugh at the thought of Tom bringing her to Conroy and dumping her off. *Dear Mother would faint dead away if she saw her.* If so much money wasn't at stake, he would have encouraged him to do it just to see the look on his mother's face.

Marty slowed the car. He had to do some careful thinking about what was the best to do. It wouldn't do to have Emmajean commited to a state hospital unless it was far away. One or two of the trustees had connections in Oklahoma. How could he explain that he hadn't told his sister or her husband about his daddy's death and about the will?

Right now he could deny that he had been to the farm and swear that he hadn't known his sister was in such bad shape. Hell, it would be his word against Tom's, and who would believe him over a Conroy?

He had been shocked to see Emmajean. She was the picture of a woman who was starving to death. If he could put Tom off for a few weeks, maybe the bitch would die and solve all his problems. It wasn't fair that the money that should come to him would go to pay for the keep of that crazy woman.

Marty turned off before he reached Red Rock and headed home to Conroy. Evidently word had not reached this part of the country about his daddy's being gone and his being the Conroy now. Marty thought that he'd just as soon keep it that way for the time being. He'd wanted to stop at Walter Harrison's office, show off his new automobile, and let him know that he no longer had to work.

"Bastard," Marty gritted. Harrison had lorded it over him for weeks. There was plenty of time to put Harrison in his place. He had more important things to think about at the present—like two thousand five hundred dollars a year.

Tom sat on the back steps and watched the sun disappear in the western sky. He thought about how Marty had refused to look at him when he promised to take the message to Mr. Conroy about Emmajean's condition. The little weasel would probably take off for Dallas or Oklahoma City in his fancy new car and never deliver the message.

What had started out to be one of Emmajean's best days had turned out to be one of the worst. He had hoped that when she went into the house, she would forget about Marty's being there. Not so.

She had come out, however, as Marty was backing out of the yard and had tried to run after him. Tom had to hold her by force and carry her kicking and screaming back into the house. She fought until her strength gave out. Exhausted, she lay on the bed and cried herself to sleep. When reasonably sure that he could safely leave her, Tom had crossed the field to where Johnny and Grant were cutting hay and had asked if one of them would take a message to Doctor Hendricks.

Johnny had gone immediately and returned with the message that Doctor Hendricks had taken a patient to the hospital in Wichita Falls and wouldn't be back until late. His wife had sent word that he would come out in the morning.

Deep in his thoughts, Tom failed to notice the horse and rider coming down the fence line from the direction of the Henry farm until they were quite near. He recognized Johnny's pony. Perched in front of Johnny was his son, Jay. A pleased smile spread across Tom's face as he hurried out to meet them.

"Daddy! Daddy! Looky me. I ridin'."

"You sure are." Tom took his son from the saddle and held him tightly in his arms. Jay wound his arms about his father's neck and clung. "I've missed you, boy."

"I Daddy's big boy."

"You sure are," Tom said again. It seemed to be all he could say.

"Henry Ann told me to bring him over. It's been a while since he's seen you."

"Five days. I count every hour of them."

"Aunt Dozie sent you a jar of dumplings and some fried peach pies." Johnny stepped down and unhooked a sack from the saddle horn.

"Bless Aunt Dozie."

"Henry Ann made me wait till it cooled down some before I brought him over." Johnny hung the sack over a fence post.

Tom sat on a stump with Jay on his lap.

"Johnny make me a swing."

"Do you swing high?"

"Johnny swing me high. Hen-Ann 'fraid I fall. But I won't fall. I big."

"You'll hold on tight when you swing, won't you?"

"Johnny say, hold tight, cowboy." Jay giggled and pointed his chubby finger at Johnny.

"What else have you been doing?"

The child tilted his head and tightened his lips as he thought. Then he blurted: "I break beans with Aunt Dozie."

"You're learning how to do a lot of things."

"I big boy."

The time passed swiftly and when it was time to go, Tom placed Jay in front of Johnny on the horse.

" 'Bye, son. I'll be over to see you soon. Thank you for bringing him over, Johnny."

"Yeah. We been riding around the yard a little. Henry Ann knew that you'd want to see him." Johnny's dark eyes noticed Tom's alert expression when Henry Ann's name was mentioned. Both he and Grant had noticed that when Tom came to the farm he watched her every move. *The man was crazy in love with her.* What a mess for a decent guy like Tom to be in.

"Be good, Jay. Mind Henry Ann."

"I love Hen-Ann."

So do I, son. So do I.

"I'm glad. I'll be over to see you soon."

As he watched his son leave the home that was no longer safe for him, Tom's dark eyes were unnaturally bright.

Doctor Hendricks came as Tom was staking his cow out alongside the road in front of the house so that she could crop the grass. He had no more than got out of the car when Emmajean bounced up off the chair on the porch where Tom had placed her and ran toward him.

"Hello, man. What's your name? Do you want me to take off my dress?"

Tom reached her and placed his hand on her shoulder. He had made sure that she was dressed this morning, but she had refused, like a balky child, to wash her face, which she smeared with another application of rouge and lipstick.

"Morning, Doc. Thank you for coming."

Doc nodded. Then turned his attention to Emmajean. "How are you, Mrs. Dolan?"

"Want to see my titties?" Tom stilled her hands when she started to open the bodice of her dress.

"No, Emmajean. Don't do that."

"Want to see my titties?" she asked again.

"Later. You can show them later."

"I'm goin' to a party!" She swung. Her fist landed on Tom cheek.

"Cut it out," he said gently, and grabbed her wrist. "Let's go to the porch and sit down."

"No!"

"Go on, Doc. She'll come."

Doctor Hendricks went to the porch and Emmajean followed. He sat down in a chair. She tried to sit on his lap, but he gently maneuvered her into a chair.

"Can we talk, Tom?"

"She's getting steadily worse, Doc. This morning she didn't know her name. I think that whatever we say will go right over her head. I need advice, Doc. And . . . help."

"I've not been trained to treat dementia."

"What the hell is that?"

"A sick mind."

"But you know enough to know that . . . there's a problem here."

"Absolutely. Is her behavior erratic?"

"If you mean, does it change in an instant, yes. I never know what to expect."

"Want me to take off my dress?" Emmajean was stroking the doctor's knee.

"No, not now." He patted her hand, then held it in his.

"She ran off the night of the rain. I had to call on Johnny Henry and the Henrys' hired man to help me find her. Johnny found her in a shed over in the Austins' woods. She'd been with a man. She had bruises on her face and blood on her thighs."

"She'd been raped?"

"I don't think it was rape, Doc. She'd . . . do it with anyone at anytime. If I find out who took advantage of her, it will be hard for me not to kill him."

"Want to see my titties? Want to see my titties? Want me to take off my—"

"No, not now." Doctor Hendricks took her hand in both of his.

"Was this the first time?"

"I've no way of knowing, Doc."

"Could she be pregnant?"

"She's not been sick in the morning as she was with Jay. But I've not noticed evidence of a monthly flow lately. Christ! I've not thought of that. She has never been very discreet and left the cloths she used at that time lying around until I made her pick them up and wash them."

"It wouldn't be unusual for her flow to stop, as rundown as she is. She's lost a lot of weight since I saw her last."

"I have a hard time getting her to eat."

"Commitment to the state hospital for the insane, if that is what you decide to do, will require having a judge of the probate court pass on her mental state. An affidavit charging lunacy would then be filed with the clerk of the court, and she would be taken by the sheriff and placed in custody so that one or more physicians could examine her. The judge would then listen to testimony of witnesses. If she is judged insane, it would be out of your hands and she would be committed."

"I don't want to do that unless I have no other choice. I've heard that they just lock them up and forget them."

"I agree that they are awful, but necessary, places. It isn't a place to send someone to get well."

"Her brother was here yesterday. He's taking word back

to her folks. In the meanwhile is there anything—No, Emmajean. Don't do that." Emmajean had pulled her hand from the doctor's and had thrust it up under her dress and between her legs.

"Don't be embarrassed, Tom. She doesn't realize what she's doing. A person of unsound mind will sometimes show strong sexual tendencies"

"It seems to be what's on her mind . . . most of the time."

"You were going to ask if I could give her something to calm her down. I'm not qualified to prescribe for her, Tom. In a hospital, they would know what to do. The best you can do now is to fix a place to put her, so that you can get some rest. You look exhausted."

"I thought of locking her in her room. But it would be hot, and she could crawl out a window if I raised one."

"Cover the windows and the door with chicken wire. You can see in, but she can't get out. It would serve for a few days until you decide what to do. I'm sorry I can't do more to help you, Tom. If you decide on the state asylum, let me know, and I'll help you arrange it."

"I'll wait on that until I hear from her folks. I want them to come and see her. After all she's their only daughter, and they can afford to put her in a private sanitarium."

The doctor stepped off the porch and headed for the car. Emmajean clung to his arm. Tom braced himself for the scene when the doctor left. When they reached the car, Doctor Hendricks reached inside and brought out a red candy sucker.

"This is for being a good girl, Emmajean." He spoke as if he were talking to a child. "Go sit on the porch. I'll come back and see you in a few days."

Emmajean took the candy, looked at it, and threw it in the dirt. She screamed an obscenity and hit him. Then she darted past Tom and tried to get in the car. He grabbed her about the waist and lifted her off the running board.

"Sorry, Doc."

Tom carried her kicking and screaming to the house. When he looked back, Doctor Hendricks was backing out of the yard. In her room, he dropped Emmajean on the bed. To his surprise she stayed there. He waited to see if the tantrum was over, then went to the kitchen and splashed water on his face in an attempt to suppress his frustration.

Tom doubted now that Marty would take his message to Mr. Conroy, and unless he was able to get to a telephone and call the man, there would be no help there. He was also disappointed that Doctor Hendricks was unable to per-scribe a medication to calm Emmajean. His head ached with the need to sleep, and his heart ached with the burden of loving a woman he couldn't have.

During the day Emmajean went into another stage of strange behavior. She sank into a deep depression and be-came so docile that she ate when Tom told her to eat, she sat when he told her to sit, and washed her face and hands when he told her to. She uttered not a single word. It was such a drastic change that it was scary.

Tom took her with him when he did chores, pushing her down to sit on a box where he could see her. She sat there until he finished, then followed him back to the house.

This behavior, although it allowed him more freedom, was almost as frightening as the hyperactive, erotic way she had been for weeks. Then, he had known what to expect.

She sat on the porch until dark saying nothing. When it was time to go to bed, she pulled off her dress and slipped a nightdress over her head.

"Do you want a drink of water, Emmajean?"

When he received no answer, he urged her down on the side of the bed and went to the kitchen for a dipper of water. She was still sitting there when he returned and drank when he told her to drink. When she lay down and tucked her pressed palms under her cheek, Tom looked down at her. She looked like a helpless child. He felt deep sympathy for this disturbed young woman whose family despised her for reasons that were no fault of hers.

Indulging in his favorite pastime of dreaming about the brief moments when he had held Henry Ann in his arms, Tom lay on his bunk in the kitchen. Time had gone fast. It was the middle of summer, and tomorrow was the Fourth of July. It would be no holiday for him. If Emmajean were still in this mode of behavior, he might be able to do the washing.

Long ago he had hidden the knives and anything else that he thought she could use as a weapon. Nevertheless, he had not been able to do more than catnap. Tonight, for the first time in weeks, Tom had a good night's sleep, although he awakened periodically to go to Emmajean's room to be sure that she was still in bed.

Chapter Twenty

Henry Ann had not missed going to town on the Fourth of July since she had scarlet fever when she was eight years old. She debated with herself about going this year, fearing she might be snubbed as she had been the day she went to town with Johnny. She talked it over with Aunt Dozie.

"Yo go and hold up yo head. Yo ain't done nothin' fer them folk to high-hat yo over."

Oh, but I have, Aunt Dozie! But knowing that Tom loves me is worth the snubs of everyone in the whole state of Oklahoma.

The festivities began with a group of war veterans marching down the street followed by the high-school band and a few cars carrying the banners of political candidates. There were vendors with pushcarts selling hot tamales wrapped in corn shucks and others selling crushed ice flavored with thick sweet syrup in paper cones. Popcorn and hot peanuts in the shell were sold along the street, as were colorful balloons tied with a string.

A high-striker machine was set up, and the barker challenged the young men to show off their muscles and win prizes by hitting the base with a mallet hard enough to make the bell ring at the top. A shell game, a penny pitch, a baseball throw, and other games lined the street. A small, six-horse merry-go-round was set up in the middle of the unpaved intersection, its music blaring. The crowd wandered along the street while they waited for the big attraction of the day, the start of the dance marathon.

In other years Henry Ann and Karen had been in charge of the church sale of crafts produced by the ladies and some of the men members, but this year Henry Ann had declined early in the spring; and now, as she came into town with Johnny, Grant, and Jay, she was glad. They had left Aunt Dozie at her church so that she could participate with the other members of the congregation in the "dinner-on-the-ground" and visit with her relatives.

They could see the striped tent over the dance platform as they drove down a rutted side lane. Johnny parked the car under a leafy tree on the street near the church. At the side, shaded by the church building, the tables holding crafts for sale and a lemonade stand had been set up. Karen came out from behind the makeshift counter when Henry Ann, with Jay's hand clasped in hers, approached.

"I wondered if you'd come today." Her eyes darted past Henry Ann to where Johnny and Grant leaned against the car, then back. She lifted Jay's face with a finger beneath his chin. "Hello, Jay."

"I almost didn't."

"You've heard. Oh, Henry, it's so unfair. That old biddy! I've told everyone I could that what she's spreading around isn't true. But some people want to believe it."

"What's she spreading around?"

"Well . . . that . . . you're having an affair with . . . you know who."

"Is that all?"

"No, she blames you for leading Chris astray and arranging for him to be with Opal."

"Oh, my goodness."

"That's not all." Karen giggled.

"Not all? What else could there be?"

"She's blaming you for *my* downfall."

"When did you . . . *fall*?" Henry Ann's grin was forced.

Jay's hand was pulled from Henry Ann's. She looked around to see that Grant had removed his battered Stetson and was lifting him to his shoulder to sit astride his neck.

"Hello, Karen."

"Hello."

Henry Ann saw the flush rise on her friend's cheeks and noted the way her eyes clung to Grant's face.

"Johnny and I will take Jay for a while so you ladies can visit. We'll be back in time to walk down to see the start of the marathon. Can you go with us, Karen?"

"I think so. I agreed to be here only for an hour, and the time is about up."

A minute or two passed before the girls spoke. Their eyes had followed Grant, with Jay perched on his shoulder and Johnny sauntering along beside him, until they turned the corner and were out of sight.

Two women came down the walk and stopped to look over the crafts on the tables.

"Hello, ladies," Karen greeted them cheerfully. "Can I sell you something?"

"I don't think so."

The one who spoke wore her hair in scallops held in place with long bobby pins on each side of her face and drawn in a small bun on the back of her neck. She kept her gaze turned from Henry Ann, who had known the woman for most of her life.

Henry Ann squared her shoulders defensively. She was being snubbed and decided to force the woman to face her to do it.

"Hello, Mrs. Oden. How's Marie? I haven't seen her since she moved to Duncan."

"She's all right." Mrs. Oden spoke without turning and with a hand in the back of her companion urged her out toward the street.

Anger and resentment forced Henry Ann to ask about Mrs. Oden's son, who was in jail in Ardmore for stealing gasoline.

"And how is Melvin? I've not seen him for a while." When she received no answer, she said, "Well, 'bye. Tell Marie I said hello, and Melvin, too—when he gets out."

Henry Ann was too angry to cry.

"Narrow-minded old biddy! She can snub me because she *thinks* I'm a homebreaker when her own son is in jail for stealing!"

"Good for you. I'm glad you asked about Melvin; he's a warthog."

"Did anyone say anything to your daddy about you being out at my place last Sunday?"

"Oh, yes! Mrs. Miller told him about Tom being there when his poor wife was sick at home, and about Chris being with Opal, and how poor Mrs. Austin was heartsick over her son being seen with a woman of ill repute. She hinted that I was too innocent to know what was going on between you and Tom out at that *indecent* place. She also told him that since your daddy died you had lost your reason and were taking vagrants in off the road."

"My goodness! What did he say to all of that?"

"Nothing. He knows Mrs. Miller. He met Grant . . . and he liked him." Karen's eyes danced. "He told me to ask him to come to supper sometime this week."

"You mean it?"

"Sure. Daddy's a good judge of character. He likes Tom, too." Karen's smile widened. "Even if he is a Catholic."

The woman who was to relieve Karen arrived, freeing her to leave with Henry Ann. The two girls walked down the street toward the high-striker, where Grant was paying the operator. Johnny sat on the running board of a nearby car. Jay was standing between his knees eating an ice-cream cone.

"Look at Jay." A slow smile started in Henry Ann's eyes. "He's got ice cream all down the front of his clean coveralls. Isn't Johnny sweet? Would you ever have believed—" She stopped speaking when she realized that Karen's attention was focused on Grant, who had swung the mallet. The ring went up to within a foot of the top.

"I don't hear any bells ringing," Karen called out just as Grant swung the mallet again.

BING!

"What was that you were saying?" Grant turned, his sun-browned face wreathed in smiles.

"What do you get for a prize, Mr. Muscle-man?"

"Do you want it?" Grant asked, and walked over to choose the *prize* from a selection offered by the operator.

"Sure."

"Do you promise to keep it forever and ever?" Grant turned with his hand behind his back.

"Not if it's edible."

"This would be a little hard to digest." Over her head he looped a silver cord with a little glass heart attached. "That's a special prize. I had to ring the bell four times to get it. I could have had four cigars."

"Oh, my. What a sacrifice." Karen's voice had a nervous quiver.

The loud bang of fireworks exploding announced the start of the ceremony preceding the marathon. Henry Ann wiped Jay's face and hands with her handkerchief and let him walk ahead of her and Johnny as they followed the crowd along the street toward the striped tent. Grant and Karen walked behind them.

They stopped at the edge of the crowd, a distance from the platform, and listened to the booming voice of the announcer crackling from a loudspeaker.

"La . . . dies and gent . . . le . . . men! The first annual Red Rock marathon is about to begin!" A cheer went up from the crowd.

"The twenty-five couples who registered to enter the marathon will now come to the floor. The last couple to leave the floor will take with them FIVE HUNDRED DOLLARS! Today everyone is welcome. Starting tomorrow, a canvas wall will surround the platform. It will cost you fifteen cents to watch, but, folks, you can come in and stay all day or all night. Now to introduce the contestants."

"Pete's supporters are here," Johnny murmured. "The Perrys are proud of their boy."

"I see his daddy and his young brother. I don't know many of the other Perrys."

"Each of the couples will have an attendant to bring them water or food," the announcer said. "They'll have ten minutes out of every hour to rest or—"

"—or use the outhouse," Johnny murmured. "I see they've set one up."

"How do you know so much about this?"

"Pete's been goin' on about it for months."

"I wonder who'll help them."

"It'll be one of the Perrys. I see Sandy over there. He's a distant cousin. All of Mud Creek is here. You don't see Hardy in town often. Even Fat Perry is here."

"There they are. Oh, goodness. Isabel looks happy as a lark. She doesn't know what she's let herself in for."

Henry Ann realized suddenly that the crowd had closed in behind them when she heard a woman's voice.

"Well, I never! How can she show her face to decent folk? It's a shame is what it is. She's taken over that poor woman's baby and is carryin' on with her husband."

Henry Ann turned and came face to face with Mrs. Austin. Their eyes met in a silent battle. Mr. Austin, standing behind his wife, turned his face away.

"Hello, Mrs. Austin."

"Don't you dare speak to me after what you've done, not only to poor Mrs. Dolan, but for pushing that whore and her bastard off on my son and turning him against me and his daddy! Every decent woman in this town knows that you're a . . . a . . . disgrace!" She raised her hand as if to slap Henry Ann. Mr. Austin grabbed her wrist. She jerked it from his grasp and forced her way back through the crowd.

Henry Ann wished the ground would open up and swallow her. She desperately wanted to cry. Pride helped her to control her emotions. She squared her shoulders and lifted her chin. She dared not look to see if the people around them had been paying sufficient attention to hear what Mrs. Austin had said.

"Do you want to go, Sis?"

"I'd really like to. But I don't want her to think that she ran me off."

"Let the old hag think what she wants. Go on with Jay. I'll tell Grant and Karen to meet us at the car."

With Jay's hand clasped in hers, her head high, Henry Ann walked through the crowd. She looked directly at each person she met, and nodded to those she knew. Several men tipped their hats, but most of the women failed to acknowledge her. Johnny caught up as she reached the almost empty street; and as they walked past the silent merry-go-round, Henry Ann stopped.

"Let's give Jay a ride on the carousel. You'll have to ride with him and hold him on."

"I've ridden only a time or two. One time one of Mama's suitors, wanting to impress her, gave me a nickel to ride. Sucker." Johnny grinned. "Mama didn't even notice."

"I'll pay. Go on and get on. Johnny'll ride with you, Jay. Won't that be fun?"

Johnny set Jay astride the gaily painted wooden horse and stood beside him. The Wurlitzer organ began to play, and the horse moved up and down. Henry Ann waved each time they came around. Seeing the broad smile on the child's face made her forget for a few minutes her heartbreak at the treatment given her by folks she had considered her friends and her despair of ever being with the man she loved.

"Did you like that, punkin'?" Henry Ann took Jay's hand when the ride was over. "Thank the man for the nice long ride."

"I wasn't scared," Jay shouted. "Johnny hold me."

"You're getting to be such a big boy."

"I a big boy," Jay agreed.

"Jay and I will go back to the car, Johnny. Go enjoy yourself. You don't have to go with us."

"Is that right?" Johnny dug in his pocket and came up with a nickel to buy Jay a huge red balloon.

"If you're not careful, I'm going to love you very much."

"Really? No one's every loved me before. How's it supposed to feel?"

The tears that flooded Henry Ann's eyes threatened to spill over and run down her cheeks. Her emotions were already raw, and Johnny's words pushed her over the edge. Embarrassed, she blinked and sniffed.

"Hey, now. Come on. I'm getting a kick out of seeing the little fellow happy."

"Did anyone ever buy you a balloon?"

"Ah . . . once in a while."

"I'll buy you a hot tamale." She smiled through the tears. "We'll take them back to the car."

They passed Mr. Phillips's office. There was still a big CLOSED sign on the corner door. Henry Ann had not heard from the lawyer since their talk about what to do about Isabel's demands. He had said that he would take care of it, and she would just have to trust him to do it.

Later, when Henry Ann and Johnny sat on the running board of the car watching Jay play with the balloon on the long string, Henry Ann saw Karen and Grant walking slowly toward the car.

"Karen is smitten by him," Henry Ann said.

"He likes her, too."

"If he decides to settle here, what'll he do? We'll not need him after the cotton is picked."

"I hope he stays around. I get the feeling that he's not worried about money or what he'll do to make a living. He's a square shooter, Sis. I'd bet my life on it."

"Don't do that, Johnny." Henry Ann gripped his arm. "Don't joke about your life. I don't know what I'd do without you."

Karen was bubbling, and Grant's blue eyes danced when he looked at her. It was crystal clear to Henry Ann that they were in love. She tried to be happy for her friend and not be envious of her freedom to be with her man.

"Guess who we saw," Karen said as they approached. "Chris, with a huge smile on his face, watching Opal and Rosemary going around and around on the merry-go-round."

"I'm proud of Chris," Henry Ann said. "It's hard for him to go against his folks. I hope he and Opal don't run into Mrs. Austin. She'll be sure to ruin the day for them."

"Have you seen her?"

"Oh, yes," Johnny answered. "If she'd been a man, I'd've punched her in the nose."

"It's not important," Henry Ann said, hoping to close the subject.

"They've started the dance," Karen announced after a short silence. "Pete and Isabel are couple number six. Pete is showing off. He's really good-looking. It's a pity he has no brains to go with his looks. If he'd not been raised on Mud Creek, he might have amounted to something."

"Good-looking?" Grant snorted. "I wish I'd known you thought that. I'd have rearranged his features when I had the chance."

"Don't worry," Karen said soothingly, and placed her hand on his arm. "I'll arrange for you to have another chance."

"Don't bother." Grant's hand covered Karen's.

The music that blared loudly on this first day of the marathon was suddenly quiet. A minute passed before anyone noticed. Then the booming voice of the announcer was heard.

"Keep dancing! Keep dancing, or you'll be disqualified. We have a problem here. The sheriff says that one of the contestants is under age and lied on the entry form. Couple number six has been disqualified." Angry shouts of disapproval followed the announcement.

"That's Pete and Isabel," Karen exclaimed.

"Well, for goodness sake! It serves her right. She thinks she's so darned smart!" Henry Ann instantly regretted her petty remark.

"Pete will be madder than a stepped-on copperhead." This from Johnny. "He's been counting on this to raise his stock in town. He thought people would look up to him if he won."

"Seems to me that honest work and being decent to folks would have done more toward earning respect than winning a dance marathon," Karen said.

A while later a car with a gold star on the side came down main street, weaving between the stands. It turned and stopped alongside the Henry car. Isabel sat between the sheriff and Mr. Phillips. The lawyer got out.

"Ladies," he said, and tipped his ancient Stetson. "Talk to you for a minute, Henry Ann?"

"You can talk in front of my brother and my friends, Mr. Phillips. They know about my problems with Isabel."

"I've arranged for the girl to be a ward of the state. The sheriff will take her back to Oklahoma City where they'll keep her until she comes of age unless you, as her closest known relative, will take her in and be responsible for her."

"I can't do that, Mr. Phillips." Henry Ann shook her head. "I tried being kind to her, and I tried being firm. She'll not put forth any effort to get along and says that she'll not go to school."

"Then she'll go into a home for wayward girls until she's eighteen. After that, she's on her own."

"Will she have to go to school?"

"Yes, and she'll have to work."

"Johnny, what do you think?"

"I think that if you don't let her go, you'll be sorry within a week. She's trouble."

"Johnny! Johnny!" Isabel called from the car. "Please don't let 'em take me. Johnny, come here. Please, tell them that I'll do what *she* says if they let me stay."

Johnny walked over to the car and leaned down to speak to her.

"You say that now, but you'd do just as you damned please. Just like you did before. You'd head right back to the Perrys. I told you when you came here that you had a good chance to go to school and make something of yourself. You threw it away."

"I'll do what *you* say. Please, Johnny. You're my brother."

"Your half brother. Thank God your pa wasn't mine."

"And I'm glad, you damned red-assed Indian!" Isabel's demeanor changed in an instant and anger made her face ugly. "Why'er ya sidin' with her? I'm as much your sister as she is."

"But you're nothing like her and never will be." Johnny backed away from the car and joined Henry Ann.

"Sit still." The sheriff grabbed Isabel's arm when she would have jumped out to follow Johnny.

"I've calculated that Ed had about six hundred dollars in assets when he died." Mr. Phillips spoke to Henry Ann. "That would be in the livestock. The cotton crop was just breaking the ground, so I didn't figure much of that in. The land and the house being yours, I'd suggest to the probate court that the rest of the assets be divided by three, and get the court to give the girl and the boy here two hundred dollars each. I'll request that I be given the right to hold the girl's money in trust until she's released at age eighteen. Any questions?"

"I'm not taking anything of Ed's," Johnny said quickly "He wasn't my pa."

"In the eyes of the law, he was. The law says you're entitled to a third of what he had when he died."

"I'm not taking anything," Johnny repeated stubbornly.

"You and Henry Ann can hash that out. When the cotton and the cattle are sold, bring in the two hundred dollars for the girl, Henry Ann. I'll hold it for her until she's legal age, and I'll see that she signs a release. You'll be rid of her."

"Thank you, Mr. Phillips." Henry Ann went to the car.

"Good-bye, Isabel. I'm sorry it didn't work out so that you could stay here with me and Johnny."

"Bitch!" Isabel yelled. "Ya want me out of here so ya can have Pete. Ever'body knows yo're screwin' Tom Dolan. Ain't he got enough for ya after he screws that loony wife of his?"

"Hush up," the sheriff growled.

"Pete'll get even with ya for this! Yo're a shitty, son-of-a-bitchin', stuck-up whore—"

"—Shut up that kinda talk." The sheriff had lost his patience. "You're a nasty-mouthed little brat. I'd not want you around either if that's the way you talk."

"Hardy'll get even, too. Pete was countin' on winnin' that money." Isabel insisted on having the last word. "They know yo're messin' with a married man, and they know how to get even with you through Dolan. They'll do it, too."

"Phillips," the sheriff said, "I'll get this nasty-talkin' little brat out of here. I'll have my deputy take her to Ardmore and put her on a train for Oklahoma City. Someone will go along with her to see that she gets there. I'll bring along some paperwork later."

"I had to wait, Sheriff, until she was doin' somethin' that'd hold in court before we could pick her up. Next time you're over this way stop by. My wife'll make us a pee-con pie and we'll chew the fat 'bout old times."

"Old times wasn't bad compared to nowadays." The sheriff tipped his hat to the ladies, and the car moved away.

"Worked out better than I thought. The girl's got a rough road ahead if she doesn't change her ways. At least she'll be in school. Whether she learns anything or not will be up to her." Mr. Phillips spoke to the group in general, then to

Grant. "Are you going to hang around the area for a while, Gifford?"

"I'm planning on it."

That Mr. Phillips knew Grant was a surprise to all of them. It wasn't until the lawyer had left them to walk down the street to his office that Henry Ann mentioned it.

"I didn't know you knew Mr. Phillips, Grant."

"I don't really *know* him. I saw a light in his office the night I brought Karen home and stopped in to asked if it was legal for a fifteen-year-old girl to enter the marathon without permission from a parent or guardian. That's all."

"Why did you do that?" Karen asked.

"The girl's still wet behind the ears. Give her three more years to grow up and she just might turn out all right. Leave her down on Mud Creek with that bunch, and she'd turn out to be just like them. I thought she at least deserved another chance."

"Don't count on her changin' any," Johnny said drily.

"Would you mind taking me and Jay home, Johnny? You can come back and stay as long as you want. I'll do the milking." Henry Ann took several quick steps to rescue Jay's balloon from drifting into a prickly bush.

"I'd like to stay, if it's all right," Grant said.

"Of course it's all right. This is a holiday." Henry Ann helped Jay up into the car. " 'Bye, Karen. See you soon."

As they drove slowly away, Henry Ann looked back to see Grant tuck Karen's hand in the crook of his arm and saw her tilt her face toward his as they walked slowly along the street.

Chapter Twenty-one

Pete Perry was well on his way to getting rip-roaring drunk by the time Hardy stopped the car behind the house on Mud Creek. Sandy Perry, with a carload of kinfolk, came careening into the yard and skidded to a halt beside the front porch. Angry Perrys piled out.

Bootleg whiskey had flowed freely in the alley behind the vacant building that had once housed the Five and Dime after the sheriff had taken Isabel off the dance floor for being under age, and all the Perrys were a little drunk. They had come to Red Rock to see their boy, Pete, take the floor at the dance marathon, had gathered around him to discuss the injustice done to him and Isabel, and had fortified themselves with moonshine whiskey.

Some of Pete's supporters blamed Mr. Phillips for calling the sheriff, and some thought it had been Henry Ann or Johnny. Others were sure it had been one of the contestants who had wanted to get Pete disqualified, thinking that it would give them a better chance to win.

Pete was furious at himself for believing Isabel when she said that her mama had birthed her in a little town outside Oklahoma City, and there was no record of her birth. She said she wasn't certain how old she was and no one really knew now that her mother was dead. When he'd asked if Johnny might remember, she'd said that he hadn't been around much. Dorene had farmed them out with other people most of their lives.

The little twitchy-twat'd had an answer for everything.

What hurt Pete the most was that he'd lost his chance to be "somebody," to be noticed for something other than being one of the notorious Perrys from Mud Creek. And he'd lost more ground with Henry Ann. It galled him that he wanted the respect of Henry Ann Henry more than anything in the world.

Why? Why? Why?

Isabel swore that there was something going on between Dolan and Henry Ann. Pete had kept an eye on the farm after Henry Ann hired the road bum, and he had seen her and Dolan out behind the house one night. He was sure they hadn't *done anything*. If they had, they'd had to do it standing up, he mused drily.

There were ways of getting even with Dolan for honeying up to a decent woman like Henry Ann when he already had a wife. Unlike almost all the women Pete knew, Henry Ann, he was sure, had never been with a man; and it wasn't right that a man like Dolan would ruin her. A load of moonshine stashed in Dolan's barn and a call to that deputy the clan had been paying off would do the trick.

The idea floated around in Pete's mind as the Perrys gathered on Hardy's front porch. The talk began to center on Dolan's woman. Cousin Wally couldn't help but brag that he'd "had some of that."

"She's not right in the head." It surprised the Perrys that Pete even cared. "Hell, Wally, ya must be pretty hard up," he continued angrily.

"Hard up! Hee, hee, hee. Ya made a funny, Pete. Yup, I was hard up! Her name's Emmajean, and I ain't carin' if she's crazy. She wanted it, and I give it to 'er."

"Are the gals down here on Mud Creek turnin' ya down?" Pete asked nastily.

"I seen her a time or two a dancin' in the woods like she didn't have no sense a'tall." Fat Perry broke into the conversation. He was wearing his "go-to-town" overalls, and enjoying being one of the crowd.

From inside the house came the voice of Rudy Vallee singing, *"My time is your time—"*

"Hardy's at it again," Sandy said, coming out to the porch with a jar of whiskey. He poured some of it in Pete's glass. "Guess he figures your girl's old enough, Oscar. Didn't she just turn thirteen?"

"If he's messin' with her, I'll whap his ass." Oscar slid off the porch and headed for the steps.

"He ain't feelin' 'er up," Sandy said hastily. "He's just dancin' with 'er."

"Dancin' with Hardy leads to screwin' with Hardy, and she ain't old enough yet." Oscar stomped into the house. "What'a ya doin' in here, Clella?" he demanded.

"Daddy! Looky! Uncle Hardy's showin' me how to dance."

"That better be all he's showin' ya," Oscar growled.

Imprisoned in his thoughts, Pete scarcely heard the voices of his kinfolk. He had come to realize that Henry

Ann would never see him as anything except Mud Creek trash. He should have known that a long time ago. He had been just too stubborn to admit it.

He'd had a crush on Opal Hastings at one time, only because she was one of the few Mud Creek women who wanted nothing to do with him. At the time, if he'd found out who had raped her, he would have killed him—kin be damned. The crush had worn off, but he still felt kind of protective toward her. Now he was glad that she had Chris Austin to look out for her. Maybe Austin would get some guts and marry her.

There was nothing left now to hang around for. In a matter of minutes, Pete had made up his mind to leave Mud Creek, leave Oklahoma, and head out for California.

But there was something he had to do first.

The day was a long one for Tom. Emmajean remained in a state of disinterest, listless and withdrawn. Although it worried him, he admitted reluctantly that it was a relief to have her sit in a chair and stay there while he went about washing his clothes and hers in the tubs he'd set up under a shade tree, and while he hung them on the line to dry.

By noon he had cleaned the house, killed and dressed a chicken, and cooked it with biscuit dumplings. Emmajean ate when he put the food before her. During the day he heard the fireworks from town and wished that he could be there with Henry Ann and Jay.

He looked down at the wasted shell of a woman sitting on the end of the porch humming softly to herself. The anger and resentment he had felt toward her during the past weeks, months, years vanished and in their place was noth-

ing but pity for her—so young and so lost through no fault
of her own.

In the late afternoon, thinking that perhaps he could
bring her out of her depression, he suggested that they
walk to the creek. Tom took her hand and walked with her
across the field and to the dugout in the clay bank where
she liked to go. The things she had taken there, the comb,
the mirror, the glass beads, a garter, and a small blue bottle of Evening in Paris perfume, were still there. Her trea-
sures were rolled up in the dirty quilt.

She sat down on the blanket and tried to pull Tom down
beside her. When he resisted, she picked up the comb and
combed her hair. Tom watched her closely. It was strange
that she showed no signs of her usual distraught behavior.
She hummed an unfamiliar tune and looked straight
through him as if he weren't there.

As he squatted on his heels beside her, he noticed large
footprints in the loose sand beneath the overhang. The
butts of a dozen or more sloppily rolled cigarettes were
scattered about outside, as if the smoker had flipped them
there. Tom wondered if it was the same man who had been
here before and if he was the one who had been with her in
Austin's shack.

Suddenly, he realized that he shouldn't have come here.
This could be the day that Mr. Conroy would come to see
about his daughter.

"Let's go home, Emmajean."

She rose and obediently followed him back across the
pasture to the house.

Mr. Conroy didn't come. No one came. Several cars
went by, but none stopped. Tom ate the chicken and
dumplings for supper and fixed a plate for Emmajean.

They sat on the porch. When it was dark, Tom took her to the kitchen and washed her face and hands. He led her to the bedroom and pulled the chamber pot out from under the bed. After she used it, he took her soiled underdrawers and handed her a clean pair.

Was this to be his life, tending to this poor mind-sick woman while longing to sneak off across the field to see his love? Suddenly, his yearning for Henry Ann was like a living force. He had only to close his eyes to see her soft brown eyes, her smiling lips, and to feel her fingers caressing his face.

He looked down at the thin figure on the bed. Today she had shown none of the anger she had exhibited for the past year. Except for not saying much or volunteering to do anything for herself, she had been completely agreeable. This morning she had stayed in bed until he took her hand and pulled her to her feet. Would she be all right if he left her for an hour? Or would she get out of bed and wander off?

The temptation to leave her here and hurry across to the Henry farm to see the two people he loved was great. Tom went to the porch, leaned against a post, and looked up at the stars, indecision clouding his mind.

After bringing Henry Ann and Jay home, Johnny refused to return to town, despite Henry Ann's urging.

"Go on back and have a good time, Johnny. It isn't every day that a carnival comes to town."

"There's nothing there for me, Sis. Beside that, I'm not leaving you here alone with Pete on the loose."

"I hadn't thought of that. Why would he come here? I had nothing to do with the sheriff coming for Isabel."

"He doesn't know that."

"He should have known better than to enter that contest with her. I told him that she was only fifteen."

"She must have convinced him that she was older. I think that deep down inside Pete's in love with you."

"What?" Henry Ann couldn't have been more astonished if Johnny had suddenly sprouted a horn in the middle of his forehead. "What?" she said again, then, "That's laughable, Johnny. For years Pete has done everything he could do to annoy me. He tried to lure you away; and when that didn't work after Daddy died, he turned to Isabel."

"Pete seemed to go out of his way to get your attention. I think he preferred that you be mad at him rather than ignore him."

"He got my attention all right. I didn't know that you were such a deep thinker, Johnny."

He grinned. "It didn't take much thinking to figure that out. Pete's a cut above that bunch on Mud Creek, even if he does do stupid things."

"He has a poor way of showing it. Do you think that he's the one who raped Opal?"

"He likes to brag about the women he's had and talk nasty about them, but I don't think he ever raped anyone. He likes to make a woman come to him."

"That's one thing in his favor. "

At sundown, Johnny went back to town to get Aunt Dozie. Henry Ann fixed supper for Jay, thinking that she would wait and eat when Johnny returned. After he ate she gave the child a bath. He'd had an exciting day and was asleep as soon as she put him to bed. She sat beside him for a while, his small hand in hers, knowing that she couldn't love him more if he were her own.

Johnny returned not only with Aunt Dozie, but with Karen and Grant.

"Surprise!" Karen called as soon as she got out of the car. "Daddy didn't want me to bring the car. He may have to use it to go out to the Hudsons. Grandpa Hudson is awful bad. So I'm here to spend the night, and I've brought food."

All through high school and in the years following, neither girl had needed an invitation when she wanted to visit and to stay overnight at the other's home.

"You're the kind of guest I like to have—one who brings food." Being with Karen always lifted Henry Ann's spirits. "Put the basket on the table, Grant. Did you have a good time today, Aunt Dozie?"

"I had me a fine time, and I is wore to a nubbin. I is takin' me off to dat bed."

"Eat supper first, Aunty," Karen urged. "I brought baked ham, sweet potatoes, deviled eggs, and I don't know what all. Daddy's ladies, the ones hoping to catch him"—Karen giggled—"loaded us up with food for the holiday."

"Honey, dis day I done et till I 'bout to pop open. I goin' to go and get off'n' my feet."

"I wonder what Tom had to eat today." Henry Ann and Karen were unloading the food basket. The words came from Henry Ann's mouth as she thought them.

There was such longing in her friend's voice that Karen thought a few seconds before she spoke.

"Why don't we send Grant and Johnny over to see. He could come back and eat supper. That is if . . . well, if he can."

"Oh, no. I couldn't ask them to go over there and—"

"I can. Johnny, Grant," Karen called as she went through the house to the porch.

Henry Ann stroked a strand of hair behind her ear and felt a delirious rush of joy at the prospect of seeing him. In the recesses of her mind she knew that it was dangerous. But the pleasure of seeing him outweighed the misery of not seeing him.

Karen had guessed her secret. Had she discussed it with Grant? How long had it taken them to recognize the signs that had evidently been there for the noticing?

"They'll drive over and see if he can come," Karen said, when she came back to the kitchen. She continued to slice the ham she'd taken from the basket. "I'm hungry for some of Aunt Dozie's beet pickles."

When Johnny turned the car into the yard of the Dolan farm, Tom hopped off the porch and hurried toward them.

"Is something wrong?" he asked before he reached the car.

"Nothing's wrong. Karen and Henry Ann sent us to fetch you over for supper, that is if you can come." Johnny turned off the motor.

"It scared hell out of me when you drove in." Tom wiped his hand across his face, then forked his fingers through his hair.

"They thought you might be able to get away for a while," Grant said.

"I'd like nothing more, but I don't know—"

"I need to put some water in the radiator while you're making up your mind." Johnny climbed over the closed door of the Model T.

"Sure. There's a bucket hanging there by the well. Need a light?"

"I'll leave the car lights on."

"How is Mrs. Dolan?" Grant asked.

"She was just the same until a couple of days ago. Do you know anything about dementia? It's what Doc Hendricks calls what's wrong with Emmajean."

"Not much. Most of the unbalanced people I've run into were in jail. Some were violent and others appeared to be in a deep, trancelike state."

"She seems to go from one to the other. One day she's all wound up and today she's been like she was sleepwalking."

"Have you had the doctor out?"

"A few days ago. He said there wasn't much to be done unless I commit her to an asylum. I've sent word to her folks by that jelly-bean brother of hers. If he kept his word and took my message, they should be here in a day or two."

Johnny filled the radiator and returned the bucket to the well.

"I'll go look in on her," Tom said. "The last couple of nights she's slept like a log."

He lit the lantern he kept on the porch and went into the house. Emmajean lay on her side, her hands beneath her cheek. She hadn't moved since he last looked in on her. Her eyes were closed. Tom stepped back and failed to see, as the light left the bed, Emmajean's eyes flicker open, then close.

The temptation to go to Henry Ann's was so great that Tom couldn't resist. He blew out the lantern, left it on the porch beside the door, and went to the car.

"She's just as I left her a couple of hours ago. She should sleep for two or three hours more. I think she'll be all right."

Henry Ann's ears were attuned to the sound of the car. When it drove in, she busied herself chipping ice and filling glasses for tea. The men, led by Johnny, came into the front door. He and Grant were laughing.

"Don't you two wake up Jay," Henry Ann scolded, glad that she had something to say when she raised her eyes to see Tom's large frame filling the doorway. His eyes, glued to her face, were like deep dark wells with little lights on the water.

"Hello, Tom. Glad you could come over for a while." Her heart thumped in her throat as she spoke.

"Thank you for asking me."

"Food is courtesy of Karen."

"Not actually, but almost," Karen said quickly.

"Sit down, everyone."

Henry Ann was grateful for Karen's ability to keep conversation going. They talked about the big event of the day—the sheriff taking Isabel off the dance floor.

"It was more excitement than Red Rock's had for a while," Henry Ann said, feeling that she had to contribute to the conversation.

"It'll be the talk of the town for months." Karen passed the potato salad. "Help yourself, Tom. After it goes past Grant, there'll be nothing left."

"Why'er you picking on me?" Grant's face was happy, relaxed, younger. His gaze went often to Karen. "How about old Hollow Legs? The kid eats like a horse."

Tom listened to the good-natured teasing, grateful that

he could be here for this little while. He tried to keep his eyes off Henry Ann's calm, beautiful face, but they seemed to wander there when he lifted them from his plate. Did the others notice?

"Jay rode the merry-go-round," Henry Ann said during a lull in the conversation. "Johnny stood by him and held him on the horse."

"I wish I could have seen him." Tom's eyes held hers as if they were the only two people in the room.

"Maybe next year . . . if the carnival comes back."

As soon as the meal was over, Henry Ann asked Tom if he wanted to see his son. He nodded. She led the way to the bedroom and opened the door. When she stood aside for him to enter, he took her hand and drew her into the semidarkened room with him. As they stood beside the bed, he reached down to touch his son's thick dark hair.

"I'm glad he has you." The whispered words came out on a breath.

"He has you, too."

Tom looked from his son to her. "I'm going to have to put his mother in an asylum."

"Oh, no!"

"I don't have a choice."

"Don't worry about Jay—"

"I don't. I envy him. Is that selfish of me?"

"There's nothing selfish about you."

"I need to be alone with you for a little while."

"We're alone."

"Will you walk out back with me . . . later?"

"We shouldn't."

"I know, but will you?"

"Yes," she whispered. She didn't have the strength to refuse him.

Grant and Karen had cleared the table and put the dishes in a pan to soak by the time they returned to the kitchen. Henry Ann stood in the doorway, loving the feeling of Tom's hand on her back.

"This is the bossiest woman I've ever known," Grant complained, spreading a cloth over the necessaries on the table. "She's got me doing woman's work."

"You bragged that you were a jack-of-all-trades."

"Doing dishes isn't a trade. It's drudgery."

"Now maybe you can understand how a woman feels," Karen retorted.

"Come on." Grant waited for Karen to hang up a cloth. "You've promised to entertain me tonight. What are you going to do? Sing or dance?"

"Don't be smug. I can dance, and I sing quite well. We'll be on the porch," Karen said to Henry Ann, as she and Grant left the kitchen.

Tom reached up and turned off the bulb hanging over the table. Henry Ann felt his arm around her urging her toward the back door.

An early moon climbed above the pecan trees. In its luminous glow Tom led her across the yard and stopped beneath the branches of the giant oak.

"We shouldn't—"

"Shhhh. Don't think about it. I want to hold you for just a little while . . . and kiss you before I go." His hand wandered over her back, pressing her closer.

Her heart was pounding with the urge to press her lips to his. All her senses were filled with his overwhelming male presence. She could feel his mouth at the side of her neck and smell the woodsmoke in his hair.

"Henry Ann, sweetheart!" The words seemed torn out of him. "How will I live without you?" He placed quick kisses along her jaw. "You've woven a wonderful web around me, drawing me to you." He took a deep quivering breath.

Her hand cupped his cheek and turned his lips to hers. He embraced her roughly, but there was nothing rough about the way he kissed her. There was a wild, sweet singing in her heart as his lips worked sweet magic with hers. He kissed her tenderly, holding her like some new-found treasure. Mindless, unconscious of time or place, she leaned on him. His mouth played on hers with infinite passion and tenderness. His tongue made small forays between her lips as his hand traversed her body from her hips to her soft round breasts.

"Tell me to stop—"

She opened her mouth to whisper her fears, but it was too late. He covered her parted lips, his tongue darting warmly in and out of her mouth, exploring every curve of the sweetness that trembled beneath his demanding kiss. Her arms tightened and she kissed him back feverishly, as though swept away on some wild force totally beyond her control.

"I . . . ache for you . . ." Tom sank down on the ground beneath the tree and pulled her down with him. She half lay at an angle across his lap. His free hand burrowed into the loose top of her dress, sliding over her bare breast. He took the lobe of her ear between his teeth and growled, "I think about you all the time."

She shivered at the touch of his exploring fingers. She

was in a timeless void where there were only Tom's hands, Tom's lips, Tom's whispered words.

"This is a little bit of heaven, my beautiful, my precious—" His rough fingertips caressed her nipple into hardness, and she trembled with the need to have him fill the empty ache within her.

She threw her arms around his neck and scattered kisses over his face. In a small part of her mind she knew that what she was doing was not right, but it was what she wanted, had wanted since the first time he had kissed her. It was as though it was bound to happen, and she had been waiting for him all her life.

Now she would know what she had been waiting for. With this wild, wonderful man she would learn the mysteries she had read about and imagined. When years of in-grained teaching of moral standards surfaced to plague her, she brushed them aside. She loved Tom Dolan, wanted him, needed him.

"I want you to love me like you would . . . if . . . if we were free to spend our lives together." A powerful, sweeping tide of love flowed over her, making her feel stronger than the hard-muscled man holding her tightly in his arms.

It was too dark for her to see his eyes, but she knew they were searching hers. Her breathing and her heartbeat were all mixed up. Her stomach muscles clenched and relaxed, clenched again.

"I want you more than . . . anything—" he whispered hoarsely; then his ragged breath was trapped inside her mouth as his lips plundered hers. The world seemed to fade away.

"You were made to be loved and . . . treasured. You are a treasure. My treasure." His hungry mouth found hers again and held it with fierce possession. His hands moved urgently over her. "God help me! I want to bury myself in you, become one with you. But I can't do it. I can't leave you with the memory of having given this precious gift of yourself here in the grass. I want to hold your naked body in my arms all night long, loving you, making you mine."

She knew that she should be shocked by his suggestions, but she wasn't. His husky whispers reached her on some instinctive level long suppressed. Adrift on a sea of arousal, she wanted only to love and to comfort this wonderfully compassionate man with the dark, worried face beneath a thatch of wild black hair.

"What better place, my love, than here where we first declared our love," she whispered, wondering how she dared be so bold. Once she began to tell him how she felt, it was easier to go on. "I want you to love me . . . make me yours. It could be all we'll ever have—"

"Sweetheart! Don't tempt me!" He made a sound of urgent longing, deep in his throat. "The past few weeks have been hell. I've got to be where you are. Otherwise, there's no life for me."

"I love you."

With great suddenness, Henry Ann felt the cool grass beneath her back. They were lying on their sides and he was holding her tightly in his arms, his hands moving over her back and hips, pressing her closer. Then his callused fingers were pushing aside the bodice of her dress and his hands closed around her naked breasts, his fingers stroking their taut rosy nipples.

"Beautiful," he whispered, rubbing his face between the soft mounds. When his mouth trailed a fiery path down her throat to her breast and closed on the nipple, the rough, seeking touch of his tongue set delicious quivers throughout her melting flesh.

"Please . . . please—" She tugged on his shaggy hair to bring his mouth up to hers.

"You don't know how I've hungered for a taste of you, the feel of you. Oh, sweet woman, I've dreamed of this—" His hands were under her dress, sliding up her legs to her hips, encountering brief panties which he thrust down, and she was open to his seeking fingers. "Sweetheart . . . I want to love you, join with you—Tell me . . . I can—"

His fingers caressed her, then eased inside. It felt so maddeningly good. She moaned and arched into them.

"Yes, yes! Please—"

In a daze of joy and unbelief she felt the tip of his eager manhood on the very center of her body. A narrow flame of pleasure begin to flicker. The flickering went on and on. Then she was stabbed with a needle point of pain that so resembled pleasure that she ignored it until finally it was no longer pain but an ecstasy so profound that she thought she would dissolve.

"Sweet, marvelous woman," Tom muttered thickly from the depths of his own careening world. He was riding the crest of the wildest passion he had ever known. Gently, with great restraint, he widened their magical circle of pleasure, taking her until she was drowning in wild, furious delight.

She felt his hard, muscular body halt and wince. She heard the cry that tore from him, and she caressed him in his trembling as he said her name with a sobbing breath, over and over. Then he lifted his body on quivering arms and lowered himself beside her.

Holding her tightly to him, Tom realized that only her

physical warmth pressed to him and the familiar lemony scent of her hair could convince him that it had not been just a dream. If he had hoped for anything, it had not been the swift and honest way which she had given herself to him. He held her, kissing her face and mouth, waiting for their heartbeats and breaths to return to normal.

Suddenly a shout came from the back of the house. "Fire! Fire! Tom, your place is . . . on FIRE!"

Chapter Twenty-two

Chapter Twenty-two

"FIRE!"

Henry Ann and Tom shot to their feet. Tom ran out into the open and saw the rosy glow in the sky.

Emmajean! "Oh, God! Don't let her die in a fire!"

"Tom, we're coming! We're loading the car with shovels and buckets," Johnny yelled.

Tom didn't hear Johnny or Henry Ann telling him to hurry. He took off running down the fence row that separated the woods from the cotton field. He ran until his breathing rasped harshly in his ears and his heart was pounding like a tom-tom. He felt as if he had a hundred-pound weight attached to each foot. The weight on his feet was no heavier than the weight of guilt he carried for having left the defenseless woman alone.

Crossing the pasture, his lungs on fire, he bounded over the rail fence and into the feedlot. He rounded the barn and skidded to a halt.

The real horror of it struck Tom when he saw the angry

flames leaping from the front of the house and lighting the sky. The dry wood of the frame house crackled and popped, sending sparks flying high in the air. Hope sprang anew when he realized the back room was still intact even though smoke poured from the windows.

He jerked off his shirt and dipped it in the horse tank as he passed it. Draping the dripping wet cloth over his head, he dashed through the back door and was stopped by a wall of hissing furious flames. Smoke burned his eyes. When he saw an opening, he dashed through it and found himself in the small room next to the kitchen.

"Emma . . . jean! Emma . . . jean!" he yelled through the wet cloth that covered his face except for his eyes.

The room was lighted by the flames, but the smoke was so thick he couldn't see. He got down on his knees and crawled to the bed. When he reached it, he felt blindly for a human body.

The bed was smooth, the sheet thrown back. She wasn't there!

"Emma . . . jean!"

Common sense told him that she might have rolled off the bed. He circled it on his knees, waved his arms beneath it and felt nothing. Feeling the heat of the fire on his back, he looked up to see fingers of fire racing across the ceiling.

God, help me find her.

Suddenly the bed erupted in a ball of flames, forcing him back. He crawled toward the door leading to the kitchen and stood. The floor was on fire and burning his hands. The only way out was to burst through the solid wall of flames. He aimed toward the back door and leaped, hoping the floor would hold him. Fire seared his hands, arms, and naked back. Yet he charged on. Momentum kept him going even when he reached the back porch. He staggered down the step and out into the yard before he stumbled and fell.

"Here he is!" Someone shouted just before he was hit with a bucket of water. Nothing in his life had felt so good.

"Tom! Tom! We couldn't find you." Henry Ann was on her knees beside him. "Are you burned?"

"I couldn't find her." His raspy voice came from a throat raw from heat and smoke. "I couldn't find her," he said again.

"Come back away from the house," Henry Ann urged. When he stood, she offered her support, but she didn't know where to touch him. "Johnny and Grant are wetting down what they think the flames could reach. Grant has moved your car. Thank goodness there's no wind."

Tom tried to get into his wet shirt.

"I couldn't find her," he groaned. "Has anyone looked outside?"

"I'll look for her. Let me see your hands first."

"They're all right."

"Let me see." She drew in a hurtful breath when she saw his blistered palms. "Karen," she yelled. "I need cloth."

"We don't have time for this. I've got to find Emma-jean."

"This will take only a minute."

Karen came with two neckerchiefs. Henry Ann dipped them in water and wrapped them around Tom's hands.

Mr. Austin and his hired man arrived in the wagon. They tied the team up in the road. With wet gunnysacks, they helped to put out the flying sparks that would spread the fire to the dry grass.

Tom, Henry Ann, and Karen searched in vain for Emma-jean, while the four men fought to keep the fire from spreading. By midnight the house had been reduced to a pile of glowing, smoking embers.

Tom was in agony from the burns on his hands and arms, but he couldn't sit and rest as the others urged him to do.

"She could be scared and hiding someplace."

"You said she was calmer than she'd been in days, Tom. Maybe she woke up and ran off." *And maybe she went to the front of the house and was overcome by smoke.* Grant knew about the guilt Tom was feeling. He also knew that he had to work through that guilt by himself.

"I shouldn't have left her, knowing she was out of her mind."

"How were you to know something like this could happen?" Karen said. "Do you have any idea how it could have started?"

"None. It could have come from the cookstove, I guess."

"If that were the case, the kitchen would have burned first. When we got here the front of the house was burning. What do you think, Mr. Austin?" Grant asked.

"Makes sense. If you say the front burned first, someone must've started it."

"I left the lantern on the front porch, and it was out." Tom walked restlessly back and forth.

"I can vouch for that. It was out when you came to the car," Johnny said. "I went up to get a new string I'd bought for the guitar and just happened to look out the window. The fire had a good start by the time we got here."

"Tom, come home with us and let Aunt Dozie tend to those burns. You can come back at daylight. You'll have a better chance of finding her then."

Henry Ann wanted more than anything to hold him and comfort him. She knew that he loved her, but she also knew that he was an honorable man and that he felt responsible for the pitiful creature he was married to and who was the mother of his child.

"I'll stay here, Tom," Johnny said. "Grant will take you and the girls back to the house."

"You should get those burns taken care of," Karen urged.

Tom finally agreed, then spoke to Mr. Austin. "Thanks for your help."

"It's what neighbors should do. If there's anything else, let us know."

Aunt Dozie was up and making bread when they reached the house.

"Aunt Dozie," Henry Ann said. "It's two o'clock in the morning!"

"I knows it. I jist can't sit an wait. I got to be doin' somethin. Is de fire out?"

"The house burned to the ground. Tom's hands are burned."

Dozie looked at the big man standing hesitantly in the doorway.

"Lawsy! 'Pears more'n his hands is burned. Come sit yoreself down right here. We gonna take care yo right now."

Karen went to the car with Grant as he prepared to leave.

"You think she's dead, don't you?" It seemed natural for her to stand close to him and rest her head on his shoulder.

"Yes. He said that she'd been really out of her head for the past few days. He hesitated about leaving her. He's in love with Henry Ann. Poor son of a gun. I understand his wanting to be with her, because I could hardly wait for today so I could be with you."

"Why, Mr. Gifford—"

"No wisecracks. I'm going to kiss you."

"It's about time."

"I've waited all day."

"Then you'd better get at it. It'll be daylight in about three hours."

With gentle hands he pulled her around to face him. Every bone in her body turned to jelly when his arms closed about her. She lifted her parted lips for his kiss. His mouth was warm and gentle and gave her room to move away if she wanted to. Karen found herself clinging to him weakly. His hands moved seductively across her hips and back, tucking her closer to him. Her mind felt like it was floating.

Grant drew back and looked into her face.

"You shouldn't kiss me like that unless you mean it," she gasped.

"I mean it." He lifted first one of her arms and then the other and placed them around his neck. "Indulge me. I want to kiss you with your arms around my neck." He pressed a sweet kiss to her moist lips

"Was it as good as you thought it would be?"

"Better. I wish I didn't have to go, but I think I should go into town and put in a call for the sheriff. It'll look better for Tom if it's done right away."

"Why? They can't think that he set the fire."

"They might think that he was trying to get rid of his wife because . . . well, because he wanted Henry Ann."

"He was here when the fire started."

"True. But it won't stop people from speculating. The sheriff will want to find the body or what's left of it. Bodies don't burn up completely, you know."

"Go, then. But . . . come back."

"Wild horses couldn't keep me away." He kissed her again, longer, harder, deeper. This time when he lifted his head his heart was beating like that of a runaway horse. "I never expected to meet someone like you."

"Is that good or bad?"

"What do you think?" He took her hand and placed it palm down over his heart. "This is a new beginning for me. I need to tell you about my past and my hope for the future."

"I'm not interested in your future if you plan to move on."

"I've gone as far as I'm going . . . alone."

"I'm glad your roaming feet brought you this way, Grant Gifford."

"Not as glad as I am, Karen Wesson."

Tom was pacing back and forth across the porch when dawn began streaking the eastern sky. He stopped in front of Henry Ann, who sat in the porch swing.

"If she's alive, she may have gone to that place in the clay bank. It would be light by the time I got there."

"I'll get a lantern and go with you."

"It's a long walk, and you've not been to bed."

"Neither have you. Oh, wait . . . I hear a car. Maybe Johnny and Grant are coming back."

The Model T turned into the yard and stopped. As was his habit Johnny hopped over the door and slipped to the ground.

"Where's Grant? Have you found her?" Henry Ann called to Johnny before he reached them on the porch.

"Grant's back at Dolan's, and, yes, we found her."

"God, that's a relief," Tom said, then, "She's all right, isn't she?"

"No, Tom. She's dead."

"Dead? No . . ."

"I wanted Grant to come tell you, but he's with Sheriff Watson. He came out as soon as Grant called him—"

"—We saw the car go by."

"They want you to come over, Tom."

"Was she . . . ? How did they find her?"

"Grant and I got to thinking that if she got out, she might have gone to that place by the creek where she went sometimes. We got the lanterns, went there, and found her. By the time we got back to your place the sheriff was there. Grant took him back, and I came for you."

"She . . . didn't burn up in the fire?" Henry Ann spoke. Tom seemed to be speechless.

"No. She was . . . she was . . . her throat was cut." Johnny said the last quickly and turned his face away.

"Someone killed her?" Tom's words were loud. "Someone killed her?" he repeated. "They didn't have to kill her, for God's sake."

"Yeah."

"Oh, my God! Oh, my God!"

"I'll take you over there. Grant made a litter out of a couple of poles and a tarp he found in the barn. He and the sheriff went to bring her in."

"I'll go with you." Henry Ann laid her hand on Tom's arm.

"You'd better stay here, Sis."

"He's right. Stay here." Tom seemed to be looking right through her. He walked to the car like a man with the weight of the world on his shoulders.

"Johnny," Karen called from the door, "wait a minute." Minutes later she came out with a bushel basket. "There's hot coffee and plenty of cups in here. Aunt Dozie wrapped the pot in a gunnysack. Buttered bread and jam are in the flour sack."

"That'll be welcome." Johnny carried the basket to the car and wedged it between the front and backseat. Tom was already in the car.

Henry Ann watched until they were out of sight. When she turned, Karen stood beside her.

"I heard. How terrible. I can't believe . . . a murder. There's not been a murder around here since . . . heaven knows when. Well . . . that is, not a woman. Who would do such a thing?"

"Thank goodness they can't blame Tom. He was here."

The acrid smell of smoldering household goods and old wood was strong when Johnny stopped behind the sheriff's car parked along the road behind Tom's roadster. Tom got out of the car and stood looking at what once had been his home. The only identifiable thing was the iron cookstove sitting amid the rubble. *What had gone wrong? Was it possible Emmajean had set the fire, then run off?*

It was quiet. Far away Tom could hear a mourning dove calling. In the morning light he looked around at things that were the same, yet so different. Mr. Austin came from the barn carrying a bucket.

"I milked your cow, Dolan. Do you want me to pour the milk in the hog trough?"

"Unless you can use it."

"Hogs got to be fed." He went toward the hog lot and when he returned he rinsed the bucket at the well and left it there. "I'll be going, Dolan. If there's anything more I can do, let me know."

"You've done plenty, Austin. I appreciate it."

Austin's horses were skittish as animals sometimes are around a smoldering fire. The hired man handled them expertly, and the wagon pulled out of the yard and headed down the road.

"Here they come." Johnny started toward the back railed fence.

Two men carrying a litter were coming across the field. Tom's eyes focused on the small form wrapped in the old quilt. Reality hit him like a blow between the eyes. Emmajean was dead. Poor girl. Her short, confused life had been anything but happy.

Tom and Johnny took the litter when it was passed over the fence. They carried it to the big shade tree beside the barn and gently lowered it to the ground. Blond hair showed from beneath the blood-soaked quilt. Kneeling down beside her, Tom closed his eyes and crossed himself. When he stood, he was looking into the eyes of the sheriff.

"Dolan, I'm sorry 'bout this."

"Thank you. You'd better know right off that if I find him first, I'll kill him."

"And you'd better know right off that if you do, I'll come for you," the sheriff replied in a no-nonsense tone.

"Some rotten son of a bitch was hanging around out there. A couple of times I found boot tracks in the sand and cigarette butts."

"That's not unusual. Most men smoke."

"Not a dozen cigarettes in one place."

"Why did you let her go out there if you knew a man was hanging around?"

"I've had an eye on her almost every minute for over a week . . . until last night. I thought she was asleep."

"There's no cigarette butts out there now. Tracks had been brushed out."

"Was she . . . raped?"

"I'm not sure. There was no blood . . . down there. She'd been knocked around . . . mauled. She had a split lip and . . . one of her breasts chewed. Bastard probably hurt her bad, she was yelling, and he killed her to shut her up."

"Godamighty! Poor girl." Tom sat down on a stump and bowed his head. "She'd taken the quilt and a few things out to that dugout—it was kind of like a kid's playhouse. I followed her many times. She'd be sitting on the quilt, combing her hair and looking in her mirror. I thought it harmless and never dreamed that anyone would hurt her until the time she didn't come home and Johnny found her in Austin's shed."

"What did she keep out there?"

"A pink comb, a small round mirror, a couple of garters, a few bows, and a string of beads. She took a small blue perfume bottle. I don't know if there was anything in it or not. When she left, she'd wrap them in that old quilt."

"Hummm . . ."

"She wasn't right in her mind, Sheriff."

"Gifford told me. You're saying she left her pretties out there?"

"They were there yesterday."

Tom knelt and lifted the quilt from Emmajean's face. Her head lay at an unnatural angle, and her face was crusted with dirt and blood. He closed his eyes and let the quilt fall back in place.

"Does she usually go out there in her nightclothes?" the sheriff asked.

"She'd go naked if I didn't make her dress. She had on her nightdress and her underdrawers when I put her to bed."

"All she's got on now is the nightdress. Gifford tells me that you were over at the Henrys'."

"Emmajean was in bed asleep when I left."

"Who besides you saw her?"

"Good God, man! Do you think I killed her?"

"I don't rule anyone out. You could've killed her and gone to the Henrys' for your alibi."

"To hell with you!" Tom's hand clenched at his sides. "I'd not gone to the Henrys' if Johnny and Grant hadn't come over."

Oh, Lord! I might have gone. I was tempted.

"Wait a minute, Sheriff," Grant said. "Tom wasn't in the house a full minute. Through the window, I could see that he went in the room and right back to the porch. He blew out the lantern and came to the car. He didn't have time to start a fire. Besides that, what man in his right mind would risk going into a burning house to get someone that he knew was already dead? Look at his hands."

"Who the hell are you? His lawyer?"

"Tom isn't guilty. He doesn't need a lawyer, but if he does, I know where he can get one."

"There hasn't been a woman murdered in this county since Indian days. This is going to cause quite a stink."

"I don't care how much *stink* it causes. This pitiful creature was my son's mother," Tom said heatedly. "I want the one who did it caught and hung. She was so demented that she would spread her legs for anyone. He didn't have to kill her."

"I could send Elmer from the funeral parlor out to get the body," the sheriff said quietly, ignoring Tom's anger. "But it'll be quicker if I take her in and have Doc Hendricks look her over. The nearest morgue is in Ardmore."

"My brother's a federal officer working out of Kansas City. I wish he was here."

"This isn't a federal case. We'll handle it here. Don't leave the county, Dolan."

"Why would I leave? My son is here."

"Yeah, that's right. The mouthy little twit told me you had sent the boy to live with Miss Henry. She said you two had something going. Never mind. Calm down," he said when Tom bristled angrily. "She also said Pete Perry would get even with whoever got him knocked out of the marathon."

"I had nothing to do with that."

"Revenge takes many paths. Looks to me like I've got several good suspects here, counting young Austin. You said that one time you found Mrs. Dolan in Austin's shed? Alone?"

"She'd had intercourse with someone. He'd slapped her and bruised her face."

"Got anyone in mind?"

"If I had, I'd a been after him. It wasn't Chris. I'd bet my life he had nothing to do with this."

"Well, we'll see. Someone want to help me get her in the car?"

"I'll do it." Tom knelt and, with Grant's help, gently rolled the body in the blood-soaked quilt in the tarp. Tom lifted it in his arms and carried it to the car. The sheriff opened the rear door, and Tom placed the body of his dead wife on the seat.

Emmajean loved to go to town and . . . she was going for the last time.

"Sheriff, would you notify her folks down in Conroy, Texas? I've been expecting them to come up here. I'd hate for them to come and . . . find out what's happened when they got here."

"What's the name?"

"Martin Conroy."

"Any kin to the Conroy that's been selling oil leases around here?"

"That's her brother. Martin is her father."

"Didn't I hear that he died?"

"Not unless it was in the last day or two. Her brother was here last week. I sent word for him to have Martin come up and help me decide what to do about Emmajean."

"Humm . . . I'll get Flossie at the telephone office to put in a call down there. Shouldn't cost over six bits. I don't think the county will raise too much cain over that."

"Thanks."

Sheriff Watson left the Dolan farm chewing on his upper lip. This was more than a bootlegging or bank-robbery case. This was BIG. A woman murdered, more than likely raped, would be front-page news all over Oklahoma. If he didn't find out and arrest the person who killed her, he could kiss his job good-bye come election day.

He was inclined to believe Dolan wasn't the one, but you could never tell about a murderer. Seven or eight years ago a couple of young fellows killed a kid named Bobby Frank up in Chicago. They were eighteen- and nineteen-year-old college boys, and one was a boy genius who spoke fourteen languages. It was hard for folks to believe that they were killers, but they finally confessed to doing it to see if they could commit the perfect crime.

The sheriff passed the Henry farm. Isabel had said that Dolan had been hanging around Miss Henry. A married man, even with a crazy wife, had no business smelling around another woman to his way of thinking. Had Dolan gotten rid of his wife so he'd be free to court Miss Henry? A well-to-do woman with a paid-for farm was a prize for any man.

And there was Pete Perry. He'd certainly have a talk with him. He'd not heard of Pete doing anything but a little bootlegging now and then. His deputy, Orlan Nelson, kept an eye on him and swore he had nothing to do with killing other folks' beef. And there was the Austin kid. Guess he wasn't a kid anymore. Orlan said he'd been keeping the road hot to old man Hastings's place, gettin' him a little tail from Opal. Maybe Opal wasn't puttin' out enough, and he decided to try Dolan's crazy wife.

Sheriff Watson was puzzled by Gifford, too. Phillips hadn't said much about him except that he'd been working at the Henrys' almost since Ed died. The man knew what he was about. It was almost as if he was familiar with procedures at a crime scene. Out at the dugout where he and Johnny found the body, he'd been careful to make no tracks. The only ones found were his and Johnny's. The place had been swept clean. There were no cigarette butts, and none of the things Dolan said his wife had taken to the spot were there. The killer had been careful to leave no sign.

Another thing that puzzled the sheriff was Dolan's not knowing that Martin Conroy had died. He remembered seeing the obituary in the Wichita Falls paper and wondering if the Conroy here in Oklahoma selling oil leases was related. It would be strange, if true, that Conroy's own daughter hadn't been notified of his death.

The sun was just coming up when the sheriff drove into Red Rock. First, he decided, he'd stop by the doctor's office and ask him to come down to the funeral parlor and take a look at the corpse, then he'd go to the telephone office. After that he was going to Millie's Diner, drink a gallon of coffee, and treat himself to breakfast.

"I just can't believe that poor woman's dead. I just can't believe it. The poor, poor thin'." Pernie Austin sat at the kitchen table with her husband and the sheriff. "I should have done somethin'. I should have gone right over there and told him that if he didn't do right by that poor thin' and get her to a doctor, I was going to the law. More coffee, Sheriff?"

"No thanks. What do you mean, do right?"

"You know. Stop spendin' his time moonin' over Henry Ann and look after his sick wife. Flitter! Ever'body knows he took the boy from his mother and gave him to Henry Ann to raise. She's almost an old maid. Guess she was gettin' desperate for a man."

"Pernie, don't get carried away," Mr. Austin cautioned.

"Land sakes! Ever'body knows they've been carryin' on. The sheriff ought to know. A married man who'd smell around after another woman right under his sick wife's nose is apt to do anything . . . even . . . even get rid of her. I knew right off that he was no good."

"Is young Chris here?"

The question came so suddenly that neither of the Austins had time to prepare for it.

"Why do you want . . . to know?" Mrs. Austin stammered.

"I plan to talk to all the men in the area. Is he here?"

"He . . . he went to Ardmore . . . to visit my sister."

"Pernie, you don't know that. Tell the sheriff the truth. Chris didn't come home last night. We don't know where he went."

"Chris-to-pher often goes to Ardmore," Mrs. Austin insisted.

"I've got to be going. I'll talk to Chris later." The sheriff moved his chair back from the table and got to his feet. "You say the fire over at the Dolans' started around ten o'clock?"

"I don't know when it started, but it was a little after that that our hired man woke me. He could see the flames from where he sleeps in the hayloft."

"Tom Dolan set it to cover up his crime. It's as plain as the nose on your face!" Mrs. Austin insisted, and followed her husband and the sheriff to the front porch. "He set his sights on bigger things, and Henry Ann was so hard-up for a man that—"

"Pernie, hush up!"

With her mouth opened to say something more, Mrs. Austin let it hang and looked at her husband in stunned silence. He had never in all their married years said such a thing to her. Her eyes shifted past him to the car that was turning into the yard.

"Chris-to-pher's home. Who's that . . . with him?" Then, "No . . . no. He'd not bring *her* here!"

Chris got out of the car, leaned in to say something to the

girl in the front seat, then came toward the group on the porch with a worried frown on his face.

"Morning, Sheriff. Is something wrong here?"

"Morning, Chris. Not here. Been over to Ardmore?"

"Not lately." Chris's eyes went to the hostile look on his mother's face. "You called him out here because I didn't come home. Good Lord, Mama. I'm a grown man. I'm twenty-five years old—"

"—And actin' like you don't have a brain in your head," his mother snapped back.

"Where were you, Austin?"

"I went to Wichita Falls and got married." Looking directly at his mother, he pulled a paper from his pocket and handed it to the sheriff. "The wedding paper, Sheriff. The preacher will have it recorded at the courthouse this morning. We left Red Rock about six o'clock, were married around nine o'clock, spent the night at the Alamo Hotel. Here's the receipt for the bill." He dug a paper out of his shirt pocket. "Cost two dollars."

"No! You didn't!" Mrs. Austin gasped. "You . . . you married that . . . whore?"

"I married a sweet and good girl that I love very much. Don't ever, ever, call her that again." Chris stood with his clenched fists on his hips.

"Congratulations, Austin." The sheriff held out his hand. "Seems like you got an airtight alibi. I'll be on my way, folks." He tipped his hat to Mrs. Austin and hurried out to his car.

"What did he mean—I had an airtight alibi?"

When Mrs. Austin didn't answer, Mr. Austin did. "Tom Dolan's wife was murdered last night. The sheriff was here about that—doing his job."

"Murdered? Good grief! Does he know who did it?"

"Her husband, that no-good, wild-eyed Catholic, did it." Mrs. Austin's voice was unnaturally loud and abrasive.

"The sheriff don't know who did it." Mr. Austin corrected his wife with a frown. He struck a match on the sole of his shoe and held the flame to the bowl of his pipe.

"Don't think you'll bring that hussy here to live," she said to Chris. "I'll not have her or her bastard in my house."

"I'm not bringing her here. I came to get some of my things and to tell you that I'm taking the car and going to California." He brushed by his mother and went into the house. She followed him into his room.

"California? You're leaving? Well! You're not taking our car."

"Hush up, Pernie!"

"Don't you tell me to hush up." Mrs. Austin turned on her husband. "If you don't have the backbone to stand up to him, I do. We've fed and clothed him all these years, and he turns his back on us for a whore that's been with every man on Mud Creek."

His wife's words seemed to float right over Mr. Austin's head.

"There's an extra gallon of oil in the shed, son. The luggage rack that fits on the fender is in there, too."

"Are you out of your mind?" Mrs. Austin was too angry to speak in a normal tone; her voice squeaked.

"Mama, I don't want to leave with you mad at me, but I'm going. I've worked here all my life, and I would stay; but I love Opal, and as long as you feel the way you do, I have no choice but to take her and make a life for us someplace else."

"Henry Ann put you up to this. It's what you expect from a woman who fornicates with another woman's husband."

Chris emptied the bureau drawers, shoved his clothes down in a pillowcase and took it to the front porch. He came back for his shotgun, his chess game, and the sheepskin coat he'd bought the winter before. Mrs. Austin stood on the porch when Chris carried his belongings to the car.

"You'd better take that toolbox in the shed, son," Mr. Austin said when he carried out the oil and the luggage rack.

"Thank you, Daddy. Opal's grandpa is going with us. He knows a lot about fixing things. No hard feelings about me taking the car?"

"None. You helped pay for it. I'd like to hear from you from time to time. You're a good boy and a good worker. You'll do all right whatever you do."

"It means a lot to me to know you think that."

"Hold on a minute. Don't go till I get back."

Chris stood by the car while Mr. Austin went to the house. Soon he could hear his mother shrieking, then loud wails as the screen door slammed behind his father.

"Here's five hundred dollars, son. You've earned it." He handed Chris a cloth sack. "You've done a man's work since you were twelve. That's less than fifty dollars a year."

"But . . . I never expected—I don't want you to be without—"

"We've got a few hundred left. We're far better off than most folks."

"But . . . Mama—"

"She'll get over it. I should've clamped down on her long ago. It was just easier not to raise a fuss."

"Thanks, Daddy. This'll really help. I wasn't as confident as I made out." Chris put his arms around his father and hugged him for the first time since he was a little boy. "I'll let you know where I am; and if you ever need me, I'll come."

"I'm glad you'll be seein' more than Red Rock and Mud Creek, son."

"Come meet Opal, Daddy. She's not what Mama says she is."

When the car pulled away from the yard, Mr. Austin waved good-bye to his son and headed for the shed, where he could wipe his eyes before going back into the house.

Chapter Twenty-three

"Henry Ann, Grant's going to take me to town, but I'll be back if Daddy doesn't need the car." Karen had walked out under the tree to where Henry Ann was swinging Jay.

"I suppose it's all over town by now about . . . Emma-jean."

"I'm sure it is. If Sheriff Watson hasn't spread the news, Elmer at the funeral home must have."

"Who do you suppose did such a terrible thing?" In her mind Henry Ann had asked the same question a dozen times.

"It's got to have been a tramp. I can't think of anyone I know who could do such a thing. Not even Pete Perry."

It was hard for Henry Ann to think that it was only a little past noon. So many surprising things had happened during the past twenty-four hours, the last of which was Chris stopping by to tell her that he and Opal were married and going to California.

"We know for sure that it wasn't Grant, Johnny, Tom, or

Chris. Chris was in Wichita Falls getting married. It took falling in love to make him stand up to his mother."

"I'm glad for him and Opal. I hope we hear from them someday. Is Tom coming back over here?"

"He'll be over for supper. Johnny was going out to see about his cattle. I tried to get him to let Johnny drive him in to see Doctor Hendricks about his hands, but he wouldn't go."

Grant came from the house. "I'll not be gone long, Henry Ann. Anything you want from town?"

"Tom will need a shirt and a pair of pants." She reached into her dress pocket for some bills and pressed them into Grant's hand. "And, if you don't mind, go by the doctor's office and get some ointment for burns. His hands are a solid blister."

"All right. I want to stop by and see Mr. Phillips. He should know the straight of what went on."

"Bring a block of ice, too. Come back if you can, Karen. It's a comfort to have you here."

"Where can we go to talk . . . and be out of sight?" Grant, driving with one hand, reached for Karen's with the other.

"There's a lane just beyond the trees ahead. It goes around a bend and on down to the creek, but the bridge is out."

"Have you been there before?"

"Not to do what you have in mind."

"And how do you know what that is, Miss Smarty?"

"Because it's what I have in mind, Mr. Smarty." Her shining eyes held his and she squeezed the hand holding hers.

Grant laughed. He was delighted with her honesty, her wit, and her ability to make him feel wonderful. After they rounded the bend, he stopped the car in the shade of a row of hedge trees and turned to her, took her in his arms, tilted her chin, and steadied her face.

"I've seen your face behind my closed lids every night since I met you. Do you believe in love at first sight?"

"Only for the very lucky ones." Her voice shook as she spoke.

He closed her eyes with kisses and heard her heart pounding. His lips moved down to hers and parted. The kiss was long and deep and sweet. When it was over he moved her face to the curve of his neck.

"Don't say anything," he whispered in her ear, the warmth of his breath caressing the lobe. The scent of him was in her nostrils. He found her lips again and sealed her sighs of pleasure with a long and hungry kiss. "I'm crazy about you."

"I like you, too."

"Like?" He nuzzled her lips with his. "You can do better than that." She liked the happiness in his voice.

"I . . . I'm crazy about you, too."

"That's better. Much better."

With his arm around her he settled her close to him on the seat and held her hand in his, bringing it to his lips and gently kissing the palm.

"I want you to know all about me before I ask you to share my life."

"Are you . . . going to ask me?"

"After I tell you that I've been bumming around for the past couple of years because my inability to do my job got a man killed. I feel so guilty that at times I put my feet in action and try to run from it. I'm tired of running. I realize now that I've got to accept what I can't help and live with it."

"Tell me about it." Her hand went to his cheek. "Tell me everything."

"I was born and raised in Tulsa. Oklahoma has always been home to me. My father was reasonably well off and could afford to send me back East to Harvard. I graduated from there, went on to law school and was accepted as a junior partner in one of the top law firms in Boston."

"I knew that you were no *ordinary* bum."

"The firm did a certain amount of *pro bono* work, and I had done my share of that. I really liked criminal law better than corporate." Grant wanted to get the telling of his story over so he could kiss her again. "I was assigned to defend a young man charged with murdering his mother."

"His mother? How awful!"

"I was prepared to despise him. They said it was an open-and-shut case, and all I had to do was to go through the motions of defending him. But the more I talked to him the more I came to believe that he was innocent. All the evidence against him was circumstantial. He was the only one who had a key to the house, he knew when she would be there alone, and he would benefit the most from her death.

"He wanted to take the stand and testify, but he was only nineteen, and I was afraid the district attorney, who had a flair for the dramatic and political ambitions, would trip him up. I advised him not to. He had an alibi. He was with another man . . . all night. The man was willing, even eager to testify to save the boy, even though he knew that he would never again be viewed the same by his family and friends."

"Why was that, if he was telling the truth?"

"They were lovers and had been sleeping together for over a year."

"Oh . . . ugh!" She shuddered. Her expression and her tone showed her revulsion.

"That was exactly the reaction of the jury. He was one of *those*—a fairy, a pansy. In their minds a man who would have sex with another man was the lowest form of humanity and capable of anything. It was easy for them to come back with a guilty verdict. Two months later, while I was trying to file an appeal, he was hanged. I dug around until I found the real killer. It was the boy's cousin. She was next in line for the money after my client. By murdering the woman and blaming the son, she had killed two birds with one stone.

"That boy's trusting eyes will haunt me for the rest of my life. I should have never let his friend come to court. I not only let the boy down, I ruined the life of the man who loved him. He was rejected by his family and he killed himself after they hanged the boy."

"It was a woman who killed her?"

"Killers come in all ages, shapes, and sizes, sweetheart." Grant gave a deep sigh. "I raised all kinds of hell with the district attorney. After I finished with him, he couldn't have been elected dog catcher. I was kicked out of the firm for unprofessional behavior. Not a firm in Boston would take me after that. But it was all right with me. I decided that I wanted nothing more to do with courtrooms and juries and crooked politicians.

"I took to the road. It was one of the smartest decisions of my life. I've met all kinds of people, I've done all kinds of things. I've learned more during the past two and a half years than I learned the first twenty-six years of my life.

"And I met you. My greatest achievement so far. I doubt that anything else I do in my life will top it. I want to settle down with you and open a small law office. I felt I had to tell you this because I may have to give a hand to Mr. Phillips if it becomes necessary to defend Tom."

"Mr. Phillips knew about you, didn't he?"

"Yes. He's a wily old codger. Got a memory like an elephant. He asked me right off if I was *the* Grant Gifford. My escapades in Boston were front-page stuff in Tulsa and Oklahoma City."

"Did you punch the guy out?"

"The district attorney? I'll just say that now he's eating with store-bought teeth, and his smile is not so pretty anymore."

"Good for you!"

"How about it? Are you game to take on an almostjailed hobo lawyer who'll have to start from the ground up?"

"I'll have to think about it. You kiss pretty good. That's in your favor."

"Daddy! Daddy!"

Henry Ann was washing canning jars in a tub on the back porch when she heard Jay shriek. She went quickly through the house to see Johnny behind the wheel of Tom's car. Tom got out on the passenger side. The two men stood beside it for a minute, then Johnny unscrewed the radiator cap and headed for the well.

Tom saw his son running toward him and bent to scoop him up in his arms. As they came toward the house, Tom's eyes held Henry Ann's. The growth of dark whiskers on his cheeks emphasized the tired look on his face. His shirt was ragged; and through the burnt holes in his trousers, she could see the bare flesh of his thighs. She noticed that he kept the palms of his hands turned out.

"I must be a sorry sight," he said when he reached the porch.

"You look awfully good to me." Her voice was husky with unshed tears as she reacted to his condition. His eyes were bloodshot and he smelled of woodsmoke. "Let me take Jay. Come here, honey. Your daddy is tired."

Tom set his son on his feet.

"Aunty cookin' pie," Jay announced, and wrapped his arms around Henry Ann's legs.

"He loves you," Tom said softly, his eyes still on her face.

"I love him, too. How are your hands?"

"They'll be all right. Thank God for the calluses."

"Grant will be back soon. I told him to stop and get some ointment from Doctor Hendricks."

"I need to clean myself up a bit before I go to town to . . . make arrangements. I was hoping Emmajean's folks would be here by now."

"Grant is also bringing a shirt and a pair of pants. I've laid out Daddy's shaving things."

"Thank you. I'll see that you're paid—"

"—There'll be no talk of pay between us. Or . . . have things changed since last night?"

"Nothing has changed except that now I have this cloud hanging over my head."

"We'll weather it . . . . together, if that's what you want."

"You know it is, but I don't want you to be hurt by any of this."

"You mean my . . . reputation?" She smiled into his eyes.

"I didn't realize that people were talking until the sheriff said something today."

"It was started by that old busybody who saw us at the doctor's office when we took Jay. Then she saw you here that Sunday afternoon. Don't let it bother you."

"It does. Anything that concerns you is important to me."

"Come on in and shave. There's a big washtub out in the barn. I'll carry out some warm water from the cookstove."

"You don't need to do that—"

"—I'll do it. You're going to have to learn to let others help you until your hands heal."

"Yes, ma'am." He smiled for the first time that day.

Grant returned, and Karen was with him. He brought the clothes and the ointment Henry Ann asked him to buy for Tom.

"Doctor Hendricks says the soda paste Aunt Dozie put on the burns is as good as any ointment." Karen was beaming even more than usual. Her smiling eyes flashed frequently to Grant and his to her.

"Tom's bathing out in the barn, Grant. Maybe you could put some of the salve on his back when you take out the clothes."

"We went by the house, and Daddy sent some underwear and socks," Karen said.

"He'll be glad to have them. He lost every stitch of clothes he had except what was on his back."

As soon as Grant left the house Karen hurried over to Henry Ann and put her arms around her.

"Grant asked me to marry him. Oh, Henry, I'm so happy."

"Karen . . ."

"Don't worry. He told me about himself," she said quickly. "He's a good and honorable man. We talked to Daddy, and he gave us his blessing."

"Then I'm happy for you. I like Grant and hoped that he would have a justifiable reason for . . . for . . ."

"Being a bum." Karen laughed happily. "He had a reason, but he'll tell you when the time is right. Where's Jay?"

"He's out in the barn with his daddy. What are they saying in town?"

"Are you sure you want to know?"

"I'll hear sooner or later."

"They're saying just what we thought they would. That Tom was in love with you, killed his wife, and set fire to the house to cover it up."

"Good grief! Tom was here when the fire started, and when he went through the flames to rescue her, she wasn't even in the house."

"Gossips don't care for the truth. It's more exciting for them to think Tom did it for love. The story is spicing up their dull lives."

"Does everyone think Tom is guilty?"

"Daddy, Mr. Phillips, and Doctor Hendricks don't think so. Don't worry, Henry Henry"—she used the pet name she'd used when they were in high school—"Grant will know what to do."

"I hope they find the one who did it . . . soon."

Grant and Tom were still in the barn when the sheriff

and his deputy arrived. Driving into the yard behind them was a shiny, new, one-seater Packard automobile.

"Who in the world?" Henry Ann exclaimed.

"I know who it is. I've seen him around town. His name is Conroy. He was in town buying up leases for a two-bit oil company."

"Emmajean's brother."

The sheriff and the deputy got out of the car as Grant and Tom came from the barn. Jay walked proudly along beside them. When Tom leaned down and said something to his son, Jay ran toward the house.

Henry Ann had never liked the deputy. He had been all right when they were in school; but the minute he was made a deputy, the job went to his head. He liked nothing more than to flaunt his authority. Henry Ann stepped off the porch.

"Sheriff," she called, "come on up on the porch in the shade. I'll bring out some iced tea."

"That'd go down right good, Miss Henry."

"I'll get it," Karen said, and disappeared into the house.

"Hello, Henry Ann." Deputy Orlan Nelson was a short man on the plump side. "Yo're lookin' mighty pretty. I haven't seen ya for a spell. Been too busy to do any callin' on the ladies."

Henry Ann thought she heard a snort from the sheriff.

"Hello, Orlan." *She'd be damned if she would call him "deputy."*

"Miss Henry, this is Marty Conroy, Emmajean's brother." Tom made the introductions.

Marty Conroy, in his fine white shirt, string tie, and dark trousers, nodded curtly as if he were a visiting dignitary and she were a servant.

"Please sit down. We'll have cold drinks for you presently." Henry Ann went into the house, but stood just inside the door so that she could listen. The sheriff began to speak immediately.

"We've got us a problem, Dolan. Conroy says he came out last week and told you that your wife's daddy had died and she was named in his will. He thinks that you killed his sister for the money she would inherit. "

Tom stared at Marty with disbelief. His face, reddened from the fire, was stoic, but when the import of the sheriff's words sank in, his eyes flashed with anger.

"What? You never told me that Martin was dead. You said you'd tell him to come out so that he could see what condition Emmajean was in and help me decide what to do."

"I never said I'd have him come out," Marty retorted staunchly.

"You're a goddamn liar! You said you'd give him my message. You never said a word to me about Martin being dead, and you know it."

"Why would I drive all the way out there if not to tell my sister her daddy was dead? I certainly wouldn't have just come visitin'. She was crazy as a loon."

"Why didn't you tell her in time so that she could have gone to the burial? Crazy or not, Martin was her father."

"You know why. She'd have done something stupid and shamed us all. Mother thought it best not to tell her until afterward."

"She had a right to be told, regardless!"

"I told *you* that Daddy was dead and that she was to get a third of his estate. Outside the trust," he added hurriedly.

"Did you think to get it if she was dead? Is that why you killed my poor sister?"

"You lying son of a bitch!" Tom was on his feet. "I ought to break you in two!"

"Just sit down." Orlan stood. His head barely came to Tom's chin. When he made to take hold of him, Tom drew back his fist.

"Don't touch me, you little pipsqueak."

"Are you threatening me?" Orlan bristled.

"Lay off, Orlan," Sheriff Watson said firmly.

Henry Ann held open the screened door, and Karen went out onto the porch with glasses of iced tea. Henry Ann stood with her back to the door, her eyes willing Tom to look at her.

Why in the world was Emmajean's brother saying such things? He was accusing Tom of killing his sister for the money she would be getting. Surely the sheriff wouldn't believe that.

All the men except Tom took glasses of tea. He shook his head when it was offered. When it became evident the discussion would not continue until the women left, Karen and Henry Ann went back inside to stand by the door so that they could listen.

"When I called down to Conroy this morning," Sheriff Watson said, wiping his mouth with the back of his hand, "I was told that Mrs. Conroy was in Dallas and that Mr. Marty Conroy was out of town. Orlan spotted him in Red Rock and told him the news."

"Hard to miss that shiny new Packard." Orlan grinned cockily, pleased to have played such an important part.

"I wasn't sneaking into town," Marty said. "I came looking for the sheriff."

"He has a paper, Dolan, from a judge in Colby County, Texas, that says Jay Conroy Dolan is to be placed in the custody of Martin Conroy, Jr. until a hearing can be held to determine permanent custody."

Tom stopped his pacing and whirled around. "What the hell did you say?"

"I'm saying the judge down there wants to take your boy and put him in the care of Martin Conroy, Jr. He says that Mrs. Dolan's mental condition renders her incapable of caring for the child and that she only got that way after you gave her child to another woman. He says that you are an unfit parent and a Catholic and that the child should be raised a Protestant."

Tom was stunned into silence. Then with a roar of rage he sprang at Marty. Johnny and Grant acted in unison and grabbed him before he could reach the man who cowered behind the deputy.

"You slimy bastard! I'll kill you before I let you take my son!"

"Like you killed Emmajean, after . . . you drove her crazy?" Marty snarled, braver now that Tom was under control.

"Sheriff, may I see the paper?" Grant asked.

"Aren't you the road tramp that's been hanging around here?" Orlan asked with a sneer.

Grant ignored him. "Sheriff, I'm Tom's lawyer. He hired me this morning." Grant warned Tom by squeezing his arm.

"Lawyer," Orlan scoffed, as he eyed the man in the worn high-top shoes and patched shirt.. "He ain't any more a lawyer than I am."

Grant took out his wallet, removed a card, and handed it to the sheriff.

"I'm a member of the Oklahoma bar, licensed to practice in the state of Oklahoma."

"Shit! Anybody can get a card sayin' anythin'.."

"Orlan, shut up!" Sheriff Watson snapped, and handed the card back to Grant. He lifted the flap on his shirt pocket and pulled out a folded document. "Take a look."

Grant studied the paper carefully, then folded it and handed it back to the sheriff.

"The judge who issued this is an incompetent fool. What were you holding over his head, Conroy, to make him issue this summons? It isn't worth the paper it's written on." When Marty began to sputter, Grant continued. "A first-year law student, much less a judge, would know that this writ is worthless."

"Are you taking the word of a bum who says he's a lawyer, Sheriff?" Marty asked.

"I may be only a hillbilly sheriff, Conroy, but even I know that a Texas judge has no jurisdiction in Oklahoma. What are you trying to pull here?"

"I'm trying to do right by my dead sister's boy."

"You didn't know that she was dead until you got here . . . or did you?"

"Well . . . no, but I knew she was crazy."

"Was Mr. Conroy's will probated?" Grant asked.

"It was," Marty snarled. "Not that it's any business of yours."

"It will be. I'll send down for a copy. My client has the right to know what was in the will."

"I don't care what was in his damn will," Tom snapped.

"Sheriff, it seems to me that Mr. Conroy came with his

summons to get custody of the child because he knew that his sister was dead and that her inheritance from her father's estate would go to her husband and her child. But if she was dead and the husband hanged for her murder, he would have control. It's clear to me that you have a murder suspect with a motive."

"You may be right. Where were you last night, Conroy?"

"Dammit to hell! Are you accusing me?"

"I'm asking you where you were last night."

"I was in Wichita Falls."

"Can you prove it?"

"I'm sure you've heard of the law firm of Shellenberger and Shellenberger—"

"—Can't say that I have," the sheriff said drily.

"You will. The Conroys have been valuable clients of that firm for over fifty years. They handle the Conroy trust. You'd better watch out, mister, or you'll find yourself going up against a law firm that will eat you alive."

"Is that so, Mr. Big-shot Conroy? Speaking of being eaten up alive. You'd better watch yourself or you'll be sleepin' on a cot in my fleahouse."

"Are you going to honor the judge's orders and let me have my nephew?"

"Hell, no. Are you deaf or something?"

"My mother doesn't give up. We'll get the boy after this murderer swings for killing my sister."

"Get out of here, Conroy. You're damn lucky I'm letting you go. I wouldn't if I didn't know where to find you when I want you."

"The service for your sister will be held tomorrow," Tom said. "If your mother wishes to come, we can delay it a day to give her time to get here."

"She won't be here," Sheriff Watson said, when Marty walked away. "I called her in Dallas, and she said she didn't have a daughter, so that's that."

"Godamighty!" Tom exclaimed.

Chapter Twenty-four

In order not to draw undo attention, because of the gossip about her and Tom, Henry Ann did not attend the burial service for Tom's wife. Karen, Grant, Johnny, Jay, and Tom arrived to find more than fifty curious onlookers gathered around the burial place. Reverend Wesson conducted the graveside service and Karen sang a hymn. When it came time to lower the casket into the grave, Mr. Austin stepped up to help Grant, Johnny, and the Reverend Wesson man the ropes. Jay, confused as to what was happening, clung to Karen's skirts.

Karen and Grant left the cemetery with Karen's father. Tom and Jay left with Johnny driving Tom's car. The crowd was quiet until Tom was getting into his car, then someone yelled.

"Murderer!"

"Why'd ya kill 'er?"

"Ya ain't fit ter live!"

Johnny drove slowly by the crowd that lined the road.

"I'm thinkin' the fellers doin' the yellin' were brought here in that 'Jelly-Bean' car over there." Johnny pointed to the Packard parked on the other side of a row of honeysuckle bushes.

"A man who'd not come to his sister's burial is about as low as he can get," Tom remarked as they drove out of town. "But I guess a mother who disowns her daughter because she has a sick mind is lower."

"Hen Ann make me new shirt," Jay said, trying to get his father's attention.

"You look very nice, son."

Tom's mind was on how he was going to pay the undertaker and for the lot in the cemetery. He would either sell the car or his cows. If it were not for Henry Ann, he would take his son and leave the place where he had had so much grief and more happiness then he thought possible. Grant had assured him that the Conroys didn't have a chance of getting Jay as long as he stayed out of Texas and away from their crooked judge.

Henry Ann, oh, my love. I could no more leave you than I could stop breathing. I never dreamed that there was a love like the one I have for you. It hurts, oh God, it hurts, to have people shun you because of me. I pray that Jay and I and our love for you'll be enough to make up for that.

Sheriff Watson observed the burial service from a distance. Damn stupid people. Imagine being curious enough to come out to the graveyard and stand in the hot sun to watch a poor murdered woman being buried. That brother of hers showed his true colors by not showing up at the gravesite. A blind man would be able to spot that car he was trying to hide in the bushes.

Last night at the Phillips's house Sheriff Watson had had a long talk with his old friend over a large cut of Mrs. Phillips's "pee-con" pie. Phil had filled him in on the story behind Grant Gifford. He was much taken with the young lawyer and was inclined to go along with him when he said Tom Dolan could not have killed his wife and set fire to the house.

Phillips, who acted as part-time county attorney, was looking into the business of Conroy's will, and he believed young Conroy had a motive for killing his sister—a two-thousand-five-hundred-dollar-a-year motive. He knew of the firm of Shellenberger and Shellenberger and said he was sure they would not be part of a scheme by Marty Conroy to take Tom's son away from him.

The sheriff waited until the crowd at the cemetery began to disperse before he got in his car and headed for Mud Creek.

When Pete rode his lathered horse into the yard, he recognized the sheriff's car. Orlan Nelson had come out late last night to tell him the sheriff would be out to question him. Hardy had been paying Orlan off for the better part of a year to keep quiet about their thriving bootlegging business.

Pete had just come from the Hastings place and had found it boarded up. There wasn't a sign of Opal or the old man. The chickens, the cow, and even the dog were gone. It puzzled Pete that they had left so suddenly. If someone had threatened Opal and scared her off, they would hear from him.

Pete unsaddled his horse and carefully wiped him down before he turned him into the corral. After he had carried a bucket of fresh water and set it inside the railed fence, he went to the house. The sheriff was sitting on the porch with Hardy and Jude.

" 'Lo, Sheriff."

" 'Lo, Pete."

"What brings you out our way?"

"I think you know."

"Yeah. News travels fast. Too bad about Dolan's wife." Pete took off his hat, reached for a dipper in the bucket of water on the porch, and poured water over his head. "It's a hell of a way to die."

"Folks tell me you had a party here the other night."

"It was more like a wake."

"I heard that you were madder than hell about gettin' kicked out of the marathon."

"Yeah, I was. You'd have been mad, too, if you'd planned on something for months, then got kicked out the first day."

"You made threats against Miss Henry 'cause you thought she had turned your partner in for being under-age."

"You got it right, Sheriff. When I get mad it unhinges my jaws, and I'm liable to say anything. Ask Hardy."

"I already did."

"I guess that settles it."

"Not quite. Isabel told me the night I took her off the dance floor that you said you'd get even with Tom Dolan for fooling around with Miss Henry—him being married and all and her being a virgin lady."

"I might of said something like that. He was married and had no business foolin' around with a nice woman like Henry Ann and ruinin' her good name."

"Don't reckon you ever fooled around with a married woman," the sheriff said drily.

"None that had a good name and didn't want to be fooled with." Pete grinned.

"Why'er ya askin' Pete these questions?" Hardy had been watching the sheriff and was afraid that he had something on his mind that he wasn't going to like.

"It's my business to ask questions. Where were you that night, Pete?"

"Here at the wake." He grinned again.

"All night?"

"Think so. I was pretty drunk."

"Some of your relatives say you saddled up and pulled out about dark."

"Who said that?" Hardy's voice boomed so loud the dogs began to bark. "Who in the hell said Pete wasn't here?"

"A couple of folks. They didn't know why I was asking the questions about who was here and how long they stayed."

"Well, he was here. Goddamnit! He was here. Wasn't he Jude?"

"I wasn't here, Hardy. I didn't get back until midnight. Everyone was gone by then."

"Where did you go?" Sheriff turned his sharp gaze on Jude, who sat on the end of the porch whittling on a stick.

"Mrs. Powell's. She and Mr. Powell are tutoring me so I can pass the college exam."

"That'll be easy enough to check out. Now back to you, Pete. Where did you go?"

"I rode over to the Hastings's place."

"Who was there?"

"The old man. Opal had gone off with Chris Austin."

"You know where they went?"

"No."

"They went to Wichita Falls and got married."

Pete said nothing for several seconds; then a quick smile flashed across Pete's face.

"He married her? Well, now, don't that just take the cake? I never thought he had brains or guts enough to latch on to a girl like Opal. So that's why the place was boarded up; they married, left Mud Creek, and took the old man with them."

"She wasn't one of your women?"

"Not 'cause I didn't try." Pete smiled again.

"Everyone thinks her baby is yours."

"Well, it isn't. She swore she didn't know who raped her. I think it was a Perry. And if I knew which one, I'd kill him, and she knows it."

Pete pulled a comb out of his shirt pocket and ran it through his damp hair.

"Don't see many pink combs," Sheriff Watson said after Pete put the comb back in his shirt pocket. "Don't know as I ever saw another one."

"It's the only one I ever saw. Most are black." Pete pulled the comb from his pocket again. "It's got all its teeth, too."

"Where'd ya get it?"

"Found it on the back porch. Guess one of the folks lost it the other night." He laughed. "They'll play hell gettin' it back."

The sheriff stood slowly. He drew his gun with one hand and pulled out his handcuffs with the other.

"You're under arrest, Pete. Turn around."

"What the hell—" Hardy came off the porch.

"Stay back, Hardy."

"Pete said he went over to see old man Hastings. Go over there and ask him."

"Hastings is gone. The place is boarded up. I was there before I came here."

"Good God, man. Go find him." Pete looked at the sheriff from over his shoulder. "You arresting me 'cause old Hastings is gone, and I can't prove I was there?"

"No. I'm arresting you because you have Mrs. Dolan's comb in your pocket. The comb she left out at that little hidey place by the creek where she was murdered."

"I found it, for God's sake. I found it on the back porch."

"Hellfire," Hardy exclaimed. "Half of Mud Creek knew about her going to that place. That woman was crazy as a bedbug."

"Maybe so, but she didn't deserve to be killed." The sheriff snapped the handcuffs on Pete's wrists.

"I never screwed that woman. I can get 'em without takin' a loony," Pete insisted. He knew better than to make a sudden move with the barrel of a gun in his back.

"Cousin Wally bragged about gettin' it out there," Hardy said. "She was willin'. More than willin'. Begged for it like a two-bit whore."

"Pete's the one I'm interested in right now. He has the comb. You'd better get busy and sell some of that white lightning, Hardy. Pete's going to need a lawyer."

Jude and Hardy stood in the yard and watched the sheriff put Pete in the car.

"Take care of my horse, Jude," Pete yelled.

"Don't worry 'bout him." The boy and the man watched the sheriff's car drive away. "He didn't do it, Hardy."

Jude's voice shook. "Pete brags and all that, but he'd not kill a woman. He talks nasty to make himself look big. He wants to be more than what he is."

"There ain't nothin' wrong with what he is," Hardy retorted angrily. "There's not a woman on Mud Creek that wouldn't jump at the chance to have him."

"Opal Hastings didn't jump at the chance to have him. Pete doesn't want anyone to know it, but he's really sweet on Henry Ann Henry."

"She couldn't see him for dirt. Damn her! I'd stake my life that Pete didn't kill that woman. If I find out who did it and blamed it on Pete, I'll break his goddamn neck."

"It'd not help Pete for you to kill someone else. Let me think on this, Hardy. You start thinking, too, of everybody that bragged about getting to Dolan's wife. Somebody dropped that comb on the porch to make it look like Pete or one of us did it. Who's been here since that night?"

"Hell, I don't remember."

"If we're going to help Pete, you'd better get to remembering."

Hardy looked at his young son with a new respect.

"How old are you now, Jude?"

"Eighteen."

"I guess I forget yo're a man now."

"Nobody's going to lift a finger to help a Perry. We've got to give the sheriff a reason to think it was someone other than Pete."

Grant came back after taking Karen home with the news that the sheriff had arrested Pete Perry for the murder of Emmajean Dolan.

"Oh, my," Henry Ann said. "The sheriff must have had good reason to arrest him, but I can't imagine him doing it"

"Pete's father came in to see Mr. Phillips and tried to hire him to defend Pete. Mr. Phillips had to explain that he was hired by the county to prosecute Pete. The man was ready to punch Mr. Phillips when the young kid with him intervened and asked who was the next best lawyer in the county."

"That would be Jude, Pete's younger brother, doing the asking," Johnny explained. "He's real smart and wants to go to college. Pete treats the kid like dirt sometimes, but I think he was proud of him, too."

Just after dark when the fireflies were out, Henry Ann caught one and put it in a glass jar for Jay. She and the boy sat in the porch swing, Tom on the steps; Grant and Johnny lolled in the chairs. All were wrapped in their own thoughts.

Aunt Dozie was in the parlor listening to the radio. Amos and Andy were having problems running their Fresh Air Taxicab Company. Dozie had never seen a taxicab, much less ridden in one, but that didn't keep her from enjoying the show. Every once in a while Henry Ann could hear her laugh. It was such a pleasant, normal sound after the tension of the past few days.

She waited impatiently for the time she could be alone with Tom before he went back home to sleep in the barn. Johnny had taken over fresh straw, bedding, towels, and soap. She had sent along her daddy's shaving equipment and a small mirror. He had to be there, she knew, to look after his stock and to discourage thieves who might think the homestead was deserted and help themselves to whatever they could find.

When Aunt Dozie turned off the radio, Henry Ann gently shook Jay, who had cuddled up beside her and was dozing against her arm.

"Time to go to bed, sweetheart."

"Can I take my firefly?"

"Why don't we let it go play with the other fireflies? We'll get another one tomorrow night and keep it for a while."

" 'Bye, firefly," Jay said sleepily.

Henry Ann, conscious of Tom's eyes on her, took the jar from Jay's hand and tilted it so that the little bug could fly out into the night. She lifted the child from the swing, and they went into the house.

When the ritual of washing and undressing was over, Tom came to the bedroom door to take his son outside to let water. He had him stand on the edge of the back porch so that he'd not get his feet dirty. His eyes caught and held Henry Ann's when they returned to the bedroom, and she felt a fluttering in her stomach.

"Good night, sweetheart." Henry Ann bent to kiss the child's cheek after he was in the bed.

"Goo'night, Mama. Goo'night, Daddy."

"See you tomorrow, son."

Henry Ann caught her breath and looked quickly at Tom. He took her hand in his bandaged one, then reached to turn off the light that hung from the ceiling in the center of the room. The house was dark except for the light that came from the crack under the door of Aunt Dozie's room. He led Henry Ann out the front door to the porch, vacant now, and wrapped her in his arms.

"Ah . . . love. My sweet love," he breathed just before he found her lips with his and kissed her sweetly, tenderly.

"Tom." Henry Ann held back. "I told Jay to call me Henry Ann. I haven't encouraged him to call me . . . that."

"Do you mind, honey? He needs a mama. He's never really had one."

"I love it. I've always wanted children and hoped I'd have more than one. It was lonely growing up an only child. I'd not want to take his mother's place. I want to make a place of my own."

"She had no place, sweetheart. And you have made a place of your own. You've been the only mama he's ever had."

"I feel like he's mine. I love him. I couldn't bear to lose him."

"You won't lose him. Grant assured me of that."

"I was surprised that he's a lawyer."

"We can talk about Grant later." Tom pulled her back into his arms and kissed her. "You love me, really love me?" His whispered words came against her lips.

"Yes, yes, and yes."

"Come ride with me."

He led her out into the yard to where he had left the car. When she was settled in the seat, he went around to the other side and got under the wheel. He backed the car out onto the road. Moonlight made headlights unnecessary. He drove slowly with one arm around Henry Ann. No words were spoken. They were content to be close together in the darkness. She leaned her head on his shoulder; he reverently kissed her forehead.

They reached the Dolan farm and Tom drove into the yard, turned off the motor, and put both arms around Henry Ann. As he kissed her, her arm slipped up and around his neck.

"Most folks wouldn't understand this, but I never, never felt married to Emmajean. I pitied her and stayed with her because she was Jay's mother. I feel married to you, my love, in my heart."

"Was it because you were not married in the Catholic Church?"

"That wasn't it at all. When *we* marry, I hope that you'll consent to be married in both churches. I'll never ask you to give up your religion for mine—"

"—Nor will I ask you." All her senses were filled with his overwhelming male presence. She could feel his lips at the side of her face and smell the woodsmoke still in his hair.

He tilted her face to his. It was too dark to see his eyes, but she knew that he was looking into hers. Her palm caressed his face. All the love, the warmth, the yearning was there in her touch.

"I love you so much." The words tumbled from her lips. She felt his body tremble.

"That's what I need to hear, sweetheart." He kissed her eyes, her cheeks, her mouth. "I've felt so guilty . . . about the other night. Your first time should have been in a soft bed where we could have taken our time, and I could have loved you all night long—"

"Hush, love." She put her fingers over his lips. "That little time we had together was perfect."

"You don't . . . regret that we didn't wait?"

"No. I'm only sorry that while we . . . while we—"

"I know. I'll carry that guilt for as long as I live."

They were silent for a long while, holding each other, content to be together. When Tom spoke it was after a series of long, sweet kisses.

"I've not got much to offer you now, sweetheart. But someday I will. I'll work this farm, I'll set up a shop here to fix cars when all this is settled. I'll have something wonderful to look forward to . . . you and Jay in a home of our own."

"How long do I wait?"

"I'm not sure. But it will happen just as soon as I can make it happen."

"Why wait at all? My home would be our home . . . yours and mine and Jay's and Johnny's."

He drew back. "I'll not have folks think that I married you for what you have. I want them to know that I married you because I love you with all my heart and that I'm taking you to love and care for, for better or for worse."

"I don't care what people think." She leaned farther back to look at him. "Are we going to let *things* keep us apart? It isn't fair for you to ask me to wait until you can accumulate as many *things* as I have. I want us to share what we have."

"I don't have much to share, love. I'm not even a very good farmer."

"I wouldn't care if you were a bum coming off the road. But you have this land to add to mine. It will be ours then. You have your ability to fix things. Someday Johnny will leave to make his own way—"

"Sweetheart, we can't make plans until this thing with Emmajean is settled. Let's not talk about it now. I just want to hold you and kiss you and tell you what it means to me to know that you love me. You gave me the most precious gift a woman can give . . ." The words came jerkily, his voice husky. His mouth closed hungrily over hers in a deep, moist, endless kiss. His bandaged hand moved over her breast, and he groaned. "I want to feel your sweet breasts again, hold them, kiss them—"

It seemed to Henry Ann that they were no longer two separate people, but one blended together by magic. She slipped her hand inside his shirt and raked her fingertips over the soft fur on his chest. She was giddy with the freedom to caress him. Their noses were side by side and their lips so close they touched when they spoke.

"I like to touch you," she whispered.

"I like for you to. Oh, God, I like it so much." Then as her hand continued to caress, "You'd better stop, sweetheart. I might have to have you right now."

"Would that be so bad?"

"The next time we come together it will be as man and wife. It's going to be perfect. I'm going to love you all night long, and there'll be no bandages on my hands so I can feel every inch of you."

"I could feel you," she said, kissing him with teasing slowness.

He hugged her hard. "Sweetheart, you're driving me crazy. If you weren't so damn sweet, I'd think you were a witch. You've put a spell on me."

"I'm glad. So glad."

"I'm taking you home before I lose control of my senses." He took his arm from around her and started the car. "Just wait, girl," he teased. "I'll get even with you for what you've done to me tonight."

"And what is that? I know about the birds and the bees," she teased.

He moved the hand on his thigh to nudge the hardness between his legs.

"A bird or a bee doesn't have . . . that."

"They must have . . . that, or there'd not be little birds and little bees."

"They don't need to pour a bucket of well water over their heads to cool them off before they can go to sleep."

"Is that what you'll do?"

"It'll not do much good. I've been in this condition every night since I met you."

"Oh, poor Tom. I know how to end that . . . torment." Her whisper was soft and seductive.

Tom put his foot on the brake and stopped the car in the middle of the road.

"Come here, woman. You're going to have to learn that backtalk won't be tolerated in this family." He kissed her long and hard.

Chapter Twenty-five

Johnny heard Tom's car leave the farm and knew that Henry Ann was with him. He came down from the attic room, went out onto the back stoop, and headed for the outhouse.

"P-s-s-t! P-s-s-t!"

Johnny dropped into a crouch and spun around, his eyes searching the darkness.

"Johnny, it's me, Jude." The boy came from behind a patch of hollyhocks that shielded the privy from the house. "I was 'bout to knock on the door. Thank God you came out."

"Jude! Mother of Christ! You scared hell out of me, considering what's happened. How'd you get here?"

"On Pete's horse. I need your help, Johnny. You don't believe Pete killed that woman, do you?"

"I didn't think so, but I'm not the sheriff."

"He found Mrs. Dolan's comb on our porch, Johnny. I've got to find out who killed her, or they'll hang Pete just 'cause he's a Perry."

"The sheriff is a fair man. I can't say as much for his deputy."

Jude snorted with disgust. "Orlan has been taking a pay-off from Hardy to turn a blind eye to his and Pete's boot-legging. Pete isn't lily-white, but he'd not kill a woman. A man maybe, but not a woman."

"I don't know what I can do to help you, Jude."

"What else did that woman have in her hidey place? Would she have had a mirror and a long string of green glass beads?"

"Yeah. It's what Tom told the sheriff she had. Some rib-bons, garters, bows for her hair, too. Yeah, and he said that she had a little blue bottle of perfume."

"Ah . . ."

"What'a you mean by that?"

"Nothing. How about drawers?"

"Underpants? I've not heard anything about under-pants."

"Well . . . thanks, Johnny."

"Jude! Wait! What do you know about those things?"

"I needed to know if she had taken anything to the river beside the pink comb. I got to get back to Hardy. He's about crazy with worry over Pete. 'Bye, Johnny."

Jude disappeared in the darkness, and soon Johnny heard the creak of saddle leather and then the sound of hoofbeats. He waited until he could no longer hear them, and then headed once again for the outhouse.

It was not long before it was all over town that Reverend Wesson's daughter was going to marry the *bum* that had been working at the Henry farm. The outrage expressed by the ladies of the church changed the instant it was learned that the *bum* was a well-known, even famous attorney.

All sorts of reasons were given for Grant passing himself off as an out-of-work transient. Some had heard—from the horse's mouth, of course—that he had lost his memory for a while. Others said that he was gathering material for a book. Still others were sure that he was in disguise while trailing a crooked federal officer.

Karen was once again the darling of the congregation. The maiden or widowed ladies gathered around and vied for the opportunity to help her with the wedding plans.

Henry Ann, on the other hand, was still held in contempt. Mrs. Austin and Mrs. Miller continued spreading their malicious gossip. Of course, it was *her* fault that Chris Austin had run away with the *whore* on Mud Creek. And it was her fault that poor Mrs. Dolan lost her mind after Mr. Dolan gave her child to Henry Ann and began his affair with her. Marty Conroy found plenty of ears willing to listen to his opinion of his former brother-in-law and the woman who stole his sister's husband.

Hard times and the lack of hope that they would soon be better, united the people of Red Rock. Henry Ann knew that there was nothing that brought folks together faster than to be against someone. At the present time it was she and Tom Dolan they were against.

After a couple of days the talk about Pete Perry died down. After all, he was in jail over at the county seat. The marathon was about to peter out. Only three couples remained, and the talk was that the prize money would have to be paid in installments because not enough money had been raised through admissions paid by spectators.

Henry Ann's newfound happiness with Tom and the

knowledge that she loved him, and that he loved her, carried her through these heartbreaking times. She had been to town, to church, and had calmly ignored the snubs from her former friends and acquaintances. Although she felt that the talk would pass when the gossips found someone else to vilify, that didn't make it any less hurtful.

Grant had contacted the Conroy family attorneys and had been sent a copy of Martin Conroy's will. Emmajean's inheritance would be placed in a trust for her son. Because of Marty Conroy's unethical attempt to get custody of Jay, his name had been removed as administrator, and the boy's inheritance was now controlled by the trustees. This suited Tom. He wanted no part of it.

A couple of weeks passed. The sheriff still came by the farm occasionally. To all appearances, he had given up looking for any other suspect. He seemed confident he had the killer of Mrs. Dolan locked up in his jail.

For the third day the wind blowing out of the west had carried with it the red topsoil of the plains. Strong gusts stung the faces of the men doing the chores and blew in under the doors and windowsills. At the Henry farm the house was hot, with the windows closed. On the west side of the house Aunt Dozie had laid wet cloths along the sills to catch the dust. The porch was covered with a thick layer of red dirt.

Sheriff Watson arrived just before the noon meal and was invited to stay and eat, as he knew he would be. Tom was there, and so was Johnny. Grant had not been at the farm for a few days. He had gone to Tulsa to see his mother and sister and tell them about his plans to marry Karen Wesson.

The meal of butter beans, turnip greens, fried okra, and corn bread was as good as Sheriff Watson had expected it to be. After consuming a second helping of sweet potato pie, he declared the dinner a feast.

"Thought I'd stop by and see if there was any news," he said, after finishing off his second slice of pie.

"You mean anything else that'd tie Pete to the killing?" Johnny asked.

"Anything. Thought Dolan might have found something over at the house."

"I poked around in the ashes and found a few things. My grandpa's Civil War belt buckle and an iron skillet. I think the lantern on the porch was lit, then thrown into the house. That would account for the front part of the house burning first."

"Sounds logical."

"Emmajean would have gone out the back door; and if she was going to set fire to the house, she would have started it there. Pete Perry, if he started the fire, did a sloppy job."

"Pete would have made sure it had a better start," Johnny said.

"You don't think he did it. Well, I can only go by the evidence, and so far it points to him."

By midmorning the wind had began to die down. When the noon meal was over, it had stopped blowing, but a veil of dust hung in the air. Clucking like a mother hen, Aunt Dozie set about opening windows and wiping up dirt carried in on the wind. The others gathered on the front porch to say good-bye to the sheriff.

"Is the date set for the trial, Sheriff?" Henry Ann asked.

"Five weeks from today. Judge Foster doesn't believe in

waiting around. Phil is preparing the case against Pete. You'll be called as a witness, Dolan. I reckon you will be, too, Johnny."

"I've nothing to say against Pete," Johnny said quickly.

"You won't be asked to say anything against him. Only what you know."

"What happens if I don't show up?"

"You go to jail."

The sheriff was on his way across the yard when two topless beat-up cars came speeding down the road. One had a front fender missing, the other the two front doors. They passed the Henry farm, then skidded to a halt and turned around.

"Who in the world?" Henry Ann exclaimed.

"Looks to be about all of Mud Creek," Johnny said drily. "Half of them anyway."

The first car pulled in behind the sheriff's, blocking him in.

"Sheriff," Jude Perry called, "we were on our way to see you."

Tom, Henry Ann, and Johnny moved out into the yard, their eyes on the occupants of the car and the one behind it. The sheriff was approaching the car when Hardy Perry stood up.

"Here's the one that killed that woman. You gotta let Pete go."

"What the hell—" Sheriff Watson looked down to see Fat Perry, trussed up like a hog going to slaughter, wedged between the front and the backseat of the car. The old lady in the front seat began to wail.

"Fat did it. We got proof, Sheriff." Jude was more calm than his daddy. He motioned to the women in the car driven by his cousin Wally. They got out and came to stand beside him. "He gave the mirror to Sudie Howell, she's Cousin Wally's cousin on the other side." Sudie bobbed her head up and down.

"He gave some of the hair bows to Betty Joy and the glass beads to Peggy. They all had to promise to let him diddle with them. None did, but Peggy." She appeared to be old enough to be the mother of the girls. "She said he had a hair ribbon tied around his balls and pecker with a bow in front. Can you beat that, Sheriff? Did you ever hear of anything so nasty? It's enough to make me want to puke."

"Yeah. Make ya puke," Peggy repeated, feeling her importance.

"He owned up to it." Hardy's angry shout broke in. "He was goin' to let Pete take the blame."

"From the looks of him," the sheriff said, eyeing Fat's swollen face and split lip, "someone persuaded him to own up to it."

"Yo're goddamn right. He was lucky I didn't kill him. He put that comb on the porch hopin' to get blame put on Pete."

"One day he came over smelling like a rose garden and I got to wondering where he got the perfume." Jude took a blue bottle and a pair of drawers out of his pocket and gave them to the sheriff. "I followed Fat. He went into a shed. I saw him get out a pair of women's drawers, smell them, and rub them on his face. Then he hid them and the bottle; but after I found out he'd given the girls this other stuff, I went back to the shed and got them."

"You're quite a detective, Jude."

"I knew Pete hadn't done it."

"Well, get that fat fart outta there, Hardy."

"Ohhhh . . . My boy! My po . . . or boy!"

"Who's that?"

"Fat's mama. She thinks we're picking on Fat."

"Natural feelings of a mama."

Hardy had pulled Fat out of the car and onto the ground. The man's feet were tied as well as his hands behind his back. A rag was stuffed in his mouth. The sheriff helped him to stand and pulled out the gag. The fat man began to cry.

"What do you have to say, Fat?"

"They . . . made me say . . . I did it—"

"But did you kill that woman?"

"I . . . I . . ."

Tom stepped up and pulled the tobacco pouch and papers from Fat's bib pocket.

"The butts I found out there were from this kind of cigarette paper and this kind of tobacco. You took her to that shed on Austin's land, didn't you? You raped her and hit her that night. I wish Hardy had beat you to death. It's what you deserve for taking advantage of that mindless woman."

"I didn't rape her. She wanted me to do it. Pulled up her dress, opened her legs—"

"She was out of her mind, you son of a bitch!"

"I didn't mean to hurt her. Ever'body on Mud Creek had a woman but me. Nobody'd let me. Ever time I asked, they laughed." As the words poured out of Fat his voice became smothered with sobs. "She was prettier than any woman they had . . . 'cepts Pete. I warn't goin' to hurt her," he repeated. "She kept . . . yellin' and yellin'. I told her to hush up, but she wouldn't and . . . had to make her hush—"

"I ought to kill you!"

"That'll be the state's job, Dolan."

"Why burn the house? Wouldn't she go with you?"

"I never burned no house. I swear it. I waited till she come out like she done other nights and followed her. I thought she was goin' to meet the man in the fancy car—"

"What fancy car?"

"The one parked in the Austins' woods. She didn't go there. She went to the place by the creek, where she always went."

"Christ! Do you suppose Marty Conroy tried to burn me and Emmajean up in that house? That little weasel! If I find out he burned my house, I'll beat hell out of him."

"Let it go, Dolan. You can't prove it."

"I could beat it out of him."

"What good would it do? Untie Fat's legs, Hardy, and help me get him in the car. The slobs too big to carry. The rest of you follow me in. You'll have to convince Judge Foster that Fat killed Mrs. Dolan before he'll let Pete out."

"Want me to ride along with ya and keep a eye on this hunk a lard, Sheriff?"

"Be all right, Hardy. Climb in."

Jude was smiling. "Told you, Johnny. Told you Pete didn't do it."

"You did good, Jude. Real good."

"I got to give Hardy credit for makin' Fat own up. Lordy, but he was mad. If he hadn't had to turn him over to the sheriff to get Pete out, he'd a stomped him to death. He thinks a heap of Pete." Jude shrugged. "It's no wonder. Folks say Pete's just like Hardy was when he was young."

*   *   *

It was late evening. Jay was in bed, Aunt Dozie was listening to the Texaco Fire Chief on the radio, and Johnny had taken the car and gone into town. The only sound was the squeaking of the chains that held the porch swing.

"Does the wind blow like this in Nebraska?"

Henry Ann and Tom sat in the gently moving swing. His arm was around her, with her shoulder tucked beneath his arm. Her hip and thigh were pressed firmly to him. Occasionally his mouth brushed undemandingly across her lips.

"Sometimes," Tom murmured. "I don't remember the dust blowing like it does here."

A contented silence followed until Henry Ann said:

"I'm glad it wasn't Pete who killed Emmajean."

"Why? You're not getting a soft spot for him, are you?"

"No, silly. I've only got a soft spot for you."

"I'm jealous of every man you look at. For a while I hated Grant being here with you."

"You didn't! Guess I'll have to get you a pair of horse blinders."

"I love you." Tom moved his face until it was only inches from hers. "I love you more every day I'll love you when you're rocking our great-grandchildren."

"But . . . I'll not have any teeth!"

"You'll be beautiful without teeth."

When Henry Ann was with this gloriously wonderful, exciting man the magic of him threatened to draw every little speck of logic from her mind. She felt the warmth of his breath and savored the thrill of being close to his hard, warm body and inhaling the very presence of him.

"When we're alone in the dark, Tom, the world shrinks until there is only you and me. It's so calm and peaceful."

"For me, too. With you I feel a peace I haven't known for years. With you, I don't feel lonely inside anymore."

The sincerity in his voice touched her heart in a way his words did not. She remembered the pain in his eyes the day he had given her and Isabel a ride home. She hadn't guessed what goodness existed in the man with the gruff voice, wild hair, and dark, pain-filled eyes. They sat quietly now, neither intruding on the other's thoughts as they enjoyed the simple pleasure of being close.

"I don't want you to go back over there." She loosened a button on his shirt and slipped her hand inside to stroke his chest. His skin was warm, and she could feel the quivering of his flesh. "Why don't you bring everything over here and stay?"

"Honey, folks are already talking—"

"I don't care. Let them talk."

"If we were going to move away, it wouldn't matter."

"We'd be foolish to give up what we have here. We'd not get half what the farms are worth."

"I realize that. I like it here, but I don't want you to be hurt by gossip."

"There are different kinds of hurt. Daddy was hurt. He was lonely. If he had found someone to love, Dorene, just for spite, wouldn't have let him go. I want to be with you and Jay and have your babies—"

Tom lowered his lips to hers and kissed her with slow deliberation. His lips caressed her mouth gently, sweetly, for a long time. When he drew back to look into her face, his eyes were smiling.

"How about getting married . . . tomorrow? I want to be with you day and night. I'm tired of long lonely nights. I love you, love you. What do we care if people think I married you for your farm? We know it isn't true."

Henry Ann laughed happily. "You're bringing far more to this union than I am. You're bringing Jay—the sweetest, most wonderful little boy in all the world."

"I thought I was the most wonderful boy in the world." Tom hugged her as if she were about to be snatched away from him and drugged her with deep, moist kisses.

"You're the most wonderful *big* boy in the world."

"Oh, God. It purely scares hell out of me to think I might never have found you." After a dozen more kisses he said, "I love you." A groan of anguish left his throat. "Kiss me again, Henry Ann Henry. Tomorrow you're going to be Henry Ann Dolan!"

Aunt Dozie had come from her room to get her snuffbox and had paused beside the door to see the couple in the porch swing wrapped in each other's arms and heard their whispered words.

Dozie chuckled silently, her rounded belly moving up and down under her nightdress.

Mister Tom be a full-blooded man. He give my Henry Ann plenty of love . . . and lovin'. Dem babies'll be comin'. Thanks to de Lawd. It's what I's been hopin' for.

SUMMER 1934

Epilogue

The hope that times would be better as soon as Franklin Roosevelt was elected president was still strong in the hearts of the people of Red Rock. The National Recovery Administration, the NRA, had been established to stabilize prices, regulate business, and initiate programs for agriculture. A public works program would be called WPA. In his "fireside chat" radio addresses, President Roosevelt urged the American people to have faith in the banks, to be patient, support the New Deal, and, above all, not to give up hope.

Henry Ann and Tom Dolan were better off than most. Henry Ann insisted that their combined acres of land be called the DOLAN RANCH. The cotton crop of 1932, for the fourth year in a row, had been a failure. That fall, after the meager crop was picked, Tom and Johnny decided to sow the fields in grass for grazing. Johnny Henry very much preferred herding cattle to chopping cotton.

He was now twenty years old and thinking about joining the navy. Pete Perry had signed up as soon as he left Sheriff Watson's jail, and his letters to Johnny had whetted the boy's appetite to see faraway places. To the surprise of everyone, Pete had finally found a place where he was accepted for his abilities and not branded Mud Creek trash.

After Grant and Karen were married and Grant had opened a practice in Oklahoma City, he took an interest in Jude and helped him enter the University of Oklahoma. Jude had decided, after a brief acquaintance with Grant, to become a lawyer.

Hardy Perry married a young girl from Ringling who liked to dance and not do much else. Prohibition was repealed, and Hardy was out of the bootlegging business; but he was scraping out a living somehow, apparently without much work.

It was a surprise to all when Fat Perry died of a heart attack in Sheriff Watson's jail before his case came to trial. His death saved his kin on Mud Creek from having to testify against him.

The big news at the Dolan Ranch was that Henry Ann was due to deliver their first child any day. Tom was beside himself with anxiety. He was never gone from the house for more than an hour at a time. Johnny was almost as bad. It was canning season. Tom volunteered to wash jars and Johnny insisted on digging and washing beets.

"Hee, hee, hee," Aunt Dozie laughed gleefully one afternoon. "We gettin' all dis help cause yo got a big belly. Yo're goin' to have ta get ya one ever' year at dis time."

That night, lying in bed, Henry Ann told Tom what Aunt Dozie had said.

"And what did you say?" He lifted her nightdress so he could rub her back. "I don't know why you wear this thing," he grumbled. "It's just in the way."

She smiled at the complaint she'd heard many times before, then ignored it.

"I said that I'd not let you in my bed during the fall months if you were going to make my belly this big in July."

"And who around here is big enough to keep me out?" He laughed, delighted with her, and nuzzled her neck. "It won't be Jay. He can hardly wait to have a brother . . . or sister."

The time Henry Ann loved the most was when she and Tom were in their bed, nothing between them, whispering important and nonsensical things. She turned to him now, pulled his head to her shoulder, and rested her protruding stomach against him. His large hand stroked the taut flesh.

"I felt him," he said in an awed whisper. "He's clamoring to get out of there and get a look at his pretty mama."

"It can't be too soon for me. Whoa! Did you feel that? The little dickens kicks like a mule."

"That's my boy. Strong like his daddy." Tom continued to run his hand over the mound that was his child growing in the body of the woman who was as necessary to him as his heartbeat.

"Stubborn like his daddy, too. What are we going to name him or her?"

"I've got that all figured out. If it's a boy we'll name him Dolan Dolan and if it's a girl," he added quickly, "we'll name her Dolan Ann Dolan."

"You'll do no such thing!" Henry Ann could feel the deep silent laughter he was trying to surpress, and began to giggle. "I'm warning you. My bladder is not too reliable these days. You make me laugh, and you'll have to go find dry sheets."

WILDBIRD™

BIRDING AT ITS BEST

Red-headed Woodpecker
P.O. Box 52898, Boulder, CO 80322-2898

He traced a ring around her navel with his fingertips and moved up to cup her breasts and stroke the dark nipple with his thumb. His lips moved along her jaw to her lips. He kissed her swiftly, urgently. He had not known what happiness was until she had come into his life.

He was hard now and throbbing, but he could wait.

"I've missed being with you the past few weeks. I plan to make up for lost time when our son finally breaks out of his cocoon. I'm jealous of him having you all to himself."

Henry Ann's heart skipped a beat, then another. He was her everything: her husband, lover, friend. She loved him with such fierce intensity that it sometimes puzzled her. Feeling loved, and cherishing this time when she could give him all her attention, she hugged his shaggy head to her breast.

Before another hour passed she was going to have to tell him to get in the car and go for Doctor Hendricks. But there was time for her to hold him a bit longer.

If you enjoyed
With Hope
LOOK FOR
With Song
by Dorothy Garlock

The Second Book of the
"Between the Wars" Series

COMING IN THE SPRING OF 1999

Set in Kansas in 1934, WITH SONG is the story of Federal Marshal Hod Dolan, Tom Dolan's brother. The Great Depression is in full swing. Outlaw gangs are terrorizing the country. Fresh from participating in the demise of the Clyde Barrow gang, the marshal is sent to Kansas to search for two cold-blooded killers who have a desperate need to eliminate a witness. The witness is a pretty, spunky country girl, who is as anxious as the marshal to catch the pair. If you would like to sample the book, an excerpt follows.

I would be pleased to hear from you.

Dorothy Garlock

Dorothy Garlock

PROLOGUE

"My baby don't care for shows. My baby don't care for clothes. My baby just cares for me—"

1934 SEWARD COUNTY, KANSAS

The long-legged girl sang in a loud clear voice as she came into the back of the store with an armload of sun-dried clothes.

"What kinda song is that?" her father asked.

"A good one. Wanna hear more?"

"Not if I don't have to." A mock frown covered his usually smiling face.

"You don't know good music when you hear it. All you listen to is that old Doc Brinkley down in Del Rio playing cowboy music," she teased.

"Don't be knockin' old Doc. If his goat glands can do what he says they can, I'm thinkin' of makin' a trip down to Texas to get me some before the crowd gets there and they run out of goats."

"You'd better not let Mama hear you say that. She'll take you to the woodshed."

"I'll woodshed him all right if he shoots off any more

of those blasted firecrackers." Molly's mother set a basket of clothes on the floor beside a table and began folding towels.

"You're in trouble now." Molly danced up to her father and kissed his cheek. *"I wanna be loved by you, nobody else but you—Boop Boop A Doo!"* She laughed gaily when he made an attempt to avoid a second kiss and ran up the stairs to the living quarters.

Roy McKenzie shook his head. It was good to have his girl home again. She brightened the place like an electric lightbulb.

The driver stopped the big Oldsmobile a hundred yards down the road from the store and slipped the gearshift into neutral. The engine purred impatiently.

"Just sittin' there. Ripe for pickin', ain't it?" He glanced at the man who lounged beside him holding the butt end of a cigar between his teeth. "I could use a orange soda pop right about now."

Didn't the bastard ever sweat? He looks cool as a cucumber, while I'm sweating like a nigger at an election.

Eyes, so light a blue that they appeared to be colorless and as cold as a chunk of ice, turned to the driver.

"What ya waitin' for? Get on down there before we sit here and use up what gas we got left." He took the butt from his mouth and held it between his thumb and forefinger as he leaned forward to scrutinize the building they were approaching.

The store was typical of many scattered over the Kansas plains. Painted above the slanting roof on the porch that stretched across the front of the two-story frame building a

444

sign read: MCKENZIE GENERAL STORE. And in smaller letters beneath it: GROCERIES-FEED-GAS.

The lone Phillips 66 gasoline pump had a post sunk into the ground on each side of it to protect it from careless drivers. Tin signs advertising everything from Garrett's snuff to P&G soap were tacked to the front of the store. On the screen door a big white one outlined in red advertised NeHi SODA POP. A few shade trees were scattered to the side and behind the building. All was still except for the clothes that fluttered gently from a clothesline situated to catch the southern breeze and the bees buzzing around a clump of honeysuckle bushes.

The cold eyes took in everything about the place. When the car stopped beside the tall gas pump in front of the store, the man stepped out and looked back through the cloud of dust that hung over the long flat road. He saw no sign of another car approaching. He dropped the butt of his cigar on the ground and smashed it into the dirt with the sole of his highly polished shoe.

"Need gas?" The words followed the slamming of the screened door.

A plump man with sparse gray hair and a white apron tied about his waist waited at the top of the steps.

"Yeah."

Roy McKenzie crossed the dirt drive to the pump. The tank that held the gas was a round glass cylinder. It was empty, and the side of the glass was marked like a measuring beaker. Roy, his hands on a lever, started pumping. The gas poured in and rose up the sides of the tank. When he'd pumped it full, he unscrewed the cap on the car tank and let the gas run down the hose and into the car.

"I 'spect it's pretty hot travelin'. 'Fraid it's goin' to be a scorchin' summer."

As he waited for the tank to fill, he glanced into the backseat of the car. The double-barreled muzzle of a shotgun protruded out from under a blanket. His eyes shifted to the men. They stood at the end of the car watching him. *City men. A fast car. A shotgun.* Apprehension rose in him as he began to hand-pump the gas into the tank.

"How much?" he asked, pulling the handle back and forth.

"Much as it'll take. Holds eighteen gallons. Was damn near empty."

"These big cars have a way of eatin' gas." When the pump registered the seventeen gallons, the storekeeper hung the hose back on the pump and put the cap back on the tank. "That'll be three dollars and six cents. Gas goin' up every day. I'm still holdin' at eighteen cents."

"Got any cold soda pop?"

"Sure do. Iceman was here yesterday."

Roy's feeling of apprehension escalated. The hair seemed to stand on the back of his neck as the two men followed him out of the bright sunshine and into the store. His eyes met those of his wife in the back of the store where she was folding clothes she had brought in from the line.

"I've got orange, grape, and cream soda."

"Orange."

Wishing the men would leave, wishing his wife would go upstairs to their daughter, Roy took a bottle of pop from the chest cooler and wiped the water off it with a cloth.

"That adds another nickel to your bill."

"Got any SenSen?"

446

"How many?" The storekeeper moved down the counter and took a cardboard box filled with small paper packets from a shelf.

"The whole box."

"The . . . whole—" The bullet that cut off his words went through his chest and into a can of peaches on the shelf behind him. He was flung back, knocking over tins of baking powder before he sank to the floor.

"Take care of her." The cold-eyed man jerked his head toward Mrs. McKenzie, who stood frozen in horror, her hand over her mouth.

"Ya . . . know I ain't got no stomach for killin' women."

"Do it, goddammit, 'less ya want the Feds down on ya. She got a good look at your ugly face." The gunman jerked open the cash drawer and pulled out a few dollar bills. "Shit! Not enough here to mess with." He lifted the change tray and found a stack of tens and twenties. "That's more like it, but still chicken feed."

The sound of the shot that killed the woman filled the store. The man stuffing the bills into his pocket didn't even bat an eye. He picked up the box of SenSen and headed for the door.

"Come on. We got business in KC."

"I'm gettin' me a couple more bottles of sody pop." Keeping his distance from the dead storekeeper and his wife, he took two bottles from the cooler and hurried out of the store.

In the living quarters upstairs, Molly McKenzie was making the bed with fresh sheets she had brought in off the line. She smiled and shook her head when she heard the loud pops. Her papa was teasing her mother with the fire-crackers again. He was just like a kid about the Fourth of July. The shipment of fireworks had come in that morning, and he had to try them out.

A minute or two later when she heard the screen door slam, she went through the rooms to the front, pulled back the lace panel, and looked out the window. Two men were getting into a big black car. One looked across the top of the car toward the store. His face was swarthy, his lips thick. Both men were wearing white shirts and brown felt hats.

"You're as bad as a kid 'bout that soda pop. Let's get outta here." His voice was thin and reedy for such a large man.

The driver of the car slid under the wheel, started the motor, and revved the engine. The wheels skidded, stirring a cloud of dust as the car pulled out of the drive and took off down the road at a fast speed. Molly let the curtain drop. She hadn't heard a car come in. Had it arrived while she was listening to *Ma Perkins*?

Her papa was fond of saying everyone had to eat, and as long as there were people, he would have customers. Times were hard. The dust storms had taken a toll on the wheat farmers, but if they had eggs or butter to trade, they would have flour and sugar.

Roy McKenzie enjoyed meeting strangers who came from the road as well as his regular customers. Over the past sixty-five years almost everyone within a hundred miles had come to the store her great-grandfather had opened back in 1870, and those who hadn't come knew about it.

Molly had spent a year and a half in Wichita going to

business school to learn typing and shorthand so she could get a job as a secretary. After the course, she had wanted to come home for a while before looking for the job she was sure she would hate. Her parents had insisted that she get out, spread her wings, as they had put it, see some of the world other than Seward County. She had lived here all her life. In fact, she had been born in the bed she had just made. She loved the smell of the store, the excitement of new goods, the involvement in the small community.

It was grand to be home!

Chapter One

Molly stood on the porch of the store and looked down the flat road that stretched to the horizon. The Kansas sun sent shimmering heat waves over the golden fields of wheat that bracketed the road.

The Fourth of July had come and gone.

Most of the shipment of fireworks her father had ordered for the celebration had either been sold or given away. Molly had tucked packages of sparklers in with the orders of several families who had been hit hard by the dust storms and the drought. Their children had gazed at the fireworks longingly, knowing better than to ask for them.

In the weeks since her parents had been killed Molly was asked almost daily if she was going to sell the store and move away? Her answer was always the same.

"Why would I do that? This is my home. There's been a McKenzie here for sixty-five years. I'll run the store as my father did."

Bertha McKenzie, wiping the sweat from her face with a handkerchief edged with lace tatting, came out onto the porch. Roy's elder sister had come from Wichita and announced that she was here to stay. She had never lived at the store her grandfather built, but she was as familiar with it as if she had. A saintly-looking woman, with a plump rosy face and a large bosom, Bertha had the constitution of a horse and the wisdom of Solomon. She didn't hesitate to speak her mind and had done so since she had arrived for the double funeral of her brother and sister-in-law.

"That preacher that was just here ain't what he's cracked up to be. He's got more on his mind than tryin' to comfort one of his *flock*. He's thinkin' to get you to comfort *him*, and to take care of that parcel of younguns of his'n, and he'd get his hands on this store to boot."

"For crying out loud, Aunt Bertha! He's at least thirty years older than I am." Molly shifted her gaze from the horizon to her aunt.

"What'd that make him? Fifty somethin'? Fiddle! He wore out his first woman and wasn't too old to get a batch of younguns off his second one. It ain't no wonder he don't have any hair on top. He wore it off on the head of the bed."

"Aunt Bertha, I swear!"

"It's true. Mark my words. Didn't his woman die around Christmas last year? By now he's raunchier than a two-peckered billy goat."

"Mama and Daddy were members of his church. That's why he comes here."

"That may be, but he's got his eye on you, too. His mouth waters ever'time he looks at you."

"How do you know that?"

"Mark my words! That ain't all! You know that farmer that came in here this mornin', the one that didn't have any

452

laces in his shoes and only one button fastened on the shoulder straps of his overalls?"

"You mean George Andrews?"

"He was givin' you and the *store* the once-over."

"George has been coming here for years. I've not said any more than 'hello' and 'good-bye' to him. He's got about as much personality as a wet rag."

"And he ain't used one in a month of Sundays. Smelled like he'd wallered in a hog lot. What I'm tellin' you is that both of them birds has got fornicatin' on their minds. Fornicatin' and gettin' a meal ticket. That Andrews looked at you like a cat after a mouse."

"That's very flattering. One man wants to eat me and the other man's mouth waters." Molly smiled.

"I ran a boardin'house for ten years. I know what's on a man's mind . . . and in his britches."

"Aunt Bertha! You're not shocking me. I got used to you when I stayed with you in Wichita."

"Oh, love, I got used to you, too. It was so darn lonesome when you left."

"Have I told you how grateful I am that you came and how much I love you?"

"A time or two. I've only been here a few weeks. Wait until I've been here a year. You'll be tyin' a can to my tail and sendin' me back to Wichita."

"Don't count on it." Molly hugged her aunt and turned away to hide the tears that sprang to her eyes. "Will the hurt ever go away, Aunt Bertha?"

"Not entirely. But it will lessen in time. Grief has a way of doing that."

"To lose both of them . . . and so senselessly—"

"I know. I lost my love during the War. I was sure that I'd die of grief. He died of influenza on the way to France. We never even got to sleep together. Oh, we wanted to, but we thought the decent thing to do would be to wait until we were wed. I wish to hell we hadn't waited."

"You loved him a lot?"

"You bet your buttons. He didn't want us to marry until he had something to offer me. Then the war came along, and he thought it his duty to go."

"Do you have a picture of him?"

"I'll show you someday. He was a handsome Irish lad with black curly hair and eyes that had the devil right in them."

"And you never met anyone else you could love?"

"All men paled when compared to Mick Shannon."

Bertha fanned herself with a cardboard fan. She loved Molly as if she were her own. The girl needed a good man to take care of her, but from what Bertha had seen so far, the pickings here in Seward County were slim. Very slim.

"Do you think they'll ever catch the monsters who . . . did it?" Molly asked with her back to her aunt.

"I don't know, honeybunch. The sheriff said that he'd been contacted by the Feds and one was coming here to talk to you. I kinda wish you hadn't told him you got a look at those fellers."

"But I did, Aunt Bertha. I'll never forget their faces. One was kinda heavyset, and the other one skinny, but he had a big head."

"How come you remember all that?"

"I don't know. After some of the shock of finding Mama and Daddy wore off, I began to remember things. The thin man had several bottles of soda pop, and the other man had an oblong box in his hand. I'm sure it was the box of SenSen that had come in a few days earlier. I remember Daddy saying a hundred packets would be a year's supply. People around here don't buy stuff to cover up bad breath when they have hardly enough to eat."

"The sheriff said they were probably big-time gangsters travelin' to Kansas City and saw the store as an easy stick-up."

"They're cold-blooded killers, not stick-up men. If the police catch them, I want to be there when they're strapped down in the electric chair." Molly turned a cold, set face to her aunt. "I mean it, Aunt Bertha. I want to be there. I've got a right to be there after what they've done." Her voice wavered, and her lips began to tremble.

"Come on in out of the heat, honeybunch, and I'll fix you a glass of lemonade. You've worked yourself down to a nubbin."

The big, black car came off the road and stopped a short distance from the porch. Molly felt an instant of panic before she saw Sheriff Mason's tan Stetson hat. She could see nothing of the driver. They were waiting, she knew, for Mr. and Mrs. Bonner and their five children to leave the store.

Mr. Bonner had led his team to the side door and was unloading several bushels of ground corn and loading a fifty-pound sack of flour and one of sugar into his wagon. Along with the corn, they had brought in five pounds of fresh butter to trade. It was already in the icebox.

"Tally up the difference, Miss McKenzie. I'll pay soon as I can."

"I'm not worried, Mr. Bonner. You've traded here for ten years. Your credit is good."

"I'm thankin' ya, ma'am. I wasn't sure now that Roy's gone."

"I know I can't take his place, but I'll do the best I can."

"That's good enough for me, miss." Mr. Bonner cleared his throat and spit, more out of embarrassment than need. "If there's anythin' I can do for ya, let me know. Hear?"

"Yes, and I thank you."

"I'll be bringin' ya in a load of stove wood."

"I'll be needing it, Mr. Bonner. We'll make a trade."

The children came out of the store and climbed into the wagon licking peppermint sticks. Aunt Bertha's heart was as big as her bosom, Molly mused. At the urging of their mother, the children uttered in unison, "Thank you, Miss McKenzie."

"You're very welcome. 'Bye now. Come again."

She watched the team pull the wagon out onto the road and waved at the children before she went back into the store.

"Aunt Bertha, the sheriff is here. I think the federal man is with him."

Bertha put aside the wet cloth she'd been using to wipe the shelves. Since the dust storms had begun a few years back, keeping the store clean had become a never-ending chore.

Molly positioned herself behind the counter. She had already decided that she wasn't going to like the federal man. If he were really interested in catching the men who killed her parents, he would have been here before now.

Sheriff Mason plodded into the store, his bootheels

456

sounding loud on the wooden floor. He removed his hat and wiped his forehead with the sleeve of his shirt.

"Howdy, miss. It's hotter than blue blazes out there."

"Hello, Sheriff. Aunt Bertha is making a pitcher of iced tea." As she spoke, Molly's eyes shifted to the man who came in behind the sheriff.

Looming over the rather chubby sheriff, the man was slim in his dark suit and a white shirt. He had removed his felt hat when he came in the door, revealing a head of thick, inky black hair. He was not what one would call handsome. His mouth was hard, and a glass or a knife had slashed across his broad forehead, leaving a scar that ended with a nick out of the end of one thick eyebrow.

Deep, dark eyes met hers. They held a combination of sharp intelligence and quiet strength. She was right in thinking that she would not like him. He was too cold, too controlled to understand the pain of loss she was suffering.

"This is the agent I was tellin' you about. Mr. Dolan wants to talk to you about . . . what you saw that day."

The man stepped forward and held out his hand.

"Hod Dolan, Miss McKenzie. I'm sorry about your parents."

His hand was rough and strong and warm, but not sweaty.

"How do you do? We can talk in the back of the store. Would you like a glass of iced tea?"

"I can't think of anything that would go down better." The hard mouth didn't become much gentler when he smiled.

Hod Dolan was a man with a photographic mind. His eyes swept over the girl locking into his memory the dark brown hair that hung to her shoulders, the slender, graceful body, and the skirt of the neat gingham dress swirling at mid-calf around her sun-browned bare legs. Her movements were coltish. Definitely not a city woman, she was as fresh and as wholesome as the golden wheat fields that surrounded her store.

"This is my aunt, Miss McKenzie." Molly looked over her shoulder and spoke to the agent. "Mr. Dolan, Aunt Bertha. You know the sheriff."

"Yes, I know the sheriff. Howdy to you, mister. Do you take sugar in your tea?"

"No, ma'am."

"It's hotter than an oven in here." Bertha had wrapped a cloth around the sweating glasses on the table. "Take your tea out back. I'll watch the store."

"If someone comes in for gas, call me."

"I'll pump it," the sheriff said. "Go on and have your talk with Dolan."

"Don't you want to sit in?" Molly asked, reluctant to be alone with the man. There was something rough-hewn, almost brutal about him.

"No, this is fed business now. Just tell him what you told me."

"I'd rather we be out of sight, Miss McKenzie. I don't want it known that I was here."

"Why?"

"I'll tell you in good time."

Molly shrugged and led the way out the back door, across the porch, and into the yard toward the screened gazebo her father had built a few years back. She opened the screened door and went inside.

"It isn't as clean as it was before the dirt storms, but it's shady, and the screen keeps the field bugs out." She took the cloth from around her glass and wiped off the bench.

"It's fine." Hod removed his coat and looked around for a place to put it.

"There's a nail in the post by the door."

His shirt was wet with sweat and, to her surprise, under the coat he wore a gun in a brown-leather shoulder holster. After hanging his coat, he stood silently, drinking his tea and looking at her for so long that she began to be irritated.

"What do you want to know? I need to get back to work."

"I imagine Mason and your aunt can tend to the store."

"What do you want to know?" she asked again.

"Everything. Start from when you first got up in the morning."

"I had oatmeal for breakfast. Will that help you catch the men who killed Mama and Daddy?"

He ignored her sarcasm. "Who all came into the store that morning?"

"The Browns, the Sadlers, and the Folkmanns. A couple stopped for gas. They were from around here, too. Daddy knew them."

"Did you see the car drive in?"

"The . . . gangsters' car? No. I didn't even hear it. I was listening to the radio. I turned it off as soon as *Ma Perkins* was over."

"What time was that?"

"Eleven-thirty."

"How long after that did you hear the shots?"

"A minute or two. I heard the murmur of their voices

first. Then I heard what I thought was . . . firecrackers. Daddy got in a shipment . . . that morning. When the screen door slammed, I looked out the window and saw the men. The heavyset man had a high voice—almost like a woman's. I thought at the time the voice didn't go with the size of the man."

Hod nodded. "What did he say?"

"He said something to the other man about his not being able to do without his blasted soda pop. Only he didn't say blasted."

"The sheriff said one of the men left with something. Tell me about that."

"The heavyset man had a box in his hand. I thought at the time it was the new box of SenSen Daddy just got in. There were about a hundred packets in it. Later, I looked for the box, and it was gone. The . . . killer . . . had taken it. Will knowing that help?" She turned her face away and cleared her throat.

"Absolutely. One has a fondness for soda pop, the other uses SenSen. I know exactly who they are."

Thank goodness! "That's a relief. When you catch them I want to be there when they strap them in the electric chair."

"Knowing who they are and catching them are two different things."

Hod watched the changing expressions drift across her face. She wasn't exactly beautiful, he decided. Not picture-perfect, but pretty. He watched as she moved the rich, dark brown hair from her neck with a nervous gesture and gazed at him with brown eyes, shining with tears she was too proud to shed. She was tall and slim, narrow-hipped, with a small waist and nice soft breasts. A man would have a sweet armful when he held her. Hod frowned, annoyed with the direction his thoughts were taking him.

Sitting on the bench, legs crossed, Molly was acutely aware of being surveyed by the intense dark eyes. She remained silent, but the swinging of her sandaled foot revealed her uneasiness.

"Well?" she finally said.

Hod cocked a brow. Her features were tranquil, but he felt the tension in her. Had she sensed his discomfort, too? He was accustomed to being on guard, weighing his words, but somehow this situation seemed to be more important. It was as if the rest of his life . . . and hers . . . depended on her trust in him.

He's a man who would know how to handle himself—in any situation, she thought, as she waited for him to speak. *Daddy would like him.*

"Do you really want to catch the men who killed your parents?"

"That's a ridiculous question." She rose abruptly to her feet. "If your parents had been killed, wouldn't you want the men who did it caught and punished?" Their eyes met; hers were the color of the tea in her glass, his dark slits between thick dark lashes. Molly felt the moment freeze into silence.

"Of course I would." He spoke softly, breaking the tension between them. Then, with his eyes holding hers, he lifted the glass and drank the last of his tea.

"Well?"

"I need your help."

"I've told you everything I know."

461

"There is more you can do. I would like for you to talk to a reporter from the *Kansas City Star* and tell him that you got a good look at the men who killed your folks and that you can identify them." He met her gaze evenly.

"They would print that . . . and the killers would see it." She spoke without the slightest bit of emotion.

"It would be dangerous. They will want to . . . eliminate a witness."

Molly was silent. She looped a strand of hair behind her ear, an acknowledgment of her inner turmoil, but she answered without hesitation.

"You . . . want to use me for bait. It's all right. I'll do whatever it takes."

"You'll have as much protection as I can give you."

"I'd do it without your protection. I've got Daddy's shotgun. If either one of them steps as much as a foot inside the store, they'll get both barrels."

He studied her for a long moment. She faced him, refusing to look away. *She may think that she could shoot a man now, but could she if push came to shove? It's hard to take a life, even scum like Pascoe or Norton.*

"It's not a sure thing that they'll come," he finally said. "But I'd bet on it."

"I don't want Aunt Bertha to be here."

"That's up to you . . . and her. I'd send you both away, but someone in the area may know someone in KC and pass the word that you're not here. The paper might get hold of it."

"And they'd print it?"

"Hell, yes! They want to sell papers and don't give a damn whether or not I make an arrest."

"I wouldn't go anyway."

"I didn't think you would." Hod took his coat off the nail and slung it over his shoulder.

"When can I expect the reporter?"

"I'll call him tonight. It'll be a few days. He'll want a picture—" He cut off his words at the loud blast of a car horn. "Who is that?"

"Sounds like the iceman. He comes about this time of day."

"What's his name?"

"Walter Lovik. Why?"

"Who else comes here on a regular basis?"

"The soda-pop man comes on Wednesdays during the summer."

"How do you get your goods?"

"From a wholesaler in Liberal."

"Do you call in the order?"

Molly drew in a shallow, aching breath. "Daddy used to go down there."

"How many on your party line?"

"There were about twenty, but some have had to give up their phones. You sure ask a lot of questions."

"It's my job. I don't want the iceman to know I'm here."

"Then I'd better get in there. He's a talker and will want to shoot the breeze for a while."

"Molly," he said as she passed him, "this is our chance to get two killers put away. I'll do my best to keep them from getting to you."

She shrugged as she looked into his eyes. This close she could see small specks of light in the black.

"I mean it," he said softly and sincerely. His hand rested for a minute on her shoulder.

Molly left the gazebo quickly. She looked over her shoulder once on the way to the store. Hod Dolan had come out and was watching her. The man confused her. *Do minds touch?* she wondered. Had he sensed the tempestuous spin of her thoughts during that last moment?

Hod stared after her, wondering if he had imagined that for just an instant they had shared something warm and intimate. It was ridiculous to imagine that he'd felt it with this woman he scarcely knew when he'd not felt anything near that, with any other woman, even some that he'd been physically intimate with. He shook his head more to clear it than to deny his thoughts.